PRAISE FOR 29

"Ever-ascending Sojourner cooks up wrenching sorrow and hilarious banter, environmental and moral conundrums, magnetizing characters, and a place of transcendent beauty in this intoxicating, provocative, and gloriously told desert tale of wildness and community, unexpected bonds and deep legacies, trauma and healing." —**Donna Seaman**, *Booklist* (**starred review**)

"This standout ecological novel from Arizona author Sojourner features picturesque prose, a vivid western setting, and sharply drawn characters."
—*Publishers Weekly* (**starred review**)

" This is a story that will stay with you and, perhaps, bring you home to your own place, and the importance of fighting for what you love." —**Susan Lang**, author of the Mojave novels trilogy: *Small Rocks Rising, Juniper Blue,* and *Moon Lily Oblivion*

"Sojourner's new novel, much like the desert landscapes in which it is set, speaks to those adventurous enough (or lost enough) to wander off to find a world bursting with fragile beauty, tenacious life, and rock hard truth." —**Giles Carwyn**, author of *Queen of Oblivion*

PRAISE FOR MARY SOJOURNER

"Mary Sojourner is tough, she's funny, she's full of wisdom, a fine outrage, and lots of hope. She sees the world as it is, heartbreaking and alive…an original, as feisty as they come, and dedicated to the struggle to forge a better world. She is also a writer of tremendous passion and compassion, expressed in a simple, lyrical, wonderful prose style that carries you along effortlessly like a beautiful ocean wave." —**John Nichols**, author of *The Milagro Beanfield War*

"Mary hides nothing. Her words will track all over your soul. Savor this stuff, this terrified, righteous nakedness of hers. It is rare."
—**Craig Childs**, author of *The Secret Knowl*

29

Mary Sojourner

TORREY HOUSE PRESS, LLC

SALT LAKE CITY • TORREY

FSC
www.fsc.org
MIX
Paper from
responsible sources
FSC® C011935

First Torrey House Press Edition, August 2014
Copyright © 2014 by Mary Sojourner

Published by Torrey House Press, LLC
Salt Lake City, Utah
www.torreyhouse.com

International Standard Book Number: 978-1-937226-35-0
Library of Congress Control Number: 2014930123

Author photo by Chris Gunn
Cover photo by Richard B. Hardman, www.ricksdigitaldesert.com
Cover design by Jeff Fuller, Shelfish, www.shelfish.weebly.com
Interior design by Rick Whipple, Sky Island Studio
www.skyislandstudio.com

Their movement is as though an invisible hand were helping...
Identification: Phycodurus eques

— Jeff Jeffords, Divegallery

Again and again
Some people in the crowd wake up.
They have no ground in the crowd
And they emerge according to broader laws.
They carry strange customs with them,
And demand room for bold gestures.
　　　The future speaks ruthlessly through them.

— Rainer Maria Rilke, translated by Stephen Mitchell

You should write a book about us.

— Monkey

To Matthew Leivas, Sr. and Vivienne Jake,
for "bringing creation back together."

For the Mojave Desert and the people of the Morongo Basin—
you saved my life and my spirit…

And thank you, Brendan Macfarlane, for the song "Money Won't."

29

1. In The Short Run

…in the short run, we are responsible…
—Walt Richardson, "Always Was and Always Will Be Love"

1

The hives burned gold in the last wash of desert sunset. A quarter moon moved up into the darkening sky, the lights of a desert city a dirty smudge above the eastern range. An agreement was reached. It was time to go.

One by one, the bees ascended, as though a coil of smoke rose from the hives. Bee by bee, the spiral thickened, swirled across the moon and was gone. The hum faded.

Deep within the hive the Queen waited alone.

The bees were gone. Nell jolted awake, opened her laptop, searched for bees leaving and was sent to the morning's *New York Times*. The bees were there. Rather, they were not there. Five hundred thousand bees had left the boxes their keeper had placed near a California almond orchard.

"I have never seen anything like it," Mr. Bradshaw, 50, said. *"Box after box after box are just empty. There's nobody home."*

She checked her email. Five messages, three of them form rejections from the last ten jobs she had applied for, one message from what had once been her bank, thanking her for having been their customer, and one message from an old schoolmate wondering if she had any openings in her department. She wrote back: *I'm no longer with Elysian. Good luck in your search.* She logged off and lay back down.

She felt as though she had come awake in an unfamiliar room, hunting clues for what to do next. The big French windows shone pewter. Dawn had begun to drift up behind the old palms in the yard across the street. The parrots that nested in the trees would be waking.

A silk shirt draped over a chair seemed a luminous after-image, the near-empty closet no longer a shock. The room was silent, the light on the answering machine steady. The only time a prospective employer phoned was if one had been hired.

It had been a year since HR had called her in and told her that the firm was reorganizing and she had a week to clear out her desk. At first she'd been frantic, then resigned, then paralyzed. This morning she could at least keep moving. She could do that much. She got out of bed, pulled her suitcase from under the bed and packed: two silk shirts, the deep plum skirt and jacket, a beige linen skirt, the old sequined flip-flops, the dark jade sandals with the baby heels, four pairs of thongs, a bra, two loose cotton workout tops and pants, a bar of lemongrass soap, a plastic vial of hotel shampoo, a bottle of Cinnabar nail polish, and a vial of pills.

The eastern window glowed pink. Nell closed the suitcase. She slipped into jeans and a t-shirt, laced up her Asics runners. The laptop and notebook would fit in her shoulder bag, her iPod, cell, and wallet in her purse. She took the last object hanging on the wall—a black pearl hung from a silver chain—and tucked it in her pocket. She would leave everything else as it was: the turned-down bed; the empty room-length closet; what was left in the kitchen, and the unopened copy of *Eat, Pray, Love* that the young woman who took over her office had sent with the note: *Best of luck on your new adventure, Nell.*

She would brew a cup of coffee from the last of the beans. She would leave the windows open, the last tangerines sliced open on the sill. Take her coffee to the front stoop. If she were lucky, the parrots would fly down from the black palms across the street. They would bend their scarlet heads and feed.

Nell swallowed the last of her coffee. The parrots had not flown to the windowsill. She couldn't wait any longer. The signal to go had come as a spiral of bees. She had been waiting for it since the long instant that the earnest young HR director had said, "We think you could find better opportunities with a different company. Of course there will be a more than decent severance—and terrific references. I like to think of this as you becoming available to the greater industry. You know Nell, you'll find something new in a Wilshire heartbeat, something more suitable to your abilities and years of experience."

Nell had smiled. "Of course," she had said. The young woman had nodded enthusiastically. "I personally wish you the very best of good fortune. You deserve it."

Endless days ground into months, then a year, and Nell could not remember a time her chest did not ache steadily. Work gone. The generous severance? Gone for survival while she chased down nonexistent job leads, and spent tens of thousands of dollars to keep her most shameful secret tucked away on a quiet street in Long Beach.

Her investments—what there had been of them—had disappeared as suddenly and completely as a desert mirage. She'd sold her good jewelry, the Japanese netsukes, the few pieces of Waterford crystal. She'd emptied the closet, the shoe rack, the drawers of silk scarves and eighty-buck t-shirts. She'd stopped paying the mortgage, retreated to her bedroom, left the rest of the house dark. What was left—the Audi—was fully paid for. The winter bonus of 2004 had been more than generous. She hadn't sold the car. She'd known it would have been futile. The money would have barely covered the late mortgage payments, let alone kept her going maybe three months in L.A. In her shock, it had not occurred to her that she might live anywhere else.

She'd understood that not only her life on King Street and her work were gone, but that nine years of university, a Ph.D. in brain science and behavior and an MBA were volatilized. She was fifty-five. She was a woman. She was a year away from her last job. In her field, high-end marketing of legal designer pharmaceuticals, she was dead—and dead broke.

There was the watchdog lawyer, Jensen, guarding a bundle stashed in a trust fund in order to keep the secret safe. That money was not hers. It belonged to the secret. What were hers were a suitcase, a laptop, six dead credit cards, and $750 in cash.

Now, a visitation of bees. Now, time to shed what was left. Now, time to leave. Nell raised the empty coffee cup. "Here's to you, Mom. You were right. Never trust The Man."

Nell drove to the Greyhound station, parked the Audi in the lot and climbed out. The faint sun, a coin of gray light, reflected off the hood of the car. Nell dug her nails into it. She looked down at the shallow gouges in the perfect wax job. "I was here," she said.

She took her bag, purse, and suitcase, put the keys, registration, and signed title in the glove box and closed the doors. She would not lock them. The car was now an artifact waiting to be found.

The Greyhound waiting room was jammed. Nell bought a ticket for Long Beach and sat on a metal bench, her bags tucked between her feet. A scrawny boy huddled across from her. When he tried to cross his legs, they shook so hard he gave up. A plump grandmother tucked her grandkids around her as though she were a quail. A girl in a spangled bikini top and cammie pants crouched at the older woman's feet and opened a microwaved burrito.

Nell waited. The couple she needed appeared outside the loading doors. They lit one cigarette, the girl holding it between her lips, the boy striking a match on his boot sole. They smoked quietly, their tense faces going peaceful as they inhaled. It was almost sweet to watch them. They stubbed out their smokes, came in through the loading doors and leaned against the wall near Nell.

The girl was a slender woman, the boy barely a man. He set a battered guitar case at his feet. The woman brushed his long dark hair back from his face. She took a bottle of Gatorade from her backpack and opened it. When she tilted her head back to drink, her earrings glinted, three gold hoops in her left ear, a turquoise stud in her right.

She handed the bottle to the young man. He drank slowly and shook his head. "I needed that," he said. "Wine coolers make an insufficient dinner."

The woman laughed. "Two basic food groups," she said. "Fruit and ethanol."

She caught Nell listening. "Just kidding," she said. "In fact, we dined on organic tofu and spring water. I bet you did, too."

Nell stood. "It doesn't matter," she said. "I don't care what you ate. I chose you."

The woman stepped sideways. She would have backed up, but the wall stopped her. The young man frowned. "Whoa. Are you okay?"

Nell nodded. "I'm okay. You're a musician."

"Yeah," he said. "We both are. That's why we dined on fruit and ethanol."

"Listen," Nell said. "Since you're a musician—do you know the musician Chris Whitley? He died three years ago. He was a junkie, but he died from lung cancer from smoking. He was a genius." She realized she sounded a little manic. "I mean, you being a musician and all."

The woman shook her head. "We don't have any drugs, if that's what you're trying to say. We're clean."

The man smiled. "I sort of remember that name. I'll look him up once we get to Oakland."

"Chris Whitley," Nell said. "He sang about dust radio." She studied their faces for recognition.

"I don't know that station," the woman said gently.

"That's okay," Nell said. "You might have."

She moved toward the loading door. "Would you come with me?" she said. "I want to show you something."

The man glanced at the woman and shrugged.

"Why not?" she said.

Nell stepped outside. The Greyhound team was loading a bus for the Mexico run. The couple followed her through the crowd.

"You see that gray Audi in the farthest parking spot?" Nell said.

The woman nodded.

"The doors are unlocked. The registration, signed title, and keys are in the glove box. It's yours."

"No," the young man said. "This is too weird. Shit, that's a $26,000 car."

The woman looked at Nell and grinned. "Yes," she said, "this is not weird. This is Los Angeles, this chick is an angel, and this is us driving to Oakland in the style to which I hope to get accustomed. We have to trust this. Bennie, you know what that psychic said. Change has gotta come." She touched the back of Nell's hand. "Thank you."

"You're welcome," Nell said and walked back into the terminal. She stood at the window to watch the couple. The woman flashed Nell a peace sign. She and the young man walked slowly toward the car.

"Car gone," Nell whispered. "House gone. L.A. gone. Ritual complete. And I don't even believe in rituals."

Five cabs were lined up in front of the terminal. The first cab rolled slowly toward her. The driver pulled over and climbed out. His bald head would have come to Nell's shoulder had he been standing next to her—which he was pointedly not about to do. He popped the lid on the trunk. "In there, please," he said. "I hope you will like some music."

She loaded her bag and waited for him to open the back door. The driver in the cab behind them beeped. The door popped open. Nell climbed into a blast of raspberry air freshener.

"Where to, miss?"

"Hollywood/Highland Metro," Nell said.

"Why there?" the driver said. "Union Station is much closer. You can take the Metro to Hollywood/Highland from Union Station. It will save you money."

"Hollywood/Highland. And I know the shortest way. I'll tell you where to turn."

The driver frowned. "As you wish."

He revved the engine and slid a disc into the CD player. "Jackie Wilson, a fine African-American musician," he said. The first song was "Lonely Teardrops."

"You see that movie?" the driver said. "That *Leaving Las Vegas*? It was not Jackie Wilson singing in that movie. Of course not. It was a white man. That movie was untrue, completely untrue. I got many cousins work up there and not one of them ever had a prostitute live with them for free, much less—excuse me, in my country, boys are taught not to say crude things to a lady like yourself."

Suck their dicks, Nell thought. Out loud, she said, "Turn here. It's a short cut."

Nell gave the driver instructions that would have broken her heart if she'd had a heart left to break. The Greyhound station had felt like a sanctuary, no sweet memories in its battered interior and bleak chaos, no beloved route to a feather of smoke rising from the Peruvian chicken joint, the shop that sold *gianduia gelati* you could kiss off a lover's lips, the tiny park off Wilshire with its scented orange trees and a bronze statue of a giant carp. Once, there had been a tall man waving her in, as though he had captured the park for her, as though the trees and scent and statue were trophies. That man would never move toward her again, his warm eyes and dark hair, his thin-lipped mouth and perfect teeth, his smile like a delighted toddler's. "I told you," he had said. "I told you this park was amazing." And in that moment, a deer that could not exist in the city had stepped out from behind an orange tree and begun to graze on a clump of white sage that did not grow that far from the seacoast. She closed her eyes.

"We are here, miss," the driver said. Nell looked up. The entrance to the Hollywood/Highland station of the Metro Red Line, which had once seemed a radiant portal into astonishment, was jammed with harried commuters and tourists.

"Did you ever," Nell said, "bring people here at night?"

The driver looked up into the rearview mirror. His eyes were shiny as olives, the whites threaded with scarlet. "Sometimes, miss. Yes. This place can be very beautiful in the rain."

Nell paid him. He opened the trunk and pulled out her bag. She folded a bill and tucked it into his hand. "Thank you," she said, "for taking the shortest way."

"Oh," he said, "but I didn't."

Nell laughed. She descended into the Metro station under the galaxy of huge shimmering eyes. You could tell the tourists. They stopped and looked up. The locals pushed past them, muttering *Fuck you*. She bought a one-way ticket to Long Beach and boarded the train.

They flew through a tunnel of dark and meteors. She remembered waking when she was twelve, knowing without question that one day she would die and that death was being trapped naked in ice-black space, ice-white sparks of light showering past. She had told her mother about the vision. Her mother had taken her hand and said, "No, sweetie. Death is just a bus stop on a long, long wonderful road trip."

Nell changed trains at 9th. The tracks rose up into grimy light, above old cottages, vegetable gardens, and tiny vineyards. Gilded plaster lions guarded the entrance to a house that had tumbled into itself. A voice came from the rear of the car. "Chocolate. I got chocolate." The kid's skinny legs were ashy, his hair twisted into a hundred tiny braids. He had a backpack slung over his shoulder. He stopped at Nell's side. "You ladies love chocolate," he said. "You know you do." The band of his underwear showed above his sagging shorts. "Ralph," he said. "Ralph Lauren. I got nothin' but the finest right there."

Nell looked up past the honed body under his muscle shirt, past the sparkling M he'd hung from a silver chain. He grinned. Then his eyes went soft. "Hey," he said. "I'm sorry, girl. I didn't mean nuthin."

He reached in the pack. "Crunch bar," he said. "For free. You eat it.

You got some sorrowful eyes."

Nell took the candy bar. "I'm okay," she said. "But thanks."

"God bless," the boy said. "You be careful."

Nell did not, as she might once have, fumble in her pocket for a few bucks to give him. If she was on her way to die, she better learn a few things. How to not be so above it all might be a good place to start. She figured if she gave him back his generosity, it would turn to dust. In her hands and his. Then she might as well just get out at the next stop, wait till the train had gone, and launch herself off the platform. There was more to do before that dive. Maybe regard words from a stranger as an opening. Maybe open the Crunch bar, for starters.

She plugged in her iPod. *Alien.* The singer's voice was fragile as old parchment. Chris Whitley, one of his later albums. David had taken her to a ludicrously delightful bed and breakfast near Venice Beach. He would not touch her. "No," he had said, "not yet. Sit by the window. Look at the ocean. And, listen."

He slid a CD into the player. "That's Chris Whitley," David had said quietly. He pulled her up into his arms. "And you are the alien. I have waited my life for you."

Nell had wondered what he believed he held, what he kissed, what he began slowly to undress. "You are not like anyone," he said. "You and I are two forms of the impossible." Three months later, he was gone. "You're your mother's daughter," he'd said. "You'll never be able to love." She'd been startled to realize that she felt released. She'd nodded and not said, "Oh, but you didn't know my mom."

The train lurched. Nell licked chocolate from her lips. Chris Whitley was dead. Just before he died, he'd sung about a prayer fallen to the ground and burned. A year later the song had become the perfect epitaph for what had become of her life—relief alchemized into a longing that burned as a cold flame. Her staff had believed she was a driven ice-maiden. They'd been only partly right.

She remembered sitting on the steps near the elevator in the Mission Palms Hotel in Phoenix. It had been February and delicately warm. The night before, she and David had floated on their backs in the rooftop pool. Palm trees had risen black and ragged against the ambient light. Huge planes flew over, their running lights flashing red and green. She had thought she knew what fish saw as ships moved above them. David had leaned toward her, sequins of red and green sparkling on his shoulders.

The next morning, Nell had sat on the hotel steps leading into the plaza to wait for David to come down for breakfast. She watched the rest of the conference people fill their plates with smoked salmon and melon and crepes from the patio buffet. She heard footsteps behind her. David walked briskly past her down the steps. Nell jumped up and ran toward him. She had one glimpse of herself reflected in the gleaming doors and had seen a girl running with the adolescent knock-kneed calculation of an actress in a meets-cute movie.

Nell opened her purse. The house keys were still there. She dropped them under the seat.

"Miss? Miss, you just dropped your keys?" The woman behind her wore a silk headscarf and filigree gold bracelets. "Here." She bent and retrieved the keys. "It is one of those days, isn't it?"

Nell let the woman hand her the keys. "Thank you," she said coolly and remembered this was a day in which she had decided to regard anything a stranger said to her as an invitation. "It is one of those days."

The woman smiled. "May I ride with you?" She nodded at the empty aisle seat.

"I don't mind," Nell said.

"I am going to Long Beach to see my grandson, Jack," the woman said. "He is an EMT. Such a good crazy boy."

"I'm going to see if I can find the house my grandmother used to live in," Nell said. "We visited her when I was little. There were flowers everywhere."

"There are no flowers where my grandson lives," the woman said, "except for some big plants—he won't tell me what they are."

Nell thought of her cottage. Nothing had lived in the four rooms except for her. She thought of her office, of the big windows lined with fuchsia and orchids and how she had never touched the plants.

"I'm no good with plants," Nell said.

"That is sad," the woman said. "I hope I do not intrude. But a woman who is alone? Forgive me, I am thinking you are alone."

"I am," Nell said. "Except for the parrots."

"Yes," the woman said, "parrots. For a woman alone, something in the home, a bird, a cat, even plants can be better than nothing. But I have seen so many American women who are alone. I did not expect to be. Where I come from, a woman my age would not be alone. But now I am. We have to be tough. I bet you are tough."

"Not me," Nell said. "I am anything but tough."

2

Nell's grandmother's house had been divided into four apartments. The stucco was still the same grimed ivory that shimmered pink-gold at sunset. "My house," Nell's grandmother had told the children, "is really a giant seashell."

The roof had been made from red tiles since long before the tsunami of red tile roofs had swept over California. Two fragrant cedars rose on either side of the front porch. There were scarlet and salmon geraniums in terra cotta pots along the railing. Nell remembered crouching in the scented shade of their ancestors during the one summer her mother left her with her grandmother.

A sheer curtain fluttered from a second story window. The silvery rill of flute music. A girl burst out of the side yard and raced toward a dark-skinned boy holding a kite at the end of the block. Both children were maybe ten. Nell couldn't remember seeing kids on her West Hollywood street, only adults and expensive dogs.

She felt as though she'd waked for an instant from a solitary dream. There was no epiphany, no golden moment of realizing she had been a child in just that place, or of knowing there could be a future for her—adopt a Korean orphan, find a dull sweet man with teenagers, decide to teach computer skills to the homeless kids at a shelter.

She took a last look at the house. A woman pulled the curtain back into the room. The flute music ended and the gut-thump of hip-hop kicked in. Nell pinched a velvety blossom from one of the geraniums and walked toward the corner. The kids and their kite were gone. The Greyhound station was a block away. She would get that far and see what happened.

Long Beach Greyhound Station was filled with sunlight. It was easy to believe that the entire shining world reeked of spilled pop and nuked burritos and that only a chicana's perfume could penetrate the stink. It was easy to watch the girl and her boyfriend and believe that love ought not end by blizzard. It wasn't easy to imagine hope, to think it might be worth it to go on waiting, become Scheherazade, saving her life night by night, story by story. But of course there had been the handsome and sociopath king—and Scheherazade's youthful beauty.

Two longhaired guys smoked cigarettes outside. They wore faded jackets with the logo of a South Dakota farm team embroidered across the pockets. The blond could have been seventeen or fifty-seven. He wore dark glasses mended with duct tape. The other guy was Mexican or Arab or what her former boss, the politically correct Christopher, would have called N.A. Nell watched the drinkers through the window. The dark man passed the blond a paper bag. "Screw-top port," Christopher would have said wisely. He believed that corporations had to have a sound working knowledge of the poor—and, of course, people of color.

A big family was sprawled across three benches. The babies and toddlers slept. A skinny woman drank from a huge Dr Pepper. Nell wondered how old the woman was. She saw her own face reflected in the window. No feature distinct. No evidence of gender or age or emotion. She walked to the ticket window.

The agent looked up from her book. She was a sweetly round young woman, her black hair streaked with blonde. "Can I help you?"

"I need a bus schedule, please."

"Where to?"

"I'm not sure. How about California?"

"You're *in* California, chica." The woman grinned. She handed Nell a schedule. "What about Palm Springs, they've got casinos there? Rich guys. Hey, you could get lucky." She checked the computer, her long silver fingernails tapping the keys. "The next bus out is at 4:35 this afternoon, next one tomorrow morning about 6:00, the next one at 11:15. Do you want a ticket?"

Nell nodded. "How much?"

"Twenty-six bucks," the woman said. "Cash or card?"

Nell opened her purse and peeled two twenties from the diminishing wad of bills. "How about 11:15 tomorrow?" The woman printed out her ticket.

"Be here by 10:30," she said. "The driver doesn't wait for anybody."

Nell smiled. "Thanks," she said. "If I'm not here, he can go with a clear conscience."

"Hey, since you got a while," the young woman said, "check out the aquarium. I take my nieces there all the time. It's awesome. Just like *The Little Mermaid*."

"I might do that, thanks."

"No big deal," the woman said. She opened her book. "'Scuse me, I gotta get back to my homework."

A bus rumbled in. The family filed out the door into the glare. Nell put her suitcase in a locker and walked outside. There was a light rail system down the middle of the street, platforms decked out with bright discs that spun in the breeze off the harbor. The platform was empty. She bought a ticket from the auto-vendor. The train whispered in and she climbed on.

They had transmogrified the harbor, engineered a charm of chrome and white brick and winding paths. She smelled the ocean. It was the same as always. Rank. Artless. Alive. She surprised herself and bought an ice cone from an immaculate little cart. The flavors were extraordinary: marionberry, espresso, key lime, mango. She ordered half espresso, half mango and sat on a bench by the water to eat.

It had been a long time since she had wanted to eat anything but the discard diet: coffee, gin—and yogurt to maintain the illusion that she gave a shit. She was fucking weary of herself. Her pain. Her narration of the pain. Her attempts at interrupting the narration. Her failure at that. The HR director had covered her walls with inspirational posters. *If you lose something you love, let it go. Choose freedom.* How the fuck could you be free of what you'd lost? She swallowed the dark trickle of espresso, turned the cone to try the mango. It blossomed orange on her tongue. For as long as it took the ice to melt to pleasure in her mouth, she was free of everything but bitter and sweet.

She watched the gulls drifting like scraps of foil in the bright sky. She finished off the cone and stepped onto the curving path that led to the aquarium. Families poured toward the big doors. She stepped into the current of moms and strollers and was carried to a ticket window, then through a turnstile into a vast echoing hall.

A diver in a black wetsuit floated in a huge tank, a mass of glowing red, purple, and blue fish looping around him. A voice threaded between the children's shrieks. "*Kids. Kids. Kids, now don't try this at home.*" She thought of the pills in her bag and imagined hiding in the ladies' room and swallowing them, then going back out to the bench at the edge of the harbor and waiting. Kids. Kids. Kids, now don't try this at home.

Nell moved out into the Great Hall. She was not particularly alarmed by the condition of her mind. A docent led a line of children up a curving staircase. Nell followed. The docent stopped at the first doorway. A dark hall lay beyond.

"Follow me," the docent said. "If you put on your headphones, you will be able to hear the marvelous stories that live under the sea."

Nell waited till the line moved ahead, and stepped into the peaceful dark. Families swirled around her and were gone. She came into blue-green light. To her right there were four dark shapes against a tank in which a huge grouper drifted above schools of brilliant clown fish. A family was silhouetted against the glow. Mother. Father. Two children. They talked in soft voices. The children crouched at the base of the tank. The mother bent to hear a question.

"No," she said, "the big fish is not the daddy. They are two different kinds of fish."

Nell walked to the next tank. It held a living coral reef. Drag queen sea anemones waved their luminous tentacles. There were filigree sea plants, pink and silver, the surface of the water sparkling. Nell pressed her fingers against her purse and felt the hard outline of the pill bottle.

"Lucent." A guide spoke to a semi-circle of high school students. "Watch the red and green lights flickering along the tentacles. They are lucent. Imagine a string of fiber-optic threads."

Lucent. I am a much-reduced bundle of fiber-optic threads. Shut up, she thought. She heard David. "You think everything's a movie, some inscrutable indie flick nobody else gets." Then she saw how the red and green lights were miniatures of the lights on the planes that had flown over her in the rooftop pool, and saw again red and green sequins reflected on David's wet shoulders.

She moved as close to the jellyfish as she could. If she cupped her hands at the edges of her eyes, she could imagine that she was in the pool, floating, knowing that this time the dark shapes were not ships that floated above her. In the next tank, a silver galaxy spun in on itself and out. A cluster of children moved toward her. She thought it might be time to make her exit.

Nell looked at herself in the ladies' room mirror. Her reflection was clear and most ordinary, haircut grown wild, thin upper lip, no make-up, gray-green eyes that showed nothing. She opened her purse and stepped into the last stall.

She pissed and flushed the toilet. All that was left was to wait until there was no one in the room, step to the sink, swallow pills, cup her hands, and drink water. A mouse-faced, bright-eyed little girl peeked under the door. Nell held her finger to her lips and thumbed her nose. The kid giggled and disappeared.

"Mommy, there's a lady in there, a funny—"

The mother's voice cut in. "Come on, Harriett, the shark exhibit starts in two minutes."

Nell stepped out to the sink and counted the pills. She had enough. She moved the pills toward her lips. Time slid sideways. She checked her watch. Three minutes had gone by. It was like waiting for the call that would tell her she was employed—time become cloisonné, each millisecond a speck of enamel that glowed the acid greens, pinks, and shuddering yellows of a migraine aura.

Nell rolled the pills in her palm. What if mango was the last thing she tasted? What if Scheherazade had submitted to her death? What if she, Nell, was nothing but a chicken shit? A spoiled woman who couldn't cut the losses a million Americans were going through. She dumped the pills back in the bottle. She should have known. A girl raised by Tara Walker could not take her own life. A girl raised by Tara Walker might have been a fucked-up mess, but she might vaguely remember that you never knew what earthly bus stop lay around the next corner. She put the pills back in her purse and went into the dark hallway of the Tropical Pacific Gallery.

The pale light rippled like moiré satin. There were the gorgeous and deadly invitations of sea anemones. And a coral reef with tiny fish darting through like animated rubies and sapphires.

She moved forward into the dark. A warmer light shone ahead. Twice, she moved into the dark and out. Twice, she stood in front of a window of water and life. She went again into the dark and came out in a dim hallway. A cool blue oval glowed just ahead. The red exit sign shone just beyond.

The oval was a tank taller than her head. There was nothing in the tank but swaying kelp. Nell wondered about the economic wisdom of maintaining a tank with no inhabitants. She was still keeping accounts. "You are a budget book," David had said. "Not about money, but everything else. I keep feeling like I'm in the red. This is not one of your assets, Nell." It had been the third of her not-assets, along with being too friendly with waiters and prone to jumping to conclusions.

The kelp shimmered. Nell leaned in closer. The kelp and shimmer resolved into a creature drifting slowly, a ripple of green and pale pink, silver and translucence. Nell dropped slowly to her knees and pressed her hands against the tank. "What are you?" she whispered.

The creature glided up and away. The body was that of a foot-long sea horse. It did not seem to flex or propel, and still it moved and disappeared into a web of kelp. Nell tucked her legs under her and sat. A second creature appeared. Blush-pink striped with silver. She saw that what appeared to be kelp were green streamers of living flesh. Tiny translucent fins beat steadily.

"You are perfect," Nell spoke without sound, imagining she was heard. "I'm the opposite. I don't know what to do. I've forgotten how to live. And I'm too scared to not live." She stared into the unblinking eye of the closest creature. "My name isn't really Nell. My real name is Aurora. It is the one my parents, Tara and Shiva, gave me. They were Debbie and Tom until they met at a hippie wedding up near Russell, New York. Debbie was sixteen. Tom was twenty-three. There was Owsley acid in the wedding punch.

"By dawn, Debbie was Tara, Tom was Shiva, and I, without anybody consulting me, was on the way. I've wondered if Shiva's sperm was tripping; if Tara's egg was spinning in a glittering matrix of night and stars and lunatic brain chemicals; if I began to divide into who I am already broken. I wonder what you are, not an acid vision, not a computer image, not an alien, but something whole and real and completely of this earth."

She was not so much talking to the creatures as to a great absence, still telling her story with the intensity with which she longed for her old life. "Okay," she whispered. "Here's the ordinary truth of it. I'm really really scared. And you are the most beautiful creatures I've ever seen."

There were voices in the dark hall behind her. She stood and studied the plaque on the tank: **Leafy Seadragon:** *Phycodurus eques, is a marine fish in the family Syngnathidae, which also includes the seahorses. It is the only member of the genus Phycodurus. It is found along the southern and western coasts of Australia. Leafy seadragons have been listed as near threatened on the IUCN Red List since 2006. These dramatic-appearing fish are in trouble because of habitat destruction, pollution, excessive fertilizer runoff, and poaching by humans. They are fully protected under Australia's local, state, and federal legislation. Special licenses are required to collect or export them. Inhabitants of temperate waters, increase of water temperature as a result of global climate change may impact their survival unless they can adapt to the changes.*

The Leafies are ocean bees, she thought. More bees. Bees everywhere and nowhere. People stepped around her, moved in close to the tank. Some of them talked to the seadragons.

"You are Scylla turned back into your gorgeous self," a woman said. "No whirlpool. No rocks. No curse."

"Hello, beautiful," a man whispered. "Where is the puppeteer?"

Finally, an automated voice with a hint of British accent told them they had fifteen minutes till the aquarium closed. Nell eased herself up off the floor and joined the crowd pouring down the stairs into the Great Hall. She walked toward the exit and dropped the pill bottle into the trash. It was clear that Sunday, April 28, 2008, was not going to be the day her cells ceased dividing—and she had damn well better figure out where she was going to spend the night.

3

Monkey stirred in his sleep. Lights glittered in the dreaming dark. Silver. Green. Pink.

"Where? What?" An EEG of An Other's brainwaves. How did he know that? Where the fuck was he?

He shivered awake. His wife did not move. She must have taken one of her new pills. They held her from dusk to dawn. She said she felt like a caterpillar in a cocoon and maybe she was becoming a butterfly. She would grow wings.

Wings. Monkey shivered. He did not want to think of wings. They made him think of flight. He did not want to think of flight. He wanted to find a way through, not out. He touched her shoulder. She didn't move.

"I'm sorry, Jackie," he whispered. He knew she didn't hear. And, if she did, and mumbled, "Why are you sorry?" and he told her only a little of it, she would run her fingers through his hair and say, "You're my crazy Monkey. I don't know what you're talking about. Go back to sleep."

Monkey slipped out of bed and walked down the dark hall. The light above the stove glowed phosphor green. 4:03. He filled a glass with water, padded into the living room, and sat at the end of the couch. When he closed his eyes, he was in the heart of a web of ripples. Wavering. Silver. Pink. He had no idea where he was, and he was surprised to realize this was preferable to knowing.

He opened his eyes. The gray cat strolled in. He was a big-head tom whose muscle and grace had survived neutering. "Hulk," Monkey said, "I do not need this. I need to crash and wake all perky. I have tricky work to do on the Porsche and the two Lexi and the Audi tomorrow. The hyper assholes—no, of course I mean the enthusiastic owners—will fuck me running with a rusty chainsaw if their babies are not ready to roll by five. Five sharp."

Hulk jumped into his lap, landing, as always, on Monkey's nuts. "You don't need to de-ball me," Monkey said for the hundredth time. "I shoot blanks. Remember?"

He scratched Hulk's cauliflower ears. As always, he felt a rush of tenderness, maybe deeper than anything he ever felt for a human. "Ah fuck," he said. "My life is good. That was just a dream, that's all. A little too much Bud, a whole lot too much bud."

He tucked Hulk under his arm and went back into bed. He had an hour of cerebral self-torment, then nothing till Jackie poked him gently on the shoulder. "C'mon babe," she said. "We gotta support the cats."

Monkey was a shade-tree mechanic, though in the guts of Twentynine Palms, California, there was no tree and, consequently, no shade. There was an old two-room adobe that he'd converted into the Monkey Biz. He worked alone. He was happiest working on cars that did not require computer triage. In fact, computer triage on a 2008 car was a fuckload nastier than anything he'd faced in his youthful days as an EMT. Computers were the anti-christ. And, since too many of his customers were rich retirees who had moved to neighboring Joshua Tree to find themselves, he figured he was already serving the devil.

He unlocked the barred security door of the Biz, then the inner door, an old pine artifact from the station's earlier days which Jackie had painted bright turquoise. She was always gracing ordinary stuff with her touch. For instance, his lunch. Even though they both worked, she insisted on packing his lunch. He opened the lid of the cooler. A cup of homemade fruit cocktail, six sushi rolls, wasabi and pickled ginger, a folded napkin and a real spoon. Jackie hated plastic. She hated anything that wasn't real. "Except for a good night's natural sleep," he muttered, and shook his head as though he could jolt out his meanness.

He booted up the computer. He kept his records in there. More or less. The computer flickered once and went dark. Monkey sat down at the desk and put his head on his arms. Last night, he'd meant to print out the records of the four lucky assholes who were his customers for the day. He'd had one toke to ease the drive home and spaced it out.

Porsche. Lexus. Lexus. Audi. What the fuck were the names of the three guys and the chick? Porsche. Lexus. Lexus. Audi. He closed his eyes and repeated what should have been memory cues. Porsche. Lexus. Lexus. Audi. He felt like he was counting beads on some infernal Papist rosary. Papist? Rosary? Those were his gramps' words.

"Shut up, Gramps," Monkey said. "Stay outta my head." His grandfather had hated Catholics and Born Agains equally, but he had to be careful around his wife. Lettie had gone down to the river and while she never pushed it on anybody, being an Okie woman and all, her eyes would go like flint if somebody made fun of The Saved.

Monkey was drifting. A bad sign. He dug through the papers in the South Park hat that was his inbox. They could have been written in Sanskrit. Hopeless. He looked up at the photo of Jackie on the computer. She was grinning into the camera. "Hey, girl," he said. "I remember you."

One toke. One toke might ignite his brain. Wrong. One toke would make the intricacies of modern automotive engineering first irresistibly intriguing, then inscrutable. A scrap of paper fell on the floor. He picked it up. Jason Stephens—2007 Porsche, timing off, 760-693-4257. The mental gears engaged. Deborah Miller, Lexus. Shane Concord, Lexus 2. Ricardo Ramirez, Audi. Check. Check. Check and check.

He tried the computer again. The screen glowed. He was in. For the moment. It was time to give up and find a part-time grunt for the office. He printed out the service orders, swallowed the last of his coffee, gazed longingly at the desk drawer that held the perfect bud in a tampon box, and went into the shop.

Miller, Concord, and Ramirez called three times apiece before noon. Stephens showed up at 5:45. Monkey's hours were posted in bright red on the front door: 8-5, NO EXCEPTIONS. Consequently, Stephens arrived as Monkey wafted the last of the dope smoke out the window into the alley.

"Oops, dude," Stephens said. "My bad." He was a full-bore charmboy so you could excuse his backdated attempt at cool.

"Yep," Monkey drawled. "Your bad."

Stephens tried to high-five him. Monkey suddenly found himself shuffling through the papers on the desk.

"Here's the damage," he said. "Normally, I'd have you come back tomorrow, but I'm feeling lenient."

"Hey, thanks, homie," the guy said. "You're a real brother."

Monkey smiled. "Whoa, pal. I see that my blue eyes fooled you. I ain't no African-American. I'm an Okie. I'm what you might call a red-bone Caucasian. And you are not a native speaker of Ebonics."

Stephens laughed. "Well, be that as it may, let's get this sewed up." He pulled out his checkbook, looked for a calendar, and froze. "Where did you get that poster? It looks like an original."

"It is." Monkey was no way going to say more. The guy didn't need to know—he didn't *get* to know—that Jackie had given Monkey the poster as a wedding gift. Because he loved the group. Because that was all she could afford. Because the picture was of a naked man and woman holding hands. Traffic and Fairport Convention and Mott the Hoople, Fillmore East in New York City, when neither of them had been any further east than Arkadelphia, Arkansas, where her Aunt Sunny lived.

"Do you have any idea how much that piece of paper is worth?" Stephens said.

"Nope."

Stephens crouched next to him and said, "Let me google something."

Monkey said, "I don't know you that well, fella."

Stephens laughed. "No worries, we're going to google that poster."

"You don't touch that poster," Monkey said.

"Google is a search engine. C'mon, you'll love this."

Monkey rolled his chair back. Stephens' hands flickered over the computer keys and there, radiant in the soft gloom of the office, was the poster and a dozen others.

"Okay," Monkey said. "Show me what you did. I want to find more."

Stephens walked him through Search. "I'll check this out later," Monkey said. "I gotta get back to my real life."

"You're welcome," Stephens said. He wrote out the check for $650, took a bill out, folded it, and tucked it in Monkey's shirt pocket. "A tip," he said. "Not for your superb workmanship, but for your even finer customer relation skills."

Monkey was too blasted by the dope and the poster to do anything but say, "Thanks. Yeah, thanks, man."

Monkey stared at the computer screen. He was pissed off, and pissed off mixed with a one-toke high was a bad combo. He called Jackie and told her he was running late, maybe an hour. He fired up the pipe and took a couple long, slow, luxurious hits.

His heart stopped feeling like it was made of ground glass. The light in the room became sweet as opal. He opened the computer and googled *Traffic. Vintage posters.*

Fillmore East 1970 appeared. He scrolled down. Traffic had had so much fuckin' class. Most of the posters were long on intricate drawings and short on day-glo. They were printed in black, brown, and then the sepia of the Fillmore East couple.

He studied the next poster in the row. Ether framed in starry blue and purple and a bright swatch of yellow. He clicked on the image. He couldn't read the words. They were yellow, in a script he knew was English but seemed foreign. There was a face and a car and a figure in full lotus in the foreground. Monkey enlarged the picture and began to decipher the words: Pinnacle. Traffic. Quicksilver Messenger Service. Crumb. Shrine.

He heard himself laugh. His heart went bone cold. There was what seemed to be the swirling skirt of a Spanish dancer and Gramps' voice and then a pure virile falsetto. Monkey was in the heart of it all. In All of It. Gramps said something about oil and a vessel and that damn foolishness.

Lumps of sludge slammed down. *I can see sound. I can...*

Monkey jolted upright. Somebody was pounding on the office door. He checked the time. 8:27.

"Dude. Dude. I know you're in there. I can smell what you been doing. C'mon. I gotta talk to you. It's Keno. Open the fuck up, *cabron*."

Monkey moved the fingers on his right hand, then his left. He lifted his foot from the floor. So far so good. The pounding got louder. "Hey, this is an emergency. Get your stoned ass out of that chair and OPEN THE DOOR."

Monkey opened his mouth. "So glad you could drop by," he said. There was no chance Keno could hear him. He cracked his jaw. "So glad you could drop by," he rasped.

"I can't the fuck hear you," Keno said.

Monkey pulled himself out of the chair. The computer was a pale blur. He looked down and saw the folded bill Concord had given him and a few words scrawled on an old envelope. They could have been written in Zulu for all he could read them.

"I'm there," he said. His voice was almost back to normal.

Monkey slid the bolt, undid the padlock, and unlocked the door. It took all his concentration. He stumbled back to the chair. "It's open," he said.

Keno Martinez filled the doorway and stomped in. "Why is it," he said, "a sensitive guy who needs a friend can't find one when he needs one?"

"Truly tragic, *gordo*," Monkey said. "Hey, it happened again. The trance thing." He might as well have kept his mouth shut. His pal was not in listening gear.

Keno sat on the stack of tires that served as a customer chair. He held a photograph out to Monkey. "Here's the reason I gotta get help right now, plus you will make out like a bandit, plus this is NOT about pussy, it's about love."

"Give me," Monkey said slowly and clearly, "one minute to call Jackie. I was supposed to be home an hour ago."

Keno subsided.

Monkey dialed. The answering machine picked up. Big surprise. It was past eight. She was down for the count. "Hey," he said, "it's me. Be home about ten. Love ya."

"So," Keno said, "look at this woman!"

Monkey took the photo and turned on the desk lamp. The woman was pale and chubby. She held a baby that was the standard redneck amorphous blob. The Madonna and Child were in a Walmart parking lot. Both of them were squinting.

"Is that not beautiful?" Keno said. "Is that not one of the most precious things you ever seen?"

"Saw. You people gotta learn to speak English if you want to be here." Monkey fired up the bowl. "Have a hit."

"No," Keno said. "I gotta keep my head clear. You get wasted, then I'll tell you the deal."

Monkey took a quarter toke. A financial deal was coming up. He was sure of it. And, somehow, always, guaranteed, a financial deal with Keno would screw him quicker than a crack ho.

He looked back at the picture. "What's the story?"

Keno took the pipe. "I guess a little hit won't hurt." He sucked in enough smoke to fell a rhinoceros. "Well, that's Amber and Kimberley Rose. Amber's the mom. I took the picture. We were on the sidewalk in front of the Walmart on that main mall drag in Kingman. Kimberley Rose was squinting because of the sun. It's that desert sun, you know, that's a brutal bitch even in April. Kimberley Rose isn't mine."

Monkey looked at Kimberley Rose's Kraft Dinner noodle-white face. "No shit, Keno."

Keno didn't skip a beat. "Amber tells me ten times a day how grateful she is that I let her and Kimberley Rose crash in my apartment.

There's more to the story than that, but when I took that picture, Amber and Kimberley Rose were moving in closer to the camera, I saw all the beauty, and I popped for breakfast."

"You're in the shit," Monkey said. Keno never bought anybody so much as a jerky stick.

"Yeah, well, love don't come to a man that often."

"What about that little dancer last month?"

"Infatuation," Keno said firmly. "Immaturity."

"So. Get it over with. What do you need?"

"It's not what I need," Keno said. "It's what Amber and Kimberley Rose need. And, good luck for you, it's what *you* need."

In the past, Keno had determined that Monkey needed a rusted-out satellite dish, an ounce of the only pot Monkey had ever thrown out, and the phone number of a gal who could hum your unit like a porch toad on a June bug.

Monkey put his head down on his arms for the second time. What could have been a pleasant and delicious dinner at home and possibly an equally satisfying conjugal relation had morphed into a hangover in a back alley in Tijuana.

"Follow me," Keno said.

He led Monkey to the street. A green 1990 Buick Le Sabre seemed to droop next to the curb.

"Look at that," Keno said.

"I am looking and what I see is a parakeet-shit green beater that'll suck gas like..."

"Wrong, you are looking at a valuable investment property."

"How so?"

"How so you buy it off of me for $150, slap a little rust remover on, gap the spark plugs, hang a Guadalupe air freshener off the rearview mirror, and sell it for $350 to some lucky Marine *guey*. The serial numbers have been filed off. The muffler is just loose enough that it roars like a fighter jet."

"Amber's ride, right?"

"Not any more. She was going to get killed in it. I let her use my pony. Why not? It's time for me to think of somebody other than myself."

Monkey held the photo to the streetlight. "What the fuck," he said.

"Maybe it's time for me to think about somebody other than myself."

"Hey, my brother," Keno said. "They didn't name me *Refugio* for nothing. And you could damn near be a real *wab*."

It was nearly ten by the time the deal was done. The celebratory sharing of the pipe took who knew how long. Keno split, Monkey pulled the Le Sabre into the side yard and returned to the desk.

He tapped a computer key. The poster leaped up into light. Nothing changed. The letters were still barely readable. The head and the car and the cross-legged figure stayed put. He put the computer to sleep and picked up the envelope.

It was his writing. He held it away from his eyes. He was starting to feel the years when he read. He was starting to feel the years everywhere but in his dick.

...all spirals toward the void, memories, color, thoughts, sound, all whirls like the skirt on a Spanish dancer, all is but a moment and infinite at once...

...Gramps...

...a pure, virile falsetto...

Monkey picked up the empty pipe and tossed it from hand to hand. "Looks like," he said, "you and me are going to take a break. Right. Who am I kidding?"

He unfolded Stephens' tip. It was a bright new one-dollar bill.

The house was dark except for a soft glow coming from the kitchen. Jackie had left a candle burning in a clay saucer and the Crock-Pot turned to warm. Monkey lifted the lid. Chicken green chili. The table was set, a napkin draped over a fat corn muffin.

He crumbled the muffin into a bowl, spooned on the chili, and sat in the gloom to eat. He knew there were chopped sweet onions in a covered dish in the fridge and grated cheese, but the munchies had taken over—and a reluctance to be pampered in his mean loneliness.

He ate another bowl of chili. He was going to have to watch it. Between a few more bowls of bud each week and the standard half bag of cookies he was about to put away, his gut was beginning to precede him by more than he liked. He untied his head rag and freed his thinning hair from the ponytail. Lovely. Spreading gut and thinning hair. And a gorgeous woman dead asleep in the room down the hall.

Monkey limited himself to eight walnut chippers. Jackie had baked them sometime in the day. He reckoned she got off work around one and managed to do her wifely stuff before she poured the vodka into her Diet Sprite. The cookies were awesome. Everything Jackie did was awesome. She even thought he was awesome.

He rinsed out his bowl and spoon and put them in the dishwasher. He heard Jackie snoring clear down the hall. He figured he'd skip a shower till morning. There wasn't going to be any reason to be sweet-smelling. There hadn't been a reason for a few weeks. Maybe if he hadn't had that second toke; maybe if Keno hadn't shown up; maybe if he hadn't been possibly going crazy. Maybe.

He crept into the bedroom. The night-light shown on Jackie's hair. He picked up a strand in his fingers. Not chestnut, not gray, it was a soft brindle, warm as the brown of fresh-split juniper. Monkey lay down on his back. He could feel the beginning of a boner. Seemed like he'd had the beginning of a boner since he'd hit puberty—"at about three," Jackie loved to say. He sighed and got ready to wait out his brain and boner till morning.

4

Nell watched the gulls be voracious and rude. The light began to cool. She wondered how she would spend the night in downtown Long Beach without checking into a hotel that would cut far too deeply into the six hundred and change she had in her purse. She'd seen people sleeping in the hard chairs of the L.A. Greyhound Station in a morning that seemed a month ago. Her bag was checked for twenty-four hours. She looped her purse over her shoulder and walked away from the harbor. She'd find a coffee shop and take it from there. It would not be the first time she'd slept in a bus station.

The coffee shop was called Affirmations. Each drink had a name. Enthuse Espresso. Motivate Macchiato. Calm Chamomile. The customers looked like they needed all of them. Nell smiled at the barista, found a table away from the speakers, opened her laptop, and logged on.

There was nothing in her private email, or her consulting account, a fiction she had maintained just in case somebody somewhere thought, "Hey, what about Nell Walker? She's not at Elysian Global anymore." In fact, she was as vanished as the love note David had once showed her. "Kate Hepburn," it had said, "was a wuss compared to you. 4-MUCH. 4-EVER." He'd wadded the paper into a tiny ball and thrown it into the wind above the Whidbey Island ferry. "Do you know there is a holiday in Japan during which lovers write poems on origami paper? They fold them into tiny boats, set them on a river at midnight, and set them afire."

He had traced her lips with his thumb. "Those people understand eternity." Nell had watched the note drop into the water. "Can you imagine," he had whispered, "those tiny fires against the dark water?" He kissed her softly. By the time she had looked down at the ferry's wake, the note was gone.

"Fuck you, boyo," Nell muttered. She wiped out both email accounts, and gave herself a new address: papercut55@yahoo.com.

To: papercut55@yahoo.com
Subject: future Nell, since apparently there is a future Nell
I seem to believe that I can disappear. A former hot shit account executive in the biggest pharmaceutical corporation in the world, the mortgagee of a 1.5 million dollar cottage in West Hollywood. The former lucky gal with a broker—not so lucky with that one—a tax consultant, a personal trainer, and two therapists who represented the sum total of her even remotely intimate contacts—can disappear.
Poof.
Gone.
Yet more or less alive.
Signed, Irrational in Long Beach

She clicked Send. It came to her that there was more to say. She replied.

To: papercut55@yahoo.com
Subject: more
Asset One in the New Lost Life: Marginal Irony

The music from the speakers grew louder. One of the baristas laughed. "Grooooooovy," his buddy said. Nell sipped her tea and waited for the sound to coalesce. A word emerged from the din. *Willing.*

Nell lost her marginal irony. She knew the song. *Willing.* One of her mother's favorite songs. She could smell the kitchen in the ghetto apartment. Mildew and roach spray. The bread her mom had just baked from U.S.D.S. surplus flour and lard. She had been fifteen. Her mom had played the song five times in a row, finally yowling along on the chorus. "If you give me..."

Nell couldn't remember the sequence in the chorus. Wine, whites, and weed? Weed, whites, and wine? And God help her, what difference did it make? She opened the laptop, checked her new account. Two messages, both from papercut55. She searched *Willing.* She opened the top link. There were a few characters in Japanese across the top of the page, some chord changes, then:

chorus;

AND I BEEN FROM TUCSON TO TUCANCARY TAHATHAPI
TO TANAPALL

DRIVEN EVERY KIND OF RIG THAT'S EVER BEEN MADE
DRIVEN THE BACK ROADS SO I WOULDN'T BET WEIGHTED
AND IF YOU GIVE ME WEED WHITES AND WINE...

Nell copied the first line and sent herself a message:

Subject: Itinerary
TUCSON TO TUCANCARY TAHATHAPI TO TANAPALL

She finished her tea, packed up her computer, and walked out onto the street. Left would take her to the light rail; right, back to the harbor. Nell headed for the water. Sequins of neon glittered on the dark surface. There were the shadows of gulls. She was hungry and afraid, which was, as her ever-hopeful therapists would have told her, better than hungry and disassociated. Which was easy to believe when you were making $300 an hour listening to a smart, funny, and numb woman.

She thought about finding a cheap place for dinner and guessed there weren't any. She needed every cent of the $600 she had left. She remembered a corpo-sensitivity retreat she'd made herself attend. It had been focused on how to prune employees with compassion. Buy-out packages were good, but they wouldn't prevent feelings. "Forgiveness," the soft-voiced facilitator had said, "cannot be bought."

"Wrong," she thought. "Forgiveness is having enough money. Tell it to my mom." She'd known that since she was a kid. Knowing that had driven her for thirty years. Knowing that hadn't prepared her for enough never being enough.

The Greyhound station was quiet. A tiny old woman had already curled up in a fleece throw. There were a few sections of the *Sunday Times* on the floor. Nell retrieved them, bought peanuts and a bottle of milk from the vending machine, took her chair, tucked her bag behind her legs, and settled in.

Nell came awake before dawn. She had slept straight through. Night after night for a year, she had waked every fifteen minutes, clenched, heart pounding in her ears. Minutes had felt like hours, an eight-hour night lasting an eternity. The spiral in her brain had been consistent: *Gone, do something, what can I do? Gone, do something, what can I do? Gone, do something, what can I do?*

The guy behind the ticket counter was asleep in his chair. Scraps of paper fluttered down to the parking lot, rose on an early breeze, and were pigeons. The morning light shifted from opal to silver to gold. She could hear distant hip-hop, then a burst of laughter. She realized she was not just hungry, but famished.

She added money to the locker. At worst, she'd go back to the coffee shop, order coffee, dump a quart of cream and three spoonfuls of sugar in it, and consider it a hot smoothie. "Thanks Mom, for the training," she murmured.

At best, she'd find a complimentary hotel buffet. The first time she had seen an elegant old lady in backdated and carefully mended clothes walk up to the buffet in a hotel without paying, she had been astonished. The woman had put four oranges, three bananas, six cream cheese packets, three muffins, a bagel, and two hard-boiled eggs in her shopping bag. She had filled her plate with bacon, sausage, eggs, bagels, yogurt, and more cream cheese. Nell had never seen a woman eat so much in her life.

Nell knew where she would go for free breakfast. The place owed her. She washed her face and hands in the restroom, ran her hands through her hair, and decided to save what was left of her lipstick for a hypothetical job interview when she got where she was going which was who knew where.

The hotel was now La Tropique International Suites. It had been La Mer International Luxe Suites the afternoon she and David had walked into the glass-walled lobby. David had found out only that morning that his wife was taking the kids to her folks in San Diego. He had called a dozen Long Beach B&Bs, all without vacancies, and given up. "It doesn't matter whether we have goat-cheese-stuffed pistachio-encrusted French toast with bilberries. It matters that we'll have each other. Let's just find some chain hotel."

The La Mer International Suites had one suite left on the next-to-top floor with a view of the harbor. There was a jacuzzi. "And amenities you might expect," the reservationist had said. "And it's only $799 for the night." David told her he had AAA. She had laughed. "There are no discounts for the Premier accommodations. This is the Katmandu Suite."

David and Nell had checked into the two huge rooms. A framed Tibetan thangka was bolted to the wall. There were amenities galore: the jacuzzi, six pulsating heads in the shower, a refrigerator, and a bed the size of Nell's kitchen. A basket of munchies sat on the entry table. Nell opened the curtains. The view had indeed been spectacular. She picked up the brochure on the glass table.

"David," she had said. "Listen to this. You have no idea what a thrilling experience we can have here."

David was on his cell. "Hold on a sec." He'd said something into the phone and hung up.

"Did you know," Nell said, "that according to this brochure, *garden ambience continues through a lounge and dining area, decorated with light colors and well-maintained but casual furniture?*"

David tugged her to the bed. "I am so relieved," he said, "that the casual furniture is well-maintained. Perhaps we might stroll down to the lounge later and sit on a nicely vacuumed patio chair. For now, we have other business to attend to. It's been three weeks." He bent to kiss her wrist.

"No, wait," Nell had said. "There's more." And, as he trailed his kiss up her arm, she read, "*Bell staff in red-and-white checkered vests wheel luggage carts toward the elevators, closely followed by young conventioneers, cruise-ship passengers awaiting boarding calls, and international businesspeople.*"

"And two aging lovers who were in such a hurry to get to the room they never noticed the natty bell staff," David said.

Later, David had hunted for food. "I am Basic Man," he said. "First fuck, then feed." He brought the basket to the bed. "Ah," Nell said, "more *Amenity Highlights*. Let's see what we've got." She opened a tiny bag of peanuts. "Protein."

David tore open the M&M's and dumped all fifteen of them on the sheet. "You have to eat the orange ones. I get the red."

"Stop," Nell yelled. "Look at this price list. It was under the basket."

David laughed. "Those peanuts were especially selected for us by Mario Batali. They had to have been. $7.75, which is $124 a pound. The M&M's must have a soupcon of cocaine. They're $200 a pound."

Nell spit her half-chewed peanuts into the packet. "We'll just return them."

"Oh no," David said. "Witty and nasty, but too easy. You see, dear one, these people do not understand Potential Marketing. You and I will never set foot in this hotel again. Nor will any of my pals."

Nell walked into the huge glass-walled atrium. A bell girl in a Hawaiian-print vest looked up from her cell, smiled, and went back to texting. Nell found the Palm and Papaya Coffee Shop and walked in. There was no host, no waiters, no attendants, nattily attired or not.

Nell found a table near the window. A sleepy waitress came out of the prep station. "You wish something to drink?"

Nell smiled. "Coffee would be perfect."

"You wish the buffet?"

Nell nodded.

"The plates are at the end."

Nell tucked ten dollars under her water glass. The waitress nodded. "And, of course, if you wish fresh fruit for later in the day, feel free to take some."

Nell swallowed the last of her dark and excellent coffee. She had put away a mushroom omelet, a quarter pound of smoked salmon, two bowls of melon, four cups of coffee, and two limp, but buttery, croissants.

You were wrong about a lot, David, she wrote on the comment card. *One of us set foot in this hotel again.* She checked five stars for service and wrote in the waitress' name.

She opened her laptop. There was no point. The only person writing to her was her. She crammed her bag with fruit, cream cheese packets, and bagels and walked out into a hazy morning.

The bus to San Bernardino was half empty. Nell stretched across two seats and folded the purple suit coat up for a pillow. A pale kid in a black trench coat sat down across the aisle and threw up in his black cowboy hat. Cheap wine and junk food fumes filled the stale air. The second time he bent over the hat, the old man in the seat ahead of the kid turned around and said, "There's a fuckin' toilet in the fuckin' back. Get your fuckin' inconsiderate ass back there."

The kid hauled himself to his feet and stumbled to the back of the bus. The old guy shook his head. "Sorry for the language, folks," he said. "I hate spoiled rich kids."

Nell closed her eyes. It was going to be a long short ride.

5

Jackie groaned. Monkey's heart leaped. "Down boy," he muttered. "Oh sugar," Jackie whispered. "Are you okay?"

She pulled off the sleep mask. "I bet I've got raccoon eyes," she said. "I'd roll over next to you, but if I move I'll break into little bitty pieces."

Monkey edged over to her. "Don't touch me," she said, and smiled. "Not yet."

There were strawberry waffles for breakfast. Monkey found a birthday candle in the Whatever Drawer and stuck it in between two berries. "What's that for?" Jackie said.

He lit it. "I'm celebrating the once this month that we had this morning." He laughed.

"Hey," Jackie said. "That was a little mean."

"Hey," he said. "I was teasing." He sat down. "I'm just a normal guy living with a real babe."

Monkey walked to work. He had a dope hangover meaner than a pissed off boar hog. He figured he might be able to sweat the poisons out. Besides, he loved the neighborhood in the early morning. A ragged banner of crows and cowbirds spiraled down to the dumpster in back of the fake French cafe. The beat of their wings *whrrrrrr*ed past his ears, not quite sound, delicate and unsettling. The feral mother cat led her mob out of the culvert and up toward the dumpster. There was nothing but fierce blue above the Marine base. The devil had arrived in town to jack up the thermostat.

Monkey unlocked the doors. There was a piece of paper on the floor. He let it be. It was probably Keno, having second thoughts, realizing there were a million women in the world, wanting to buy the Le Sabre back—for less, because somehow in the night, something had gone bad, shitty, disastrous.

Monkey considered cleaning. The coffeepot had an inch of industrial sludge in the bottom. A black widow spider web laced the one window. There was a pile of spare hubcaps (thanks to Keno) toppled on the floor. There was at least a quarter inch of perfectly good bud in the ashtray. Monkey put the bud back in the envelope in the tampon box. He picked up the coffeepot and set it back down. He breathed on the spider web. There were a few new strands since the day before. "I spare you," he said. "You spare me."

He opened the computer. The screen did not light up. Nothing. He rebooted. Nothing.

He picked up the note from the floor.

M-man, call me pronto. Don't matter how early. It's bad. Real bad.
K-rip

K-rip stood for Kryptonite, code for *I ain't woofin' ya*. It wasn't just high-grade cannabis, one-sided deals, and respect for vehicles built before computers that linked him and Keno—they both clung to seventies street talk as though it were a soul line.

Monkey dialed Keno's cell. He figured he'd go through the desk and find the day's work orders while he listened to Keno. Keno picked up on the first ring. "Oh man, thank you," he said. Monkey knew it was bad. Keno said *thank you* maybe once every five years. Silence, then a choked breath. "My nephew. Lucero. You remember him. Lucky Luc. He's dead."

Lucero Diaz had enlisted in the United States Marine Corps in January of 2006. He had been eighteen. He was—he had been—the father of three kids. By three different mothers. Lucero had been a real punk. Lucero Diaz was dead. Monkey realized he was thinking formally, his thoughts honed by shock.

"What?"

"Fuckin' Humvee went off the road. Luc ate it. That's all we know."

"I'm on my way," Monkey said.

"Not now," Keno said. "I'm at my mother's. It's fucking insane here. I'll come by later."

"Copy. You know where to find me." Monkey started to hang up and didn't. "Hey. K-rip? I am sorry."

"That little *pendejo*. Twelve years on the street...he was runnin' you-know-what when he was six. Keepin' alive the whole time, keepin' his spirit. Two months in Beirut. Powder dry, cajones tucked up where they belong. Then, bam. Fuckin' *pinche cabron*."

"The dangling dirk..." Monkey said. It was Keno's and Monkey's favorite summation of all that was both heinous and unavoidable: *Dorked by the dangling dirk of fate.*

"I gotta go," he said.

"Me too."

Monkey hung up. Two work orders lay in front of him. Both computer tuning jobs. No phone numbers. He *had* to slack off the *mota*. He had to call the Classifieds at the Hi Desert Star and place an ad. They had a cheap and dirty special on weekends. Ten dollars for two days, as long as you kept it to three lines. People sold everything. Carburetors. Iguanas. Velvet paintings of John Wayne.

Monkey grabbed another of an endless supply of old bill envelopes

and wrote: 1984 Le Sabre, cherry, $350. obo + wanted: part-time
computer genius. $11 an hour. Call 8-5 weekdays. 760-673-8889.

Jackie called just after he finished off the last job. "I was thinking,"
she said, "maybe I could pick you up and we could run over to Sally's
for dinner, then head down to the casinos for a few hours." Her voice
was clear and sweet. Under those circumstances, Monkey would have
agreed to a Thursday evening at Super Walmart.

"Sounds good," he said.

"I wasn't finished," she said. "I bought a new candle."

New candles were code for long, luxurious blow jobs.

"Mmmmmmmm," he said.

"I'll bring your Hawaiian shirt," Jackie said.

"Wear the mini-skirt," Monkey said.

"And you-know-what underneath," she laughed and hung up.

He heard Keno's Bronco a block away. Dual pipes, glass-packs, and
the sullen thump of "96 Tears" blasted on Kicker mid-bass speakers.
Monkey shut down the computer. It was going to be a long half hour
before Jackie picked him up.

He walked out into the yard. Keno pulled up and sat tight till the
last of the song faded. Monkey walked up to the driver's window.
Keno was wiping his face with his sleeve. "I'm sorry to bother you,
M-man," he said. "I had to come back. I never heard those lyrics the
way I hear 'em now...how they're singing to somebody who's gone,
who's looking down at us laughing. Like Luc's up there, you know, and
he's lookin' down. He's laughin'. Shit, he's happy.

"Ah fuck, man, like Sam Kinison...the dude was lyin' on the
highway near Needles and he looks up and says, 'Oh. Okay then,' and
he dies. Right there. Just got married and all to that stripper broad
with the humongous *chichis*."

Monkey waited. Keno passed him an open tequila bottle. "If I'm
gonna make sense, you gotta catch up," he said. Monkey took a hit. He
loved it. Tequila was the closest booze high you could get to the fine
vegetable buzz of weed.

"Jackie's picking me up in a half hour—oh shit, and I've got to call
in an ad to the paper. Come on in."

Keno climbed out of the Bronco, wrapped his arm around Monkey, and damn near drove him down into the hardpan. "Lean on me," Monkey warbled. They stumbled into the office.

Monkey finished the call just under the wire. The ad would be in the weekend's paper.

"It's the miracle of computers," the rep had said. "I don't know how people got along without them."

"We just tied our messages to our dinosaurs," Monkey said.

Keno handed him a photo. "Here's the three kids. Look. My more or less nephews." The little boys' eyes were solemn. They held white roses in their hands. "That was Luc's second old lady's idea. Everybody was all kissin' and sobbin', these three ho's who hate each others' guts. It was beautiful."

Keno held the tequila bottle to the light. "Two more swallows," he said. "One for you, one for me. Have at it, *companero*."

Monkey shook his head. "None for me, two for you. I need a clear head for my date tonight."

Keno was too muzzy to make a joke. "Monkey," he said, "I always wondered about somethin'. You and Jackie are tight. Yes?"

"Tight as a toad's tush," Monkey said.

"Then why, ah shit, this ain't none of my business, but why no kids?"

"Couldn't have 'em, didn't want 'em. That's my half of the story. The other half is Jackie's. That's confidential info."

"Respected."

Monkey looked at Keno's wet eyes. He saw a softness in the big face he'd rarely seen. "K-rip," he said, "here's about ninety-nine percent of my half. I see red. You know what I mean?"

"*Mal loco? Mala rabia?*"

"Yeah. I've always been scared that if I had a kid and the kid fucked up, I'd fuck the kid up."

"*De dios*," Keno said, and finished off the bottle. "Thanks, man."

"Always," Monkey said. "Any time."

Saigon Sally's was a Vietnamese joint tucked in between a massage parlor and Jen's Hair and Nails. They had two menus. One for customers, one for adopted family. The co-owner, Mr. Anh, had fallen in love with Jackie. "You are not like American women," he had said.

"You are soft."

He appeared in the doorway. "We have fresh fish tonight. My uncle caught them over at Parker. Please come in."

He led them to a red-curtained booth. "You are early," he said. "Please eat at the Wedding Table. Like newlyweds."

Jackie smiled up at him. "Twenty-five years next month," she said.

Mr. Anh laughed. "No, no, you are only teenagers. Not possible."

Jackie ordered salt and pepper shrimp for both of them. "I will choose the rest of the meal," Mr. Anh said. "You will be happy."

Monkey leaned back on the padded seat. "I am beat," he said. "Between the computer and Keno, it's been a long, long day."

Jackie took his hand and drew it under the table. He felt the silky skin of her thigh. When he moved his hand higher, she tapped his wrist. "Not yet, Mr. Man, you're so greedy."

He looked at her sweet face. He thought about telling her about Lucky Luc, but she had picked up her purse and given him a guilty look. "I'm going to grab a smoke," she said. "I've been good all day." She slipped through the red curtains and was gone.

Monkey couldn't remember why he had thought the casino would be fun. He'd run through fifteen hands of poker and four hundred bucks he didn't have. Jackie had disappeared into the maze of slot machines. His head ached and he wanted some bud more desperately than he wanted to. It was getting out of control. As were the miserable cards fanning out in front of him.

He zoned out during the last hand, tipped the dealer, and got up. He figured Jackie was on one of the animal slots. Some tech genius had jacked right into the Cute neurons in most women's brains. Give 'em puppies and talking chickens and they were happy. Jackie loved the Poker Pigs, a nine-liner on which the bonus featured five pigs in turn-of-the-century outfits playing cards. He filled a paper cup with Coke at the Bottomless Free Drinks! near the video poker.

He walked to the back door. Tail-lights glowed like animal eyes through the smoked glass. He pushed open the door and walked out into air as soft as a woman's skin. For some fucking reason, his eyes were wet. "I got nothing to feel sad about," he thought. "Nothing."

6

"San Berdoo," the driver called out. "Palm Springs transfers, you got an hour and a half. Nothing but vending machines in the station. Mickey D.'s a few blocks away."

The kid with the black hat was asleep. The old guy nudged him. The kid nodded, hauled himself up, and wobbled toward the open door. The old guy waited till Nell moved past him to creak out in the aisle. "Kid's gonna be dry," he said. "Stash your stuff in a locker and let's scout out a burger."

"Give me a minute," Nell said. "I need the ladies' room."

There were no doors on the stalls of the ladies' in the San Bernardino Greyhound Station. Nell hunkered just above the toilet to pee and looked down. Two tampon wrappers, one stained thong, and a used condom lay at her feet. She finished and stepped carefully over the mess. There was a sign on the sink. Out of Order. She leaned against the wall next to the sign, thought about taking a picture with her cell, and figured there was nobody she could send it to.

The bus ride from Long Beach to San Bernardino had been a stretch of near-hallucinogenic nostalgia for the man that didn't exist. She had felt as though she had a full-body migraine aura, one that ebbed and flowed, ebbed and flowed, and never resolved into clean pain. She'd forgotten the tiny glow of I Will Survive vengeance she had felt when she had walked out of the La Tropique International Suites breakfast buffet scot-free.

Why did she miss David? Worse, why didn't she miss anything else except the parrots? Not her neighbors, not her former staff, not the gorgeous boy barista in King's Road Coffee. Not her friends, because there hadn't been any. There hadn't been time.

The cottage had receded in her memory, along with twenty thousand dollars worth of furniture, three pairs of Manolo Blahniks, two pairs of Uggs, three sets of 900-thread-count sheets, one never-lit thirty-dollar Sage/Coriander candle, an unused espresso machine, two blown-glass goblets etched with Mimbres designs, and a cup full of plastic forks.

She added up the scores in her Life Tournament: Nell—0, Mom— winning. Nell had ceased to give a shit about material things. It did not feel pious. It did not feel Green. It did not feel like some fucking noble truth of Mahatma Gandhi. It felt like giving up. "Right on, Mom."

The glare in the McDonald's was only a little less painful than the glare outside. The old man stepped over to the next register. "One plain burger," he said, "large coffee, and large Coke. Make that Coke to go."

The place was packed with white-haired couples uniformly dressed in beige and denim shorts and pastel polo shirts. She wondered what it would be like to sit across from a hubby for an hour, eating darn well what you wanted no matter what the young doc had said, while you and hubby didn't say a word. It occurred to her that she might need a reason down the line to be grateful she'd tossed the pills, and not being The Wife with The Hubby would be a good one.

She looked out the window. A couple hitched at the side of the road. The skinny one's hair was a silvery fall down a long back; the chunky one's a luminous halo. The skinny one held a sign. She remembered hitchhiking with her mom. Her mother had never held a sign. The Rule of the Road had been: *We go where we are taken.* Score one more for Mom.

Nell thought about the working mothers in her office and their cell phones, their parenting magazines, how they juggled schedules and au pairs and the kids' relentless play dates and lessons. "According to *Parenting*, I should be dead. How did I make it to being a grown-up?"

The counter girl called her number. She picked up her food and ordered four more burgers and two Dr Peppers. She and the old guy ate. He told her stories about hard time on the road. "I wouldn't have it any other way," he said. "Except there's no fine woman in my life."

Nell smiled. "Somebody's missing out."

The old guy laughed. "You can say that again."

The counter girl called Nell's number. The old guy shook his head. "You eating more?"

"Nope. Just a little payback." She carried the burgers and the drinks out to the couple. The skinny one was a boy, the short one an old woman.

"Whoa," the kid said, "the Good Samaritan." He bowed and took the food. The old woman took Nell's hand. "Thank you," she said. "Me and my grandkid are headed for Indio. His ma's a cashier in the casino."

"God bless," the kid said. "Travel light."

There was an abandoned lot across from the station, one skeletal tree twisting up from the broken ground. The bus to Palm Springs left in twenty minutes. Nell checked her watch. She had time to walk. A girl leaned against the bus station wall. She stretched out her arm. There were watches from wrist to elbow. "Y'all need a new watch," she said. "Rolex. Genuine. Ten bucks."

Nell remembered that she was regarding human contact as an invitation. She stripped the Piaget from her wrist. "I'll trade you," she said.

The girl's eyes were dead. "Uh uh," she said. "That's a fake, besides I needs the cash."

Nell shook her head. "So do I."

"Ho," the girl said. "White bitch ho."

Nell crossed the street, stepped over a tumbled rock wall, and picked her way over shattered glass and beer cans to the tree. The lower branches were dead. A few glossy leaves sprouted from the top. The ground was littered with blood-red globes. She picked one up. It was an ornamental orange, months desicated, the skin rough as sandpaper. She held it to her nose. The scent was sharp. She dropped it in her bag.

She wondered why she wasn't frightened by the emptiness stretching ahead of her. She had spent at least thirty years awash in essentially solitary busyness. The company had had to force her to take vacations. Until David. Until he had escorted her out of the Fortress of Solitude. Shut up, brain. The bus driver came out of the station and waved at her.

"We're heading out, ma'am. Time to board."

The drunk boy lay across two seats. Nell sat well away from him. The driver closed the door. The old guy tottered across the parking lot and pounded on the side of the bus. The driver snarled and opened the door.

The old guy climbed on. "Hey," he said. "Thanks for your

graciousness."

The driver waited while the old guy made his way down the aisle. Nell turned to watch. The old guy leaned over the back of his seat and poked the kid. The kid whined and shook his head. The old guy poked him again. When the kid slitted his eyes open, the old guy handed him the Coke. The kid sat up. "Thank you," he said. "I'm sorry."

"Shut the fuck up," the old guy said. "Drink that slow. If you puke again I'll bust your face wide open."

"Palm Springs," the driver called out. "Be sure to grab your bags." Nell, the old guy, and the hung-over kid climbed out and headed for the little station. The place was empty; nothing but a vending machine and a sign telling customers there'd be a ticket agent at 5:30.

The bus pulled away. Nell, the old guy, and the kid waited outside. A beat-up van squealed into the parking lot and stopped in front of the kid. The driver leaned out the window. "You dumb fuck. You are in deep shit." The kid pulled open the passenger door and dropped into the seat.

The old man lit a cigarette and nodded. "You can see where it comes from, can't you?"

The van stalled out. The driver pounded his fists on the steering wheel, tried again, and rooster-tailed out to the highway. The parking lot was empty except for a taxi idling at its edge. Nell sat on her suitcase. There was nothing in any direction except for shimmer, sky, and railroad tracks. The old guy shaded his eyes. "Did you ever see anywhere as beautiful as this—except for those damn wind towers over there?"

"What's wrong with them?"

"You one of those green beans?"

"What?"

"All about solar power, all about wind power, thinking we can get a free ride from this desert?"

"I guess I believe that. I haven't thought about it much," Nell said.

"You need to learn something, missy," he said. "Those friggin' things are like bird blenders. I saw a picture of an eagle cut clear in half. You green beans ought to educate yourselves about how it really is out here. It's not nothing out here. It's everything."

He lit a cigarette and shook his head.

"I'm sorry," Nell said. "I will learn about that. I'm kind of new to everything these days."

"It's okay," he said. "I just get fired up about certain things. I'm Harrison, by the way."

Nell looked away from the wind towers to a horizon that contained fierce white light, low mountain ranges, and not, as far as she could tell, much else.

"It might take me a while to really see this," Nell said. "Meanwhile, how do you figure we get into town? Maybe walk?"

"Are you nuts, darlin'?" Harrison said. "It's gotta be ninety degrees and rising."

Nell stepped out from the shade. The sun slammed down. "Damn," she said.

"See what I mean? Look. I've got an idea. First off, my intentions are pure. I've got no choice. My blood pressure pills run the show. Why don't you and me split the cab fare? It'll run eight bucks apiece. Where you headed?"

"I'm not sure. It's my first time here. Maybe a cheap bed-and-breakfast. I need to get some sleep."

"Where you been, missy?" Harrison said. "Nothing's cheap in Palm Springs except the millionaires. This is Palm Springs, home of the rich and getting richer."

Nell looked away. She'd forgotten that she wasn't the woman who could stay in a bed-and-breakfast anymore. "Sorry," she said. "Let's just say I'm getting used to new circumstances."

"Tell you what," he said. "I'm heading into a casino. I've got enough comps to get a room. I won't use it. Never do. Blackjack's kind of a hobby of mine. I play all night once I get started. You can stay in the room. I'll get just one key—for you. You can bar the door.

"We'll use my comps in the dinner buffet and fuel up. You can grab some of the fruit and rolls for later—seeing as how you're traveling economy class—sit by the pool, do what you damn well please and get a good night's sleep."

"Thanks for your offers," Nell said. "Let me think for a second."

"Women," Harrison said.

Nell grinned, reached into her bag, and pulled out cream cheese and three apples. "You gotta love those buffets," she said. "And I'm Nell."

"Well, goddammit," Harrison said. "I'm glad to see you're not one of those uppity broads who has to run the show. Let's get out of this blast furnace."

Harrison had signed in and handed her the key. "Come on over to the tables so you know where I am," he said. "Then check out the room. I won't budge from my seat. You can come and get me and we'll hit the buffet."

The room was almost elegant, a view out across Palm Springs to a low cobalt mountain range—and there were no solid gold M&M's. Nell dropped her suitcase and bag on the bed, undressed, and stepped into the shower. She couldn't remember when she'd felt so grateful for hot water sluicing over her skin. She leaned back into the stream. She remembered one of her mom's boyfriends saying, "Getting in the shower after two weeks on the road is the best high you'll ever feel." Rusty, he'd called himself. He'd brought Nell a string of beads he'd found in the parking lot of a truck stop. He'd been nothing but kind in the month he had been her mom's zillionth final, permanent, forever sweetheart. "I swear it, honey, this guy's the real one."

Nell toweled dry and pulled on clean clothes and the rhinestone flip-flops. They'd been a gift from the guy briefly known as Liberator from the Fortress of Solitude. She opened the patio doors. The sun was a white diamond, dropping down toward the mountains. She took her laptop outside, sat and put her feet up on the railing, the flip-flops sparkling, a hot breeze ruffling her wet hair.

The vanishing bees spiraled in her mind. She opened her laptop and checked. They were still disappearing, more and more of them. No one knew where or why. There were opinions, dozens of opinions: trucking native bees out of their home ground to pollinate crops; a new disease brought on by climate changes; the proliferation of microwave signals. She thought of the Leafy, endangered by habitat loss and the human need to collect all things beautiful. Echinacea disappearing from over-harvesting, because herbal medicines had become the next hot item. Nell had sussed out that echinacea was going to be the next wave in the greenies' health fad…and blue-green algae…and acai berries… and her bosses had believed her and jumped on the vegan gravy train.

If the bees and the Leafies, the echinacea, and whatever had once thrived in the desert eaten by Palm Springs were going, were gone, then what? Teach people to change? Teach herself to change? She shook her head. Get real, Nell. It was too easy to conjure up Scheherazade, too maudlin to think one day at a time, too Oprah/Chopra Deep Lite to believe she could "reinvent" herself, much less 6.7 billion others. And still, a creature that could move as though invisible hands propelled it? *I better propel myself down to find Harrison,* she thought, *before I decide my next stop is Sedona or another one of those other crystallated bliss-seeker high-dollar towns.*

Harrison was at a far poker table across miles of migraine-inducing carpet. He sat ramrod straight, his truck hat tilted down. The dealer had just flipped her last card. Three of the players shouted, "Bust!"

Harrison muttered, "Amateurs."

Nell sat next to him. "You gonna play?" he said.

"No way. And I'm starving."

"Just like a woman," Harrison said. "Your gender really knows how to bust up a guy's affair with Lady Luck."

He tipped out the dealer, gathered his chips and cigarettes, and stood. "Truth is, I could definitely go for a slab of prime rib right now."

The buffet had been a mile long. Prime rib. Crab claws. Mexican. A pile of fry bread. "Skip the salad bar," Harrison said. "You look like you need protein."

Harrison told more road stories while they ate. He had that condition of an old guy: holding forth. It had driven her furious all the times one of the older execs in the company had trapped her between him and the coffee machine and lectured her about her area of specialization. But Harrison's stories were on a par with the Leafy, endangered species in a world that was forgetting three-dimensional stories. He told about buying breakfast for the one aging hooker in a Utah Mormon town, and the night he'd hitched a ride with a drunk kid up near Flagstaff and they'd run over a frozen Indian, and the old lady gambler he'd seen neatly throw up in her nickel bucket and go right back to her machine.

"Get some dessert, Nell," Harrison said. "You need to put some meat on your bones. They've got a carrot cake that'll sugar you up for the next week." He paused. "Look. Hope this isn't pushy, but where are you going?"

"I don't know," Nell said. "Not back where I came from, that's for sure. I suspect it's better if I just let the road take me, the way you do. I've got enough to live on for a month."

"More or less?" Harrison said.

"Less," Nell said.

"Well, darlin', what the hell. Maybe you ought to try your hand at a wager or two. You never know. If you don't play, you can't win."

They finished up. Harrison handed his comp card to the waitress. "Nell, go back to the buffet and get whatever you can put in that bag," he said. "I'm going to try some foreplay with Lady Luck and see if she'll put out."

Nell wandered through the slot machines. They weren't the three-reel bandits she remembered from a brief stay in Tonopah with her mom. These slots looked like video games, their designs clearly pimping to the sentimental. There were Elvis and I Dream of Jeannie, and I Love Lucy. They were penny machines on which you could bet five bucks. "Okay, Leafy," Nell murmured. "Show me the way."

Leafy had a wannabe side. Nell found herself in front of a machine with Aztec graphics. A silver-gold sun and blue moon glowed on the screen. Nell sat down. She had no idea what to do. A hefty Indian woman next to her said, "You new to this?"

"I am."

"It's easy. Just take all the money in your purse, tear it up in little pieces, and call the waitress over for a free drink. Just kidding. You slide a bill in that slot, then pick how many lines you want to play and how many pennies a line. Then hit Spin. When you want to stop, hit Cash Out. You get a paper slip and take it to the cashier—if you got the sense to cash out."

"Thanks," Nell said. She slid a dollar in the slot, hit one line, one penny a line, and Spin.

"Jesus Christ," the woman said. "You've got to play more than that."

"I'm just practicing," Nell said. "Last time I jumped in with both feet, I damn near drowned."

Two dollars, seventeen cents and one hour later, Nell had been up, down, up, down, up. The Indian woman had hit a bonus, cashed out, and patted Nell on the shoulder. "Good luck, honey. Don't spend it all in one place."

A tall young guy with a weird haircut sat down next to Nell. He shoved a hundred in the machine and took a long pull off a twenty-ounce Red Bull. "Keeping it clean," he said. "They get you drunk and they get your money." He glanced over. "You need to bet more. Hey, I've got a system, want me to teach you?"

"I'm okay," Nell said. "Just getting up to speed."

"Seriously," the kid said. "Just once, play two bucks."

"That's half my credits," Nell said. "What if I lose?"

"Duh. What if you win?" Music pounded through the casino jangle. The kid froze. "Holy shit, listen to that. It's more than coincidence. It's a sign I'm going to hit big." He bet five bucks. "Fuckin'—'scuse me—'29 Palms,' Robert Plant," the kid said. "It's a sign. Want to know why?"

"Sure," Nell said. She bet two dollars. A faux-Mayan glyph, what might have been a golden bowl, an ace, a moon, and sun came up. Nada.

"I'm stationed over at the base in Twentynine Palms. I'm a Marine. I love that heat in the desert heart. Get it? Hoo-ra, here I go." He hit Spin. Five blue moons leaped up on the screen. "Fifty free games at five bucks a game. I told you." He handed Nell a twenty dollar bill. "Come on, ma'am, go for it."

Nell watched the kid's credits launch. $20. $160. $540. He handed Nell another twenty. "You and Robert Plant made that happen," he said.

Nell bet a penny. She didn't need any more luck than what the stranger had just handed her—she knew where she was headed. "What's Twentynine Palms like?" she said. "I'm relocating."

"Even hotter than my machine here," the kid said. "Damn near as friendly. They got low rent and almost no jobs, but you seem pretty smart. You should be able to find something. It's about an hour from here."

"I don't have a car."

"There's a bus that leaves from in front of the casino in the morning, goes straight to Twentynine. Once you're in town, you can walk just about near everywhere."

"Thanks," Nell said. "I think I'll give it a shot. Meanwhile, I better get out of here with most of your generosity still intact." She cashed out her credits and slipped the second twenty in her pocket. "I'd say good luck, but doesn't look like you need it."

Harrison sat in front of a big pile of chips, back still straight, hat still down over his forehead. "That you?" he said without turning around.

"It's me," Nell said. "I figured out where I'm going. Twentynine Palms. I'll get a good night's sleep and say goodbye in the morning."

"You know where to find me," Harrison said. "Here's a comp for breakfast. You know the drill: lots of protein and fill up your purse."

Nell bent and kissed him on the top of his hat. "Thank you," she said, "for being a gentleman. I hope Lady Luck French-kisses you dizzy."

7

The morning after the night before was weird. Monkey wished it weren't. Jackie had lit the Special Treats Candle. She had done her best which was, as always, superlative. After the first rush of her warm lips on him, Monkey had found himself thinking of other things. Not other women, but other things. He'd remembered the way the Traffic poster had dissolved and how the colors had swirled. He'd finally caught the edge of a purple-blue ripple and let himself be carried out and away.

She had rested her head on his belly and said, "Was that okay?"

He'd stroked her hair. "It was a Rembrandt, baby." She smiled against his skin.

She had moved up from him and rolled to her side of the bed. Her cats, as opposed to Hulk, who was his cat, curled up around her. Monkey had gone out into the backyard to take a leak. He could hear the old pit bull next door snuffling in his sleep.

"You and me, *viejo*," he said. "You and me."

Sleep had not come. Finally, he'd fired up a bowl, stretched out on the living room couch, put five CDs in the player, punched Random, and headphoned up. Traffic. Chris Whitley. The Gourds. Van Morrison. Big Head Todd. He made it intact through *The Low Spark of High Heeled Boys*; a Whitley cover of "China Gate"; The Gourds'

"Jesus Christ with Signs Following"; even The Man's "Raglan Road." Then, Big Head Todd kicked into "Bittersweet" and the vortex was back. He had just long enough to think, "New Age bullshit," and he was gone.

Jackie found him asleep in the morning and slipped the headphones from his ears. Monkey stared up at the ceiling. Fragments of the trance lingered. Teapots and a hearth and flowers as big as his head. And somewhere far far away, metal rods spinning. Just as he had begun to know the sequence of their pattern, they had disappeared. The voice had been unfamiliar. It had whispered in his mind. "Pay attention. We've got you." He had no idea if that had been a comfort or a horror.

"Be right out," he called. "My shoulder's acting up again. Want to stretch out a little."

Jackie appeared in the door. "You feeling funny again?"

"Naw," he said. "Everything's great."

The Biz was an oven. He opened the doors and started the swamp cooler. There was a minor miracle of the computer booting up instantly with the day's schedule already on the screen. He printed out the invoices and washed out the coffee pot.

"Okay, Rando," he said. "I ain't full up." Rando had been one of the guys on his graveyard EMT crew. He was a lumberjack from the U.P. Rando had taught them his dad's favorite saying one night when they'd been back to back with four messy and unfortunately unsuccessful suicide attempts. "We," Rando had said, "are full up for rats." When Monkey and Ed D. Washington had said, "Say what?" Rando said, "Full up for rats! Like, sometimes everything is mellow and you got no rats up your ass. Other times, you got a few, but you still got room. Then, like tonight, you are fucking full up."

Monkey poured water into Mr. Coffee. "Rando," he said, "I got room. This coffee pot is clean, the work is mindless, and you couldn't really call that little glitch last night true erectile dysfunction. Not me, Rando, nope, not me."

By the time Monkey heard the stutter of a beater vehicle

malfunction in the side lot, he was full up for rats.

Keno loomed in the doorway. "Monkman, we are here."

"What's that noise?"

"You calling me a noise?" Keno said.

"No, the other noise, the sound of a wounded beater crying out for free medical care."

"You got me wrong, brother. I'm here to introduce you to Amber herself. Solely. Exclusively. No vehicle freebies needed."

"I can deal with that."

"She's out in her new car," Keno said. "Wait'll you see what she's done."

They walked out into the lot. Amber was in the driver's seat of a gray '94 Camry. She turned off the engine, checked herself in the rearview mirror, opened the door, and unfolded her abundant self from behind the seat. Monkey stepped forward and reached out his hand. She wrapped her arms around him. "You are Monkey," she said. "I am so glad to finally meet you."

Monkey eased himself away from abundant tatas and even more lavish perfume. "And you," he said, "are Amber. And the gorgeous kid in the backseat must be Kimberley Rose."

Keno looked at him and mouthed, "Nice."

Amber nudged Keno. "Monkey," he said, "check this out." He and Amber walked to the back of the Camry. "Maybe you better get the baby," Monkey said. "It's about a hundred and eighty out here."

Amber lifted the baby out of the car seat and to her shoulder. The kid looked like an irritable albino lemur. "Ta da!" Amber said, and pointed to the Camry's back window. Two flag stickers, Mexican and American, iridescently painful to the eyes, flanked a bi-lingual advertisement of Zen-like simplicity.

Amber Waves
Mobile Hairdressing Salon
She brings your beauty to you
Salon Movil de Estilista de Cabello
Ella trae la belleza a ti

"Amber translated it herself," Keno said. "She is a poet as well as a cornrow and dreads artiste."

Kimberley Rose yelped. "She's hungry," Amber said. "Can I take her into the office and feed her?" She blushed. "You guys. Don't come in, okay."

She took the baby into the Biz. "She's breastfeeding," Keno said. "It's healthier for the baby plus it's the ancient way."

Monkey shook his head. "*Viva la Raza*, dude."

Keno punched him in the shoulder. "*Venceremos*."

"By the way," Monkey said, "those plastic stick-on letters give that vehicle real class."

"It's a Camry," Keno said. "It couldn't have much more class."

"Understatement," Monkey said. "This has been lovely, but I have to get back to work. Maybe you guys, me, and Jackie can get together this weekend. Puff a few, hoist a few, grill a few. Give me a call later."

Keno opened his cell and dialed.

"Who're you calling? I said I needed to get back to work."

"Amber," Keno said.

"She's in the office."

"She asked us not to go in. You don't get it, Monkey. Amber is a real lady. Maybe the first real lady in my life except for my moms and grandmoms."

"Okay. Come on. You can watch me not kick the shit out of some rich retiree's Beamer."

Twilight had drifted in by the time Monkey pulled his head out of the Beamer's engine. He kicked the shit out of the right front tire, closed the hood, and locked the car. His head ached, not so much from frustration as from the thoughts that kept running through his head like a punk band on loop delay. He shouldn't have started the day thinking about Rando. Thinking about Rando led to thinking about the old job in Vegas led to thinking about smothered babies and skeletal old ladies and teenage girls raped to mincemeat.

At first, the job had made sense. He'd felt like he was making something of his life. He'd believed he'd been serving humanity. He had never forgotten the look in his Gramps' eyes when he learned that Monkey was full certified. "Son," he'd said, "hardly anybody in this family made it past eighth grade till your mom. Now, you're an EMT, that's damn close to being a doctor. You've made me a proud old man."

Then the hospital had started paring the budget with a butcher knife. He and Rando and Ed D. found themselves out on more calls with less respect. Crack cocaine arrived in the neighborhood, then tweak. AIDS was more than a scary rumor. The 3 a.m. had come that found him and Ed D. bent over the blue face and twisted body of a twelve-year-old ho named Tulip. The girl who had called it in told them Tulip had thought she was shooting up heroin the john had given her for two blowjobs and an ass-fuck. She'd shot up China White.

Monkey looked at Ed D. Ed shook his head. "When the going gets tough," he said, "the tough…it'll have to wait." They stepped away from the body—forever to be known in Monkey's mind as The Tulip—and gently led the other girl away from the scene. There was a siren in the distance. They knew not to contaminate the scene more than it already was.

Later, he and Ed hid out in a storage room in the hospital basement and toked up. Getting high didn't work as planned. Monkey found himself lying on the cement floor looking up at Ed D., who looked more scared than he had ever seen him. "The fuck, Monkey," Ed said. "You okay?"

"What happened?"

"Motherfucker, your eyes rolled back in your head and you dropped like a rock."

Monkey had tried to keep breathing. "I don't know what happened, but I gotta get out of this business."

Monkey sat in the desk chair and punched in the bill for the Beamer. He shut the computer down, thought about the tampon box and his lighter, shook his head, and went out the door.

8

Nell woke after her second full night's sleep. She took her coffee to the patio and watched the reflection of morning sun move across the mountain range. She wondered if the parrots had found the tangerines. She'd washed her travel clothes the night before and hung them on the patio balcony. They were dry. She finished her coffee, showered, dressed, packed, and headed downstairs for the breakfast buffet and goodbye to Harrison.

Harrison hadn't moved from his seat. Nell wondered when he peed. He had a cup of coffee next to his right hand and a cigarette in his left. "You on your way," he said without looking up. It wasn't a question so much as a statement.

"I am. I want to thank you for your kindness," Nell said.

Harrison shook his head. "Don't thank me. Pass it along. Now you got a road story."

"I'll do that," Nell said. "How will we catch up to each other?"

"We won't. We don't need to." Harrison looked up and tilted back his hat. "You're a real sweetheart. Hope you catch up to that." He set down his coffee and took her hand. "Thanks for indulging an old guy. Now git."

Nell bent and kissed his cheek. He turned back to his coffee and cards. A voice spoke over the loudspeakers. "Morongo Valley bus departing in five minutes. Meet in front of the casino." Nell picked up her bags and walked away. She tried not to look down at the carpet until she was through the big smoked-glass doors.

The Marine was nowhere in sight. She climbed on the bus, found a seat away from the sun glare, and took her notebook out of the case. *I'm not going back*, she wrote. *I didn't check out. I don't know anything more than that.* She turned to the back of the notebook and wrote:

$750.

3/3/08: Greyhound Coffee (L.A.)	$1.29
taxi fare to Hollywood/Highland Metro	$35.00
gallows tip	$25.00
Metro - ticket to Long Beach	$1.25
Greyhound locker	$2.00

Light rail fare	$1.25
Aquarium ticket	$20.95
tea in cute coffee shop	$2.85
tip	$1.00
2/4/07 Breakfast at La Tropique	free + $10 tip
San B – Palm Springs bus fare	$26.00
McDonald's	$15+
Tips at Spa Casino	$10.00
Palm Springs to Twentynine fare	$10.00
Sub-total	$161.59
Balance:	$588.41

The balance seemed impossibly low. For twenty years, she had not paid attention to how she spent money; she had not *had* to pay attention. Her broker and advisors had taken care of everything, until she realized they hadn't. She had kept track of the trust fund only. And that was sealed off from her as thoroughly as those twenty years. She closed the notebook and opened her laptop. It was time to do some research.

The bus headed north, turned right, and began a climb up a long hill, the road curving between gray-brown cliffs and through desert studded with low bushes and black rocks. They crested the slope and drove past old trailers, empty stores, houses that looked as though the sun was pounding them down into the sand. An old woman bent near double stepped out of a motel room and waved at the bus. The driver honked. Nell shivered. She tapped the shoulder of a Marine sitting in front of her. "Is this Twentynine Palms?"

"No, ma'am," he said. "This is luxury compared to Twentynine Palms. There's shade here. This is Morongo Valley. You headed for Twentynine?"

"I am."

"You got a son in the Corps?"

"No. I'm relocating."

The Marine shook his head. "Why Twentynine Palms? It's a tough town. No work. No water. Nothing but shacks and trailers far as you can ever see. I can't wait to get deployed."

The bus stopped at a gas station. A few passengers stepped down and shaded their eyes. Two of them pulled out a map and pointed south.

"Tourists," the Marine said. "I bet they'll be on the next bus headed out."

The bus stopped next in a town that seemed to be mostly strip malls and antique shops, went past a meditation retreat that Nell's smartphone told her had been founded by a gentleman with a forties' movie star gaze, a brocade jacket, and possibly lipstick. He, Edwin John Dingle, the driver told them, "or Ding Le Mei in his brocade incarnation—had taught Mentalphysics, whatever that was." Nell suffered a flashback to a colleague's effort to recruit her for an organization that was referred to only as The Process. "We breathe," the woman had said. "It is so simple. We breathe." Nell had checked out The Process. Her colleague had been simply breathing for fifteen thousand bucks for a three-day weekend.

"Joshua Tree next," the Marine said. "Last stop for rich hippies."

The bus stopped in front of a coffee shop. Four kids with backpacks and gorgeous bodies climbed in, followed by a graying middle-aged guy toting a patched suitcase. "No animals, John," the driver said. "You know the rules."

"What animal? You see an animal?"

Something scratched inside the suitcase. "Cripes sake, John, I've told you twenty times. No animals. Besides, did you punch holes in that suitcase?"

"I did."

"What for?"

"Emily's in there. She don't count. A horned toad isn't an animal. It's a reptile."

The driver shook his head. "Pay me," he said, "and let's get this show on the road."

They rolled through a bleached-out landscape, the only relief low dark mountains in all directions. "Folks," the driver said, "Twentynine Palms coming up. The Marine base is our last stop. Climbers, it's a short hitch to the Park. We're stopping at Stater's. If you're not going to the base, people, that's where you get off."

Corporate and weathered local motels lined both sides of the highway. Nell opened her notebook and checked her balance. She'd give herself one night in a motel, get the local paper, and start pounding the pavement. She wondered if people still pounded the pavement. She could hear her mom: "Honey, the fridge is almost empty. It's time to pound the pavement." They'd wander the downtown streets of whatever podunk town they'd landed in, picking up cans and bottles, checking for Help Wanted signs, smiling at people and asking, "Any change you can spare?"

The driver pulled into a little mall. There was a secondhand store, a Redbox, a chain pizza place, a smoke shop, and empty storefronts. Heat waves ripped up off the asphalt. "Twentynine," the driver said. "Named for the twenty-nine palms at the oasis where you'll find twenty-nine palms and a fancy hotel."

The Marine handed down Nell's suitcase. "The El Yucca Motel is a pretty nice place," he said. "It's down the highway a little ways. My wife's picking me up. We can give you a lift."

"Thanks," Nell said. "Is the motel cheap?"

"For this time of the year. Maybe run you thirty bucks."

"What are rents like here?"

"Really low if you aren't picky. And there's a storefront mission that helps people out. Not that you look like you'd need that, but it's always good to know the territory."

"Thanks. I'll try the El Yucca."

A young woman pulled her Geo in front of them and smiled up at the Marine. He bent down and kissed her. "Come on, traveler," he said. "We'll run you over to the motel."

They parked in the motel lot. Nell stepped out of the car. The Marine's wife rolled down her window. "You take care," she said. "You're in the dead end of the world, but the people are nice. And it's real pretty at dawn and dusk."

"Thank you both," Nell said. "You helped a lot."

"Just one thing," the girl said. "Do not ever get your hair cut at Jen's Hair and Nail Joint." She shuddered. "*Euuuuu.*"

"I'll keep that in mind," Nell said. The girl rolled up her window and they pulled out onto the highway. Nell walked around to the back of the motel. There was a little suburb to her right, beige houses, red roofs, a couple aboveground swimming pools. Low shadowed mountains that seemed stripped of anything living rose in the north under a cloudless sky. Something flickered in her cells. The mountains, the sky, the hugeness were eerily familiar. But she and her mom hadn't come this way. She was sure they hadn't come this way. Her mom had loved wet green air. Nell grabbed her bags and went around to the motel.

The desk clerk was skinny as an egret, her copper dreadlocks gathered into a beaded ponytail. She caught Nell checking out her nametag—Zirconia. "It's a joke," she said. "My real name is Diamond, but no way I'm going to let most of the losers who check in here know that."

She laughed. "Didn't mean you. I don't know what you are and I don't want to know what you are, but that purse tells me that if you're losing—just saying—it might be a recent condition."

Zirconia's cell rang. "'Scuse me."

"Hey, girl," she said into the phone. "I gotta be the Mo6 Ho right now. I'll call you back."

Red and blue lights flashed briefly outside the window. "Cops," Zirconia said. "Just popped a gang of low-rent tweakers in the last room. Everything's cool now."

"Can you take cash?"

Zirconia narrowed her eyes. "Say what?"

"I have to pay in cash. Is that okay?"

"Okay, I changed my mind about you. You *are* lost, but you're from another planet so that's okay. Of course we take cash."

Nell paid.

"You're in 118," Zirconia said. "You only got that one case to carry, so I'd give you a room on the second floor where it's quieter, but I've only got done-up rooms on the first floor, plus this way you're closer to the donuts in the morning which, believe me, you really want to be." She looked down into her coffee mug. "Whew, I've gotta lay back on the caffeine. You need the phone? I have to take a deposit if you do."

"No," Nell said. "Is there WiFi?"

"Hard to believe it, but there is. No charge. Hard to believe that, too."

Nell handed Zirconia the money. "Bet you're not getting rich off all these amenities."

Zirconia grinned. "Thanks. You got that right."

Nell bent to pick up her case. "Hey," Zirconia said, "I'm off at midnight so I won't be here in the morning. Just a suggestion: stay out of that chain restaurant down the street. My girlfriend works there. When anybody fucks up, they gotta write their name and their crime on a big old bulletin board. It's called the Wall of Shame. Plus the food is toxic."

There was a muck-brown, primer-blotched '80 Caprice station wagon on blocks at the far end of the parking area and crime scene tape across the door next to 118. Nell shrugged. It would guarantee a quiet night. She opened her door and went into a room almost as plain as the one she'd occupied during her only excursion into self-awareness. The Simplicity Retreat had been held in a monastery in the Santa Catalina foothills. The monks had dispensed silence, a windowless cubicle, and acacia honey at twenty bucks a jar.

Nell set her purse on the plastic shelf, tucked her bag underneath, and fell back on the bed. She would get up in a few minutes, take a shower, wash out her underwear, and lie on her back staring at the ceiling till morning.

Morning. Nell smiled. She had three solid reasons to be willing to wake up. A drag queen seahorse, the kindness of a blackjack fiend, a town with low rent. Not bad for a woman who once had it all.

The phone rang. Nell dragged herself off the bed and answered.

"It's me—Ms. Diamond. I just wanted to let you know we really do have free coffee and donuts in the morning. Actually, they're *churros*, you know, Mexican crullers? Connie's mom makes them. They're usually gone by eight."

"Thank you," Nell said. "Give me a wake-up call at six."

Reason four. Free churros.

She lay back down. The last thing she saw before she fell asleep was a hairline crack in the ceiling, and a flicker of green and pink. "I remember you," she whispered.

Nell woke. The room was dark except for the LED blinking on the fire alarm. She remembered she was in a motel room. With a shower. And coffee. And Mexican donuts in the morning. She flicked on the light and checked her watch. 10 p.m. She went into the bathroom and started the hot water. It was icy. She let it run and stripped off her clothes.

She tossed her bra and panties on the bed and looked at herself in the mirror. All she could seem to focus on were her anything-but-abundant and anything-but-young breasts. Nell: A-cup. David: "I love tits." Game over.

She stepped into the warm water and felt her tears begin to slip out of their eddy. She thought of the woman turned to salt, then Isak Dinesen, from a women's lit seminar she'd taken a century ago: "The cure for anything is salt water—sweat, tears, or the sea." For an instant, she imagined a vial of tears left in the desert, a desert aeons ago ocean, more aeons, glass gone back to silica, salt glittering in the sand and gone.

She washed herself, turned off the water, and stepped onto the worn bath mat. The mirror was cloudy. She ran her finger over the moisture one time, a wavering clarity at the level of her eyes. She looked into her own gaze. Gold flecks, wrinkles fanning out. Her gaze.

She logged on and almost sent a blank message to David. A reflex. A tic. She closed the computer. It was time to stop. You can't disappear if you aren't willing to lose sight of the known earth.

9

The scent of strong dark coffee filled the front office. A plump woman with skin the color of cinnamon and eye shadow the gleam of casino neon looked up from the front desk computer. "I'm Connie," she said. "You're 118. Diamond told us to look out for you."

"Really?" Nell said.

"She's like that. She said I should ask you whether you are a tourist or not, and when you said you weren't, I should tell you about La Paloma, which is a women's shelter house run by her and her ladyfriend, Shiloh. *La Paloma* means a dove, not the white kind, more like your average homey pigeon."

"Homing?" Nell said.

"Naw, " Connie said. "*Homey*...rat with wings, but looking sharp, all green and purple on the feathers, like oil on a puddle." She laughed. "You're looking for coffee. I can tell. I got the good stuff back here. You take cream? Real cream, not that powder *caca*?"

A tall balding guy in a Jesus Loves the Raiders muscle shirt came though the Employees Only door. "You must be 118," he said. "Connie taking care of you?"

"I am," Connie said. She set a big mug of coffee and a plate on the counter. "These are churros," she said. "My mom makes them fresh."

"Go ahead," the man said. "It's all on the house. I'm the boss. I get to tell you what to do. Those are like donuts. But better. They're real Mexican."

Nell sat on a mustard-yellow vinyl chair. "That's a collectible, you know," the man said. "Corporate hasn't replaced the furniture here in thirty years."

Nell bit into the churro. It was not much more than a trace of good grease and cinnamon-scented air. "Oh, this is gorgeous."

"Now drink a little coffee quick," Connie said. "Churros and coffee are better than sex."

They were. Connie and the boss walked outside for a smoke. A hefty red-haired woman in a powder-blue tracksuit and gold sandals came in. "They are going to kill themselves," she said. "All the time, smoke smoke. I can tell you don't smoke. You got that what-you-call fitness look about you."

Nell ate the last of the churro in one bite. "Not me."

"Not smoke?"

"Not fitness."

The woman patted Nell's shoulder. "I'm Shirley," she said. "I am the boss of Housekeeping. You need anything?"

"I'm leaving today," Nell said.

"Okay, but if you want anything before you go, fresh towels, shampoo, let me know. We take good care of our people."

Connie and the boss came back in. "So?" Connie said. "La Paloma's about a mile away. I'll drive you if I can take a break."

"You had your break," the boss said.

Connie laughed. "No, you had the pleasure of *my* company and *my* cigarettes."

"Go ahead. It's slow. I'll cover the desk."

"It might seem weird," Connie said, "how the boss is, but you lucked into El Yucca: The Real Reality Show. This place has been here since 1939." She opened the back door of her car. "Put your bag in there. Everybody who works here is loco. It's partly the boss. He's got Jesus, but not in a sucky way."

Nell climbed in the passenger seat. Connie pulled onto the highway. "La Paloma isn't far. Once you get there, you have to keep it a secret."

"I'll do that." Nell remembered all the times she and her mom had gone under the radar. In those days, it had been a do-it-yourself itinerary. They'd ducked down in San Jose, California, and surfaced a couple weeks later in northeastern Wyoming, disappeared from there and found themselves in a dingy by-the-week motel in Missouri.

"Not to change the subject," she said, "but how do you get Jesus in a not-sucky way?"

"You saw that big Scooby Doo plastic bowl outside the back door of the office?" Connie said. "There's this pregnant stray dog. Kinda flippy. Not mean. Just scared so bad she shakes if a human comes anywhere near. The boss puts food out. You saw that wrecked car at the edge of the parking lot? The dog sleeps in there. We tried to tell the boss dogs mean vet bills, but he just said, 'J.C. will provide.'"

"That's definitely not sucky," Nell said.

"So then, another example but different, he burned a hole in a guy's arm with a cigarette because the guy was ragging on a woman with their kid in the back seat. The boss walked up to the driver window, pinned the guy's arm to the metal, and held the cigarette just above the guy's arm. 'Shut your hole,' the boss said. 'You got a lady and a kid in this car.' The guy was fucked up on crack. He tried to yank his arm back and the boss jammed the cigarette down.

"Did the woman get out of the car? No. Did she rescue the kid? No. So, while the asshole was all hunched over and whining about his burnt arm, the boss pulled out his gun, shot out the two front tires, hauled the woman and kid from the car, and called the cops.

"The cops showed up and noted that the front tires seemed to have mysteriously deflated. Broken glass maybe. They made the guy. Tons of warrants out for him. They took the woman and kid into protective custody and told the boss he needed to check the parking lot for glass before somebody else had a blow out."

"Definitely what Jesus would have done," Nell said.

"Outlaw Jesus," Connie said. "That's what the boss calls him, like that Johnny Cash song about his personal Jesus. Me, I'm your average *chica*...Jenni Rivera rules. You gotta check out *Mi Vida Loca*. What about you?"

Nell laughed. "Beats me. Maybe the Church of Picking Up the Pieces."

"Oh yeah," Connie said. "I know that one."

She pulled out her cell. "I'm letting Diamond know you're on the way."

La Paloma was a sun-faded ranch house on a suburban street a few blocks from downtown. There was a big front porch, three scrawny leafless trees, and a cammie-painted mailbox. Zirconia met them at the front door. "Walk in this door and I'm Diamond," she said. "Welcome, Nell."

"Thanks," Nell said.

Connie grinned at Diamond. "You've got you a new fish here, girl. Take it easy on her."

"You're one bad chica," Diamond said. "You need to stop hanging out in bad company. Thanks for bringing Nell over. And tell your mom that I have to lay off the churros. Shiloh says so."

Connie hugged Nell. "Welcome to Twentynine," she said. "Free churros 6 a.m. sharp at the motel every morning. Come visit sometime." She walked down the sidewalk to her car and took off, the wail of a woman's voice on the radio fading away.

Diamond took Nell to her second floor room and told her the rules: *No booze. No smoke. No dick.* "I'll leave you to get settled," she said and closed the door. Nell hung her suit in the closet and lined her one pair of shoes up on the floor. She noted her new furniture consisted of a twin bed, TV tray, sage-green armchair, and dresser. There were white gossamer curtains over the eastern window, and a new bright red bath towel hanging from the back of the chair. There were, to Nell's relief, no affirmations or cheery sayings on the walls. There was a calendar, an alarm clock, a notebook, and a pen.

Nell set her shampoo and brush on the dresser, and hung the chain with the black pearl from the closet doorknob. She left the computer in her bag. She looked out the window. There was a dusty yard below. A skinny brown and white dog was curled in on itself in the shade. She sat for what seemed hours, then lay down on the bed. She could not sleep. She hadn't been able to take a nap since she'd been a kid. If you had a sweet dope-dealer mom, you had to be a girl vigilante. Girl vigilantes did not take naps.

The light outside the window had gone apricot. Nell went downstairs to the front stoop and sat. She was on a quiet street, with old houses in pastel yellows and greens and pinks, and a burnt-orange sun floating down into the dark ragged mountains far to the west. The concrete was still warm. The stucco wall between the dirt yard and the sidewalk went rose-gold. Nell remembered again how her grandma's house in Long Beach had seemed to be a huge shell at sunset. She had stood in front of the place not three days earlier and she had thought that, and thought just as lucidly that she was on her way to her death.

"Mind if I join you?" A tiny blonde woman with a late-for-it mullet stood next to her.

Nell nodded.

"I'm Shiloh. Diamond thought you might like some company, and to know she's at the crucial point of her fried chicken."

"I'm Nell. She was right."

They were quiet long enough for Nell to understand she was being given room to say what came next.

"You give the new kid a little time to open up," Nell said.

Shiloh laughed. "We do. We've sat right where you're sitting."

"He didn't hit me," Nell said. "Nobody's ever hit me." The words were the first she had spoken to anyone about David.

"You know," Shiloh said, "how cops can beat somebody and there aren't any marks?"

The sun was gone. A blurred arc of light hung above the mountains, going molten to pink to the rose-blue of Connie's eye shadow.

"It's beautiful here right now," Nell said. "But it's strange, there's something familiar about the place. And I've never been here before."

"You mean La Paloma?"

"No. I'm not sure what I mean." Nell figured it was time to change the subject. "Those mountains out there, see how the sunset is. It made me think about Connie's eye shadow. Over at the motel."

"She is a true artist," Shiloh said. "What I love that those Chicanas do is how they outline their lipstick with a perfect darker line of a different color. Me?" She laughed. "What you see is what you get."

"I worked in a place," Nell said, "where you had to wear make-up that looked as though you weren't wearing make-up."

Shiloh smiled. Nell knew the smile was not a question. She took a deep breath. It was sweet and unsettling to have enough time to talk, enough time to be silent.

"I'm not used to this," Nell said. "I haven't talked to anybody in a long time as much as I've talked to all of you. Does that seem weird?"

"No. Yes. Doesn't really matter whether it does or not."

Diamond carried a bowl of fried chicken out through the door. "I don't expect our other ladies, Chelsea and Judy, back till after nine," she said. "We can have us a picnic on the front porch. Maybe tomorrow, me and Shiloh'll take you out to see something you won't believe."

Nell grinned. "You'd be surprised what I'm starting to believe."

Nell pulled the camp chair to the open window of her room. She looked out toward the tiny backyard of the house to the east. There was a garden, a shed, and the dog that she had learned was a goat staked to a clothes pole. She could see a shadow on the back steps and the red coal of a lit cigarette.

I keep being alive, she thought. She wasn't sure what had brought her through the day or what had made her leave the laptop in her bag. She closed her eyes. A breath of cool air washed past her face. There was the stink of exhaust, the scent of rain on earth. She heard a faint sibilance and when she opened her eyes, she saw that the shadow at the edge of the garden was watering a thread of new plants. She tried to remember what her cottage had smelled like, how the neighborhood had sounded in the twilight. There were no memories beyond the parrots and the absence.

She pressed her hands to the windowsill. The old wood was cool. She understood that she had not lost her memory, but that she had ceased, sometime in that old life, to smell and hear and sense. *How obvious*, she thought. *It should be harder to know this kind of thing, maybe have to pay twenty thousand bucks to know—just know.*

She watched the person stop watering, coil the hose, and light another cigarette. The goat curled up on the ground. A helicopter searchlight strafed the yard. The goat startled, then tucked its head back into its belly. The smoker shook a fist at the sky. The thump of a car speaker faded in, boomed, and faded out.

She had no idea what time it was. She didn't care. She must have dozed in the chair because she saw a luminous ribbon of pink and green drift around her. It coiled again and again, as though the earlier breeze had returned and enfolded her.

She wasn't sure when she had gone to her new bed. She woke once in the early morning and padded down the hallway to the bathroom. The house was silent. She didn't turn on the light. The last of a quarter moon shone in the window.

She went to the toilet. When she stood, she saw her face in the mirror. Her skin and hair were silvered. Her eyes were dark ovals. She traced her lips with one finger. She could imagine drawing a wine-red line carefully around their curve.

Shiloh tapped on Nell's door. "If you want to eat, Diamond's making omelets."

Nell sat up. "I'll be right down." She thought of how she had once waked alone morning after morning. Then, after David had come into her life, woke already tucking the cell plug into her ear, already logging into the laptop on the nightstand, not quite being able to draw a full breath till she saw his wake-up email. He'd created a secret address. Only for her: Tristan4thee@gmail.com. "Though," he had laughed, "I am married in my spirit to you."

Nell had saved every email. She considered logging on and reading one, just one. She would wait and dole them out for a while. She had no idea how long that while would be.

Then she was more interested in what Diamond had folded into the omelets. She swung her legs over the bed and stood. "Whoever you are inside me who is hungry," she thought, "I might be glad to have you back." She remembered the hungry ghosts the Tibetan Buddhists believed roamed the earth. They were insatiable. They were doomed. Whoever was inside her who was hungry might not yet be doomed.

10

Shiloh and two women sat at the kitchen table, one young and sweet-faced, the other near emaciated. Shiloh waved Nell to a chair. "I assume you drink coffee," she said. "It's on the counter." Diamond turned from the old stove. "Chelsea, Judy, this is Nell."

"Hey," the younger girl said. "I'm Chelsea." The woman next to her looked up at Nell. "Judy," she said and touched her face. "I ain't sick. Don't worry. You can't catch anything." Shiloh patted her shoulder. "It's okay, girl, give Nell a chance to settle in."

Nell took a mug from a collection next to the coffeepot. There were chipper rehab logos and lizards in cowboy hats and the standard New Age wannabe neutered Kokopelli. Her mug reminded her that Goddess didn't make junk. "There's a marker next to the cream," Shiloh said. "You can put your initial on the bottom if you want." Nell filled her cup. "I don't know how long I'll be here."

Chelsea laughed. "Doesn't matter, it'll wash off eventually. I hope I never have to leave."

Nell poured her coffee and sat down between Shiloh and Judy.

Diamond set a platter of green-chili omelets, sausage, and hash browns in the middle of the table. "Help yourselves."

Chelsea and Judy had left. Shiloh poured more coffee for Diamond,

Nell, and herself. "Is Judy anorexic?" Nell asked.

"I can't really talk about her," Shiloh said. "We keep things confidential, though we can't control for gossip."

"And me," Nell said, "don't you need to know anything about me?"

Diamond smiled. "We've got time. Don't you want to know about us?"

"You're part of Planned Parenthood or something, right?"

"Wrong."

"Social services? A church outreach?"

"We don't work that way."

"Then how?"

"Threads," Diamond said. "Threads that run everywhere, threads that you can't see till they light up. We're just one part of a greater Morongo Basin network. There are animal shelters, foster homes for old people, crash pads for runaway kids. We're one of two women's shelters. There are networks like this beginning all throughout the country. You could think of us as a way to pass through hardship under the radar."

"I haven't known hardship for the last fifteen, twenty years," Nell said. "Till a year ago. And now." She shrugged.

"Hardship's a chameleon," Shiloh said. "If you don't know how to look, you don't always know it's there. That's what we're for, giving women a place to rest—sometimes just so that they can figure out they're lost—until they can take the next step, maybe even just have the next thought about taking the next step."

"And if there don't seem to be any next steps to take," Diamond said, "we hang out together till there are. This particular network started a few years ago when some women caught on that the existing social systems were breaking down. Budget cuts. Burned-out staff. Too many people slipping through the cracks. Me and Shi were caught on the game. Pimps. Crack cocaine. By the end of it, both of us were living in a car on the outskirts of Barstow.

"One early morning, we looked at each other. 'You're a dead woman,' Shi said. 'So am I. We've got to do something.'"

"Something turned out to be hitching into town with our last two dollars and fifty-two cents," Shiloh said, "and seeing a sign on an old storefront that said 'Need help? Come on in.' We could smell coffee.

We opened the door and found ourselves in the middle of one of those alcoholics meetings. There was a full pot of coffee, a tray of donuts, and about five people who looked as rat's ass as we did. An old lady smiled at us and said, 'Grab some coffee and donuts, ladies, and have a seat.'"

She laughed. "Nobody had called me a lady, ever. We sat down, tried not to slam down our breakfast, and listened. I was raised God Is Watching You Catholic, so God blah de blah makes me want to puke. But these folks were just talking about trying to get by, feeling pounded down to the ground, wanting to give up. Diamond looked at me. I nodded. We sat tight and hung around after the meeting was over. By the time we left there, we had been given a room in a woman's house.

"We picked up odd jobs. Diamond cooked. I cleaned. Both of us had paper out on us so we didn't dare go to Welfare. We met some other ladies at a junkies' meeting one night and turned out everybody had survived pretty much the same way. This Mexican chica said, 'We're doing this like my aunties and *abuelas* did. Keep it simple. Do it ourselves.' So, we started getting together every few days to figure things out. We kept the rules simple. We knew we were constantly in danger of making another bureaucracy.

"Nobody keeps paperwork. There is no infrastructure. People offer their homes or their apartments. We have a crew of visitors—kind of like mystery shoppers—to make sure nobody takes advantage of anybody. The whole crew except for a few of us retires every six months. No internet presence. It all works by word of mouth. We keep the secret. We are the secret.

"And it's a little web, just between Yucca Valley and here. That's the only way something like this can work."

"It's nothing new," Diamond said. "In fact, it's about as old as anything human is. Given human nature, somebody will narc us out someday, but for now every person, every animal we help is a person or animal who would have slipped through those cracks."

"Does it have a name?" Nell said. One of her Non-assets According to David had been needing to name things—"You and I are, Nell, just simply are," he had murmured against her bare throat.

"There's no formal name," Shiloh said. "You could think of it as a Black Widow, the web asymmetrical and full of holes."

"Nice," Nell said. "Now you can fall through the cracks and land in a web with holes."

"Exactly."

"Who funds Black Widow?" Nell asked.

Shiloh glanced at Diamond.

"Look," Nell said, "I knew a woman in a nursing home. She had dementia. I know what it cost." Her mind rattled. *And who paid for it with money and not one visit, ever? Not one visit. Not one phone call. Not one card or present.*

"We're mostly funded by donations from nice, ever-so-self-aware, guilt-ridden and hugely wealthy liberal benefactors," Diamond said. "Bless their hearts."

"Expiation," Nell said. "Speaking of which, I'll wash the dishes."

"I'll be in the back office," Diamond said. "Holler if you need me."

There was a window above the double sink with three budding cacti on the sill. Nell set their dishes in the left basin, the plates mismatched flowered china, plastic, and faux-Fiestaware, the silverware not silver. She poured in detergent and turned on the hot water. She couldn't remember the last time she had washed dishes. She turned off the tap and plunged her hands into the soapy warmth.

Her fingers began to relax in the water. She took a deep breath, pushed her hands deeper in the water, pulled up a handful of silverware, washed each piece, and rinsed it. She held a knife in the fierce light that poured through the window and carried it out to the back stoop. In seconds the knife was dry, in another second it was too hot to hold. She wrapped it in the hem of her t-shirt and went back into the cool kitchen.

"I won't wash dishes like this again," she thought. "As though it were a ritual. I won't take time. I won't feel the water. It will become a chore." She remembered her mother telling her the day would come when she would be happy to have a kitchen to clean. They had just washed their bowls and spoons in the stained bathroom sink of a motel that could have been any motel. Her mother had spread a clean washcloth on the dresser and put the two bowls and spoons on it to dry. They had gone through the busted screen door to the parking lot curb and sat in the fading light. There was New Mexico opal light or Texas big city skyline or strings of glittering headlights along an interstate. Her mom had lit a cigarette and sucked the smoke in deep.

"On the other hand," she had said, "this is freedom."

There was a faint knock on the front door, then another. Shiloh yelled, "Come in!" Another knock. Shiloh ran to the door. "Oh my god, Mariah," Nell heard her say. "What happened to you?" She led a sturdy black-haired woman into the kitchen. The woman leaned against the sink. "Just give me a minute," she said. "Don't touch me. Don't say anything." She closed her eyes.

Shiloh glanced at Nell and nodded. They sat in silence. The woman was dark-skinned, arms blotched with darker fingerprints. She wore shades, a Havasu Landing t-shirt, and capris cinched with a beaded belt. She folded her arms across her chest and looked down.

"I just got grabbed," she said. "Some guys jumped me from behind. They told me that if I told, they'd get my grandbaby. They knew her name. So I came here. We've got to get my grandbaby. Punkin. They said her name. They knew it. I want to kill them."

Nell looked at Shiloh. "Make a fresh pot of coffee," Shiloh said. "Then soak a couple towels."

"Get Punkin first," the woman said. "Sorry. I'm kind of running on, just spitting stuff out. Excuse my manners. I'm Mariah."

"That's Nell," Diamond said. "We won't call the cops unless you decide you want to. Chelsea's on runner duty. I'll send her for the baby."

"Good. She's at daycare, over on Two Mile Line. You know the place. And really really don't call the cops." Mariah reached out and shook Diamond's hand, then Nell's. Her handshake was a whisper touch. Nell remembered an Elysian meeting with a group of traditional elders and healers. The Cultural Resource folks in HR had taught the team to shake hands gently. "That tells them that you mean no harm." Much later, after Elysian had made tens of millions of dollars catering to one of the hot new herbal medicine fads, Nell couldn't forget the delicate touch of one of the old women's hands.

Nell soaked a dishtowel in cold water and handed it to Shiloh. "I'll get the coffee going, then I need to look for a job. I'm glad to meet you, Mariah. I'll be back tonight.

"And, Shiloh, how about if I take over dish duty?"

"Oh no, not that," Shiloh said. "It's yours, Nell."

Nell made her bed and put her clothes in the top dresser drawer.

She looked out the window. The glare drained any color out of everything. The goat was nowhere in sight.

She closed the curtains, lay down, closed her eyes, and saw rosy filtered light. She thought of scarlet-headed parrots, of paper-thin tangerine slices, of the creature that had been pink, green, and silver. Animal. Vegetable. Mineral. She remembered how it had seemed to drift only in two planes. How had that been possible?

She sat up and pulled the computer to her lap. She opened it and nearly closed it. There would be no job offers; no message upon which she had once thought her life depended. But there was the question of how the Leafy Seadragon seemed to move. She searched the Leafy and clicked on the first link.

The Leafy unfurled. She scrolled down: *...the leafy appendages are not used for movement. The body of a seadragon scarcely appears to move at all. Steering and turning is through movement of tiny, translucent fins along the sides of the head (pectoral fins, visible above) and propulsion derives from the dorsal fins (along the spine). Their movement is as though an invisible hand were helping...*

She logged off, closed the laptop, and opened her notebook to check her accounting. The numbers were not good. She was going to need more than an invisible hand. It was time to pound the pavement. Black Widow work if she could find it—no social security number, no records, no benefits. Maybe David had been right. She was becoming her mother's girl.

She slung the bag over her shoulder and went downstairs into the empty house. There was a phone in the kitchen, but she had no idea who to call. She poked through the kitchen drawers for a phonebook. There was none.

She stepped out on the front porch and slammed into a solid wall of heat. She closed the door behind her and waited. She'd thought she would check out the main street, find a cafe and a newspaper and do whatever it was that non-executives did to find work. In fact, stepping away from where she stood, much less out into the glare, was impossible. She sat down in a plastic chair in the meager shade.

The street was empty. Heat waves rippled up from the asphalt. The searing air had no scent. Old houses, sidewalks, even the shrines that had been built in some of the yards—shrines she knew were near brilliant with garlands of paper roses and tinsel—were the same no color the backyard had been. And it was April.

She had six hundred bucks—and no coordinates. She needed more. She needed to be able to remember what she had known so long ago: how to stop, how to wait, how to move slow. No motivational speaker was telling her this. The heat spoke. Her blood answered. There was no possibility of anything but compliance.

She remembered the wet green heat of the trees in a fish camp in Missouri, and the river she and her mother had floated on. The water had been no deeper than her waist. They lay back, lifted their feet, and were carried. They heard pebbles clicking along the river bottom. They had drifted what seemed a long time, then climbed out onto a sandy bank. Nell had found a pebble. It split when she set it in her palm. There had been a thread of tiny crystals in its center that seemed to spell a word in a language she had never seen.

She and her mother had walked slowly up a worn dirt trail. Dragonflies caught in their hair. There were songs from a thousand birds. Her mother led her back to the little beach from which they had entered the river. They had stepped in again and drifted down. Nell couldn't remember how many times they stepped in, drifted down, walked back, and stepped in. At last, the light began to go blue-gray. They drifted a last time under a sky that seemed the color of the touch of the water. A great blue heron fished in the shallows. They climbed out and walked slowly back.

Fireflies shimmered in the dark leaves. Nell and her mother came off the trail into the camp and saw a woman frying fish on a campfire. She had fed them and told them they could stay the night in a shed behind her house.

Nell had fallen asleep in her mother's lap, both of them held in the scent of pine smoke and river and wet green air. The last thing she heard was the woman saying, "You know, down here we learn to go slow and smell the mosquitoes," then her mother's husky laugh.

Shiloh and Mariah pulled up in front of La Paloma and parked, the little Neon vibrating with the whomp of hip-hop. Shiloh bent forward, turned off the engine, and held her cell to her ear.

A few seconds later, she and Mariah carried a suitcase and a baby carrier into the house. "Ah shit," Shiloh muttered. "Fuckin' Judy." She tossed a newspaper into Nell's lap. "Classifieds. Local. There's a computer job in there." She slammed through the front door.

Nell followed her into the house.

"Give me a minute," Shiloh said. "I've gotta call Diamond."

Nell opened the paper. Shiloh had circled an ad and written: *A job, a car, just what a woman needs.* The ad read: "1984 Le Sabre, cherry, $350. obo + wanted: part-time computer genius. $11 an hour. Call 8-5 weekdays. 760-673-8889."

Mariah carried the baby upstairs. Shiloh sat down. "Judy discorporated," she said. "Big surprise. Customer told the boss the ladies' was locked. Boss picked the lock. There's Judy going down on the dishwasher. Boss decides that's not in Judy's job description. Dishwasher's been there fifteen years. Judy's been there a week. Guess who gets fired.

"Shit, I'm breaking confidentiality, but I've got to vent. Boss goes in to cover Judy's tables, hears somebody laughing like a maniac in the parking lot. He discovers Judy crouched on his brand new Cruiser, butt naked, laughing her tits off and pissing all over the windshield. Boss calls Chelsea. Chelsea calls me. Welcome to La Paloma."

"What happens to Judy now?" Nell asked.

"Hard to say, but it won't happen here. Part of how Black Widow works is we don't take on more than we've got the set-up and smarts to deal with." Shiloh checked her watch. "It's ten fifteen. One nutted-out former resident. One beat-up Chemehuevi tribal matriarch. One six-week-old baby. This is a personal best for La Paloma."

"What's Chemehuevi? You're talking about Mariah, right?"

"She's an elder in the local tribe. The Chemehuevi had been here long before whites showed up. A few folks live here in Twentynine, a few down near Banning, most of them on the rez east of here on the river. There's a little cemetery down off Adobe. They've paid a shitload of dues—hassled by the government, by white settlers, by other tribes; their kids shipped off to boarding schools. You'd think they'd be pissed off all the time, but most of them are pretty mellow and openhearted."

"And now somebody tried to scare one of their elders," Nell said. "I wonder what's going on?"

"Who knows? All we can do is give her a safe place for a while and see what happens. I better call Diamond. She's going to be absolutely thrilled by all the good news."

Shiloh called, told the bones of the situations, said uh-huh a few times, and hung up. "She said to let the cops sort it out." She tapped the newspaper. "Meanwhile, what do you think of this?"

"Is this job close by?"

"Five blocks. I think I know the guy. He's an underground mechanic, one of the best in the Basin, maybe even in Southern California."

"He's illegal?"

"No. He's licensed and all, just not under the umbrella of a normal garage. They call them shade-tree mechanics. He took Diamond's dying Cherokee and got it not just on the road, but legal. By the way, we don't call our Mexican guests 'illegals.'"

"Point taken," Nell said.

"If it's the same guy, his wife Jackie's an R.N. in a Black Widow— I've got to stop using that name—old peoples' home. Mariah's a nurse at the same place. Tell you what, give the garage a call." She dialed the phone and handed it to Nell.

"Yeah?" The voice was a silky abrasion. The music in the background wasn't.

"You're looking for a computer genius," the former corpo-Nell said crisply.

"I am."

"Shiloh sent me."

"I'm here. Come on over. 237 Smoke Tree."

"I'll be there. I'm Nell."

"I'm Monkey. You'll recognize me. I'm the only one here."

"Hey," Nell said, "is that Van Morrison?"

"*Rave on, John Donne*." He hung up.

"Monkey?" Nell said.

Shiloh grinned. "Meet Monkey. He's a man of few words till quitting time."

Nell put on her clean underwear, purple suit, and the Manolo Blahniks. She didn't have any stockings and she refused to wear pantyhose. David had loved that. Stockings and a garter belt under a business suit. The afternoon he'd slid his hand up her bare thigh in the annual budget talks had been the afternoon he'd called her into his office and told her to close her eyes. He'd clasped a chain around her neck. "It's a Tahitian black pearl," he'd said. "They are the rarest pearls. Next year, there will be a pink diamond on this chain. It's even more rare."

They had then set the world land record for the fastest and most quantitatively orgasmic fuck in a global pharmaceutical corporation, after a meeting in which it had been decided to admit to most of the dangers of the company's most profitable product and issue genuine regrets.

"Stop, brain," Nell said. "That is enough. It is next year. There is no pink diamond. And the black pearl turned out to be a fake. Now I am here—and I need to lose that fucking pearl somewhere soon—and these." She opened the computer, found the document with David's emails, deleted them, and emptied the trash. "In for a dime, in for a dollar."

Shiloh looked up. "Oh my god. You're wearing that?"

"It's all I have," Nell said.

"Those shoes?"

"I don't think my flip-flops effectively pull the ensemble together."

Shiloh grabbed her car keys. "Come on, girl. No way you can walk even a block in that outfit. I'll drive you. Call me if you need a ride home. And you'll want to get rid of that suit. There's a resale store on Adobe. It used to be crappy, but since Joshua Tree turned the new place hip, slick, and groovy, there's some decent stuff. Diamond said to front you the cash for a couple outfits." She held out a few folded twenties.

"Thanks, I can handle that."

"You sure?"

"I'm sure."

Shiloh shook her head. "Okay. Grab your laptop. Just in case Monkey's killed his PC."

11

A woman stepped into the garage. Monkey looked out from under the hood of the second not-really-a-real V-dub of the day. The woman was sturdy-built, her face expressionless, her curly hair pulled back in a mousy knot. She wore a purple suit and had a big leather bag slung over her shoulder. He figured she was a tourist on anti-depressants and had wandered into the wrong neighborhood.

"I'm Nell," she said. "I called about the car and the job."

Monkey ducked back under the bug. "I'll be right out. The office is through that door. Grab a seat."

He pretended to do something in the guts of the bug. He needed to suss her out. Shit, what if she were an undercover narc. He couldn't remember if he'd left the ashtray on the desk. He wiped his abruptly sweaty hands on his pants.

If she were an undercover narc, it was either a Keno slip of the lip or that brain-dead fuck, Wendell, or... He made himself stop thinking. He knew he wasn't paranoid. Paranoia was when you were afraid of something that didn't exist.

He stood up. "Be right there," he said. She was silent. Bad. Oh, bad. They were always quiet. He remembered what his cop pal, Ron, had told him. "Whatever you do, don't talk. We can be quiet forever—or as long as it takes for you to start telling us everything we already know."

He walked into the office. The undercover narc sat on the stack of tires. She was the only woman to have ever done that. Monkey acted as if that were normal and sat in the office chair.

It was quiet for a long time. Nell looked around the office. There was a metal desk, an old computer, and a two-drawer battered file cabinet. The office chair tilted perilously. There was a four-cup Mr. Coffee on the file cabinet containing an inch or two of swamp bottom sludge. Grease-stained coveralls hung on the back of the front door. There was another door into the garage bay and a window on the opposite wall. The light was more gloom than light. The place smelled like her only memory of her mom's one decent long-term boyfriend, of mechanic grease, cigarettes, a hardworking man, and the faintest echo of pot.

The boss was a chunky guy in a Bob Marley muscle shirt, tie-dye head rag, and cargo shorts. His copper-gray hair was pulled back in a scrawny ponytail and she would have bet he was starting to get bald. His eyes were washed-out blue. He had the skinniest wrists and legs she had ever seen on a wide-shouldered guy.

He cleared his throat. "You are here about the car and the job?"

"I am."

Narc, for sure.

"Why?" He'd blown it. She'd know that he knew that she might know.

"I need a car and a job."

"Why?"

Nell remembered the last of the series of interviews that had landed her in the middle of the Elysian corner office with a fat salary, fatter stock options, and fattest benefits. The final question the team had asked had been: "What is your time limit on having a baby?"

"I think," she had answered, "I could nail you on at least three counts of discrimination on that one."

The team had stood as one and smiled. "Congratulations."

"So," Monkey said. "I repeat myself—why? And I forgot your name."

"I need to earn money so I can pay rent, eat, and pay my bills. I need a car so I can drive to the job at which I earn that money. I'm Nell."

Monkey looked at her suit. "I don't know much about chick fashion," he said, "but my wife does. I bet she'd figure that suit at eight, maybe nine hundred bucks. You need money?"

"She'd figure wrong. It was $1250. What's more, once you decide to hire a vastly overqualified computer genius for an even more vastly underpaid eleven bucks an hour, I am taking the suit to a resale store and hoping to acquire a few office casual outfits, i.e., tank tops and cotton pants. Why I need money is my business."

"Hey," he said. "I shouldn't have asked. Shit happens, right?"

She nodded.

"Okay, just one more detail before I maybe hire an overqualified computer genius for a measly eleven bucks an hour: Why Twentynine Palms? In—oh yeah, there's no global warming—late April. Right as the devil moves in."

Nell hesitated. But the guy looked genuinely curious.

"I'm nosy," he said. "I'm an Okie. I come from a breed of people who love a good story."

"Are you online?" Nell said.

"That?" he pointed to the computer. "The Fiendish Thing? Yeah.

More or less. Mostly less."

"Get us into Google," she said. "It's a search engine."

"That thing." Monkey frowned, opened the computer, and logged on. "You find it." The interviewee narrowed her eyes. "Please."

Nell sat at the computer. "Don't look," she said. Monkey covered his eyes. He felt like a kid. He reckoned he liked the feeling. "Okay," she said. "Here's the deal. Don't ask me any more questions. Just read this."

LITTLE FEAT: WILLIN
AND I BEEN FROM TUCSON TO TUCANCARY TAHATHAPI TO TANAPALL

"So?" Monkey said. "So there's one Asian in the world who can't spell English?"

"I couldn't find a bus to Tanapall."

Monkey stepped back from the desk. He was in trouble. He wanted to say something dumb like, "Where have you been? I've been waiting my whole life for your whip-smart, subtle, and fucking funny mind." For Chrissake, he'd known the chick ten minutes, and that was not the kind of thing he would let himself feel or say. Twenty-five years of technical fidelity, twenty-five years. What the fuck.

"Are you okay?" she said.

"I. Yeah." He shivered. "Things have been a little weird lately. That was funny. Your remark. That was very funny."

Nell nodded. "Me too. Things weird, I mean. But, while we've got the computer open, let me take a look at your records."

"Here," he said and handed her a South Park hat stuffed with papers. "This is the Inbox."

She worked through the day. Quitting time, he walked her out to the LeSabre. She leaned down to open the door. "Wait," Monkey said. He pulled off his head rag, folded it, and offered it to her. "That handle will blister you." She looked up. Bets were off on advancing baldness. She'd guessed right.

She took the head rag, opened the door, and leaned in. The car smelled like old beer, old puke, and something else she didn't want to analyze. She squared her shoulders. It was no time to be fussy.

Monkey watched her. "I was going to get an air freshener, but I didn't get around to it."

"That's okay," she said. "How much? You said three-fifty. OBO."

"One-fifty. That's your best offer, and you can work it off."

"Oh no," she said in a Cockney accent. "I say one hundred, then you say three twenty-five, then I say one-fifty, then..."

Monkey closed his eyes. This was going to be a challenge. She knew Little Feat. Monty Python. She was funny. Brassy. What the fuck. Twenty-five years faithful. Not easy on his part, what with guys like Keno and their lady friends, to say nothing of two lapdance joints less than a block away.

"One-fifty," he said. "You work it off, ten bucks a week. We open at 8:00. That hunkajunk is gassed up and good to go."

The woman slid into the driver's seat. She looked up.

"Wait," he said. "Get out. I want to show you something."

He led his new computer geek to the front of the shop. "Check that out." He jutted his chin toward a sign above the door.

There was a four-foot-high monkey sumi-brushed in black on an off-white panel. BIZ had been painted in delicate calligraphy next to it.

"My wife Jackie did that," Monkey said. "She's amazing."

"It's beautifully done," the woman said. "And it's funny. That's my favorite combination in life. You're a lucky guy."

They walked back to the car. Monkey tried to think of something to keep the conversation going. "Seriously, girl. Get rid of that suit. You'll scare the customers."

"Yes, boss," the woman said. "Just in case you need a reminder, my name isn't Girl, it's Nell." She reached out the open window. He took her hand. Her fingers were fine-boned and strong.

"Nell," he said. "Little Nell."

"Curious," she said.

Monkey laughed. "A Dickens fan." Who was she? A yuppie who knew real music and movies and one of Charles Dickens' more obscure works. For that matter, who was he—a washed-in-the-blood-of-the-Lamb Southern Baptist Okie stoner who played air guitar when nobody was looking and slept maybe four hours out of eight most nights of the week.

"When the going gets tough," Nell said, "the tough get reading."

Monkey logged onto the computer and found the Little Feat lyrics. He fired up a bowl and read the words over and over. Nothing strange happened. He was just a gob-smacked guy sitting in front of a machine he barely understood, a guy getting older and balder by the second, a guy who was going to have to start wearing loose shirts down over his package while his new computer geek was around. He sucked in a second toke. And he was a lucky guy married to a woman gorgeous, sweet, and talented.

He logged off. He didn't know Her—shit, he was thinking of Nell as Her—he didn't know her last name. It probably didn't matter since he wouldn't be reporting her income. He didn't know her phone number in case he suddenly decided it would be wise to fire her before she showed up at the door with her sad eyes and big brain.

Okay. It was simple. He'd fire her before things got weird. He knew where La Paloma was. But then he'd have to see her. He'd have to give her the back-pay. Fifty-five bucks. Cash. When you paid under the table, you didn't write a check. So he'd have to hand her the money. In which case, he'd have to see her. Again. So if he had to see her again, he might as well at least let her exorcise the demons from the computer. Yeah. That made sense. More or less.

"When in doubt," he said and fired up a third time.

12

Nell turned out of the Biz parking lot onto a street she didn't know, kept going, and realized she was lost. She could have gone back and asked Monkey, but she needed to figure out her new life herself. Who was he, anyhow? A back-dated extra from *Spinal Tap* who'd read *The Old Curiousity Shop*, knew how to *Life of Brian* bargain backwards, and the lyrics to a stoner seventies anthem. He had the face of a football coach—high school, not NFL—and the eyes she had too often seen when a cop who had stopped her for speeding had taken off his shades.

Saigon Sally's. She saw the sign for a Vietnamese restaurant in a strip mall and pulled in. She'd get an iced coffee and see if she could get online. The cafe was open and empty. Candles burned in front of a little bronze Buddha. A Vietnamese girl in a fuchsia *ao dai* and green high-top sneakers brought her a menu. "Iced coffee," Nell said. "And can I get online?"

"Of course," the girl said. "But you *have* to eat. My grandma is an awesome cook. Don't get the pho. It's good, but it's ordinary. Let me pick you out some stuff to nibble on. How much can you spend?"

Nell remembered the rule about invitations. She decided to celebrate. She had a job, even if her boss was a cypher. "Fifteen bucks," she said.

"Excellent choice," the girl said and giggled. "Don't you hate it when the waiter says, 'Hi, I'm Josh. I'm your waiter,' and then no matter what you order even if it's totally boring or something like oysters with peanut butter and ice cream, he goes, 'Excellent choice.'"

"I do."

"So I'm Keri. I'm the boss of you for this meal."

She picked up the menu and disappeared through the beaded curtains in the back. Nell logged on. The map of Twentynine jumped up in front of her. It was pointless. She didn't know the address of La Paloma, and Shiloh had said they didn't have a presence on the web. Keri brought her a glass of ice and condensed milk covered by a tiny metal pot. "Watch."

The coffee dripped down over the ice. When it had stopped, she took off the pot and stirred. The milk swirled up through the coffee. "It's a lava lamp," Nell said.

Keri laughed. "All you older people say that. But I know about those thingees. My mom has one an American boyfriend gave her a long time ago."

"My mom had one too," Nell said. "It was turquoise and white and orange. She dragged it with us all over the country."

A bell rang. "Your food is ready," Keri said. "I'll be right back."

Nell sipped her coffee and watched the light outside begin to cool. She was lost. She was not afraid. The coffee was dark and sweet. She had a job and a Buick LeSabre with the serial numbers filed off. Keri slipped through the beaded curtains with four plates of food balanced on her arms

"Wait," she said. "I have to get the other stuff and I have to give you the guided tour."

Nell nodded. "I am here to obey."

The girl came back with plates of raw vegetables, rice paper, toasted baguette slices, pickles, mint leaves, and finely chopped cilantro. She had three cruets hooked through her fingers. "Okay," she said. "This gray mooshy stuff is eggplant and herbs dip. You scoop it up with the toast or the long beans or the cauliflower. The goopy stuff on the sugarcane is *Chao Tom*. It's shrimp. You take the rice paper, pile mint leaves, pickle, those rice noodles on it, put the shrimp paste on top, roll it up, and dip it in this sauce." She touched one of the cruets. "I'm not gonna tell you what the sauce is, okay? Because sometimes white people get grossed out?"

Nell grinned. "It's *nuoc mam*. Fish sauce. My boyfriend took me to Vietnam a few years ago. But we never ate these."

"Omigod," Keri said. "Where?"

"Hue, it was gorgeous."

Keri poured a dark sesame sauce onto Nell's plate. "Ohmigod. I've got to get my grandma."

Grandma was a tiny, impeccably made-up woman who spoke flawless English. She had fled Saigon at the last minute. She had never been to Hue. She had been too busy working and raising her kids. And she knew where La Paloma was.

"I have a friend," she said. "They helped her out." She narrowed her eyes at her granddaughter. The girl looked away. "Keri can give you directions."

She went back into the kitchen. The girl stood by Nell's chair. "I'm good," Nell said. "I don't need anything else."

Keri bent down. "No," she whispered, "I just wanted you to know. That friend my grandma said about?"

"Yes?"

"That's my mom. She got mixed up with an American guy. Big mistake."

"Me too," Nell said. "Big mistake."

"Not me," Keri said. "No guys till I find my dream. After my mom got straightened out at La Paloma, she started learning about where she came from. Check this out."

She hunkered cross-legged on the chair across from Nell.

"My mom taught me this old saying. *A thousand years of Chinese domination. A hundred years of French colonization. Twenty years of daily civil war. The heritage my mother left me. The heritage of my mother is my country of Vietnam.*'

"So, I started researching Vietnam. It is so amazing. My mom and I are going there after I graduate. She was only two when they came here. My grandma isn't sure if she wants to go.

"Plus it's not just Vietnam. There are some Indian kids from around here in my classes. They were talking about what it's like being Indian in America. I told them the saying and they were like *totally, that's how it is for us.*

"Plus this is really weird, you being in Hue and all. Look."

She held out her arm. *Hue* had been tattooed on her wrist.

"It means lily and intelligence. Don't worry, it's just indelible marker. But after we get back from Vietnam, I am going to make it my real name."

A couple came through the front door. "Thanks for talking," Nell said.

Keri stood. "Thank you, too," she said. "My grandma made some food for you to take for the ladies at La Paloma. No charge. I'll get it when you're finished."

Nell ate slowly. There was a delicate under-taste in the sesame sauce, a little familiar. She put a dab of it on her tongue. Lemony, something else. She remembered. She opened her bag and took out the withered orange she'd picked up from the field in San Bernardino. The scent was the same. Bitter, pungent, a whisper of citrus. She wondered if the parrots had found the tangerines and if there were slivers of peel on the ground outside the window, arcs of orange against the dark grass.

Keri brought a stuffed plastic grocery bag. "My grandma said to tell you that we hope you come back to eat with us."

"Thank you," Nell said. "I will come back." A guy at a nearby table waved his check in the air.

"Gotta run," Keri said.

Nell tucked two twenties under the empty plate and left.

Monkey went in the back door. Jackie was playing computer solitaire.

She smiled muzzily up at him. "I've got supper already to go," she said.

She was ripped. He was ripped. Compatibility was the key to a satisfying marriage. He was surprised to hear himself say, "I, I gotta shower and shave. It was a full day."

She sighed. "No big deal. This dang solitaire. I haven't won in ninety-six games."

He rubbed her shoulders.

"How was work?" she asked and logged off.

"I got me a new computer geek," he said.

"What's he like? Some nerdy kid?"

Monkey pressed his thumbs into her shoulder blades. "Nope. He's a she. Probably in her fifties."

Jackie spun in her chair. "A she? I don't know if I like that." She winked.

"Computer geek," Monkey said. "I said I got me a new computer geek in her fifties. You've got nothing to worry about."

No one was at La Paloma. Nell put her food in the refrigerator and went out to the front stoop. She watched the last sliver of rose-purple light disappear behind the mountains. She wondered what lay out in the desert beyond Twentynine. She'd take a few weeks to get her bearings and let her blood adjust to the heat, then she'd go. Alone. It was a relief to be truly alone. She had been in constant contact with people so much of the time in Los Angeles. Meetings, phone calls, email, IMs, faxes, text messages. In all of that, she had been absolutely alone. David had been the only person to come close enough for her to step away from herself, the only person to touch her, the only person to go what he called "gaze-to-gaze."

And when she had been alone, she had been jammed full with what she hadn't done at work, then with what she had done with David, would do, then wouldn't. Always, there had been subtext under subtext under what you believed was the true surface. In work. In love. All the same.

She looked up toward a ribbon of green afterglow above the mountains. A soft breeze drifted down the street. She could smell the cooling asphalt. This solitude was different. She could feel it swirling around something in her that had yet to emerge, or something that might be changing.

She realized that she had stopped looking for subtexts the moment she had given the Audi to the couple in the Greyhound station. The puking kid had been the puking kid. Diamond was Diamond. Keri was Keri. Mariah was a grandmother who worked in an old folks' home. Even Monkey, brilliance seeming to run molten under his redneck hippie appearance, was not a man with a secret intention.

Nell considered "appearance." It could mean surface. It could mean an emergence. She looked up. The ribbon of green was gone. The mountains were dead black, the sky a cool silver. She closed her eyes. For the first time in as long as she could remember, she was happy to be right where she was. And where she was, again, was strangely familiar.

Monkey could not sleep. Why should this night be different than any other night? Jackie breathed softly, snored, jolted in her sleep, snored, jolted again. It drove him nuts. It drove him psycho that it drove him nuts.

When he closed his eyes, the swirling colors of the trance began to drift in. Just as he started to go, there was a twitch or a chain saw buzz from his wife's side of the bed. There was no peaceful dark, no memories of sweetness to draw him into sleep.

He glanced at the clock. 11:30. He wanted it to be morning, wanted that first hit of coffee, wanted to get to work early because Nell was coming in to help him alchemize the computer. Those were her words, "Alchemize the computer. Turn dross into gold. You know?"

"Yeah," he had said. "Like Fantasia. But, when I so much as touch the fucking thing, I've got nothing but a million broomsticks."

He pulled himself away from the memory. "Uh uh," he whispered. Jackie murmured. "What's wrong, Monkeyboy?"

She wiggled over to his side of the bed and pressed herself against him. "Tell Mama." She fell instantly back to sleep. He held her. He whispered. He told her about the trances and how his hair seemed to be receding like a monsoon puddle in July and that he was scared he couldn't remember real passion. And if she heard that, he was sorry, so fuckin' sorry.

Nell went up to her room. She stripped off her clothes and pulled on a t-shirt. She took the orange from her bag and set it next to her laptop, opened the curtains to a cool breeze, and sat. There was a soft knock on the door. "You asleep?" It was Diamond. Nell didn't move. Diamond knocked again. Nell slowed her breathing. "I'll catch you in the morning," Diamond said. "Sleep tight."

13

Jackie was gone from their bed. Monkey heard the shower. He pulled on his pants and walked out into the hall. The sun glowed on the wall just ahead, bright as a puddle of mercury. It was going to be touchy if the trances started kicking in when they wanted to. It was worse that mercury made him think of alchemy, which made him think of Her.

The light shifted a millimeter and he realized that what he had thought was a hallucination was a crescent of silver satin stitch on one of Jackie's patchworks. The price tag was still on the piece. $45. She had pulled it and all the others from the gallery in which they had been exhibited for a few months. There had been one sale. "No point," she had said. "My dad was right. I'm not an artist."

Monkey ran his fingers over the patch of silver light. It was the center of a ragged flower, a flower that twined up from what might have been a woman's soft belly or a sweep of pale sand. Jackie opened the bathroom door. "Don't start," she said. "I feel like shit. Don't start in on how I'm wasting my life."

He reached for her. She sidestepped. "I'm sorry," she said. "It's an ugly morning."

"I'll start the coffee," Monkey said. "You want me to make toast?"

"Don't bother," she said. "Everything's already made."

Diamond knocked on the door. "Rise and shine."

Nell padded to the door and opened it. "I'll be right down. I need to shower and dress. I've got a job."

"And a vehicle," Diamond said. "You move fast."

Shiloh looked up from her book. She'd been shanghaied into going back to college for an Associate's. "No degree, no workee," her boss had told her. "Fifteen years busting my hump for Down Home Cooking," she said, "a restaurant that's owned by a Shanghai conglomerate, that has all its Miss Wanda's Waffles, Bad-boy Fried Chicken and Kiss a Peach Cobbler shipped in frozen, and makes us write our names on the Wall of Shame if we so much as drop a napkin, much less suddenly go mental and bitch slap some pitiful old Snowbird to death because he tried to flirt. Fifteen years working my way up to Graveyard Shift Manager and they tell me I have to get a degree." She slammed the book shut. "Hey, Diamond tells me you have a job—and a car. You must have met Monkey."

"I did." She started to say that he seemed a puzzle and stopped herself.

"I already put in a few hours on the job," Nell said. "I hope I can stay here a little while longer till I get a nest egg."

"You can stay here as long as it takes," Diamond said. "Long as you solve the mystery of the bucket of *Hu-Tien* in the fridge. How'd you find Saigon Sally's?" She set three bowls on the table and ladled soup into their bowls. "Sally taught us to eat this for breakfast. It's weird how it somehow makes the heat less brutal."

Nell poured herself coffee and sat down. "I got lost. I barreled confidently out of the Biz, drove a couple blocks, and realized I had no idea where I was. I saw a sign for pho, knew they'd have good coffee, and went in. Keri told me her life story. Her grandma told me not much. But, she knew La Paloma, gave Keri a look that said, 'Keep your mouth shut,' and gave me this soup for free."

Diamond looked at Shiloh. "That damn Black Widow, definitely asymmetrical. Speaking of holes, Nell, what did you think of Monkey?"

"He seemed pretty nice."

Shiloh looked hard at Nell. "He is very very married," she said. "His wife is a friend of a friend of ours."

"Not my type," Nell said. "And..."

"Don't worry," Diamond said. "You notice Shiloh is a little chunky and how her late-for-it mullet sticks up. No accident the local kids call her *gallinacita*."

"Spanglish," Shiloh said, "for mother hen."

Nell concentrated on her soup.

Shiloh scattered chopped cilantro over the bowl. "Hey," she said. "In my former life, I fucked everybody's husband."

Diamond laughed. "And a few of their wives."

Shiloh grinned. "So, whatever you want to tell or not tell, it's chump change compared to our dance cards."

Nell carefully put down her spoon. "Okay. Monkey's married. Brilliant. First man in my whole life who seems to be as smart as I am. Married. Funny. Married. Fighting getting old. Who isn't? Did I mention married."

"Nice. Concise. And modest," Shiloh said. "I'd like to hear more, but the Down Home Grits and Grease Special is calling." She grabbed her pack and left.

Diamond poured Nell a second cup of coffee. "I'm serious about you staying on as long as you need to. Judy won't be out of treatment for a long time. Mariah and the baby are in one room. We have plenty of space."

"Thanks," Nell said. "I like feeling I don't have to panic. Can I tell you tonight what I want to do?"

"Of course. And we won't even require a deposit."

"I better get going," Nell said. "I cleaned out most of the garbage in the Biz computer yesterday, but there's three years of records to enter. In all honesty, I don't think Monkey really cares."

"He doesn't," Diamond said. "And? What Shiloh said? About him being very very married?"

"Yes?"

"Watch out," Diamond said.

"Because he's really a scum bag?"

"Because he really isn't."

"Lovely." Nell picked up her cup and headed for the sink. "There will truly be no problem. He's short. I like tall. He's chunky. I like buff. He's almost bald. I like hair. He's got pale blue eyes. I like dark brown. He's married. He's married. He's married."

Diamond's voice was both quiet and amused. "You know? In five hours, you sure managed to get a lot of details on that boy."

"Look," Nell said. "He's also maybe ten years younger than I am, which means he's Mid-life Crisis Man, which means younger chicks, which means I am nothing but a flat-chested old broad."

"Oh jeez," Diamond said. "You better plan on kicking it with us for a long long time. And tonight's the Mystery Tour. We leave at 5:30."

Monkey unlocked the door. The Biz was cool and dark. Not for long. "*It's the time da da da of the season...*" He couldn't remember the next line. He bet Nell would know how to find the lyrics. Nell. Cut it out, Monkeynuts.

The planet swung a fraction. Eight a.m. May sun blasted in through the east window. He lowered the broken blind. A bar of light slashed the floor. *There are spinning rods. There is a pattern. I know what it is. I know...*

Monkey looked away. There were four jobs today. Nell was coming in. He needed to be tip-top. He turned back to the sleeping computer. He droned, "Da Da Dum, da da Dum Dum...."

"Is he rich like me?" Nell stood in the doorway.

"Fuck me running," Monkey said. "Don't, do not, DO NOT ever creep up on me like that again." His voice was flat.

"I'm sorry," she said. "The door was open."

"Okay," he said. "Okay, I have rock n' roll Alzheimer's. I can't remember the lyrics. It's The Zombies. Chris White."

"He discovered Dire Straits."

"And that other guy, Blunstone?"

"Colin Blunstone," she said crisply. "He had a voice like a demented choir boy."

"Jaysus," Monkey said. "You think any of them are alive now?"

"If they are," Nell paused, "we can find out."

He touched the computer screen. "This," he said, "the Fiendish Thing, will tell us, right?"

"The Time Machine," she said. "It will take us almost anywhere we want to go."

Monkey stood and waved her to the chair. He wasn't sure how many more time machines he could handle.

"So," she said and logged on. "Let's start with *Time Machine*. I think you'll like this. Pull up the tires." She was startled to feel at home. "Look."

Monkey leaned in. There was a photo. The man's eyes were sorrowful. "I know why he looks so sad," Monkey said.

"That's H.G. Wells."

"I know." He almost told her Wells was sad because he knew too much he couldn't talk about. Spinning rods, layers of the real and unreal, voices telling him to keep going into nothing known.

"Check out his hairline," he said. "It's receding. That's why he's sad."

Nell turned toward him. "At least you guys have a hairline to recede." She looked down at her chest. *This is crazy*, she thought. *I can't believe I made a joke about my boobs. Or relative lack of them.*

Monkey looked away. Anything he said would be dangerous. When he turned back, she had brought the words under Wells' picture into sharp focus: *I seemed to see a ghostly, indistinct figure sitting in a whirling mass of black and brass for a moment—a figure so transparent that the bench behind with its sheets of drawings was absolutely distinct; but this phantasm vanished as I rubbed my eyes.*

"Listen," Monkey said, "I've got to get to work." His voice had gone flat again. He stood and put the tires back in their place.

"How long," Nell said, "do you want me here?"

Monkey didn't turn around. "How long do you want to be here?"

"It's going to take a few days to get all the records set up."

"Cool. How about you eight-to-five it for a couple months. Put things in order. Maybe make us one of those website things. For today, you can dig into the files, take a lunch break, you know, like a straight job? There's a killer *taqueria* a block down. My wife packs my lunch, but you could bring me back a *horchata* around noon. You fly, I'll buy."

The hypothetical files were crumpled in a cardboard box by the laws of Chaos Theory. She thought longingly of her former genius assistant, Lillie. She thought of her former large and immaculate desk and grinned.

"Why the Cheshire Cat face?" Monkey asked.

"Partly your incredible office skills," Nell said.

"What else?"

"I think it would be fantastic to make you a website."

"More business, right?"

"That's the point. And, Jackie's an artist?"

Monkey looked away. "Yeah," he said. "More or less. A little too much less right now. I gotta get to work."

Nell was quarter-way through the stack by noon. She put the sorted records on the desk and logged on. She'd set up the system, get a break from crouching over the box. Glare blocked the bottom of the screen. The window blind was broken.

She hunted through the desk drawers for tape. There were no office supplies. No paper clips, no pencil sharpener, no pens or pencils or tape.

"Hey," she yelled. "You got any tape?"

There was a long pause. Monkey walked in. "Just this," he said. "It's called duct tape."

"Based on that remark," Nell said, "I could sue you for gender assumption. If I was actually employed here. If I existed. If I believed you had any money."

"Non-existent employee cranky," he said. "Time for fud."

"Dog looks at clothes dryer," Nell said. "There is a sign taped above the open door. 'Fud.' Arrow points into the dryer. We see a cat's eye and whiskers peeking out from behind the dryer."

"Little Feat. Monty Python. Gary Larson. Duct tape. You're the World Book Encyclopedia of crucial trivia, girl."

Nell taped the blind back together. Monkey pulled a ten out of his pocket. "This will get you an abundance of taquitos. Get me one lengue. And a horchata."

Nell put the computer to sleep. "I'd like to use the computer for some personal stuff on my lunch break. Is that okay?"

"Hell, no," Monkey's voice was ice.

Nell went stiff.

"Hey," he said. "It was a joke. Do you really think I would give a shit what you did on your lunch hour?"

"Gracious me, no," she said. "I was faking shock."

She tucked the ten in her pants pocket and left.

Monkey sat down on the tires. How the fuck could it be so easy with a woman he'd met less than twenty-four hours ago? He'd had crushes before. His crush on Jackie had lasted twenty-four years, eleven months, and sixteen days. Most of his other crushes had been based on the curve of a hip or the perfection of cleavage. Once there had been something different, but that woman had been a colleague and he'd not been so much ethical as chicken. To her sorrow—and his loss.

Nell picked up the food and started back under a blowtorch sun. She checked the horchata to make sure the lid was still on and snuck a taste. The sweet cold flooded her mouth. She could see why Monkey liked it. He liked a lot. *You're the World Book, girl.* David thought that too, till he didn't. David. David who? Not only am I learning about horchata, I am learning I'm one shallow babe. Stranger danger, Nell. Watch out.

Monkey took the horchata. "You sneak any?"

"Not me."

He carried his lunch out to the garage. Nell set the taquitos on the desk, logged on to Yahoo, and started to send herself an email.

"How do you do that?" Monkey stood beside her. She jumped and logged out. "Payback," he said. "For scaring the bejesus out of me this morning."

"It's easy," Nell said. "You create an account, then you drive yourself crazy waiting for somebody to write."

"My wife tried to get me to do that. She handles all our email. She's great at stuff like that. Besides, I can't type."

"It'd be cool to surprise her. Pull up the tires and sit here," she said. "I'll walk you through it."

"Fem-dominatrix."

Nell glared at him.

"I almost said, 'You're cute when you're angry,'" Monkey said.

"I'm ignoring that," Nell said. "I'll get out of Yahoo. Now, you go back in. See where it says Set Up New Account?"

Five minutes and a dozen inventive and disgusting Oklahoma country boy cusses later, Monkey was oilinmyvessel47@yahoo.com.

"Oil in my vessel?" Nell said.

"It was my gramps' favorite gospel song. Mine, too. Though neither he nor I were exactly what you might call saved."

Nell packed up the plastic forks and salsa cups. "I'll leave so you can write your wife in privacy."

Monkey grinned. "You might as well go for a long walk. The way I type, this is going to take an hour."

"Walk? It's hellish out there. I'll take a couple of those tires into the garage and just sit. I'm getting pretty good at that."

By five, Nell's eyes felt sanded. Monkey was gone. She saved the records and logged off.

The phone rang. "Hey, it's me."

"Which me?"

"Who else would call you?" Monkey said.

"Nobody. But this is the Biz phone. Customers, you know? State inspectors."

"Oh. Yeah. Flinch."

He was stoned. She was sure he was stoned. Fourteen years of navigating through the skunky fog of her mother's smoke had made Nell an expert.

He giggled. "Check your email. I'm the boss." He hung up.

Nell logged back into Yahoo. One message:

oilinmyvessel47@yahoo.com
Subject: Duct Tape.
Tomorrow's Casual Day. You'd look good in this:
http://www.oz-q.com/humour/duct%20tape.jpg
The boss

Nell clicked the link. A young woman in jeans and a flannel shirt was duct-taped to a wall. The tape extended up away from her body like gleaming wings. There was an ugly couch and an uglier floor lamp next to her. It might have been sinister, except for the whole-hearted grin on the girl's face.

The silver wings held her in place.

Nell hit Reply.

Subject: oxymoron
The silver wings hold her in place.
The Flunky

She logged off, grabbed her bag, locked the door, and left.

Monkey waited for Nell's reply. Minutes, hours, days, whole centuries went by. He realized the trance was calling him. "Uh uh," he said and held himself together. Then, her email. Subject: oxymoron.

You bet, he thought. Hypoxia due to hyperweedia + moron = him. She had a way with words. He heard Jackie fixing up their coffee for morning in the kitchen. Next, she'd come in, kiss the top of his head, evade his hug, say, "Sleepy-bye time, Monkeyboy," and be gone. He logged off.

He went in to Jackie. "We gotta talk sometime," he said. He imagined she might take his hand and lead him to the back patio. They would sit in the quiet dark. He would tell her about the trances. She would put her arms around him and say something like, "It's just the dope, honey. That's all."

Jackie looked at him. "Oh no," she said. "That's what husbands say when they got the twenty-four-almost-twenty-five-year itch." She set his hands on her hips.

Monkey pulled her close. He didn't say what was racing through his mind: *there is no twenty-four-almost-twenty-five-year itch, there will be no thirty-year-itch, no so-old-we-forgot-how-to-do-it itch*. He could hear his asshole EMT instructor. "Listen up, you sick puppies, don't ever, ever let your mouth make promises your lame rookie ass can't carry out."

"No," he whispered into Jackie's hair. "No itch. Except for you. I just wanted to figure out how we're going to celebrate the Big Twenty-Five."

She snuggled into him. "We could start now."

Mariah and Shiloh were eating *posole* in the kitchen. A tiny baby slept peacefully in a washbasket in the corner. Mariah filled a bowl for Nell and offered a plate of biscuits. "That's my grandbaby," she said. "She's not but six weeks old. I take care of her now and then, so my daughter didn't care that we brought her here."

"She's beautiful," Nell said. "Her name's Punkin?"

"We haven't found her real name yet," Mariah said. "My mother's people like to wait till the right name turns up, so we just call her Punkin."

"Are you feeling better?"

"Yeah. I had some plants in my bag. We boiled them up and put them on the sore places. Plus I ate a bunch of Diamond's chocolate chip cookies. They helped a lot. But I still feel shaky."

"Do you want to say what happened?" Nell asked.

"Sure. I'd gone out to a little wash that I go to to talk to my grandmother's grandmother. Not a cemetery, just a place. I go there mostly to thank her for the good stuff in my life. I came around a bend in the wash and these plastic ribbons and stakes were all along the edge. I was going up closer to see what name was on them, when somebody grabbed my arms hard from behind. I never saw them. They tied a rag around my eyes. A guy said, 'This didn't happen. You stay away from here and if you tell the cops, we'll get Punkin. Don't move till you hear a horn honk. If you do, something worse could happen.'

"I waited till I heard the horn. Then I took off the rag and climbed up the side of the wash. There wasn't anything but a bunch of dust moving away toward town. I checked the stakes. They were marked with a name: FreegreenGlobal. I went back down and sat on the sand for a while and talked with my great-great-grandma, then I got myself here. I checked out FreegreenGlobal on the internet a few days ago. It's a huge international solar power company. I tried to track if there was an owner company but there were nothing but dead ends."

"I might have a way to help with that," Nell said. "But, in the meantime, we need to get the cops out there."

"No," Mariah said. "No cops. But I'll tell you more or less where it is so you *don't* go out there. It's off Mesa, out west of the Base. You'll see a compound with barbed wire and a lot of dogs. The wash runs to the west of it. Don't go out there. Even if I hadn't gotten jumped, it's not a place for white people. Plus the old guy that lives in the compound is a crazy man."

"Don't worry," Nell said. "I'm just getting used to being here. I'm not ready to go much beyond town."

Diamond sat down. "You better get ready," she said. "There's just enough light for you to see something you won't believe. Mariah, we're taking Nell up to Luna Mesa. Want to go?"

"I'm whipped. I want to get Punkin and me settled in for the night. You ladies have fun."

Diamond parked at the side of a dirt road. "That's the dump straight ahead," she said. "Don't let it prejudice you."

Nell looked out at miles of sand, shrubs, and Joshua trees.

"You're wondering what the big deal is, aren't you?" Shiloh said. "Let's get out."

They walked along the dirt road. The air was soft, the sun dropping toward the mountains. Diamond stepped off the road into the sand. "I'll walk point," she said. "Snakes and scorpions just love city girls in blinged-out flip-flops."

"Shut up," Nell said. "I've walked scarier places than this in these."

"Uh huh. You so bad." Diamond stopped. "Okay, we're here."

"Where?"

"In Oz. Watch out for the flying monkeys."

Nell almost believed her. The twisted silhouettes of the trees and the absolute silence were not of any earth she'd known. "Where are the monkeys?"

"They're not out yet."

"Where's Oz?"

"Just look," Shiloh said. "Let your eyes be desert eyes."

Shiloh and Diamond went quiet for what seemed like a long time. Nell looked out toward a cluster of big Joshuas. A trail of pebbles led out from them, as though water had once flowed there. Then it seemed as though her gaze softened. She saw a pale yellow mist running along the edge of the pebbles.

"What is that?" she asked. "The yellow."

"Coreopsis," Shiloh said. "Now check what's growing near that creosote."

"What's creosote?"

"The shrub right in front of you. See the purple flowers next to it?"

There was a patch of dark green crinkled leaves and spiky buds with tiny purple flowers on them. "Chia," Shiloh said. "You can eat the seeds, grind them into flour, make a gel that's good for your skin. Mariah takes Diamond and me on walks out here. She says a person could feed themselves just from this desert." She spun in a circle. "And there's Smoketree and Mojave Aster and primrose and, right here on the edge of this wash, a desert lily. Look down into it."

Nell looked into the lily. Delicate yellow sepals sprang up in its white throat. She thought of the Leafy, of the living green streamers, the translucent fins. Diamond and Shiloh stood next to her. "Can't talk, right?" Diamond said. "That's what this place will do to you. If you're lucky."

It wasn't until it happened that Nell knew she had been waiting for it. They had come back to the porch at La Paloma. Mariah had joined them. Shiloh had brought out more cookies. They told stories, the details not mattering, the threads different and the same. Bad choices on top of bad choices for three of them. A little grace leading to a little grace for all four. "Sometimes it's hard to believe," Shiloh had said, "that humans are at the top of the food chain."

Nell went up to her room and sat by the window. The man on the steps smoked steadily. He untethered the goat. It curled up at his feet. Now and then, he leaned down and scratched its head. A helicopter searchlight strafed the yard. When it had passed, the man was gone. Nell went to her bed and fell instantly asleep.

The creature drifted in front of her. Pink and green and silver. Animal, vegetable, and mineral. It hovered at the end of her bed, filling floor to ceiling. *Shiloh was wrong*, it said. *You are not at the top of the food chain.*

Nell couldn't tell if the creature smiled or if that were just the curve of its mouth. It drifted in two planes. Up. Down. Always in full sight. It spoke once more. *Anything can be a doorway. Any doorway can be a way forward. Any way forward can be a map. Mariah can tell you about the map.* Then it was gone. Nell jolted up. Tremors began deep inside her and moved through her body. She lay back down. The shaking deepened. She considered getting up and trying to get to the chair by the window. Maybe she needed air. Maybe she needed to look at something other than the ceiling she couldn't see.

Da da da, da da, dada. Did your daddy show you how to live? What daddy? She remembered a seminar about compassionate management the boss had paid a weaselly shrink and his smiley-face crew to put on. Nell had been stunned when the facilitators told them they better go pee because they were not going to be let out of the room for the morning. Then, some idiot had played "Cat's in the Cradle." By the end of the song, half the group was sobbing. "I'm leaving," Nell had said. There had been silence. She had walked to the door and tried the handle. It was not locked. She had opened the door and walked out.

She could get off the bed and walk out of La Paloma. She could sit in the LeSabre till the shaking died down, then hit the road till her not quite six hundred bucks was gone. She could find another city, another job. She could go back to being a hungry ghost.

The shaking began to slow. She spiraled through dreams and waking. She saw the tangerine slices on the windowsill. The parrots flew down and took the fruit in their yellow beaks. Dawn drifted up from the dark hillside.

Nell woke. Words lingered from her sleep. *Anything can be a doorway.*

She picked up the notebook and pen on the dresser and wrote:

Premises

1. *My species is not at the top of the food chain.*
2. *Anything can be a doorway.*
3. *Any door can be a way forward.*
4. *Any way forward can be a map.*

She turned the page.

To do

1.

14

A month or so of molten days and sweetly cool nights settled into an easy rhythm of decoding Monkey's paperwork, fencing with him about the Biz website, fencing with him about everything, wishing she didn't like his brain so much, liking her brain more and more, hanging out with the women at La Paloma, and waiting for more visits from the Leafy. She'd stopped keeping the budget book. The To Do list hadn't grown, but there was a new premise: *Human interactions are not opportunities to network for personal gain.*

She woke to the scent of waffles. Morning blasted through the curtains. She opened them and looked down in the yard. The goat was in its shed. A scruffy brown bird picked at what was left of the goat's breakfast. Nell pulled on her clothes and went down to the kitchen. Diamond turned from the stove. "How do you want your eggs?"

"How come you do all the cooking?" Nell said. "I could pitch in. I cook a mean *huevos rancheros,* which is pretty much the only thing I cook."

"I love cooking," Diamond said. "I love having a pan. I love having a spatula. I love having a stove. In a real kitchen. In a real house. I love having eggs. How do you want yours?"

"Over easy," Nell said. Maybe it was time to issue a few invitations of her own. "Yeah," she said, "my mom didn't have a regular kitchen till I was already gone from the home." *Home* caught in her throat.

There was no RSVP. "One time," Diamond said, "this ho showed me how to make s'mores with a cigarette lighter and two dollars' worth of stuff out of a vending machine. We were always jonesing for sugar in those days. A. We were junkies. B. We were kids. But, you know back then, all any of us had to sell was pussy and blow jobs."

"There's more than one way," Nell said, "to be a ho." Another invitation, albeit facile.

"Yeah, girlfriend," Diamond grinned. "But the occupational hazards in those other occupations aren't quite as deadly."

Yep, facile.

Diamond carried the pan to the table, slid eggs onto their plates, and sat. "The waffles are in the oven. Bring them over."

The waffles were full of toasted pecans. The maple syrup was real. "I used to love s'mores," Nell said. "My mom and I camped a lot."

"I couldn't put one in my mouth to save my life now," Diamond said. "I think I'd puke. When do you have to be at the Biz?"

"I don't exactly punch in," Nell said. "I can call and tell Monkey when I'll be there." She took five twenties out of her purse and put it under the sugar bowl. "I want to start paying you. A hundred a week. Does that work?"

"You don't have to do that," Diamond said. "Take a while to get on your feet again, save enough to rent your own place."

"Nobody's going to rent to me. My credit rating is non-existent. Besides, you're right, I'd like to stay here as long as I can. I need it."

"It's my cooking," Diamond said. "And Shiloh's mullet and fashion sense. It's your call."

"Thanks. Now take the money."

"Let's talk a little more. Mariah asked me to tell you more about what's been going on."

"Sure," Nell said. "Where's she been?"

"She took Punkin to her daughter's and went back home. They got word to some of their cousins in San Bernardino. Big boys. Once were gang-bangers, but got popped and cleaned up their acts. They're temporarily in residence with Punkin and her mom, and Mariah and Daryl. Oh, and one of Monkey's bad boy buddies drops by. The Chemeheuvi gossip line made sure that word got around. Some mess has gone down and the visitors from San Berdoo are staying for a while."

"I'm glad," Nell said. "I didn't understand what she said about talking to her great-great-great-grandmother. Do you?"

"Not a lot. Mostly what I know is from books. We don't get very many of the Native women in here. They tend to take care of their own. You probably know that the white justice system is by and large not a friend to people of color."

Or poor white people, Nell thought.

"I think what Mariah was talking about is a place that's associated with her ancestors' spirits, like the great-great-great grandma. There's a trail or something. I figure the plastic ribbons and stakes were survey markers, maybe a new development going in, though it doesn't make sense way out there."

"FreegreenGlobal," Nell said. "It's the solar power arm of a huge oil conglomerate. I need to start researching the connections. They're murky."

"What is clear, though," Diamond said, "is that somebody doesn't want Mariah out there."

"Or maybe anybody else."

It was mid-morning by the time Nell got to the Biz. The door was locked. She let herself in and found a note on the desk. *Out for parts. I left today's work orders next to the Fiendish Thing.*

She pulled out the stack of un-entered receipts and went to work. She liked the quiet. She liked the smell of oil and dust from the garage. She lowered the pile of receipts by a couple inches and leaned back in the chair. A car pulled in next to the garage.

The office door flew open. She turned. A huge man blocked the light. "Who the fuck," he said, "are you?"

Nell grabbed the phone. "Who the fuck are *you*?"

The guy moved into the light. His head was shaved except for a queue of braided black hair hanging down to his butt. His eyes were red. He smelled like very expensive perfume. She knew she was amassing details in case a police report would be required. If she was going to be lucky enough to be alive to give one.

"Hey," he said. "Put down the phone. I'm Refugio. Where's Monkey?"

Nell held on to the phone. *Refugio?*

"Refugio?"

"Keno?" the guy said. "Monkey told you about me, right? I'm his best friend. I sold him that LeSabre out there."

"I bought your car," Nell said.

"Oh jeez, I'm sorry." The big guy sat down on the tires. "So, where's Monkey and who are you?"

"He left a note, said he was out for parts. I'm Nell. I'm the new office administrator."

Keno held out his hand. "Good to meet you. The last time I was in here there was papers all over the place and an inch of crank-case oil in the bottom of the coffee pot." He glanced at the coffee maker.

"I'll make some." Nell understood what was soothing about being an office administrator. Whatever came next would drop in front of you. You did it, then there was something else to do. She set the phone back in its cradle.

"Here's the deal," Keno said. "My heart is broken. If I don't tell somebody immediately, I'm gonna have a coronary. Immediately. Monkey's not here. You got kind eyes. I'll tell you."

Kind eyes? Nell put the computer to sleep. Premise Two was in operation and she'd opened the door.

"You know how to do a people search on that thing?" Keno asked. "You know, like a missing person? Like a missing broad? And her kid?" He buried his head in his hands and started to cry.

Monkey walked in. "What the fuck is this, Dear Abby?"

Keno looked up. "Dude. She's gone!"

"*Que?*"

"Her. She. Amber. And she took Kimberley Rose with her."

"Maybe two days ago," Monkey said patiently, "you bought her a car. What happened?"

Nell stood. "Do you two need to be alone?"

"Sit down," Monkey said. "I mean, please sit down. We might need a woman's viewpoint."

Nell poured coffee. "What do you take?"

Keno shook his head. "Don't matter. Just give it to me. Please." He looked at Nell. "I'll catch you up. Even though every time I say her name my heart shatters into little pieces like a broken mirror." He sipped the coffee. "She is Amber. Kimberley Rose is her little baby daughter. They were living with me. Not a shack-up. They needed a place to stay. And then, this *diablo*, this *cabron*, this pustule, this fake gangstah *malevencio*, this spawn of a mutated maggot who just happens to be the sperm donor that made Kimberley Rose—don't think about it—he comes back.

"Plus, Amber found out that she couldn't call her travelling beauty salon *Amber Waves* because that was the older chick in *Boogie Nights* and like copyrighted and we figure out she could call it Amber Ouaves, like a joke, but legal, and then somebody tells her Ouaves sounds too much like *huevos* which is a dirty joke. And she goes, 'I can't take this anymore. I give up. Thank you, Keno. You are a dear,' and she packs up all her stuff, grabs the baby, gets in the Camry, and goes."

"She won't get far in that Camry," Monkey said quietly.

Keno punched him on the leg. Monkey reeled a little, then hunkered down on the floor. "Where's the sperm donor? Sorry."

"With her. Who knows where? She didn't tell me much about her past. I didn't ask. It was more of a holy thing between us, you know, like respecting each other's boundaries and shit.

"Hey. You. Nell. I need a woman's perspective."

"Frankly," Nell said, "I don't know jack about other women. I know even less about men."

Monkey nodded. "This new computer geek here is a woman who

could be a dangerous bitch. This is a woman I could love."

"Illusion harassment," Nell said. "I got two counts against you now. You're lucky I don't exist."

Keno raised his hand. "Excuse me," he said, "I'm the one on suicide watch here. Can you two hold whatever that is that you're doing till later? Besides, cabron, you're married."

"What Nell and I are doing," Monkey said, "which is not in any wedding vow I took, is called bantering. It's what an educated man and woman can do. It indicates both wit and intelligence."

Keno looked away. "My brother," he said, "what you got in the way of education is nothin' but a GED and a revoked pretend doc license."

Monkey's gaze went flat. He slowly rose to his feet. "You got thirty seconds, bro."

Keno waved his hands in front of his mouth. "Erased, consider it erased. I'm kind of delicate right now."

Monkey hesitated.

Nell sank down into herself.

"Hey, Monkey," Keno said. "One two three four...remember what your mama once taught you...five six seven eight nine ten. Count to ten and remember who you are. You're a good Oklahoma farm boy; I'm my mom's *Refugio*. We are not supposed to scare a lady."

"I'm not a lady," Nell said. "I'm a computer geek."

Monkey hunkered down next to Keno. "I'm thinking," he said, "you and me got low blood sugar caused by a lack of munchies caused by a lack of dope. How about we unwind, send Nell out to Saigon Sally's for whatever she deems suitable for a scorching Mojave Friday, put the Closed sign on the door, and medicate your broken heart?"

"Dr. Feelgood," Keno said. He handed Nell a hundred bucks. "Knock yourself out. Me and Monkey*mota* here—that's not Japanese, it's Spanglish, means he is a *curandero*, that is witch doctor specializing in the judicious and entirely medicinal use of weed—which will cure everything from glaucoma to diabetes to impotence to a busted ticker caused by a woman too myopic to see her true love right in front of her."

"Saigon Sally's is right around the corner," Monkey said.

"I know. I'm on it."

By the time Nell came back with three bags of takeout, Keno

and Monkey were hunched over the computer. "No shit," Keno said. "This is unbelievable."

Nell coughed delicately. Guys would be guys. Who knew what they were looking at. Keno turned and smiled innocently. "Check this out," he said. Nell leaned in toward the screen. A serious young man held a cat. He told the camera he had a project. The song was one of the parts of the project. The camera cut to the young man playing acoustic guitar. "I can't hear," Nell said.

"How do you turn this fucking thing up?" Monkey said. Nell reached in between them and jacked the sound. As she did, she checked the URL. "Code Monkey? This guy is singing a song called Code Monkey?"

"Yeah," Monkey said. "I'd think, if I *could* think right now, that he had written it for me."

"Hang on," Keno said. "I'll start it again."

Monkey handed her a set of headphones. "Put these on, it'll help." Nell listened. The kid sang about being a code monkey in a boring job in a boring place with a cute receptionist who found him boring.

Monkey reached up and took the headphones off of Nell. "Don't take it personal," he said. "I was kidding about the song being for me. I'm a happy man."

Keno logged off. "The thing about you, Monkeymota, is you cannot handle weed."

Monkey fumbled with a takeout bag. "Never never smoke on an empty stomach." He opened a box of spring rolls. "Keno, you get two; Nell, you get two. Monkey, you get six."

"That was my hundred bucks," Keno said.

"That was my dope."

Keno and Monkey ravaged all but one bag of the takeout. Nell settled for her two spring rolls and a tall iced coffee.

"The computer geek here thought I was after your fortune," Keno said. "Racial profiling, I figure."

Monkey looked him up and down. "Right. You got a three-inch-high platinum and diamond Guadalupe hanging over your hairy chest, which Nell can see because you're wearing a Raiders muscle shirt. You got T-Mac's on your feet with no socks, like you're so fly you just buy another pair when you get stank-foot. And you're gonna go lawsuit because Nell pegged you for a *cholo* bad boy?"

"That's redundant," Keno said calmly.

"I didn't think you were a cholo," Nell said. "I figured you were undercover, and I *had* found some bud in a tampon box and I figured I was going to have to cover Monkey's butt."

"Euuuuuuuuu," Keno said. "Run, Nell, run."

He took another toke and smiled. "Life is hard. I'm going over to *Grrrlz* to drown my sorrows in Shaleika's tits." He hauled himself up.

Monkey looked up. "Thanks for sharing. You have definitely harshed my mellow."

"It's better somebody do it now, than later when you get home." Keno winked. "Listen Nell, he's got one of the sweetest and most patient wives anybody could have. You gotta meet Jackie. You'll love her."

He picked up the last bag of takeout, bowed, and dropped it into Nell's lap. "*Muchos gracias, mi hermana.* You give great listening. I'll catch you up later. I think I'm gonna live."

He opened the door and was gone. Monkey spun the chair around and faced Nell. "You can take off," he said. "I'll pay you for eight hours. It's payday. Yeah, and a bonus to get you to forget what I said about not feeling so great."

Nell was quiet. He pulled out a roll of bills. "What? Eleven bucks an hour. Five times seven times eleven. Can you figure it out? I'm having a little trouble with complex equations right now."

"It's three hundred and eighty-five dollars," Nell said.

"Plus the bonus makes it four hundred."

"Are you crazy? You don't have to pay me fifteen bucks to forget— what was that you wanted me to forget?"

Monkey shook his head. This was too much fun. He was going to have to fire her very soon. Or they were going to have to write a screenplay. "I am the boss. You are the flunky. You will take what I pay you. You are working for Monkey. You are not a code monkey."

Nell put her pay in her bag. Monkey fired up another bowl. The smoke drifted toward her. The room seemed to close in on Nell. "I've got to get out of here," she said. "I'm the Queen of Contact Highs and dope makes me crazy."

"Suit yourself," Monkey said. "I'm going to get crazy, listen to some tunes, and then go home to my sweet and patient wife."

Nell grabbed her purse.

"Hey, lady," Monkey said. "Oops, I mean woman person, don't forget your supper." He handed her the sack.

Nell took it. "What about Jackie? Wouldn't she like a night off from cooking?"

His eyes went flat. "Hey. No offense. But managing my marriage ain't nowhere in your job description."

15

The LeSabre wouldn't start. The oil light wasn't on. The battery light wasn't on. There was gas. Nell opened the hood and tightened the battery cables. For the second time since she'd come into her new life, she thanked her mother for what was beginning to seem like a useful, if sometimes scary, apprenticeship in being a girl taking care of herself.

The LeSabre continued to not start. She'd walk home. She was not going back into the office, not with a cold-eyed and semi-coherent Monkey there. She climbed out of the car and was slam-dunked yet again by the sun. She could barely stand, much less walk ten blocks.

She locked the LeSabre and went back to the Biz door. It wasn't as though she hadn't caught sleet storms in a man's eyes before. What was he going to do? Hurt her feelings? There had to be more than what the two of them had to give him the power to sucker punch her heart.

The door was locked. She thought again about walking. She heard a voice. It wasn't Monkey's. She unlocked the door, opened it a crack, and looked in.

Monkey was slouched in the office chair. The computer was on. There was a video of a swarm of bees. They swirled up out of a hive. Once. Twice. Again and again, the bees flew up and away. Monkey was talking. Nell moved in closer. His eyes were closed. His eyelids fluttered. His right hand was pressed to his chest.

"Yes," he said. "Particles. Going. Oh fuck, the solar wind."

His body jerked. The phone was just past his right hand. Nell hesitated. She was afraid to reach across him. She knew what a person could do in a drug blackout. And there was this: not only did she not know his home phone number, she did not know his last name so she could look it up.

She waited. The spasm died away. She went into the john and soaked a paper towel. "Nurse Nightingale," she thought. How many times had she soothed her mother with a wet cloth? How many times had she waited for her to open her eyes and say, "'That was soooooo beautiful."

Monkey slouched to his other side. A new computer screensaver had gone on. It was an old psychedelic poster, with a translucent man meditating and a translucent green car. Lacework grids rose on either side, sky blue shading to aqua shading to lilac. There were letters in chrome yellow: *Traffic.*

Monkey stirred. "Hey, Mr. Fantasy," she said. "It's Nell."

He flinched away from her. "You can see through me?" he said. "No."

"You can taste the solar wind?"

"No," she said and for an instant felt something cold and crystalline on her tongue.

"Are you okay?" he said. His eyes snapped open. He looked at the screen. "That wasn't the way through," he said. "Not the poster. Something else took me. Can you get me a glass of water?"

Nell folded the wet towel and laid it across his forehead. "Oh god," he said. "That feels good."

She filled a cup and brought it back. He took his hand from his chest and wiggled the fingers. "Something is happening," he said. "Something is happening to me. I might be going crazy."

He took the glass and lifted it to his lips. "Might dribble," he said. "Early dementia, probably. Everything else is going."

"Dementia, maybe," Nell said. "Hair, for sure."

He smiled weakly. "What was on the Fiendish Thing when you came in?" Nell touched a key. The computer woke. The swirling bees were gone. There was an orchard of blossoming trees.

A narrator said, "No one knows what's happening. In this case, these almond trees cannot do their work without the bees. Almonds are one of the largest crops in America."

Monkey grabbed the desk and pulled himself upright. "Yes," he said. "Do you know what's happening to the bees?"

"Nobody really knows."

"Christ," he said. "Yeah, and no matter what cosmic riffs I'm getting in the trances, the bees are leaving."

He untucked his work shirt and pulled it off. "I'm sorry," he said. "I probably stink. Hope you don't mind. I'm suffocating in that shirt."

Nell looked. He was not radiating funk. He gave off light. Monkey wore the tie-dyed muscle shirt with the photo of Bob Marley silk-screened in the center of concentric ovals of pink, orange, and yellow. He was a solid figure bathed in concentric waves of desert sunset. She did not believe in auras. She would not believe in auras. Auras were something for over-stimulated losers.

"What's wrong?" Monkey said. "Don't you like Bob?"

"No, he's perfect. You aren't going crazy," she said. "You can't be going crazy, because if you are, so am I. You're—I hate to say it—giving off, well, a gorgeous aura."

"Did you sneak some bud?"

"No. Never. It hates me."

Monkey sat on the tires. Nell sat in the chair in front of the computer. "Please turn the Fiendish Thing off," he said. "It makes you look like a zombie. We need to have a sit-down."

"Do you think you ought to call your wife?"

"No," he said. "She doesn't know about my psycho speed bumps."

"Besides," Nell said, "managing your marriage isn't in my job description."

"Ah," he said. "I see our in-service training sessions have taken hold."

Nell wondered where he'd learned about in-service training sessions.

"When did you come in?" he asked.

"Maybe five minutes after I left. The car wouldn't start. I was going to walk home, but it persisted in being Twentynine in early June out there," Nell said.

He nodded. "I go into these trances. That wasn't the first time. The first time, Keno found me out on the street telling an old homeless guy that he needed to call the television guys. I had something really really important to tell all of Southern California. Something that could...and at that point, Keno says, I started talking in what the homeless guy thought might be Pentecostal.

"He drove me to the nearest Emergency Department. I started to come out of it on the way over, tried to talk him out of the doc visit. He is large enough to guarantee that almost anybody does what Keno thinks is required.

"They gave me a workup, a CAT scan. I was clean. Nothing. No brain lesions. No occluded arteries. I don't know why they didn't take a urine test for THC, but they didn't. I suspect Keno smoothed that one out. Between him and his family, he's got connections with half of the *barrio*, and half of the so-to-speak lower echelon medical providers are his people.

"So, no brain damage, nothing organic. A fucking cosmic blow job. The only preacher I have even a pencil dick's worth of faith in is Sam Kinison, and he died outside of Needles telling God, 'Oh, okay.' Where does that leave me?"

"A fucking cosmic blow job? Not even a pencil dick's worth of faith? You've got an elegant way with metaphor," Nell said. "But, tell you what, consider this—you go home to your sweet and loving wife; I go home to sitting alone by the window watching an old man smoke one cigarette after another in the yard across from me. No more penile references—no matter how puny they might be."

Monkey looked at her. Her jaw was set. Her eyes were narrowed.

"Okay," he said. "Respected."

"Appreciated."

"It's your turn, partner. Why are you crazy?"

"I can show you," Nell said, "but I've got to turn on the Fiendish Thing."

"I'll be okay. So far, the trances haven't double-dipped me."

Nell logged on and searched "Leafy Seadragon." The image leaped up on the screen, silver and green, pink and serene. "This creature cannot be real. But, it is. I saw it in an aquarium in Long Beach."

Monkey pulled up the tires. "Holy fuck."

"That's what I thought the first time I saw it," Nell said. "Emphasis on the holy. And *I* don't believe in anything I can't measure. It's visiting me."

"Nell," Monkey said. His voice wavered. She turned and saw his eyes roll up. He laughed. Later, she would tell him that his laugh was that of someone coming home to a place both familiar and terrifying, an alien place for which the exiled one had longed.

She caught him as he fell forward. "I'll stay here," she said. "I'll be here when you come back."

The light in the office window went salmon, then pink, then dark. Monkey's hands were cold, his pulse slow and steady. Nell's shoulders began to ache. She propped him against the desk, took the coveralls from the door, spread them on the floor, and eased him down on them. She sat next to him. It seemed to be important to keep her fingers on his wrist. The pulse was slow but steady.

The phone rang once. The office fell silent. She could hear the traffic on Smoke Tree thin out and fade away. Monkey's chest rose and fell slowly. Every now and then his eyelids fluttered, his body trembled.

She couldn't remember when she had felt so necessary, or so peaceful. She thought of the mountains she had watched from the front stoop of La Paloma, of the old man's cigarette an ember in the dark. She knew she would write Oilinmyvessel47 later and tell him all of it. The salmon light, the pink; the throb of *norteno*; how traffic could grow from a hiss to the roar of a motorcycle; how a woman could be at a man's side and on a front stoop and sitting at her window all in the same instant.

Monkey rolled on his side, then back toward her and pressed her hand to his chest.

"Cold," he said. "Freezing cold. If it spreads out. I don't know." His eyes opened. He smiled. "Nell, that's twice in one night. Not bad for an old guy."

"Hey."

He took her hand from his chest. "Sorry. Thanks."

She started to stand. "No," he said. "Give me a minute. I want to try to tell you what I saw before I decide it was all nothing but gobsmack."

Nell waited. He shivered. "Can you grab that poncho on the chair and toss it over me?"

She covered him with the poncho. He pulled it up to his chin. "The whole thing is scary," he said, "but the only part I don't like is that I can feel a coldness in my heart. It feels like a little seed of my death."

He shook his head. "I don't talk like that, you know? I talk like

Everything's cool. Monkey's a lucky boy. It's alllll good."

Nell's knees ached. "I've got to get up," she said. "I'm not going far." She sat in the chair.

"Here is where I go," Monkey said. "First, there is a swirl of colors and shapes. There are ordinary things like the Mr. Coffee in the foreground, the window, then the background moves forward, kind of slips in and out of what I'm seeing. Sometimes there are metal rods. They move in lattices and patterns. Just when I think I know what they are, they disappear.

"Sometimes I'm floating in black outer space with meteors flashing by me, a lot like that embryo in the movie *2001*. There are voices. They don't speak out loud. They talk directly to my mind. Each time, they tell me something that connects with what they've told me before, a lot about a cataclysm on the way, one that only humans can affect.

"Mostly I'm not freaked. But this time there was something new. I saw a stream of animals race around me. They were mutants, made from animals and parts of people I know. My wife's head was melded into an elk. Keno's face was grinning at me from the side of a lizard. I saw my mom's hands at the ends of a rabbit's legs. There was more. I saw the head of a woman I once knew sprouting from a javelina's neck. It was as clear as something you'd see in ordinary daytime."

"I had started to look at a Leafy Seadragon on the computer," Nell said. She hit a key. The seadragon floated on the screen. "Wait, don't look. What if you go out again?"

"Don't worry," Monkey said. "A specific door opens once, that's it."

"Here it is," Nell stepped aside.

"Jumpin' Jesus," Monkey said. "It's everything at once. Animal. Vegetable. And those silver stripes—mineral. The things in the trance weren't beautiful. They were fucking horrible."

"This creature is what's stalking me," Nell said. "That's why I keep wondering if I've gone crazy or like that movie *Jacob's Ladder*—I'm actually dead or lying strapped to a bed in the loony bin."

"If that's true, then so am I," Monkey said. "I don't think that's it. I cannot believe I just said that. We sound like New Age bliss-heads."

"Then where's the bliss? I believe this: the Leafy is real. I saw it in the aquarium in Long Beach. It's why I'm alive. It's why I am here in Twentynine. And it's why I'm your not-on-the-records computer grunt."

Monkey closed his eyes. "I'm whipped. How about we close up shop for tonight and I buy you breakfast tomorrow morning? You can fill me in on a few details about the planet that sent you here and I'll tell you more about what I'm being told."

"Free food," Nell said. "Once a hippie, always a hippie."

Monkey sat up slowly. "But, you know," he said, "no matter what's going on, the bees are leaving."

"I can't forget that," Nell said. "We can't. We haven't even talked about that."

He grabbed the desk and pulled himself up. "See you here at seven. We'll talk about everything."

"Wait," Nell said. "That black space with lights flashing by. When I was a kid, that's what I thought death was."

"Ah shit," Monkey said.

16

Nell stepped out into sweetly warm air, the moon a fat chunk of silver above her head. The LeSabre was dead. Monkey was in no condition to drive. The street was empty. She decided to walk home.

She remembered the MTA driver's warning. "Don't be walking around here in the dark. This town looks pretty, but pretty like a green rattler." She'd heard his words a little over a month ago. It seemed time had gone glacial in the Mojave heat. The days had been a slow, easy pulse. The nights, except for the fit of shaking, had been peaceful. She checked her watch. What had seemed to be an all-nighter at the Biz had been less than three hours.

She walked west on Smoke Tree. Her thoughts began to slow. It was good to be out of the office and away from Monkey. He was a jolt for her, a jolt of hope that she wasn't crazy, she wasn't a woman who had faced into her time running out and panicked. And he was his own aftershock. There was no way to know what would settle out.

A helicopter throbbed in the distance. The throb became a ratchet shredding the air. She stepped into the alley to her right. She had nothing to hide, but her past moved her before she could think. The searchlight strafed the street and caught a glint just beyond her. It looked like an animal's eye. Nell stepped back onto the sidewalk and stopped.

She looked back into the alley. The glint was less than five feet in. Her mother's voice was in her mind. "What if it's an animal? What if it's hurt?"

Nell clicked the penlight on her keychain and walked toward the glint. The speck of light resolved into an eye, the dark mass around it became a big stuffed Tyrannosaurus Rex with green sequin scales, an open red mouth, and white felt teeth. It sat on a full recycle bin. Nell shown the light over its body. It was intact and clean. She picked it up by the tail and shook it. No roaches. No scorpions. No spiders.

The chopper was gone. She tucked the dinosaur under her arm, stepped out onto Smoke Tree, and headed home. Punkin might need a guardian. And she needed a shower.

Diamond and Shiloh were settled into the swing on the front porch. "Big date?" Shiloh said. "Who's your scaly pal?"

"I found this lady on top of a trashcan," Nell said. "I figured she'd be a guardian for Punkin. I thought about the Biz, but I realized Monkey's got his brain for a pet."

Diamond snorted. "Do you want to take some geranium cuttings in to the Biz? Maybe make a curtain to cover those busted blinds? I bet you even cleaned out the coffee pot."

"He did," Nell said.

"That," Shiloh said, "is a miracle. A born and bred red-bone Oklahoma panhandle Southern Baptist boy cleaned out his own coffee pot! Woo hoo."

"You got a guy cleaning out a coffee pot," Diamond said, "you got a guy wants something."

Yeah, and there was a lady starting to want something, too.

"How is work?" Diamond said.

"The files are a challenge. Everything else is easy. I met Keno today and thought I was going to have to call 911, but it was a false alarm." "Keno has helped us out a few times," Diamond said. "And he's helping out Mariah. He can be extremely persuasive."

"And his fashion sense is impeccable," Nell said. "I'm headed up for a quiet evening. See you ladies in the morning."

Nell set T. on the foot of her bed. She opened her laptop and logged on. There was one email in her Inbox from Oilinmyvessel47. She decided to send her message before she opened his.

To: oilinmyvessel47@yahoo.com
Subject: Portals
I haven't read your message yet. I want you to have this before I do. You were on the floor. I sat next to you. I thought of the mountains I watch from the front stoop of La Paloma and of the old man's cigarette an ember in the dark. I knew I would write Oilinmyvessel47 and tell him all of it. The salmon light, the pink; how traffic could fade from a hiss to the roar of a motorcycle, the throb of norteno; how a friend could be at a man's side and on a front stoop and sitting at her window all in the same instant. How anything can be a portal.
I guessed when you read it we would both know we weren't crazy.
n

She sent the message and opened his. He had sent it while she was on the way home.

Subject: Transport
I fix cars. Cars are transportation. I have read dictionaries for fun since I was a little squirt. There is a dictionary on the Fiendish Thing. Here is what it knows about "Transport."
verb: *take or carry (people or goods) from one place to another by means of a vehicle, aircraft, or ship...*
figurative: cause (someone) to feel that they are in another place or time: for a moment she was transported to a warm summer garden on the night of a ball.
(usu. be transported) overwhelm (someone) with a strong emotion, esp. joy: she was transported with pleasure.
historical: send (a convict) to a penal colony.
noun:
1. a system or means of conveying people or goods from place to place by means of a vehicle, aircraft, or ship
the action of transporting something or the state of being transported: the transport of crude oil...
2. (usu. transports) an overwhelmingly strong emotion: art can send

people into transports of delight. See note at rapture
ORIGIN late Middle English: from Old French transporter or Latin
transportare, from trans- 'across' + portare 'carry.'
m

Nell re-read his email twice. "Lovely," she said. "Just lovely." She re-read her own message and closed her laptop. She went to the window. Music echoed from all directions. The old man was not on his stoop. She set the laptop on the floor and put on her headphones. It was a good night for Chris Whitley. It was a good night to be reminded that there were no fixed numbers on the dial of Dust Radio.

Monkey surfed electrons for a while. He learned more about Leafy Seadragons and bees, too much about ice caps. The news was heavy. He decided to go for something more suited to his Okie redneck scorched earth personality. Keno had told him about a whip-it site called Girls Gone Wild.

He found the girls. They bored him. Besides, what he really wanted to do was check his email. He clicked on Yahoo.

She'd written. He opened the email and read. He read the first and last sentences more than once.

Subject: Portals.
I haven't read your message yet. I want you to have this before I read it...
...I guessed when you read it we would both know we weren't crazy.

He went back to his message: *Latin transportare, from trans- 'across' + portare 'carry.'*

He had hated English when he was a kid. All those rules. All those dumb diagrams. All those boring essays on what some dead fuck had meant in some dead book about some dead time. The books hadn't started out dead. It was the writing on the writing that had killed them. And now, his office administrator and he were trapped in some Alice in Wonderland living fairytale. And they were writing it.

He grabbed his pipe and walked out into the back lot. The moon was a cool burn in the west. He remembered a summer night he and Jackie had camped a little north of Yucca Valley. How the stars had been, how Jackie and he had felt such wonder. He shook his head and went back into the Biz. That night had been five years ago. They had not slept under the sky since then. It was time.

He turned off the lights, locked up, and saw the LeSabre in the lot. Nell had walked back to La Paloma. She really was crazy. He figured he'd hotwire the car and leave it parked in front of the safe house. He crawled through the open driver's window and tried. No go. Things were getting very complicated.

Jackie was asleep when he got home. He crouched next to her and took a deep breath. She smelled of lavender shampoo and woman, her scent—as endearing to him as it had been twenty-five years ago. She turned his direction. "Hey," she whispered. "There's food in the fridge. Gotta sleep."

He stroked her hair. "Tomorrow's going to be different, babe," he said. "I promise."

Monkey worked by the light of the candles Jackie had left on the kitchen table. The knife was chef-sharp. She was fastidious about her work tools. He was just stoned enough that cutting the oranges and mangoes and kiwis was like slicing minerals. He watched lozenges of translucent carnelian and rose quartz and jade fall away from his knife into puddles of candlelight.

He squeezed lime juice over the fruit, drizzled in a spoonful of honey, and covered the bowl. Mixing up his mom's buckwheat pancake batter was a little trickier in the soft gloom, but once he got started it was as though his hands knew the dance. He set the fruit and the batter in the fridge. He would wake Jackie with breakfast in bed. And then, he would call Saigon Sally's and order a picnic to go. Those Vietnamese sandwiches could make you forget to buy American.

He blew out the candles, went into the living room, set the CD player to Random, stretched out on the couch, and put on the headphones. There was no trance. He fell asleep to the almost mathematical perfection of Robin Trower's guitar.

17

Nell woke from a dreamless sleep, no visitations, no silver and green trails. It was Saturday—the Weekend. The Dread Weekend. There was nothing to do, nowhere to go. For decades, her weekends had been lacunae that could not be filled. Not with workouts, not with shopping, not with DVDs and popcorn and ice cream; not with grown-up play dates with people who bored her stuporous—not even with work. Till David. At least she was spared *that*—all of it, all of the dreary hope that time could be filled with what you grimly made yourself do, all of the incandescent hope that a lover could be a cornucopia of the future.

Chrome light burned behind the curtains. She checked the clock again. Eight thirty. She remember the LeSabre was in the Biz parking lot. She opened her laptop and logged on. There was nothing new for papercut55. *Shit.* She suddenly remembered. He was going to take her to breakfast, they were going to tell stories, she was to have been at the Biz at seven. She didn't know his home phone number. She figured she'd cut her losses. There was the matter of the purple suit and the Manolo Blahniks. When the fuck ups fuck up, the fuck ups go shopping.

The black pearl hanging from the doorknob glinted in the morning light. She reached for it, then stopped. It wasn't time yet. And maybe a secondhand store wasn't the right place to take it.

The kitchen was empty. There was a note near the phone. *Mariah called. New info. Here's her number and her email. We'll catch up later. Loose lippies bust hippies.* Nell poured a cup of coffee and sat at the table. It had been a long time since she had forgotten an appointment. She could see Monkey's tired face. And the words: *Latin transportare, from trans- 'across' + portare 'carry.'*

She picked up the phone a few times, put it back, then picked it up and dialed the Biz. There was no answer. She dialed Mariah.

"Mariah here."

"It's Nell. Diamond and Shiloh said you called. What's up?"

"How about you and I talk a little? Soon."

"When? I can get free any time," Nell said.

"What about this morning?"

"Give me an hour. I've got an errand to run."

"I'll be there at 9:30," Mariah said.

"I have some new info on Free—"

"Don't say anything more," Mariah said. "Save it for just between us two."

They hung up. Premise Two was cranking up.

Monkey woke. Jackie was already out of bed. He closed his eyes. He bet she had found the fruit and the pancake batter and resumed her command of their breakfast. He felt like shit. He was going to have to smoke up the last of the bud and then take a break. Right. He swung his legs over the side of the bed and stood. He couldn't hear any sounds from the kitchen. Maybe she was in the shower. Maybe he could accidentally stumble in on her. Maybe she would pull the shower curtain aside and take his face in her hands and kiss him. Not a sexy kiss, a kiss of tenderness. He rubbed his hand over his face. Two days' beard stubble. Dream on, Monkey, dream on.

The john door was open, the kitchen empty. He poured himself coffee and sat at the table. There was a note under one of the candles. *Girls Day Out, Mr. Man. I waited up for you till 9. Jerilynne and I are going to Casino Del Sol. Triple slots points for the ladies. I should be back by seven, but if the machines are hot we're going to get a room. J.*

Monkey lit the candle and burned the note. He took the fruit salad out of the fridge. The batter would keep. He popped the plastic lid on the fruit and dug in. Hulk coiled around his ankles.

"Not the breakfast I was hoping for," Monkey said. "You know, pancakes and butter and syrup, all romantic-like with lit candles and then we run up to Luna Mesa and sleep under the moon like we used to." He dropped the spoon. "I'm a fool. I told Nell to meet me at seven. I gotta get a calendar—or a conscience—or lay off the dope."

He checked the clock. It was 8:15.

He covered the bowl and stared at the phone. No point. Nell didn't seem like the kind of woman who would wait longer than two minutes—much less let herself into the Biz to wait for two hours and forty-six minutes. He had now officially screwed up with two women.

He yanked the pancake batter from the fridge, opened the back door, ripped the lid off, and threw the bowl against the garden wall.

Hulk watched the batter dry instantly on the bricks. A cowbird skittled from an ocatillo and started to pick at the batter. Monkey saw Hulk shrug. Fat domestic cat vs. feral bird? No contest.

"Hang on," he said. Hulk ignored him and walked back into the house. "I need to look at the bright side. A. There's still some bud. B. If you fuck up with one woman, you only got one shot at making it right. If you fuck up with two women, you got two chances. No way I'm going out to the casino for Ladies' Day, but I can go to the Biz, finish up that bud, fix the LeSabre, and drive it over to Nell. Yes. Wait. LeSabre first. Bud second."

It didn't escape him that he was talking to an ocatillo and a cowbird. He wished it were nothing new. His mom's laugh came to him. "You know, Carl, you and Jackie have the quietest house in the Mojave."

"Right, Mom," he said. "That's why we're still so happily married."

He checked Oilinmyvessel. There was nothing. He logged off. No way was he going to apologize to Nell in little units of 1 and 0. He would be a man. The worst that could happen is that his overqualified, underpaid computer geek would quit. He'd be back to zero. He knew how to do that. His license for being at zero was up-to-date.

Nell virtuously opened a cup of low-fat yogurt. "I hate yogurt," she muttered. "And yoga and breathing deep into my essence to know reality, which if I do right now, I know I need real food." She found two of Diamond's fresh-baked cinnamon rolls in the breadbox. She smeared them with butter and took her real breakfast out to what was left of the shade on the front porch.

There was the matter of the purple suit and the Manolo Blahniks. There was the matter of not checking her email every ten minutes. She could take care of both. If she slathered on sunscreen, cut holes in a pillowcase, and pulled it over her head, she might be able to walk very slowly the three blocks to the secondhand store. Plus she would not be near email for as long as it took to trade the suit and shoes for work clothes.

The plan fell apart. She did not own the pillowcases. She ate the last bit of cinnamon roll, went back into the house, and checked her email. Nothing. She packed the suit and shoes, found a silver Grrrrrl Pow!er cap on the rack downstairs, and stepped out into the glare.

Shiloh had lied about the proximity of Noo to Yoo. Nell had crossed the entire Mojave Desert west to east by the time she pushed through the door. A perky young man in a paisley sarong and sandals looked up. "Ohmigod," he said. "You get in here, ma'am." He dashed up to her and undraped the suit from her arm. "Luisa," he called back over his shoulder, "bring us a glass of water. There is a lady out here in dire straits."

"I'm not a ma'am," Nell said. "I'm not a lady."

"Why of course, I didn't notice your hat," he said, then yelled, "My mistake! There is a *girl-thang* out here in dire straits."

Nell leaned on the counter. Her breath caught in her throat. She had not factored in the possibility that even a snooty secondhand store would have the dusty scent of despair. It had been forty years since her mother had been able to drag her into a Salvation Army store. In high school, at part-time jobs, in college and a full-time job, she had worn the same combinations of a few cheap but new tops, skirts, and jeans over and over rather than set foot in a secondhand store. She looked down at her hands. They were not the hands of a girl. She took a deep breath and pulled the suit out of her bag. "I need to get rid of this suit."

"You certainly do," the young man said. He held out his hand. "Welcome to Noo to Yoo. That's N-O-O to Y-O-O, not to be confused with New to You, which is a corporate chain who would joyfully slap us with a big fat lawsuit. I'm Danny. I'll be your personal assistant today."

"And I'll be your personal customer."

"My boss makes me say that, " Danny said. "This place may look like a grungy little indie alt-shop, but he has dreams."

He looked closer at the suit. "Ooooo, girl. Where did you steal this?"

"It followed me home."

"This is a bad time of year for something like this, but I'm going to believe in the future. Come September there is going to be some tight-wad, planning-to-bust-through-the-glass-ceiling, silk-shirt, Communist, Women's Studies prof up from the college in Palm Springs who will snatch this up."

"I need tank tops and cotton pants," Nell said.

Danny took her elbow and guided her to the racks of summer clothes. "Luisa," he called, "get your thumbs off your cell and get out here. I need your expert eye."

He stepped next to Nell. "It makes her feel better," he whispered. "Even though everybody here knows I am the undisputed judge of what other people should wear."

Luisa was silent.

"Get out here, bitch."

The voice from the back was sepulchral. "You do it. I'm too suicidal right now."

"Must be an epidemic," Nell said. Danny raised his eyebrow.

"Joke," Nell said.

"Believe me," Danny said, "it's gone wayyy past funny. Every day, every day I go through this shit."

"Fine," he yelled. "If you get blood on that adorable Désirée Webers vinyl thingy, I will personally kill you myself and deny you the satisfaction."

He leaned toward Nell. "In fact, this is all a clever ruse on my part. I knew if I pushed her she wouldn't come out. Which means I will decide what I am going to give you for that thing, I mean that suit. To your advantage, honey. The Manolo Blahniks are a different story. I am praying in my deepest soul that you and I have the same size feet."

"Ladies' ten medium."

"It is a perfect day." He clutched the shoes to his bosom.

"I could use that water Luisa was going to bring before she killed herself," Nell said.

"Promise not to shoplift. Okay?"

"On my honor."

A half hour later, she left Noo to Yoo with four cotton tank tops, five pairs of loose cotton long pants, three pairs of shorts, and a pair of never-worn red Keen sandals. "These are perfect for summer walking," Danny had said. "They are ug-LEE but outdoorsy types love them. I almost said 'more mature types,' but there is that silver hat." The walk home was longer than the walk to the shop, even in her ugly but comfortable shoes. "I scored," she called out.

Shiloh opened the door and looked at Nell's haul. "You did."

"Danny was an angel."

"Danny's a shrew."

"I think it was the Manolo Blahniks," Nell said. "They were grafted to his feet by the time I left."

She started up the stairs. "Your boss was here," Shiloh said.

"What?"

"He drove up in your LeSabre. I told him you weren't around. He said he was going to take the car to the car wash. I told him he ought to take himself to the car wash. He looked like shit."

"I'm going to wash my new wardrobe," Nell said.

"You need quarters," Shiloh said. "The washer and dryer are the only money makers in this sorry place."

Nell dumped her new old clothes in the machine. She knew they were clean. The musty scent that drifted up from them was not in them—it was in her. She fed the washer four quarters and went into the kitchen. Shiloh was at the table cutting out food coupons. "I called Mariah," Nell said. "She's on her way over."

"Yeah," Shiloh said. "And Monkey called. He said he'd bring your car over about 1:00."

Nell felt a sudden need for a glass of water, maybe three glasses of water. She let the tap run till the water was cold. "I wouldn't drink that," Shiloh said. "It's Twentynine water. God knows what's in there. Residue of anti-depressants, hormone disruptors. You could go zombie or sterile."

"Thanks. It's a little late for the warning, but no big deal," Nell said. "Thanks to age, I already am sterile. And I do mean thanks."

Shiloh took a jug of water from the fridge and poured Nell a glass. "Here you go. And I'm just realizing Diamond and I didn't give you our newcomer orientation—partly because we're crazy busy, but mostly because you seemed like a sister right from the beginning."

"Let's do it tomorrow."

There was a knock on the door. "It's me, Mariah. I need to kidnap Nell for a while."

"I'm ready," Nell said.

"Great. But before we go, do you have internet here?" Mariah said.

"We do. My computer's up in my room."

"Let's go check a couple things. They'll help you understand what I'm going to be telling you."

Nell logged in. "Let me find what I'm looking for," Mariah said. "It's easier than telling you." She typed in a few words and hit enter. "This is the heartline." She handed Nell the earphones. "It starts with a prayer."

The video began, a soft voice murmuring while a ray of light moved slowly over a panel of burnt orange and apricot stone. Then, the words: "The Salt Songs are the traditional songs of the Southern Paiute people who live in Arizona, Utah, Nevada, and California. The Songs are sung at memorial ceremonies to assist with the transition to the next world, and to contribute to community healing. The songs are also sung to revitalize Southern Paiute culture.

"The Salt Song Trail represents the sacred journeys of ancestral spirits and serves as a map of Southern Paiute sacred and historical sites and communities. Salt, along with other medicinal herbs and other important resources, was gathered along the Trail."

Mariah paused the video. "Some of us took the songs to the Sherman Indian High School, which used to be the Sherman Institute. That's where the government held our children after they had taken them from their families. Many of the children died there without ever returning to their homes. We sang to bring the little spirits home.

"You can watch the whole video later. We need to go where we're going before it gets too hot. But I would like you to hear what the head of the singers says. Mr. Eddy has worked with us to teach us these old songs. He's one of a few of my people who remember."

She hit play. Flute music trilled, the notes silvery, as images of petroglyphs pecked in stone, wind-rippled desert sand, blue mountains, and acres of coreopsis scrolled past. A hefty man with warm eyes spoke: "I'm going to teach you this song. But before I teach you this song, I'm going to break your hearts." The singers in front of him nodded. "If you are broken-hearted when you are singing this song," the man said, "you'll learn this song."

Mariah stopped the video and bookmarked it. "We can go now."

Mariah led Nell out to a late model, quarter-ton green crew cab. "This is my baby. Daryl gave it to me for my last birthday. Not bad for an old lady, huh?"

She pulled out onto the highway. "It's a good thing it's not high noon. I'm taking you to a place where we can talk safely, and there's shade."

They turned onto a dirt road that led into a maze of other dirt roads and two tracks. There were ramshackle cabins and trailers with busted-out windows everywhere. Mariah parked in the driveway of a tiny shack with a tall white post next to it. The words *Magic Electric* were painted on the post.

"What's Magic Electric?" Nell said.

"Back in the day, a homesteader got the idea he could make electricity from heating the sand. He was going to make a fortune. He painted the sign before he tried his great experiment."

"What happened?"

"No magic."

Mariah grabbed a fanny pack with two water bottles and climbed out of the truck. A wash ran along the back of the property. "We're going down into the wash." They switchbacked down the side and walked north toward a big rose-gray boulder. Mariah held up her hand. "I need to say a prayer." She murmured a few words and scattered something in the sand at the base of the rock. "We can sit here."

They settled into the soft earth in the shadow of the east wall of the wash.

"Welcome," Mariah said. "This is part of my home, part of my family."

"Which reminds me," Nell said. "How's Punkin?"

"She's bigger every day," Mariah said. "Next thing you know she'll want to borrow my truck. Do you have kids, if you don't mind my asking?"

"No. No kids. No husband. Almost no family. My job was my life."

"Jackie tells me that now your job is diving fearlessly into Monkey's computer," Mariah said. "She and I work together in one of the old peoples' foster homes. That woman is a dynamo; she's always running the old folks on errands or out to play bingo. She even started an OFC for the three men."

"OFC?"

"Old Fart Club. They get to play cards, drink beer, and eat pork rinds." Mariah laughed. "And, of course, she has Monkey."

Nell raised an eyebrow. "He's not that old."

"He might as well be. He's what you call high maintenance."

She handed Nell a water bottle. "Drink up. The dry heat is sneaky out here. Next thing you know, you're dehydrated."

Nell grinned. "I know you know that I know you want to tell me about Monkey being high maintenance."

"Well, for starters," Mariah said, "he's the lightest sleeper in the world. So Jackie snores a little. Big deal. He pokes her with his elbow and cusses and frumps out of bed fast so she'll wake up. Sometimes she has to take an allergy pill to get back to sleep. Plus he thinks she wouldn't survive without him. That's plain crazy. She's a strong woman. She walked him through a big mess in his first job and she supported them till he could get a loan from his folks to get the Biz going."

Mariah looked over her shoulder as though somebody were listening. "Ooooo, my grandma would give me the stink-eye if she heard me. She hated gossip. Of course, that didn't keep her from her stitch-and-bitch sessions with her pals."

"Guys call it gossip," Nell said. "Women call it CINS, Classified Information Necessary for Survival."

"Funny you would say that. I want to talk about some CINS, some things that you won't tell anyone else—not even Monkey or Jackie."

Nell remembered the web of sworn to secrecy and don't repeat this that had tangled her and her co-workers into a knot of loyalty to the Big Dogs—and disloyalty to each other.

"This could be a matter of life and death," Mariah said. "Not just for my people—though what is coming could be a form of extinction. We need your help."

"Why me?"

"You're a stranger, meaning you're not part of the powers that be in this town, this county, or this state. You're a computer genius. And you have eyes that aren't easy to read."

Nell thought of the bees, of the Leafies, of the ravaged Echinacea meadows, of, of, and of. "I promise I won't repeat anything you tell me," she said.

"There have been two more attacks," Mariah said. "One up here—a white guy riding his mountain bike in a wash near the Base. Another on the outskirts of the Park. This time it was a native healer looking for medicine plants. Nobody was hurt badly. The message was the same. 'Don't come back here.'

"Our elders talked about this a long time. They believe that this is the beginning of a threat coming to this desert that can tear the Salt Song Trail apart. There are many well-meaning white people who believe that what's coming will be good for the earth. We have to stop what's coming. And we have to teach the people who don't know any better. We have to start now."

"You're talking about FreegreenGlobal."

"Exactly, and more—corporate solar and wind power installations. The old people told us that we have to teach the world about the real danger of this so-called 'green' invasion. That's where you come in. Some of us have good internet and media skills, but we've never organized against something before. The young people act rebellious, but it's mostly show. A few want to learn the real ways, but too many are lost. And if we lose what we stand to lose to so-called sustainable energy development, there will be nothing to help them find their way back. When it comes to getting something done, it's falling to us older, more traditional folks. This is where you come in, because I've guessed something about you."

"What?"

"You were an executive in a big company."

"How do you know that?" Nell asked.

"Rumors. Besides, you've got you-won't-read-me eyes and those mega-bucks shoes Shiloh told me about."

"Your hunch is right, but the shoes are gone."

"My people and I need what you can do," Mariah said. "We don't care where you learned to do it. We don't have any money. We can't pay you in cash."

Nell thought of the bees, of the Echinacea, of the Leafies drifting in a dwindling sea. "You're an endangered species," she said.

"We are. And there aren't that many of us to begin with, especially us Twentynine Palms Chemehuevi."

Nell raised the water bottle in a toast.

"Okay. You've got me. I'd like to ask for one thing in return, something you might be able to give me."

"Ask me," Mariah said. "If I can give it, I will."

"I had a dream that you could show me how to make a map."

"In fact," Mariah said, "a map is exactly what we're talking about. A map of a trail." She took a long drink. "It's getting hotter already. Each year the hard heat comes earlier. You know what I'm talking about."

Nell nodded.

"You drink some more too," Mariah said. "You're going to get a lesson about this desert—and maybe how to survive in it. First off, though we're also called Chemeheuvi, we call ourselves Nuwuvi, The People. We're one of the bands of what the white anthropologists have labeled Southern Paiute. We've lived here forever, though we were scattered by the white man and other enemies for a long time. Those who could came back home.

"I'm Twentynine Palms band of Mission Indians Chemeheuvi. We once lived at the Oasis of Mara in Joshua Tree Park. We were what they call 'displaced.' And not for the last time. We came back. My reservation is here and down by Coachella, and we live throughout this whole area, though since there's so little work here, many have gone to the cities because they can find jobs, especially our young people. There are also Chemehuevi in Banning and a few other towns. The main Chemehuevi reservation is on the west side of so-called Lake Havasu."

"So-called?"

"Lake Havasu is really the dammed Colorado River. We lost so much when the Parker Dam went in. We haven't stopped losing since. That's why I'm telling you this.

"No matter where we Chemeheuvi and other people of the Southern Paiute live, we are all connected by that Salt Song Trail the video talked about. They didn't say too much about the spiritual trail, but it's the path the soul takes to go to the afterworld so that it won't be trapped here. We have one hundred forty-two songs we sing that are places on the trail. We sing them after someone has died to help the soul on its way to the afterworld. As the trail moves through different places, the songs change to be in the language of the bands that live in the area. As the people sing, the songs become the trail.

"My friend Leonard over on the river rez, the Paiute woman you saw in the video, and a white professor worked with the remaining Salt Song singers who are left to map the trail. They've taken the singers to museums where the stolen bones of our ancestors are locked up and to those BIA—Bureau of Indian Education—schools.

"Our ancestors marked some of the places on this trail with piles of stones, rock carvings, lines of crushed rock on the sand, but other places are natural—a hill, a cave, a mountain, a place you can look and see that mountain a certain way. This boulder is on one of the side trails. I was shown it by my grandmother, who had been shown it by her grandmother.

"Some of us believe that FreegreenGlobal wants to put a solar development close to here. One of the companies has already damaged a sacred site down near Blythe. I'll send you a link to the place. You won't believe it. There are huge figures the early people made from lines of rock. You can only really see them from the air. It's not a site on our trail, but really all of this weaves together."

"If destruction like that occurs to places on the Salt Song Trail, terrible things will happen. For us there will be dozens of spiritual wounds—a kind of cumulative genocide—but the damage will spread throughout the whole world. It's crazy to us that white people think it's okay to destroy our sacred land for cheap solar power."

"Mariah, I need to tell you something that may fit with what you've told me," Nell said. She felt her pulse jolt. She and Monkey were a secret containing a greater secret. If she told Mariah what Monkey was seeing, she would leave a hidden place dearer to her than any she had ever known.

"But please don't tell anyone else," she said. "Not Jackie. Not Monkey. Not anyone."

"I promise."

Nell looked up beyond the edge of the wash. The sky was cloudless, the sun burning white. Dry desert lilies shuddered in a small breeze at the edge of the wash. A year ago, she hadn't known the flowers existed. Now she knew what lay in their hearts.

"Monkey has been seeing and hearing things," she said.

"That boy smokes too much weed," Mariah said. "Jackie tells me all the time."

"It's not exactly that," Nell said.

"Then how exactly is it?"

"I've been with him when it happens. Yeah, there's pot, but he isn't just high. He's in a trance, and he's being told things that might be like what you've just told me, not about the trail, but about destruction."

"Some plants are sacred," Mariah said, "even weed. What's Monkey hearing?"

"There's a cataclysm on its way. I think that the ones telling him this have seen the consequences."

"Who's talking to him?"

"We don't know."

"Our old medicine people knew that the Ones speaking to them might be good, might be bad," Mariah said. "That's why the old folks served as apprentices for a long time to a teacher who had also served an apprenticeship."

"Monkey's been on his own with this till I came along."

"What's he seeing?" Mariah asked.

"Swirling colors. People and animals mutated into each other. Spinning rods that made themselves into a web. Just when he has almost figured those out, he comes out of the trance. And his heart feels cold."

Mariah shook her head. "This is really weird. I took my nieces to see this sci fi movie, *The Last Mimzy*. It was about people in the future talking to us through time, trying to tell us to change our ways. They had decided that adults wouldn't listen, so they sent a message for kids, a box in the ocean with toys in it. But the toys were actually teaching devices. A brother and sister found it. The little boy learned how to build a web of rods. The little girl believed in what they had found. Are you sure Monkey didn't see that movie?"

"He's never talked about it," Nell said. "Besides, I was with him when he went out. He wasn't faking anything. I believe in this. I believe in him. And when I can let myself think things that aren't logical, I believe the future is talking with him."

"My people believe that the past, the present, and the future are all flowing in us all the time," Mariah said. She stood and brushed sand off her jeans. "What kind of destruction is he being told about?"

"I don't know, but that's what convinced me. I look around. How can I not see what's happening? I left my other life partly because I dreamed that the honeybees were leaving. Then I learned that they are—and nobody knows why. The destruction is well under way."

"I know about the bees," Mariah said. "The animals are talking to us all the time, but we've forgotten how to listen. I have a Havasupai friend who's fighting a uranium mine proposal near the Grand Canyon. She believes the same things we're talking about. I want to know more of what you know, but I need to go to work for the rest of the afternoon. We're having our first organizing meeting next week. I'd like you to come.

"Leonard is coming over from the river rez. He's the real deal, not one of those puffed-up red headband guys who travel from demo to demo scoring with the white wannabe ladies. He's going to tell us about what's happening with the new solar project proposal down near Blythe. He thinks the FreegreenGlobal stakes I saw mean that the solar guys are going after land up here. Down there or up here, it's all the same."

"Everywhere," Nell said.

Mariah looked hard at Nell. "I just wonder about one thing. Why did you work for that company?"

"They offered me a job when I was twenty-one, then the offers got better and better," Nell said. "I thought I'd do work that mattered. Then I became trapped—mostly by myself."

"Why'd you leave the job?"

"I was 'made available to the industry,'" Nell said. "That's corpocode for fired."

"Why?"

"For being a woman who got old—and maybe messing with the wrong man."

"You're not old. I'm older than you are."

"They would have fired you, too."

"If they'd ever hired me in the first place. Those big corporations don't have time for Indians—unless they think we've got secrets that can make them money."

Nell flinched. "I know that one. I saw it."

"Well," Mariah said, "now you're here."

"And I need to make a map."

"I don't really know what your map is," Mariah said.

"It's not songs," Nell said.

"What if you sit for a while and just wait? See what comes up.

Sometimes when I don't know what I'm looking for, I'll do that."

"I know this much," Nell said. "The map is real. It's not just in my mind."

Mariah dropped Nell off at La Paloma. "See you Friday?"

"Hang on a minute," Nell said. "I've got something for Punkin."

She ran up to her room and brought down the big green T-rex. Mariah laughed. "She might be a little young for this, but this is a good mascot for us in the battle coming up. We'll give it to her when she's old enough to understand, and tell her the story."

18

Nell walked into La Paloma and found Monkey crouched in front of the living room bookcase. "Man, this could be Saphiro's Book Store before it went bust. This is a serious collection of books, look." He held up *On the Road* and an old leather-bound collection of Yeats. "They've got *Dune* and *The Invisible Man*, a shelf of desert guides and a shelf of high-brow, pissed-off chick books."

"Speaking of the invisible man," Nell said, "were you here when I just came in?"

"I was. You were zooming. You can take the girl out of L.A., but you can't take L.A. out of the girl."

Nell was grateful for his light tone. She was going to have to apologize for standing him up. She hadn't apologized to a man since she had found herself groveling repeatedly to David.

"I owe you an apology," she said.

Monkey looked up. "You do. I was heartbroken. I waited two hours for you. Got up early and everything, walked away from Jackie's homemade pancakes."

"Oh jeez," Nell said. "I hit the bed at eight and didn't wake up till seven. That's a personal best for sleep. For the first time in maybe twenty years."

Monkey sure as shit knew that drill. He decided to let her off the hook. "I lied," he said. "I screwed up, too."

"Ha," Nell said. "How could you forget me?"

"Hang on. Don't push your luck. See what a sweetheart I am?"

He pointed to two grocery bags of Sally's takeout. "I bought lunch because I felt like such an asshole. And I spliced a wire in the LeSabre."

He looked her up and down. "Man, those are some ugly shoes."

"Don't change the subject," Nell said. "How'd you forget? I told on myself. It's your turn."

Monkey stood. He flinched and pressed his hand to his lower back. "I do not like what is happening to me," he said. "This getting older shit. But, considering the alternative..." He stretched out to each side and felt the muscles loosen. "I was going to make breakfast for my wife and persuade her to go up into the hills with me, but she had other plans. See, it's Summer Solstice. If you live in Twentynine, you have to celebrate Summer Solstice."

"Hang on," Nell said. "You asked me to go to breakfast, and you didn't get up early enough to make Jackie breakfast. So you broke two dates." Nell regretted "dates" immediately. "Never mind. So what's the deal with Summer Solstice?"

"It's the longest day of the year," Monkey said. "From then on, the days get shorter and eventually cooler. And the nights get longer. You've seen the nights—black velvet and diamonds, more moon than anywhere else in the USA. There's a lot to celebrate. Jackie and I used to always sleep out in the desert on Summer Solstice.

"And I got high. That's how I forgot." He kept his voice light. It pissed him off that he had to *keep* his voice light. "Are we even now?"

Nell thought about the emails. They were running two for two. By the end of the time with David, she had written three hundred and sixty-three; he had written one hundred and four. Monkey was her boss. She was his genius nerd. That was all.

"We are," she said. "Even."

"Good," Monkey said. "I was hoping I could persuade you to go out in the desert with me. We'll find a grove of Joshua trees, eat our picnic in the shade and talk. Now that you've got those health-nut shoes we can explore once it cools down."

"Give me five minutes," Nell said. "I need to put my wash in the dryer."

She walked into the kitchen. Monkey picked up the Kerouac. It had been twenty years since he'd read it. He'd been late for it then. He hoped he wasn't late for it now.

Nell and Monkey drove to the Biz. He grabbed his pack and stashed their food in a cooler. They climbed into his old Nissan pickup. He set the cooler between them. "No air-conditioning," he said. "Doesn't matter. Both windows won't roll up and I am a desert boy." He reached into the cooler, pulled out a wet bandana, and draped it around Nell's neck.

Water dripped down her back. She closed her eyes. "Once," she said, "just once, I took LSD. I didn't feel anything for what seemed like forever. Then it felt as though liquid silver was trickling down my spine. This is better."

"How so?"

"There will be no eternity of being born, giving birth, and dying all at once. At least not for today."

"While we're on the topic," he said carefully, "I *am* a little stoned."

Nell opened her eyes and looked at him. "Bossman, we've all got our medicine."

"West and the road are two of mine. We're headed west," he said and laughed. "Yeah. Jimbo. Ride the highway west…"

They drove past a trailer compound with a tall fence around it. "Mormon family," he said. "You know much about those folks?"

"They're the only religious zealots dedicated enough to knock on motel doors," Nell said. She remembered her mother inviting two lanky boys in suits into their room. The Mormons had not cast a curious glance at her mother's statue of Kali, her shrine to Janis Joplin, the garlands of beads hanging from the mirror. They talked a long time. Her mother was stoned gentle. They loved her questions. Nell saw something in their eyes that did not frighten her. After they left, her mother fanned the pamphlets they had given her out on the bed. "They said they believe in a Mother God," she said. "They said they were more like hippies than they were like normal people. And when they spoke the name 'Jesus', they said it with love."

"You going to say more about that?" Monkey asked.

"Probably not."

"I thought so."

He turned on a dirt road, dust rising behind them in a red plume. He slowed down. "We've got all afternoon. I don't know how I get racing on Yuppie Time, but I do."

"I don't think there are yuppies anymore," Nell said. "That was twenty years ago. I think most of them have become scuppies."

Monkey snorted. "Senior Citizen Upscale Scum, right? My mom hates that term *senior citizen*. You've got to meet her. You two will love each other." He tilted a water bottle to his lips.

"Fuck sake, I can't believe how much I'm talking. To anybody, but especially to a woman who does not have a last name. This was supposed to be breakfast and we were supposed to tell our names."

"You first." Nell was deciding that Monkey was a boy with no boundaries. Meet his mom? What? Next thing, he'd decide she should meet the wife.

"Yeah, it'd be cool if you met my family," he said. "And Jackie. You're going to fit right in."

"Hang on here," Nell said. "I asked you to tell me your real name. Suddenly you're setting up a family reunion. *Maybe* we'll negotiate that later—I tend to be allergic to happy family get-togethers. What's your name?"

"Carl," Monkey flushed. "My mom calls me Carl. My last name is Barnett, Bar-NETT. My middle name is known only to immediate family and Jackie. My family's from Spiro, Oklahoma, three generations back. If you look the town up on the Fiendish Thing, you will note that Spiro's historical tornado activity is slightly below the Oklahoma state average, but 113% greater than the overall U.S. average. My brother and I were held responsible for at least thirteen percent of that figure."

"Your brother?" Nell figured at the rate he was yakking, she'd buy herself some time to decide whether or not to tell him her real last name.

"Just the one brother. Deacon. I'm the oldest."

"Why Deacon?"

"He is a man of deep principles. Next to Keno, he's been maybe my best friend.

"Your turn. Your name?"

Nell thought fast. She didn't know why she couldn't say her real name. "Silver," she said. "My name is Elinor Silver. Nell Silver." She tilted her head. "My hat's my colors."

They rode a while in comfortable silence. Monkey turned south off the highway.

"We're here," Monkey said. "Back door to Joshua Tree National Park. Gram Parsons loved this place. You know him? You know the story?"

"I do."

Nell had been at college when her mom had called from a payphone. "Honey, I've got real sad news. Gram Parsons is dead. His friends cremated him somewhere in the desert. I can't stop crying. It's like I lost a brother."

The road curved up to a sandy wash. There was a handful of short twisted trees, a slope of purple wildflowers and coreopsis. Monkey eased off onto a strip of patchwork shade under the chunky trees. Seedpods scattered the ground. Monkey hauled the cooler to the trees, came back and pulled a double pad and tarp from the camper shell. "We'll eat and caffeinate, then we'll head up the wash."

Nell climbed out of the truck. The air was still. Hot. Crystalline. She walked around the trees. The scent was not desert, but almost tropical. Fat white buds tipped the branches.

"Stubborn Joshuas," Monkey said. "Not just surviving in hell, but making it beautiful."

"Poet," Nell said.

"Not me. Jackie thought that up. She used to stitch the trees in her art. She painted those words on one of her pieces."

"You said she's an artist...why the *used to*?"

"She kind of stalled out. She'll make art again," he said in his don't-ask-me-more voice. He spread the pad and tarp on the ground and opened the cooler. "Come on, Greenhorn, time for some chuck wagon chow."

Monkey took a flower-print oilcloth out of his pack and laid out their picnic. Nell closed her eyes and rested her fingertips on the *bánh mì gà*. "Ah," she said. "I have psychic powers. Two chunks of fresh-baked French bread, sliced chicken, pickle, lettuce, tomato, and a mayonnaise that's so good you want to eat it with a spoon." She opened the paper. "*Voila!*"

"How did you know that?" Monkey asked. "It's time I put you through a real job interview. Who the fuck are you?"

"Therein," Nell said, "lies the tale." She bit into the sandwich. "Or tells the lie."

Monkey took the lids off their coffees. "These are still icy. I'll give you yours after you tell me two honest real facts about yourself."

"I was a yuppie," Nell said. "I was a cool, ruthless, nasty, charming, inscrutable executive who pretended she didn't know that her staff called her Dragon Lady. That's seven honest real facts."

She picked up her coffee.

"I fell in love with a cool, ruthless, nasty, charming, scrutable executive who was so hip it made your teeth hurt to listen to him. He and his pals had a computer program that designed outrageous getaways. They named it William Blake—Bill for short. He flew us to Hue for a long weekend. The second day of the trip, we ate bánh mì gà in a riverfront cafe in Hue."

"The guy was scrutable?"

"Very."

"Then what?"

"He bailed. I was let go from the company 'for my own good,'" Nell said. "My own good didn't happen. I lost everything. For the first time I wanted to die. I dreamed about the bees leaving and I knew it was time. I met the Leafy and figured I was being premature. I might need to mention that Scrutable was married."

Monkey nodded. "So you headed for Tanapall?"

"Yep."

Monkey pulled off his head rag and the rubber band that held his ponytail. He shook out his hair. "There," he said. "I should do that more often." Sun glinted in the copper and gray strands.

"Shake your head again," Nell said. "You have a corona."

"Light around an eclipse," Monkey said. "That's an improvement on my normal condition. Usually I just have the eclipse. You really love words, girl."

"I do," Nell said.

They finished the sandwiches and coffee in easy quiet. Nell remembered the silence that had fallen between David and her toward the end and how she had felt as though it were crushing the air out of her lungs. She lay back on the tarp and pillowed her head on Monkey's pack. He stretched out at the base of the Joshua.

"I was last up this wash five years ago. In this same spot," Monkey said. "Me and Jackie came out for the longest day of the year. This

Chemeheuvi nurse where she worked told her it was good for a couple to do that—spend the longest day away from people. It would mean we would never get divorced.

"Once it cooled down, we walked for hours. There was a half moon. When we got back to this tree, Jackie got out her paints, making moon cloud sketches for her art. She used up all the silver in her paintbox."

He closed his eyes and fell quiet. Nell watched his breathing slow. The Joshuas softened the glare above them. She couldn't remember ever being in the kind of dry heat that held her. She thought that if she closed her eyes and went to sleep, she would become mineral. The bushes trembled in a tiny wind, rattling as though they were a web of tiny bones.

Monkey leaned up on one elbow. "Catnap," he said. "Learned to do it in my former profession."

Nell let the clue drop away. She didn't want to know about his past. She didn't want to talk about hers. She just wanted to be held by the gently insistent heat.

"Imagine being trapped here," she said. "No water. No escape. You could disappear, particle by particle. You could sublimate straight into the air, end up nothing but salt."

"People do," Monkey said. "South of here not too far, Keno's aunt lost two daughters, her son-in-law, and one grandbaby. They were trying to cross. They got lost. They didn't exactly disappear. The Border Patrol found chewed-on human bones, water bottles, a kid's sandal."

Nell was quiet. For the moment, *sublimation* was obscenely facile. She thought about the word *facility*. She remembered that the root was something like *unimpeded opportunity*.

She looked up at Monkey. "I have a fuckload to learn," she said.

He shook his head. "I never heard a woman cuss as much as you."

"You never met a woman as pissed off as me." She turned away.

He set his hand on her arm. "You've met your brother, girl."

She looked down. Their skin was laced with intricate shadow.

Nell sat up. "Let's walk up this wash. I want to know more."

Monkey scrambled up a boulder the soft orange-red of an apricot. Nell followed him and sat. "What are we on?" she asked.

"Monzonite granite. We're sitting on what once was liquid rock."

Nell pressed her hands against the warm rock and looked up the wash. She could see the Joshua under which they had sat, under which she had felt his touch on her arm. She felt light-headed. "What you said? About the bees? Do you remember what you said about the bees?"

"*What! I said.*" He laughed. "I need play you this old funk tape I made. Classic stuff—'Get the Funk Outta my Face,' 'Fight the Power,' 'Brick House.' I alternated the tunes with Jim Morrison reading his poetry. *Enter the hot dream/Come with us/ Everything is broken up and dances.*"

Nell remembered reading Morrison's poetry and thinking it was overwrought and sentimental. She didn't remember those words, words that could have been written about the Leafy's mineral shimmer or the way the Joshua tree's branches shattered the light. Or this man's touch on her arm.

"*What!* I said was that no matter what cosmic riffs I'm getting in the trances, the bees are leaving."

She looked at him. "Do you care?"

"About the bees?"

He was quiet. Nell waited.

"I care about the bees," Monkey said. "I care about the desert tortoises. I care about little bugs you can't even see. I care about the dirt bikes ripping the shit out of ancient Indian geoglyphs. I care about how the big biz solar companies are going to nuke this desert. I care about all of it. And I can't do a fucking thing. All I seem to be able to do is promise myself I'll change and watch myself fail."

Nell knew better than to hold his hand on that one. She waited him out.

He hesitated. "I know what you're not saying. 'What about the cosmic riffs?'"

"What about the riffs?"

He looked away. "I was raised as close as you can get to the South without crossing the Mississippi. My Southern Baptist elders told me tarot cards and ouija boards were instruments of the devil.

"Then I worked a job where I saw the real devil. I'd started out a true believer. I was going to beat the devil at his game. The game was bigger than me—no credit to me. I saw kids punched to death. I saw people alive with half their brains outside their skulls. I saw little girls die in childbirth, little girls.

"I had an EMT supervisor called Custer. It wasn't his real name. He hated Blacks and Mexicans and Indians, and he was always in the middle of the worst blood baths, so the guys called him Custer. He was a nasty motherfucker, but he taught me one thing: *There is no Big Other. Good or Evil. Death is the only guarantee.* If you can live with that, you can live.

"And now I'm getting invitations I can't turn down from something I can't see, some Big Others who put their words in my head and make my heart freeze."

He hunched his shoulders. "Sometimes I wish I could just shake till I shook it out of me. But I can't. Brave Okie boys don't do that. We don't be titty-babies. Not us. Even if some who-knows-what-fuckers seem to be the bosses of me."

"Do you know the story about the king who didn't know fear?" Nell asked.

"Nope."

"There was a great king who had everything, except the ability to feel fear. So, of course, that is all he wanted. He was young and handsome and unmarried. 'If only I could shudder,' he told his wizard, 'I would be a happy man.'

"The king sent messengers out into his kingdom, then throughout the known world. He promised that the woman who could make him shudder would become his bride. Day after day, women lined up outside the castle. There were beautiful women with ugly hearts, ordinary women with ordinary hearts; there were sorceresses and witches. None of them could make him so much as flinch.

"One day, a woman waited till just before the gates of the castle closed. She slipped through and found the king and his wizard about to dine. 'Let me sleep in your antechamber,' she said. 'By morning you will know what it is to fear.'

"Her eyes were bright. She held her back perhaps a little straighter than the other women, her head a little higher. The king agreed to her request."

Nell stopped. She watched cloud shadow drift across the wash below them.

"So? What happened?" Monkey said.

"I'll let you know."

Monkey grinned.

"I'll cut you a deal. Tell me what you've been hearing in the trances," Nell said, "and sooner or later you'll learn how to shudder."

"Okay," Monkey said. "But believe me, woman, Okie boy or not, I sure know how to shudder."

He was quiet a long time. Nell watched him gather himself. He bent his head. "In the last trance, I heard Stevie Winwood, then my gramps. I knew it was Winwood because even though there were no words, his voice sounded like molten silver. Gramps was bitching about Born Agains just like he was alive."

"I thought you were raised Southern Baptist," Nell said.

"I was. Gramma was Born Again. But Gramps knew Jesus lived in everything. He'd stop at the end of his very long day and watch how the sunset came through the old trees. He'd eat a peach and smile like he'd been sanctified. 'God—you spell that with a small g, Monkeyboy,' he'd tell me. 'No religion owns god.'"

"What else? What about the Big Other?"

"Nell, you're going to think I'm one of those woo woo nut cases."

"Maybe. But if you don't tell me what they said, you might not hear what happened to the handsome king."

Monkey looked down at his hands. His voice was measured. "That cataclysm I told you about is coming. We humans can forestall it. If we can, there might be hope for everything that lives on the planet. How's that for cosmic?"

Nell remembered her eerie sense of peace as she had watched the Leafy Seadragons move without moving and as she had sat in the office gloom with her hand on Monkey's heart. She remembered Mariah's words. She felt the same quiet certainty about Monkey's.

"How do the Big Others know this?" she said.

"I don't know," Monkey said. "But it feels like they're going to keep at me until I pay attention."

Nell grinned. "They really are the boss of you," she said.

"They're the Bosses. Fucking lovely."

"They're the same as the bees. They're the same as the Leafy."

"Okay," Monkey said. "You're real. I'm real. They're real. It's real. Stay tuned, kiddies. The Bosses coming at you on *Dust Radio*."

Nell turned back to him.

"You know that song?"

"I do."

"So did Mr. Scrutable."

"I'm not him," Monkey said.

"I intend that to be the truest thing you ever said," Nell stood.

"Wait," Monkey grabbed her wrist. "So what happened to the king?"

"You'll find out. I'm ready to head home." She wasn't. The thought of her empty room felt anything but comforting.

"Hey," Monkey said. "How about we stop by my place and see if Jackie's there? I'd like for you two to meet. She's curious about you."

Nell didn't answer. She bet Jackie was curious about her. She bet Monkey had told his wife that there was no threat from a computer nerd. She wished she had a few cosmic bosses to tell her what to do. Monkey was clearly on another planet in which the inhabitants had never heard the term *emotional affair*.

She knew what not to do. Go back to La Paloma. Sit at the window and let the fading light carry her into a story of a future that held Monkey. Monkey alone. Monkey free.

"Hey," he said. "There's a big world out there full of lots of different kinds of people. We've got to spring you from your cubicle."

"First of all," Nell said, "it was a corner office, and second of all, the last time a guy wanted to free me from my solitude, he left me alone in it."

"As I just pointed out," Monkey said, "I'm not him. You willing to see how the other half lives?"

"Sure," Nell said. "Let's go."

They were almost to the Bronco when Monkey stopped and bent down. "Holy shit, I never thought I'd find one of these, much less two of them. Hold out your hand. Be careful, it's sharp." He picked up two twisted gray stones from the sand at the base of a scorched Joshua and set one of them on her palm. "It's lightning glass."

She touched the pocked gray glass. A facet in it glinted. "Lightning," she said, "hits sand. Right?"

Monkey nodded. "Alchemy."

19

The house was tucked away in a little cul-de-sac, the front yard a soft olive replication of the desert hillsides, wildflowers brilliant orange and purple against the pale sand.

"Jackie did the landscaping," Monkey said. "The plants are all native."

"She has a wonderful eye," Nell said.

"Wait'll you see the inside of the house. It's all her touches."

Monkey unlocked the door and motioned Nell in. There was no one home except for a big gray tabby with ragged ears and prizefighter shoulders who pushed past Nell and twined between Monkey's feet.

"This," Monkey said, "is Hulk. He is my good boy. He is long on nuts and short on discretion."

Nell looked down. There seemed to be no nuts.

"Hulk refuses," Monkey said, "to accept the reality of that long-ago trip to the bad man. That trip was nothing but a bad catnip hallucination."

Monkey took Nell on the grand tour. They began in the living room. "This is the gibbon lair," he said. "I have the couch, the sound system, the TV, and the headphones. I have all I need. Check this out." He turned on the sound system. A galaxy of LED lights sparkled. "Now, watch over here." Vacuum tubes began to glow softly orange. "See the difference? LEDs are icy. Vacuum tubes are warm. It's the same with the sound. That's an original Dynaco Stereo-70 tube power amp."

Nell crouched in front of the vacuum tubes. "You haven't listened to Hendrix," she said, "till you've listened to him through one of those old amps."

"You're not my sister," Monkey said. "You're a bro. Sit back in that recliner. I'll play you one tune. It's not Jimi, but it might be about you."

Nell sat and closed her eyes. The song was "Western Plain." When Van Mo got to the line about letting the shack burn down, she opened her eyes. Monkey stood in the doorway. "I see those tears," he said. "Don't you be going titty baby on me."

He walked her down a long hallway and flicked on a light over a display of unframed photos. Hulk as a stubby kitten. Monkey with his arm around a petite woman whose face was shaded by a big straw hat. "That's Jackie," Monkey said. "That's the reason you don't see a *Sports Illustrated* Identikit tits and ass poster over the Biz desk. Jackie's my pin-up girl. Would you believe she's fifty-two? Put that girl in a pink t-shirt and no bra and we're talking groinalicious."

Nell stared at him.

"I mean, you can see wrinkles if you look close," he said, "but she's in great shape for her age."

Nell continued staring.

"What?" Monkey said. "What? Don't go chick on me."

"And what," Nell said, "do you see when you look in the mirror?"

He touched his hair. "I like him," he said. "Got a few gray hairs, little extra chin-event here. Hey, I'm forty-seven."

Nell kept quiet.

"Okay," Monkey said. "Now what?"

"Groinalicious? Penile reference alert?"

"Hey," he said. "Groins are not gender specific. Lighten up." His voice had gone somewhere between neutral and sub-zero. "Shall we continue the Grand Tour?"

"Indeed," she said easily. "Let the tour continue."

There was a glint of silver at the end of the hall. "What's that?"

"Jackie's work," Monkey said. "Her real work. Come look."

The glint was a silver crescent impeccably satin-stitched within the pale yellow heart of a cactus flower, the upper right curve of the blossom touching the side of a red satin hand. Fragments of photoscreened cloth drifted below the hand: a sepia petroglyph of a mountain lion, a black and white photo negative of a comet, vapor rising from a city street. Words in chain stitch trailed across the moonflower and the hand. *Only connect.*

Monkey ran his finger over the comet. "Do you know those words?"

"I don't."

"I found them in *Howard's End.* I'll show you."

He took her into a guest bedroom, its walls lined with bookshelves. He pulled out an old hardback. "Listen," he said. "Only connect! That was the whole of her sermon. Only connect the prose and the passion, and both will be exalted, and human love will be seen at its height. Live in fragments no longer. Only connect, and the beast and the monk, robbed of the isolation that is life to either, will die."

"I thought Keno said you didn't go to school?"

"He said I had a GED," Monkey said quietly. "I hated school. I love to read." *Or I did*, he thought, *before I started living so deep in mota mondo.*

They returned to the patchworks: five wiry hares appliqued across a pair of satin-stitched lips. It took a second for Nell to see that the mouth had tiny scarlet beads scattered on it, as though the hares' claws had pierced the lips.

There was a cotton patch silkscreened with a picture of Monkey and Jackie taken in a dollar photo booth. She had embroidered dark glasses over her eyes and a crooked halo above his head.

"So much ferocity," Nell said. "So much tenderness. You must love each other very much."

"We do," Monkey said. "We have a lot. Thank you for what you see." He leaned forward and kissed Nell's shoulder.

"You're welcome." Her voice was steady.

He looked into her eyes. "You're really intense, you know?"

"Sometimes I am."

"That was okay?" he said. "Yeah? That little kiss?"

"It was. But, if you really want to thank me, make some coffee."

Monkey led her into the kitchen and nuked coffee. "My only kitchen skill."

"You don't cook?" Nell said.

"Jackie's an Arkansas gal," Monkey said. "The only reason a man should be in the kitchen is to eat. I've tried a couple times, but it gets very tense in here when I do."

He poured them coffee and led Nell back into the living room. "Do you mind if I toke up?"

Nell looked at his face. He could have been seventeen. Hulk laid his head on her foot and fell asleep.

Before she could answer, Monkey said, "Jackie's probably socked in for the long haul. We could watch a DVD or listen to some tunes. I've got mixes I must have made knowing you were on your way to me."

"Actually," Nell said, "it's almost lights out for me. This has been a long full day."

"You sure about passing on that DVD? I've got this incredible

French movie, *City of Lost Children*. It'll mend your broken heart."

"I never said my heart was broken."

"I am a master diagnostician," he said. "Of vehicles and lost girls."

"I'm not lost," Nell said. "I am exactly where I want to be." She leaned in close to him. "And I'm not a girl. Look." She touched the lines around her eyes. "I'm just like Jackie. Not a girl."

"Some girls are always girls. Please? Stick around? You one-hundred-per-cent hard dragon lady sure you don't want to soften up with a movie? You sure you want to go hang with your lonesomes?"

"I'm sure," Nell said. "I like my lonesomes. They've been my best friend for a long time." She laughed. "And I've only got tomorrow to wax my legs, shape my eyebrows, do my nails, and get ready for another demanding day at the Biz."

Monkey pulled up in front of La Paloma. "We could sit on the stoop a minute," Nell said. He climbed out, came around, and opened her door.

"Duane Allman," she said.

"Say what?"

"A stoned southern gentleman."

"Yeah, but I'm not dead," Monkey said.

"I'm not going to say it," Nell said. "The next part of that."

"You don't need to."

"The part about 'You will be,'" Nell said. "I won't say that."

They settled in on the stoop. Doves cried out from the oleander. "Those are Inca doves," Monkey said. "I love that mournful sound." The street was quiet. A western cloud went copper, rose gold, then pale green just above the dark mountains. Monkey's face was gentle. "Would you come in for a minute?" Nell said. "I have something to show you."

She led Monkey up the stairs and opened her door. The evening breeze blew the sheer curtains into the room. "Sit here." She pulled the chair to the window.

Nell stood in the doorway. "Pull back the curtains and look down to your left."

Monkey obeyed. He saw a goat curled on the dark earth, the man on the steps, and the tiny Mars of the lit end of a cigarette. "Does he smoke all night?"

"For hours."

Monkey knew that later—in his marriage bed, alone—he would see Nell at this window. She would be watching.

"Imagine being old like that," Nell said. "So peaceful. I just wanted you to see him."

She waved him into the hall.

"Thank you," Monkey said. "I'll say good-night."

Nell waited till she heard the truck pull away. She opened the computer. Her mailbox was empty. She typed in Monkey's address.

Subject: What comes next

The king fell asleep in his great carved bed. The woman, on a soft pallet on the floor, did not. She lay awake until she heard him snore. Then, she crept down to the goldfish pond in the castle garden and scooped up a bucket of fish.

She slipped into the king's bedroom, gently pulled back the covers, and threw the bucket of fish over his sleeping form.

They were married the next day. The End.

n

She sent the message, closed the computer, and took her chair to the window. The waning moon was a smudge beyond the lights of the Marine base. Someday soon she would meet Jackie, and when she did she would show her the Leafy Seadragon on the computer. She would ask Jackie to make its portrait in satin and sequins.

The house was dark except for the orange glow of the amp. Monkey wished Nell were there, or Jackie, even Keno stretched out in the recliner, a big grin on his big face. Monkey did not know when he had first become afraid to be alone in an empty house. Or alone anywhere except the Biz. He felt dried out and jittery. He checked the pocket of his shorts. The last nubbin of pot was there.

He made a pipe out of a soda can, toked deep, trashed the can, and went into his lair. It was a night—like all other nights—for tunes. He loaded five CDs into the machine, hit Random, and stretched out on the couch.

For a while, he was in the company of sound, of The Doors and Big Head Todd and Etta James. Then, the first guitar notes of the Allman's "Crazy Love" rasped out, and he thought, "What if there were steel guitar strings stretched unbearably tight across a human heart and Dickey Betts could reach in and play them..." and Monkey was no longer alone.

This is how it is, this is how it was. Once you were fragile. Once you did not know how to hunt or move on water. Once you put feathers in your hair. You carried shells.

Your feathers were blue. The Others' feathers were orange. Orange was the color of death. Beyond alien moons, a pebble rolled down a mountain. It gathered what could not be shed. Now We know the color of a seashell in the ear of a child who hunts for rats to bolster the family stewpot. The dead rat is carried home in a bandana. The bandana is blue and orange.

You cannot move. Look at this.

Then Monkey heard Nell's voice—"Yes."

A network of rods began to glow and spin against pure black. The pebble rolled out of the web and became an ice ball. It spun into the heart of the body lying on the couch and grew. The rods spun faster and faster. The web began to heat up, to glow; the rods were nothing but an orange blur.

We tell you again. We have seen it. It is coming. You and your kind did not set it in motion. It is immutable. What you and your kind have set in motion can be altered. And, with it, your DNA. We will show you the trail.

Monkey heard the *hushhhh hushhhh* of a rattle. His flesh and bones were diffused. He was a particle in an icy orange radiance. He studied the body on the couch. It did not disappear. It put its hand over its heart.

It was nearly three by the time Monkey inched upright. The music was over. He knew without looking the exact color of the vacuum tubes. He knew how it felt to be that glow. His chest was ice. "Do not fucking kill me," he said. "Please, Bosses. That is not in any job description I ever agreed to."

He stumbled down the long hallway to the bed and collapsed

without pulling back the sheets. He reeked. Jackie would slaughter him for stinking up the quilt. With luck, he'd wash it before she got home.

He closed his eyes. He saw, not the spinning rods or the glacial orange light. He saw the tiny glint of a stranger's cigarette. He saw the moon dropping toward the western mountains—and a woman watching.

The last thing Nell remembered before she fell asleep was the patch of silver shimmering in the gloom of the hallway, the ragged silver crescent Jackie had stitched in a flower that just touched the side of a red satin hand.

20

Diamond tapped on Nell's door. "It's Orientation Day. And there are raspberry muffins."

Nell closed the computer. There had been nothing from Monkey. She'd waked before dawn and taken her coffee out to the stoop. Doves had called from the telephone wires. She'd thought about Jackie, about a woman she knew only by Monkey's words—and by her house. There had been candles everywhere, and stained glass in the colors of a desert wash. There had been fine-woven Indian baskets and, in the long hallway, gorgeous patchwork panels from which price tags still hung.

"I'll be right down." Nell closed the curtains. She thought of Monkey sitting quietly at the window. He had looked down on the little goat and the man and the dark. He had watched long enough to see the man light a new cigarette. Nell wondered if he had understood how that was, to be peacefully alone. She wondered if she did.

Shiloh and Diamond walked her through the Twentynine basics: Don't walk the streets at night. Don't set foot outside without water for the next six months. Don't head out into the desert without your cell phone, even if it won't work most places. Don't drink tap water. Seriously. Even more, never trust a cop. And do NOT get your hair cut at Jen's Hair and Nails Joint.

"I feel so much safer," Nell said. "Those are the same rules for L.A.—except for Jen's."

"There's more," Diamond said. She glanced at Shiloh. Shiloh shrugged. "Do you believe in anything?" Diamond said.

Nell felt herself step aside without moving. "Like a god?"

Diamond hesitated. Nell remembered the ad exec at the Corp, the jolly guy with the tiny gold camel in his lapel. He'd kicked booze, by Jesus; he'd kicked coke, by Jesus; he'd kicked reefer, by Jesus; heh heh, all by the grace of Jesus. He'd say Jesus and then he'd pause and study her. "Well," he'd say, "cat got your tongue?"

She'd never said what she wanted to, which was to point out that she was reasonably certain Jesus hadn't worn Brioni suits, or driven a bright yellow Hummer, or owned three houses, one in Beverly Hills, one in Belize, and one in Jackson. Mr. Saved had been missing the part about the camel and the eye of the needle, and the rich man and the kingdom of God. But she'd scarcely been in the position to criticize.

"Is this multiple choice?" Nell said.

Shiloh smiled. "It better be."

"Last April I would have told you I didn't believe in anything but hard work, luck, and hard luck. Now, I don't know."

Diamond laughed. "That's my religion. The Church of Don't Fucking Know."

"So why did you ask me if I believed in anything?"

"Twentynine is complicated," Shiloh said. "We've got mysterious stuff on the Base and their creepy orange flares at night and who knows what floating around in the air. We've got perps on the lam, greed, and mutations of dope the rest of the world has yet to discover. We've got a ripple of air on a day of no wind. We've got a fifty-nine-year-old grandma going out to talk to her ancestor and getting punched out by two guys. We've got weird stuff we don't talk about because if we don't, maybe the weird stuff we don't talk about won't come calling."

"You've got the Dementors of Corporate Solar threatening to fuck with a bunch of sacred sites," Nell said.

"We do," Diamond said. "And there are a few old people in what's left of the tribes who've got a power arsenal that makes the Base look like Sesame Street."

"So, it's easy," Nell said. "Don't walk around at night. Don't drink the water. Don't piss off the long-time locals. And don't get my hair cut at Jen's."

"That last one for sure," Diamond said. "Pay attention to what the locals say. Pay attention to your hunches."

"I will," Nell said. "I want to show you something. I met it right before I came here. I was thinking about eating my gun. Then I saw this and figured why not hang around to find out what other impossibilities exist. Open your laptop and I'll show you."

They had just searched Leafy Seadragon when there was a knock on the front door. Shiloh left to see who it was. Diamond leaned in to see the text. "*Their movement is as though an invisible hand were helping,*" she read. "That's what Shiloh and I were trying to get at."

"That is real," Nell said. "I saw one. It moved exactly like that. I think I'm ready to join the Church of Don't Fucking Know."

Shiloh came in and leaned over her shoulder. "Oh my god, what is that?"

"It's real," Nell said.

Shiloh sat. "Let me check this out. Nell, your boss is here again."

"I'll be right back." Shiloh and Diamond didn't answer. They were lost in the Leafy's cyberworld.

"This might sound weird," Monkey said.

"What with everything being so normal and all," Nell said. "Try me."

"Jackie invited you for lunch."

"When?"

"Today. I'm supposed to bring you back to the house if you want to come."

He sat down on the couch. "Please do it."

"Why?" Nell said.

"Because she wants to meet you. Because I told her about you. Because if I didn't tell her about you, it would seem weird."

He folded his arms over his chest. "Because I am thinking about you too much. Because we, that is you and I, need to get this defused."

He started to reach for her hand and stopped.

"Because the Bosses visited again last night and I heard your voice and I need to have you in my life probably for a long time because you're the only one who believes this impossibility—and this is how we have to do it."

"Right," Nell said. "Let me tell Shiloh and Diamond I'm leaving and let me put on some real clothes."

"Not the suit."

"The suit is gone."

Monkey drove. Nell felt the same way she had always felt going into a meeting with the sharks. She remembered what she'd told the kids who interned in the Corp. Research till your eyeballs fall out, then put on your headphones and research till you've gone deaf. There was no way to google Jackie.

 He pulled the truck up in front of the house and shut off the engine. "Okay. This is not a big deal. Computer nerd meets wife. Wife meets computer nerd. No big deal."

He led her into the kitchen. The house was quiet. Nell looked back toward the front door. She was glad she had memorized the route to the house. She could, if necessary, walk back to La Paloma. Yes, it was a Bessemer furnace outside, but it might make sense to risk death by desiccation in order to nicely say, *I quit, goodbye,* to Monkey before she had to nicely say hello to his wife.

She'd spent thirty years knowing it was critical to have a backup plan. She'd leave, walk back to La Paloma, and ask Diamond and Shiloh to help her find a job. She could feed and wash old people, she could make sandwiches for runaways, she could listen to women much worse off than she was—for hours, for as long as it took.

Jackie stepped into the kitchen from the sunroom. She was everything Nell was not. Tiny. Long auburn hair. Gray-eyed. She had the body of a teenage girl, a very lucky teenage girl. "I'm sorry, babe," she said. "I was on the phone with your mom." She stepped forward and took Nell's hands in hers. "I'm so glad to meet you. He needs you."

"You've been on the Biz computer?" Nell said.

"Once. I never went there again."

"It's amazing," Nell said, "what a guy who can listen to an engine and hear a subliminal whimper can do to a simple spread sheet. I'm happy to meet you, too. He showed me your art."

Jackie's face stiffened. "When?"

"Last night. Didn't he tell you? He brought me over to meet you, but you weren't here."

Jackie swatted Monkey on the butt. "Bad man," she said. "You should have called. I would have come home."

Monkey pulled her in close. Nell made herself look. She hated it. "I figured," he said, "you had those little piggies dancing on your machine. No way I was going to interrupt what was going to fund me a free dinner."

"Those little piggies," Jackie said, "must have been on happy pills. They kept nodding out."

"Kinda like me last night," Monkey said.

"Now there's a surprise," Jackie said.

Nell remembered the years when the Corp had instituted drug and alcohol abuse seminars. For a while, it seemed half her staff was valiantly drinking Perrier at business lunches and sneaking a smoke in the stairwell. David had called the clean and sober people *Huggies not Druggies*. Nell hadn't had anything to give up except him.

Here was her stoner boss and his devoted wife cheerfully discussing what Nell was beginning to suspect was what HR called Mutual Substance Difficulty. And she was finding it increasingly difficult to look at the two of them, entwined and radiantly obtuse. She glanced around the kitchen. "Oh," she said, "I love that lamp." It was a ceramic Joshua studded with tiny lights. "Could you turn it on?"

"Sure," Jackie said. "But before we do anything, you've got to meet the cats." She led Nell and Monkey out to the patio. There was a Joshua tree in the corner, a profusion of Oriental poppies, and a ramada shade woven from vines.

"Jackie designed the roof," Monkey said. "She can make anything she puts her mind to."

Jackie looked at him, her expression cool. "When I want to." The cats uncoiled from under the lounger and lay down at Jackie's feet. There was, in addition to Hulk, a cringing tortoiseshell named Titty Baby.

"Are you thirsty?" Jackie said. "We've got beer, lemonade; I can make iced tea, coffee. There's a pitcher of margaritas in the fridge, but I figured that for lunch."

Monkey leaned in close to Jackie and sniffed. "You quality checked them?"

Jackie stiffened. "I took one taste to make sure they tasted right. You can make them the next time."

Monkey put up his hand. "Whoa. Just checking."

Jackie ducked out of his hug and walked into the kitchen. Monkey shrugged. Nell considered it would be appropriate to step away into the bathroom. When you lived in your own little fortress of solitude, you could duck out anytime you liked. Especially when you felt as though you had no skin, especially if you knew that later, minus that skin, you might no longer like the company of your reliable lonesomes or your knowledge of other peoples' secrets.

"I need to hit the ladies."

"Bathroom's in the hall," Jackie said.

Nell found the bathroom, flushed the toilet for effect, splashed water on her face, and opened the door. Jackie was reaching for the knob.

"Don't tell me," she said. "Those damn hot flashes. Can I come in?" She slipped past Nell, turned on the cold water, and soaked a washcloth.

Monkey looked in on them. "Hey, babe," he said. "Show Nell the paintings."

"Shut up," Jackie muttered.

"What?"

"Sure," she said and tossed the dripping washcloth in his face.

"You're very lucky," he said, "that we have company." His grin was tight.

"No," Jackie said, "*you're* lucky." She took Nell's hand. "Come on. I'll show you what he's talking about. If you like what you see, that doesn't give you a license to nag about making more of them."

Monkey started to say something. Jackie put up her hand. He folded his arms across his chest.

Jackie led Nell down the hall to a closed door. "Give me a second," she said. "This room's a mess."

Nell turned her back. She heard Jackie moving things around. When she looked down the hall, she saw that Monkey had not moved. He flashed her a peace sign.

Jackie said, "Come on in." Three big paintings leaned against the far wall. Jackie touched the light switch and the wall seemed to shimmer. "These are completely different from the patchworks," she said. "I painted them at a different time."

Jackie kneeled next to the first painting. She toasted the painting with the soda can she'd brought from the kitchen. "Here's to you," she said. "Here's to my kudzu heart."

"What?"

"That's what Monkey says sometimes. He says I'm as beautiful and everywhere as kudzu."

Nell moved closer to the paintings. "But," she said, "kudzu is a parasite."

Jackie smiled. "That too. He thinks I couldn't survive without him. You know we Southerners love stories." She steadied herself on Nell's arm and pulled herself upright. "You want a little refresher?" She held out the soda can.

Nell remembered the Second Premise. She tilted the can to her lips. It was icy and sweet and laced with what had to be three shots of vodka. "Whoa, girl," she said. "High octane."

Jackie took back the can. "Yeah. I need it on certain occasions." She closed the door.

Monkey had not moved. He saw the light from the back room shrink and disappear. He heard the soft click. He had no idea which woman had closed the door.

Nell hunkered down in front of the first painting. *Kudzu Heart* in the lower lefthand corner, *JBarnett, 1/99*.

"Did you name this?" Nell said.

"No, it was him. He's the word man." Jackie dropped down next to Nell and sat cross-legged.

Kudzu Heart was at first glance a green bowl done in pale watercolors. As Nell studied it, she began to see it as a heart with its top amputated, its interior black and yellow and darker green. The background was the same color as the outside of the heart, so that the heart seemed translucent.

"Those string things dripping off the side?" Jackie said. "Monkey says those are the kudzu vines."

"Are they?" Nell asked.

"No, the paint just ran. He's always going way deep into stuff. For instance, when I painted this, I had brought a bowl home from the flea market and it was a cloudy day. The light was a weird green, the same color as the bowl, so I painted it in about forty minutes."

She stood and set the painting to the side.

"This next one is just a sketch. When I studied art, the instructor had us draw ordinary things. This is a bowl that got broken. Later, when I looked at all three of the paintings in order, it made sense to me."

The painting was in orange. Again, there were darker shadows. This bowl was low and wide. Again, the background was the same color as the object. There was a black line from the upper left curve to the lower. Monkey had titled it: *Busted*. Jackie had not signed it. Only the date was in the lower right-hand corner: *2000*.

"How was the bowl broken?" Nell asked. "And the black line—what is it?"

"Monkey broke the bowl," Jackie said. "And the line was just paint dripping because I put the painting away too soon."

She moved to the next one. "Bet you can guess who loves this one."

Nell saw a flat black oval against pale peach light. Around the oval, Jackie had suggested the shape of a tall pot with strokes frail as clouds, the pot a mirage.

The black opening seemed to say, "Come inside."

"Does it have a title?"

"*Ghost Vessel*," Jackie said. "He named it. I painted it in December last year on the thirtieth anniversary of his gramps' death. I gave it to him for Christmas. He didn't say a word when he saw it." She paused. "He's a crazy one."

Nell was grateful for the vodka in her blood and for Jackie's calm presence. She took the can and drank. "My favorite patchwork," she said, "is the furious rabbit one."

"You got that!" Jackie said. "I'm amazed. Most people don't. Some people think I'm this cute little fuzzy bunny. I'm not."

"Some people?"

"One people, okay? He needs it to be that way. Maybe I do, too."

Jackie set her hand on Nell's shoulder and pushed herself up. "Good thing you're strong, girl," she said. "You may have to be."

Monkey and Hulk were settled in on the patio. "Grab a seat, Nell," Jackie said. "I'll bring lunch."

"Let me help."

"Nope, it's easier for me to do it myself." She walked back inside.

"What's with the breathalyzer test?" Nell said.

"Job description: no marriage counseling," Monkey said.

"Listen, boss. You bring me here. You want me to get to know Jackie and Jackie to know me—but only parts of us?"

Jackie pushed open the patio door. She set a bowl of gazpacho, a plate of taquitos, and the pitcher of margaritas on the patio table. "Pour yourself a margarita, Nell," she said. "I guarantee you it'll be perfect."

Monkey looked down at his hands and took a breath. Jackie ladled gazpacho into deep blue bowls. Nell figured she couldn't get away with another trip to the bathroom, so she poured herself a margarita. "Monkey told me he took you out to the Joshua wash," Jackie said.

"He told me you love the place."

"We used to go out there a lot. It's amazing at night. Monkey gave me a telescope for our twentieth anniversary. We'd go out and look at the stars for hours. Sometimes we'd take my friend Jerilynne and Monkey's folks and Deacon with us when he was around." She shrugged. "I don't know what happened. Seems like the last few years have been a blur."

Nell thought of the West Hollywood sky, so little difference between dusk and midnight and dawn, and still the parrots knew when to fly back to their trees and when to come down to feed. She wondered if there was a compass in living things, a compass that had yet to be tugged off true north. And she wondered if the bees were going crazy or if their departure was one of the last sane acts left.

Monkey drove her home. "Listen to this," he said and slid a CD in the player.

As Chris Whitley's voice rasped from the speakers, Nell closed her eyes. "I know the song," she said. "It's about an alien. I felt that way a few times during this visit."

"It gets a little complicated sometimes," Monkey said.

"It does."

"It's going to be fine. Jackie likes you. I could tell."

"I like her, but there be dragons here," Nell said. "I know that."

"Shit," Monkey said. "I bet you love breathing fire."

"I do. And Jackie can breathe underwater."

Monkey shook his head. "Women are a different species."

"Not species," Nell said. "Elements."

To: papercut55@yahoo.com
Subject: The King
He is subject to anger. He cannot do Disagreement Lite. Now you have seen this. And still, he asks you for one promise.
m

To: oilinmyvessel47@yahoo.com
Subject: One?
What promise do you want from me?
n

To: papercut55@yahoo.com
Subject: Vow
Promise me you will not throw a bucket of water and fish on me. I already know how to shudder.
p.s. Are you an alien?
m

To: oilinmyvessel47@yahoo.com
Subject: Chris
He is dead. It was a great loss. How eerie that he died not from heroin, but from smoking cigarettes. How ordinary and extraordinary that he still sings to us.
I make no vows. I've never been able to keep even one.
n
p.s. You're safe. We are in the middle of a desert. We're in the middle of a drought. There is no water. There are no fish.

To: papercut55@yahoo.com
Subject: Taxonomy
You are a dangerous bitch.
Etc. etc.
m

Nell logged off. She sat by the window and watched the moon drift above the stained rose of the town's ambient light. She saw how the glow alchemized the scruffy little town into mystery. She knew she now lived in two worlds—not the hermetically sealed bone-room of her mind, but a world in which a woman ate dinner with new friends, talked and listened intently, and found herself liking those with whom she ate, and a world in which a woman and man connected nearly every second, without words, without touch, in the company of his wife.

She opened the window all the way, drew the curtains closed, and lay on the bed. The curtains danced in the night breeze, as she had known they would. She slowed her breathing and watched them. Anything could be a ghost vessel. The Leafy was instantly with her, drifting in and out of the curtains, shape shifting, creature in one instant, a filigree of pink and green the next.

This is how it is for Monkey. This is how we help him see. This is how we help him hear.

The words were in her mind. The fog of pink and green began to grow. The Leafy hovered motionless in the haze. Shapes and scintilla appeared in the fog. A word came into focus. *Taxonomy.* The Leafy became a shuttle trailing a silver thread. The word faded. The voice resumed.

Nell, there is more than one way to weave. There are infinite looms. Shuttle is an ancient word.

The thread flowed into the shape of a music CD. The shuttle skimmed along points that were sound. It cast rainbows. It cast a man's high, angelic voice.

Nell sat up.

Good. You are not dreaming. No more than always. You're safe.

The Leafy resumed its form.

Pay attention. Pay attention to everything. The map will have no numbers on it, no grid.

Nell pushed herself up from the bed. "Why do I need a map? Am I leaving? I don't want to leave."

The map will take you as far as you will be carried. Pay attention to what Mariah told you about finding the map. You have your own trail.

Nell watched the Leafy melt into the light beyond the window and disappear. She sat at the computer and logged on. No more messages from Monkey. She opened the dictionary and typed in *shuttle*.

Origin: Old English *scytel* [dart, missile]

She closed the dictionary and opened Yahoo.

To: oilinmyvessel47@yahoo.com
Subject: the loom
Old English *scytel* [dart, missile]

She saved the message to Draft, re-opened it, sent it, and went to her bed.

21

Nell watched the lace curtains ripple in the dawn breeze. She had jolted awake at three a.m., then four, then five, each time more afraid. She gave up trying to sleep and checked her email. No message from Monkey. Her gut knotted. He'd changed his mind. He'd seen her and Jackie together and made a choice.

She knew the fear. She remembered it, her increasing terror as David's emails and texts became fewer and fewer. Monkey wasn't David. It was 6 a.m. and he probably wasn't even awake yet. She could hear her last shrink telling her she was simply reacting to meeting Jackie: "You must learn to keep it simple, Nell." She could do that. She'd take a shower, eat breakfast, give Shiloh and Diamond money, find out how to get in touch with Mariah, and go to work.

Shiloh was bent over a map on the kitchen table. "Look at this," she said. "Mariah called with details about all the attacks. There have been more, out near the Oasis of Mara in the park and down near Blythe at the edge of the geoglyphs. They told the woman up here that if she told the cops, her old mom would get hurt. It was a tourist couple down near Blythe. The attackers blindfolded them and said, 'Tell people to pay attention.' She wants you to call. Here's her cell. It's okay to call her at work."

Nell dialed Mariah. Voicemail asked her to leave a message. "It's Nell," she said. "Call back anytime."

Monkey was deep in the engine of a pale blue pickup with raven wings painted along the side. "You okay?" he said.

"More or less. You?"

He pulled his head out of the truck. His eyes were bloodshot, his face puffy. "More or less. Let's keep it just business today. Nothing personal, I'm on overload right now."

Nell's gut knotted. "I'll pull the work orders," she said. Business as usual. Yep. Keep it simple. Get through the day, then go home and play computer Scrabble till your brain melts and maybe you'll be able to sleep—what with having thrown the Xanax away. Nell knew how to do that. Her cell rang. "Yes?"

"Hi, it's Mariah. How are you?"

"Fine," Nell said. "And you and your family?"

"We're doing much better. My nephews are helping a lot and that big Mexican guy Keno checks in every day. The meeting is next Tuesday. I'll pick you up at six. I sent you a new link to the geoglyphs. Check it out."

"Sounds good. I'll be at La Paloma next Tuesday."

"See you then."

Nell checked her email. Nothing except her message to herself about the shuttle and Mariah's link. Nothing coming from the garage but a silence she swore she could feel. She took the work orders out of the South Park hat, wondered why she'd ever thought it was funny, and booted up the computer. She decided to take her lunch break at Sally's and check Mariah's link later, at home.

Two year-long days passed. Monkey was pleasant and nothing more. No banter. No response to her last email. No code talking. Nell woke, checked her email, studied his every move, and fell asleep with the *he's leaving* knot in her gut.

Nell repeated to herself every bland idiocy she'd ever read in the "healthy love" books—healthy love?—an oxymoron if she'd ever heard one. *Go within and find your inner lover. You can't be loved if you don't love yourself. When he pulls back* (It was always "he" who pulled back), *step back, let go, blah blah blah.* She'd thought about climbing into the paid-off LeSabre and heading east, but the only inner wisdom she seemed to find was: *There's no off-ramp. I can't go back.* And there was work to do here. She logged on and found Mariah's link to the sacred geoglyphs.

She looked down on an expanse of sand and rock, at gods scraped into the darker earth. The beings were huge and elegant, an elongated man and a creature that looked like a mountain lion. Tire tracks swirled around the fenced in figures. A fierce-eyed old man led a little group out to pray at a second site, where the giant flute-player god Kokopelli, and Cicimitl, who guides souls into the afterlife, had already been damaged by the solar installation surveys.

Nell traced the figures on the screen with her finger. She knew they were not just powerful, but beautiful. She was numb. She thought of Sylvia Plath's bell jar, the way obsession could close around a person and seal them safely and terribly away from the real world. She thought of David's words: "You're your mother's daughter. You'll never be able to love." This death-in-life wasn't love. She traced the figures again, more slowly than before. "I see you," she whispered. "I won't forget."

Thursday morning, Nell opened her email to a message from Monkey. No words, just a picture of an orb weaver spider. She made herself not reply, choked down coffee and a cup of yogurt, and drove to work. Monkey had just opened the hood of a beater station wagon. A spool of thread lay on her desk. She held the end of the thread and tossed the spool through the garage door. Monkey picked up the spool and walked into the office. "We need to talk today."

"We?"

"Come on. I'm sorry. I've been a little weird. I got smacked by some good old Baptist guilt."

"Thanks for clarifying."

"Don't go corporate on me. We're not in some business meeting, Nell. This is real life."

Nell let go of the thread. "You don't talk to me like that."

Monkey reeled the thread in. "I'm sorry. I'm no good at this."

"It might help if we knew what 'this' was," Nell said.

"Really, we need to talk today. I have to know more about where you come from. You have to know more about me." He touched her shoulder. "Please."

Nell didn't move. "Give me a few minutes. I need to go for a walk." Monkey stepped back and tossed her the spool of thread. "Maybe you could get us some juice. I couldn't eat this morning."

"Me either," Nell said. "I'll pull the work orders, get the juice, and be back in a half hour." She paused. "Please. Please don't get high."

His face went tight. "I won't. I wouldn't have. But that's my business. Drug counseling isn't part of your job description either—besides, there's no bud left."

"No," Nell said, "I'm not a drug counselor. I had a mother who got high all the time. And being high all the time is not part of the Mom with Little Girl job description."

She felt her pulse thud in her wrists, *Leave. Leave. Leave.* She saw David, she saw the CEO of the Corp, she saw the drunks and stoners and cops who had patiently explained to her mother why they were right and she was dumb.

"I'll be back in a half hour," she said.

"Hey," Monkey said. "While you're there, nuke me a burrito, will you?"

Nell flashed him a peace sign.

The Quik Stop was jammed. Hung-over street people and red-eyed teens and old guys who'd snuck away from The Wife were lined up to buy cold cheap booze. Nell put a burrito in the microwave and took orange juice from the cooler. Somebody touched her arm.

She turned. It was Danny from Noo to Yoo. He wore beige summer slacks and a white shirt. He'd knotted a black string tie around his neck.

"This tie is actually a noose," he said. "In memory of Luisa. She's gone. She did it. The tie is more than just the right thing to wear to the funeral of a twenty-year-old tweaker who killed herself. It is to commemorate the manner of her death."

Nell started to say something, but she had no words despite all of Elysian's in-service training in compassionate corporate communication. Danny set his finger gently on her lips.

"Nothing. There is nothing anyone can say. I came in Saturday morning and she was there. She didn't make a mess. No blood on anything. Why did I say that to her—about getting blood on the Désirée Webers? Don't give me some woo woo answer. Please."

The microwave pinged. Nell took the burrito out and put it in a bag.

"Would you possibly have any idea of how many friends I have lost in the last two years?" Danny said. "And not from AIDS, which you might think."

"No."

"Seven. Two in car wrecks; one from a drive-by shooting; two in a suicide pact because they couldn't, as they say, live with or without each other; two from tweak, one of those from a heart attack, one because his brain blew up. I am twenty-one years old and this shit has got to stop."

"Dear god," Nell said.

"Not dear god," Danny said. "Not dear god at all. You tell me, where the fuck is God?"

A flabby kid in a Diamondbacks muscle shirt bumped Nell's arm. "You gonna stand there forever dissing God? Some of us like Jesus. Some of us gotta go to work."

Nell and Danny stepped forward.

"I'm working at Monkey Biz," Nell said. "Come over if you want. It's not exactly a regimented job."

"I know the guy's wife," Danny said. "Jackie. She's an astute shopper. She's always coming in looking for retro shirts for him. Hold my place. I have to get my fix. I'm a Dr Pepper addict. Bad."

Nell waited. The line was the standard slow-moving, convenience-store-in-a-grim-neighborhood line. Every customer pulled handfuls of change from their pockets and carefully counted it out. She grinned. "Time for the Jacket Safari," her mom would say. Then they would hunt for spare change through every pocket of every piece of clothing, take the cushions off the couch when they had a couch, scour the parking lot of wherever they had landed.

Danny stepped in next to her. "Did you ever just want to bail? And then, you realize there's nowhere left to bail? 'Cause everywhere's the same?"

"I did bail," Nell said.

"Did you find a place you could be—I don't know—new?"

"Not all the way. I don't think it works like that."

Danny opened the Dr Pepper and took a few slugs. "Then how, girlfriend, how the fuck *does* it work?"

"I don't know."

Danny hesitated. "I don't know if you're into that woo woo Sedona stuff. I'm not. But a woman came into the shop a week or so ago. She was old, maybe in her mid-sixties, had these almost black eyes that just burned into me. 'Do you know about the changes coming?' she said. 'Some people think it is about earthquakes and UFOs. It isn't.' She said she could email me a link to some information.

"I was like *oh please*. But, later that night, I couldn't sleep. The Base choppers were tearing up the night. If a guy is wired from a day of serving impossible customers for minimum wage, that chopper roar is like the end of the world. And the searchlights? I grew up Catholic and the priests told us God could see everything we did or thought. Pervert! Why would God have to peek into a little boy's shorts? I'm OCDing here. Sorry. So I couldn't sleep and I checked the article out. You got a pen?"

They had almost reached the counter. A girl behind them handed over a pen. "You can keep it."

"Thanks," Danny said, bought his fix, and scrawled the web address on his sales slip. Nell paid for the juice, burrito, and sack of ice. "I put my email address down too just in case you want to get in touch with me," Danny said.

He touched Nell's arm. "Really, I hope you get in touch with me. If you want. Or something. Good grief, I am completely insecure."

Nell opened the juice and put the burrito on the desk. "Food."

Monkey came into the office. "Thanks," he said. "You talk. I'll eat."

"Wait a second," Nell said. She logged on and typed in the web address Danny had written on the receipt. A yin yang of turquoise and chrome-orange luminous threads leaped up on the screen.

"What the fuck is that," Monkey said. "I swear I'm not high."

"Give me a second to read," Nell said. "Oh, it's nothing much. The polarity of the earth is shifting. The ozone layer is going to be stripped away. There will be cancer and mutations. No big deal. Business as usual."

Monkey set his food on the floor. "Let me look."

He leaned over her shoulder. "Holy shit. That blue and orange gridwork. It's like the trances. And it's real science. If it's in *Science* magazine, it's real science, right? Promise me we'll read it later. See, because I couldn't sleep last night. Every time I started to drift off, there was something there. It was so weird, so out of line, that I finally got up and sent myself an email. No thought. Just my fingers moving on the keys."

He opened his account. "Check this out."

He stepped back. Nell opened the message.

They are real. We have the human longing to tell Them, "We are here. We are here."

And so we speak our prayers in high mountains…our words are ice crystals that once were breath, gate gate paragate parasamgate.

We pour blood down the steps of our pyramids, it dries into a shellac from which the southern sun reflects, broadcasting a code the old ones still know: "We are here. We are here."

We hold mountain air on our tongues. We pierce our tongues. We breathe and we bleed. Nothing can be the same.

Nell picked up his glass and drank. Monkey logged off and sat down. "What does *gate gate paragate parasamgate* mean?" she asked.

"Gone, gone, gone to the Other Shore, attained the Other Shore having never left."

"Where did you learn that?"

"Nope," he said. "No more about me. It's your turn. I need to know a whole lot more about who my cosmic partner used to be."

"She was me," Nell said. "A person doesn't change in a month. I'll give you the bones."

She felt weary. The bones were stripped of anything that had once lived. She had cast them out for therapists. She had cast them out for David. He had thrown them back at her.

"Promise me," she said, "you will never throw these bones back at me."

"No fish water tossed, no bones thrown." His voice was gentle.

"My mother," Nell said, "was a petty dope dealer and what they used to call a free spirit. I was born in 1955. My father was her first high school boyfriend. He bailed. My mom jangled us around from one weird choice to another. I knew how to steal a balanced meal at a convenience store by the time I was seven. I knew when to smile at the stranger my mother was greeting at our motel door. I knew how to say, 'I'm going to the movies with Mandy,' so my mom and her date could be alone. I knew how to find the town library and spend the day there. In fairness to her, she never hit me and I was never abused. More than anything, I learned how to watch, to remove myself from my fear and watch.

"I ran away when I was sixteen. All the newspapers and TV were talking about the Summer of Love. I couldn't find it. It was my summer of almost raped and almost killed and almost locked up. I learned even more than I already knew about how to watch."

"I watch," Monkey said. "I am always a millimeter removed from the mess. You and I are made from the same DNA." He touched her hand. "I'm sorry. Keep going."

"I hitchhiked," Nell said. "I was picked up by a Jack Mormon family in Utah. They cleaned me up, fed me, gave me The Book and told me their way was The Way, but I was probably going to have to find my own way. They had a little truck garden and nine kids and I spent the summer working the hardest physically I've ever worked.

"That fall I got a job at the burger and shake joint and enrolled in two satellite community college courses. Geology and Psychology. I was going to figure out the planet, and if I couldn't do that, myself. One late afternoon, I borrowed the family's truck and drove up to a place called Muley Point.

"Up there you walk out on huge rippled slabs of sandstone. There are tiny potholes filled with water. You find a flat spot on the rim of the point and sit. You just sit. The light changes. It goes from quartz to pink-gold to opal. You think how much light and minerals can be the same. Below you, there is blue air and violet desert.

"I heard something clatter behind me. A young doe picked her way across the rock. I told her I would never be like my mother. I told her I would come back someday and thank the place for keeping me alive. Later, when things got really rough in L.A., I'd find myself hearing the clatter of her footsteps. I'd know that if worse came to worse, I could walk out to that edge and go into the blue air."

Monkey shivered. "You don't know," he said. "You have no idea what a body looks like after a long fall."

"No," Nell said. "But nobody would have found me till the sun and the birds and the insects had eaten every speck of me but bones."

"Like Keno's relations who tried to cross," he said. "Jesus, you're a romantic."

Nell looked up at the Traffic poster. "Not you."

"And then?" Monkey asked.

"And then, more community college and university and business school till there were no more glass ceilings and I found myself sitting in a corner office with windows in a corporation that pretends it is an alchemist and is in fact a drug dealer—which means I had brought myself full circle. I managed a huge staff and I orchestrated global ad campaigns, all of which were filled with pretty lies. You've seen the ads: a lily out of focus, a woman's sad face, words in a Victorian font. The side effects are in tiny letters. The inconclusiveness of the trial studies are hidden somewhere on the internet—until the shit hits the fan, somebody ends up on life support, and earnest apologetic press releases are issued.

"As a consequence of my fine mind, labor, and ability to ignore hypocrisy and exploitation, I owned a cottage in West Hollywood, an Audi, many many shoes, two crystal goblets, and, for an almost three-month hallucination, the love of the terminally hip guy. I didn't own the scarlet-headed parrots that flew down in the morning to eat fruit from my bedroom windowsill. The birds are the only things I miss."

"What happened with Scrutable?"

"The second-to-last thing David said to me was that I was my mother's broken daughter, and I was hardwired to never be able to love. The last thing he said was that he was relieved it was over because I was so relentlessly intense. I didn't point out to him that my intensity was what he first adored."

"Did you thank him for the pep talk?"

"No. He had already walked away. Maybe he was right about my wiring being shot. I was thinking last night about contacting somebody in L.A. to find out if I am a wanted woman and I realized I knew no one I could call. Nobody."

Monkey stood and walked to the door. "I swear on my grandma's Holy Roller soul, women don't know jack about men."

"There's an insight," Nell said.

Monkey leaned against the door. "See how calm I am," he said.

"Just kind of leaning all casual-like against this door."

"I'm impressed."

"So, while I'm still calm enough to talk, I'm going to tell you what happened with David. I almost called him that dick, David, but I didn't want to stir up any happy memories for you."

"What happened? You tell me."

"I reckon somebody started sniffing around about him. Plus he knew your brain was pulling him further and further from safety. He's a junkie for potential and safety, which makes him a guy who lines up the next chick before he leaves the one he's with—the wife doesn't count. So, he lied, then he started noticing all the things about you he could make himself not like.

"Oh yeah, then there was what Keno calls the SOB factor. After a while, when the shine on the chrome has worn off, it's a case of Same Old Boobies. D-cup, C-cup, all same-same."

Nell looked down at her chest. "O-cup."

"O-cup?"

"Ordinary."

"I'm studiously ignoring that," Monkey said. "Pretty soon, David couldn't not notice when you were too quiet, when you chattered, when you wanted to make love more than he did, how you were too friendly with a waiter, how you weren't friendly enough. Worst of all, how you seemed to have started needing him. And then, he thought that if he just pointed those things out, you'd change, it'd all be amazement and meld again.

"He started to believe himself. You could tell something was up— or not—and went a little insecure. So David started making walls— fuck I hate that pop-psych shit, but it says it, right?"

"Yes."

"It would have worked with some ordinary chick, but you with your Trinity sensors, the same deep down radar that means you believe in the Bosses even more than I do, you suss it out. It gets worse. You start calling him on it. He really hates that. He denies anything's wrong. Then you bail."

"Trinity is the chick who loves Neo, right?" Nell said. "She's Isis to his Osiris."

"Like us, maybe."

Nell felt the wall between their two worlds begin to thin. No good. "Don't try to sweet-talk me," she said. "How do you know David so well?"

"What do you think?" Monkey crossed his arms.

"I don't think. I know. You. You and Jackie. And, if you're such a psychoanalyst, then you know what a transition object is—and, I will nevuh, evuh be a transition object for some greasy muthuh-fuckuh again."

"James Caan. In *Thief. You will nevuh evuh be a transition object in my life.*"

"Agreed. So no tongues go down throats. No clothes are removed. So what are we going to do?"

They were quiet. Monkey reached out his hand. Nell reached back. An abyss between their fingertips began to close.

Nell pulled back her hand. Monkey believed he could see what it cost her, as though he saw the incandescent threads that ran between thoughts and muscles. He wondered if a trance was threatening. "There's more to the David story," she said. "There's the Nell half of the story."

Monkey waited.

"So," Nell said. "You were right. As soon as I knew the walls were going up, I was terrified. It had been years since I'd been touched. It had been my whole life waiting for a mind like his, a wit, a playfulness. I believed he saw me. All of me. I had never felt so sure, so confident, so beautiful in my life."

She laughed. "I am not a babe. I know that. There is a French term, *jolie laide*—no Monkey humor please—that means unusual beauty in a woman. David told me the first time we made love that he had seen that I possessed that kind of beauty.

"You can't know what it is like to not be touched with love for twenty years, to fall asleep alone, to wake alone. You can't know what it is like to have known since I was a little girl that I would always be not quite enough in a man's eyes. You can't know how that scars a woman."

Nell stood up and walked to the door. She was a rigid shadow in the glare. "So. David began to pull back. I asked him what was happening. He told me I was making things up. He told me I was scaring myself. And he began doing exactly what you described. I remember the precise moment I knew it was over. I was teasing him in a way he had loved and he looked up and said, 'Okay, that's worn thin now.'

"Then one night, he showed up for what was to have been dinner on the Santa Monica pier. He told me he'd had a call from one of his field reps and that he had to cancel. And, worse luck, he'd be gone out of the country for a month.

"I looked at him. I knew that if I pretended anymore, I'd lose what little was left of me. I said, 'It's over.'" She sat back down on the tires. "That was pretty much it." She turned her face away. "I lie. I emailed him right before I ran away."

"And?" Monkey's voice was flat.

"Nothing. Of course, nothing."

"Nice," Monkey said. "We could go back to not quite holding hands, or we grab something at Sally's and go out to the desert while I ask you one question and tell you damn near all of my deep dark secrets."

"What's that Bonnie Raitt line about down where it's dark and tangled?" Nell asked. "We both know that place."

22

Saigon Sally's was empty. Monkey tapped on the open kitchen door and waited. Sally came in through the front door. "I was watering the cilantro," she said. "I planted it in that empty lot behind the building. How come you Americans got all these spaces and you don't grow things in them? You could sit out by them in the evening and smoke your cigarettes and watch the children play."

"We Americans put in our earplugs, jack in our brains, and disappear."

"Such a philosopher," Sally said. "What can I do for you?"

Monkey ordered and headed for the men's room.

Sally ran the order to the kitchen and came back. "So, you know each other?" she said to Nell.

"He's my boss," Nell said. "It's Loyal Assistant Day. He's buying me lunch."

Monkey walked up.

"I am?"

"It's tradition," Nell said.

Sally handed them water. "Take your time," she said. "I ordered a surprise for you." She walked back to the kitchen.

Monkey drank his water glass dry. "I'm a little nervous." He knew he was more than nervous. Keno, Deacon, and Jackie knew some of it, but the whole truth had been his alone. Nell looked at him.

"If I don't start confessing now, I might never."

"Fair enough."

"Number 1: I killed a man," Monkey said. "He was a coke-head, a dealer, a pimp scumbag who'd put more than a few of his hos in my ambulance. He deserved to die. But it wasn't my job to kill him. I was high. I made a mistake. He died. His family blamed me. They were right."

He looked down at his hands for a long time. "Man," he said. "This is a soap opera scene. Guilt-jammed-up guy stares at his hands. I can still feel it in my hands, feel his heart going slower and slower under my palm.

"But by the time it happened, I had seen so much shit. I'd seen so much evil. I was sick to death of mangled babies, rich bitch suicide attempts and drug overdoses and drunks braindead from choking on their own puke. I didn't see people anymore. I didn't even see animals. I saw grievous errors."

Monkey's eyes were wet. "I was twenty-nine. I'd been at it since I was twenty-one. If I hadn't had Jackie to come home to, I would have eaten my gun."

"You carried a gun?"

"Not on the job. I had my own gun. Sometimes, I'd get off nightshift, shove the gun and my Walkman into a daypack, and ride around the nastiest parts of the city on my mountain bike with my earphones in. I'd be looking for some scum to take out. I figured I was the Litter Patrol. I never took a shot.

"Being an EMT in a city is a lot like being a cop. They got the power of The Law and The Gun. We had the power of waiting a minute too long to do what might keep some parasite alive."

"Are you telling me you killed the guy on purpose?"

"I'm telling you I didn't."

"Jackie knows this part, right?" Nell said.

"Yeah. I don't know what I would have done without her comfort."

"What doesn't she know?"

"Let's hold it till we get to the desert. Even Keno doesn't know this part."

Sally came towards them. She held out two bowls. "Eat this while you're waiting. We make this only for ourselves. Me and my family, we are hillpeople, like your Indians. Our food is different from the city people."

She set the bowls on the table. There were chunks of dark meat in a clear green-flecked sauce. There was a pile of dark leaves. "This is buffalo. You wrap meat in leaves and put on sauce. It is cold, good for a day like today." She wrapped a chunk of buffalo and put it on Nell's plate. "Loyal Assistant Day. You eat."

Nell bit into the bundle. The outer leaves were pungent. The sauce was spiked with lemon grass and chiles and fish sauce. The buffalo was so tender it seemed more like essence of flesh than flesh. "Heaven," she said. Sally nodded to Monkey.

"You're a modern guy. You make your own."

They ate in silence. Monkey was surprised he could taste how fine the food was, much less swallow. He leaned back. "Isn't it weird that you can have an experience that haunts you every day and now, when you, I mean I, can tell it to somebody, I don't want to find the words. Shit."

Sally brought their takeout. Monkey reached in his pocket. "I left my wallet in the car." He walked out.

"You and he are friends," Sally said.

"More like co-workers," Nell said. "His computer was a mess. I needed a job. Shiloh turned us on to each other."

"He is not a happy man," Sally said. "And he is still a boy. Be careful."

Nell nodded.

Monkey brushed through the red bead curtains. Sally smiled. Nell had seen that smile on consultants who had picked up on every subcurrent in a meeting and weren't talking.

Monkey sat. "You know, Sally," he said, "that smile will fool a fan, it won't fool a player."

"Women-talk, Mr. Barnett. Just like me and your wife do."

"I'll tell my wife you mentioned her," he said. "My wife, that is. Jackie. My wife."

Sally motioned to their food. "You go now. Noon rush in a few minutes. Very noisy then."

They headed west. "Should you call Jackie?" Nell asked. She heard her mother. *All those nice buttoned-up hubbies coming in through the door at 5:05, just so the wife won't be mad and they might get a little lovin' after* I Love Lucy. *Don't ever forget, darling, that marriage is just a racket set up by religions and governments. It keeps the citizens on short leashes.*

"In twenty-four—plus some change—years," Monkey said, "she and I got the *mi casa, su casa; mi vida, su vida* worked out. She takes off with a girlfriend once a year. I hang with my brother and Keno out in the Badlands a few times a year. So, my computer geek and I hang out in the shade of a Joshua tree. No big deal. Besides, my computer geek, may I remind you, is not my marriage counselor."

"There goes my raise."

"I know some back roads you'll like," Monkey said. "And one of the sweetest saddest places I know—acre after acre of abandoned houses. It's spooky. Sometimes there's a wind out there on a calm day. I swear it's all the broken dreams and lost hopes drifting around the trailers and shacks. Open me a water, will you?"

Nell handed him the bottle. She did not look at his small strong hands on the steering wheel. She did not let herself feel how much she liked how much she felt like one of those wives seeing hubby come in through the door at 5:05.

Monkey pulled into the cheapest gas station to fill up. The cheapest gas in the cheapest gas station was $4.85 a gallon. He shoved his credit card into the slot and watched the numbers rocket. A middle-aged fellow in a puke-green El Camino loaded with ladders and painting gear drove up to the opposite pump. He looked at the prices and put his head down on the steering wheel.

"That good?" Monkey said.

The guy climbed out. He wore faded cargo shorts and a Metallica t-shirt. He shoved his long graying hair back out of his eyes, glared at the pump, and nodded.

"Let me tell you, pal," he said. "I work steady at odd jobs. Right now I'm handy-manning for a real estate dude. Me and the truck are racking up the miles. In the last week, the raise in gas prices has cut my wages by half."

Monkey nodded. "Hey," he said. "They—and I do mean capital

T-H-E-Y—who are getting rich off of the rest of US are headed for a big wake-up. It's going down. And when there's no US to shove money in their pockets, who the fuck are THEY going to drain next?"

The guy pulled off his shades. "Call me a conspiracy nut," he said, "but there is something really fuckin' weird going on. They are lying to us. The price of oil dropped. Gas keeps going up and now they want to screw up this desert with their goddamn yuppie solar factories."

"They got us trapped," Monkey said. "And we pay for the trap."

The guy laughed. "We sound like a bunch of commies, don't we? I never figured I'd have to deal with this."

"No commie," Monkey said. "Just a red, white, and blue guy with his eyes wide open."

He climbed back in the driver's seat. "You hear that?"

"I did," Nell said. "It's the sound of an invisible shuttle weaving."

"Whoa. Talk about inscrutable."

He took two bandanas from his pocket, dipped them in the cooler of ice water, and handed one to Nell. "That good old Okie air-conditioning," he said. "Better than LSD."

23

They drove up a long slope between sun-beaten ranch houses and trailers. "Check this out," Monkey said and pointed at a street sign to the east that read *Security*. "And this." The next street to the west was *Memory*. "Who knows what somebody meant when they were named? Who knows anything for sure out here? That's why I love living in this desert so much."

He turned on a dirt road and drove out into raw desert. "We're going to the neighborhood of lost dreams," he said. "You can't see much from the road. I'll park and we can walk for a while."

He pulled over on a sandy road that shrunk to a two-track parallel to a wash. "We'll go along this wash," he said. "You'll feel the lonesome dreams wandering around." There was a ridgeline to their right, jagged black boulders scattered at its base. Tiny green leaves sprouted at the sides of the road. Shacks and trailers seemed to spring up from the sand.

Nell knew where she was.

"I haven't been here in a while," Monkey said. "Nothing looks like it's changed. Let's head for that purple double-wide."

They walked along the edge of the wash. The dry lilies still swayed in the pale sand. "Those are desert lilies," Monkey said. The sand around the flower was traced with circles. "The wind moves the leaves," Monkey said. "See? All these dead dreams circling around."

"I looked into one," Nell said. "It was the heart of a galaxy."

He took her hand. "Remember when the kids are in the planetarium? James Dean. Sal Mineo."

Nell nodded. "I remember. 'In the infinite reaches of space the problems of man seem trivial and naïve indeed. And man, existing alone, seems himself an episode of little consequence.'"

They walked up to the trailer. The pole leaned into the wind. Magic Electric. Nell saw what she hadn't seen before. Dead geraniums trembled in two big truck tires under the shattered front window. *Hustler* and *Woman's Day* magazines lay just inside the broken-out door. "Should we go in?" Nell asked.

"Sure," Monkey said. "Just check ahead of you. Sometimes rattlers like to go into the shade. I'll come with you. I've never been in this one."

Nell stepped into the front room of the trailer. Rodents had chewed out chunks of the sofa's upholstery. A blue recliner was smeared with bird shit. There was a photo album on a dusty coffee table and an old television with the screen kicked out. She picked up the album. Inside, there were photos of dark-haired kids, a late-model El Camino, a family standing in front of the pirate ship at the Treasure Island Casino. There was a matchbook cover from JT Basque Bar & Dining Room, Gardnerville.

The kitchen looked as though the family had just stepped out for a grocery run, except they had taken off the refrigerator door. The rest of the trailer was the same—a dining room table and chairs, beds and dressers in the bedrooms, the shower curtain still hanging in the bathroom, kids' toys scattered on the floor.

"Why did they leave everything?" Nell said.

"When people hit bottom," Monkey said, "they can't afford a trailer, much less a moving van. You see this everywhere out here. That ranch we saw still has most of its heavy equipment."

They stepped out into the sun. "Going into a place like this," Nell said. "It's like driving by an accident and stopping so you can see the corpse. You don't feel right looking and you just have to look."

"Yeah," Monkey said. "Welcome to real life. Let's go down into the wash. That's even realer life."

They zigzagged down the side of the wash. There were shotgun shells and shredded tires that looked like dead crows.

Monkey stopped. "Don't go any further," he said.

"What's wrong?"

"I don't know. Something's not right," he said. "Not dangerous, but more like we don't belong here."

"I don't feel anything."

"Seriously? I don't know what it is, but I've got enough weird on my plate."

"Okay," Nell said. She thought of Mariah's story, of property markers visible and invisible, of secrets that weren't to be told. "Let's go back. Let's find a place to talk."

Monkey drove for hours on the web of backroads. He stopped a few times and they walked out through Joshua groves, climbed up to basalt ridgelines, and looked out over more abandoned homesteads. They were silent. Nell loved the ease of their quiet.

Finally Monkey pulled up next to a cluster of boulders at the base of a creosote-covered slope north of the abandoned houses. He unloaded the cooler. "We've got shade here for the rest of the day." He spread a sleeping bag out on the sand. Nell sat and leaned back against the still-warm stone. Monkey opened the horchata and passed it to her. She drank.

"Cinnamon," she said. "Almonds."

Monkey settled in next to her. "I better say what I have to say now while I have the courage."

"Is this one of those we-have-to-talk conversations?" Nell said. "If it is, I'm hiking back to Twentynine."

"In a way," Monkey said. "But not in that way. I doubt we'll ever have that conversation." He took a deep breath. "This is in the dark tangle. This is Number Two."

Nell waited. She knew what he would say next would make him far more unfaithful to Jackie than any orgasm. She knew she could tell him to stop. She knew she wouldn't.

"There was a woman, a girl more," Monkey said. "She was wandering around talking to herself and she was bipolar nuts. Custer was my instructor for the night. He and I picked her up because the cops decided she needed help, not jail. We let her ride in front with us because she told us she was terrified of the back of the ambulance. We put her between us. As soon as I climbed in and Custer hit the gas, she unbuttoned her blouse. Her breasts were the most beautiful I'd ever seen—to this day. It wasn't just that they were young and natural. I looked at her and I saw my first girlfriend. I remembered myself before I'd become the cold motherfucker I was that night.

"Custer winked at me. He turned down an alley. The girl was street smart. 'The fuck you doing?' she said.

"'It's a shortcut,' he said. He parked the rig, climbed out, and nodded to her. 'Follow me. You play nice and we'll fix you up with something better than they'll give you in the Emergency Department.'

"He told me to sit tight and keep guard. They went a ways down the alley. I could not believe how turned on I was. I was two years passionately and happily married and I couldn't wait for Custer to finish—because then it was my turn."

Nell watched him. He couldn't read her gaze. He turned away and made himself keep talking. "Look, I didn't do anything. But the only reason I didn't do anything was because I heard a scream. The girl came running down the alley and stopped by my window long enough to spit in my face. Custer limped back. 'The cunt slammed me in the jewels,' he said. 'And none of this happened.'"

Nell was quiet. She felt the bell jar close over her.

"What," Monkey said.

"I don't quite understand why this is such a big deal," Nell said. "*If* you really did just sit there with a hard-on and really didn't touch her, then it's just a medium deal. And, if you felt that spit on your face, you paid your penance. You really are a Southern Baptist, boss." She took a sip of coffee. "What's more, boss? If that's all there is to your deepest darkest secret, I'm sure not going to tell you mine."

"You don't get it. I was all the way faithful to Jackie. I had been since our first kiss. If things had gone different, I would have been down that alley getting my joint copped. Doesn't matter if it happened or not, it could have. For nothing but dumb carnal lust."

"I think carnal and lust are redundant," Nell said.

"Excuse me? Why are you being so hard?"

"I'm always hard. I have to be honest, I'm not impressed by much of anything human."

"You're really not getting it," Monkey said. He looked at Nell's closed face. "Where have you been for the last twenty years? On some planet where people didn't look out for each other? It wasn't just that I would have cheated on Jackie. The worst part was that I could have stopped what was happening. I knew that Custer had physically hurt some of our customers—not accidentally. He'd told the rest of us stories about what he liked to do to hos. 'Ride the edge,' he said, 'always ride the edge.'"

"The planet I was on was all edge," Nell said. She couldn't seem to stop her mouth. She couldn't stop seeing Monkey as a naïve kid. He should have gone after Custer and the girl. She didn't want to face that. Even more, she didn't want to say it to him.

"Thanks for the peptalk, sweetpea." Monkey stood. "Let's go."

"What are you doing?" Nell asked. "We're just having a disagreement. People have those. We're seeing something differently."

"You don't get it, Nell." Monkey turned away. "You really don't get it. We're not having a policy meeting. We're both spilling our guts. And I told you that I don't do Disagreement Lite like some whiney yuppie. Who the fuck are you? Have I read you wrong?"

"I'm me," Nell said. "I'm not you." The details of everything around her leaped into adrenaline focus—a cluster of white pebbles, the liminal between shadow and bone-white sand, the blue lines on the back of her hands. That was a skill your mind learned when you really did not want to be in the middle of whatever it was that was being foisted on you. She felt herself step away from herself.

"Let's drop it," Monkey said. "Let's just eat—if we can." They didn't talk. Not through their noodle salads, not through the coconut custard, not through the last sips of iced coffee. Nell remembered how it was to eat something delicious and not taste a thing, to swallow past a tight throat, to wonder how anything could enter a clenched belly.

"Ready to go?" Monkey said.

She nodded.

"Let's hit the road."

Monkey was gray, his shoulders hunched and rigid, his hands clamped to the steering wheel. He had what one of her mother's Nam vet boyfriends had called a thousand-yard stare.

Nell felt her throat knot. All she had to do was touch his arm and say, "Hey, we can talk this through." She couldn't. She tried to breath slowly. Sometimes that would hold off what came next. It didn't work. She felt herself begin to go hollow. In seconds, a skin bag of what looked like Nell sat at Monkey's side. It said nothing. It was too busy watching, far too busy gauging their silence.

Monkey shook himself and laughed. "You know," he said, "you'd almost think Sally wanted to make the point that I'm married."

Nell managed to smile.

"Oh fuck," Monkey said. "You've got that Stepford Wife smile. What's wrong? What's going on?"

Nell shrugged. It was all really simple. David had been right. She'd had a little grace period here. She'd felt whole. She'd met a guy with whom it had been somehow both astonishing and easy. But really she was a shell, and she had shattered herself. She'd quit. She'd go back to La Paloma and look for a new job. She'd meet Mariah and learn to make a new map.

"Nell," Monkey said. "Come on, lighten up. That was nothing. Just a speed bump. Just me going postal. I get like that."

"I don't know," she said. "I just don't know. I shouldn't have said what I said about it being no big deal. The world I come from, everybody had affairs. It was part of the deal. The men were married, had to be married in perfect marriages so there were no demands on them. Most of them fooled around. The pressure on the women was different. That doesn't matter, I had no call to be so harsh."

Monkey touched her elbow. "Come on, I'm taking you back to the Biz. We'll put the Closed sign up and sit for a while. We don't really know each other. It just feels like we always have."

She looked at him. She could feel tears sliding down her hot skin.

"Let's go," he said. "You don't have to say anything. I'm here."

He led her to the Biz, unlocked the door, and let them both in.

"We'll leave the light off," he said. "God, you're shaking. Don't do that. Don't shake."

He sat her in the office chair and crouched at her feet. "Why are you shaking? You can't be cold. It's a hundred and fuck out there."

Someone knocked on the door. Monkey wrapped his arms around Nell's legs. "Go away," he whispered against her skin. "Whoever that is, go away." He felt her fingers on the top of his head. Her touch was cool. "Now I know how Hulk feels," he said. "Listen, Nell, I've got a big problem. I really cannot do Argument Lite. Keno calls me *cacahuete*. Monkey Nuts. Sometimes it's funny when he says it, but sometimes I am a hand grenade with the pin pulled. Then it's just a matter of seconds till I'm not in my body and the world is a cartoon."

Nell was quiet.

"I didn't mean to scare you," Monkey said. "Jackie got used to it. Now, she just walks away from me when it happens."

"I'm not Jackie."

"I know. But you and I connected right away and it's been so easy, I keep thinking you know everything about me."

"It's not just you," Nell said. "I think I'm pretty fucked up. Maybe we're getting too close. I didn't have to deal with it for twenty-five years because nobody got close. That's part of the deep down tangled and dark. I don't expect anyone to go the long haul with me. Easier to not begin. I don't know what's happening to me with you."

"Me either. I said I've been faithful to Jackie for twenty-four years. I have. Yeah, I check out women all the time. I'm a brainless dog. Then you walked in."

"And you looked up."

Monkey sat back on his heels. "Let's take a little more time to just be together. Sound good?"

"Sounds good. It's not just you and me. I had another visit from the Leafy. It talked to me. It morphed into a shuttle, not a rocket, but weaving in a loom."

He leaned into her legs.

Here are a grown woman and man, Nell thought. They are in a garage in a desert city. You can smell brake fluid and oil and a faint trace of pot smoke. The woman and man touch each other respectfully. The woman has just told the man that she saw a Leafy Seadragon in her room, a saltwater creature that lives off the southwest coast of Australia. She tells him it became a shuttle. She tells him it talked to her.

The man listens. His face is calm. Neither the woman nor the man doubt her words; neither the woman nor the man know what will come next.

"The Leafy said there were infinite looms." She stood, went to the desk, logged in, and opened the polar shift article. "Look at those grids on the magazine cover. They look like weaving.

"The Leafy told me I would learn the ancient meaning for shuttle. After the Leafy faded away, I looked up *shuttle*. The word derives from the Old English *scytel* which means dart, or missile. I copied the definition in a message, started to send it to you, and sent it to myself as well."

She took a deep breath. "I sent it to myself because you have become the only other person I can tell this to. And you are married. Then you didn't write back. I knew instantly that you were backing out."

"So fast?"

"Fast enough to have the exit door knob in my hand."

She looked away. Monkey waited.

"None of what is happening with the Leafy is remotely like anything else in my life, before or now," Nell said.

"Or with me?"

"Yes."

"And there are more dark tangles, right?" Monkey said.

"Yes, but not for now. You know more about me than anyone I've ever known. I need to rest."

"You have more of me than anyone I've ever known." Monkey spread a tarp on the floor and lay down. "Join me?"

Nell shook her head. "Not yet."

He smiled. "That means eventually."

"I went cold back there because I didn't tell you something I was thinking. It was the first time I went behind my eyes with you."

"What?" he said. "Tell me now."

"You should have gone after Custer and the girl."

"I know. I wake up most nights thinking that, then I might as well forget sleep. I reckon I'll carry this with me forever. It's a small price to pay."

He patted the tarp next to him.

"Please come on down and let's hold each other."

Nell lay down next to him, rested her head on his shoulder, and set her palm on his chest.

Monkey put his hand over hers. "What is happening for me with you is not remotely like anything else in my life, before or now. I am a man who was divided into compartments. Each cell was sealed off from the others by a watertight wall. I am a mechanic. I am the founder and owner of Monkey Biz. I am the Good Husband. I am the Good Son. I am Wild Boy Bro. I am the undisputed King of Accurate Rock 'n' Roll Lyrics. I am Crown Prince to Deacon's King of Obscure Movie References. I am a one-man World Book Encyclopedia—not Britannica. I am myself, the guy who smokes too much dope, and checks out every pair of tits he sees—in that, I am Everyman.

"All of these personalities got along great with each other. Nobody stepped over the line. Then one day about two years ago, I was chilling in the office and I figured I'd relax a little before I went home. I'd huffed one little toke of my recreational anti-depressant. I had on my headphones and was letting the local hip-hop station take me wherever it wanted me to go. It apparently told me to get lost. 'Cause one second I was listening to Eminem and the next second I was on my back on a gurney in a side cubical of the ER, looking up into a big white light, with my pal Keno sitting next to me.

"Twenty months later, a fierce-eyed woman in a truly ugly suit walks into my office and tells me she couldn't find the bus to Tanapall. Shazam. My brain scrambles. And the Bosses aren't sending in Red Cross Flood Relief."

Monkey took her hand and shivered. "If I do this," he said. "If I do this, I will have to be way behind my eyes when I am with Jackie. I've almost never had to do that. And you must burn this into your hardwiring. I will never leave her. She would self-destruct without me. She's already got her sleepy pills and a little too much booze."

Nell sat up. "If *you* do this?" she said. "First of all, I don't need to know those details about Jackie. That's her business. Most of all, *doing* this is not your decision. It's ours." As the words left her mouth, she wondered if there were a third party in on the contract negotiations, a third party she wasn't sure she believed in, which somehow made the contract non-negotiable. Nobody with whom they could set up meetings. Nowhere to appeal when the predictable deal-breakers began.

"Stop," she said. "No, slow down. Slow it all down. You do not know me. Not really."

"I do," Monkey said sadly. "I'm afraid I do. Worse yet, I know me." He looked up. "What I don't know is what *this* is." He laughed. "This ain't *The Matrix*. I've seen that movie five times. I think *this* is one of those medieval beasts, can't remember the name. Body of a lion, head and wings of an eagle."

"That's a gryphon," Nell said.

"Yeah, that's it. So it doesn't really exist, but it's made up of parts that are real." He shook his head. "Please lie down with me again. It helps me think."

Nell lay down next to him. He put his arm around her. "We're a gryphon," he said.

"You're right. We are a creature that doesn't really exist," she said. "Made up from parts that are as real as the spark plug or whatever it is that's poking me in the butt."

Monkey kissed her forehead. "It has to be like this," he said. "I mean touch, for us to surf that other thing, for that trance thing to make any sense."

"I'm not ready for more," Nell said. She realized she had just agreed to exactly that—the eventual more—to letting the warmth in their hands move not just through all of her, but all of him, too.

"Me either," Monkey said. "So just close your eyes, listen to the soothing hum of the swamp cooler, and take a rest."

24

The roar of the end of the world woke Nell. "Friggin' yuppie bikers," Monkey said. "Probably German nihilists." He pulled Nell closer. "Was that so bad?"

"I hated it," Nell said. "When can we do it again?"

Monkey hauled himself up and opened the front door. An envelope and two messages were tacked to the wall. "I need to skedaddle in a few minutes," he said, "but I want to read these and check out a couple orders on the Fiendish Thing."

The first note was from Keno. Monkey opened it and shook his head. He studied the words for a second and handed it to Nell.

Kappa-man, do you believe this? He's Japanese. This new dancer turned me on to him. He's you, cabron. There was a delicate ink and brush sketch of a monkey with a fish tail. "Oh fuck," Monkey said. "It's just like the animal humans I saw in the trance. And I'm not high."

There was a second message from Keno. *There is something weird going down. Familia. Call me as soon as you get this.* "Now that's a surprise," Monkey said. "Keno and something weird. I'll call him, then lock up."

The envelope was for Nell. It held a reprint of the *Science* article. Danny had written in the margin: *This geo-magnetic shift stuff is the real deal. My sister's a geologist. Email me. You've got the address.*

P.S. Can you imagine this design worked up in sequins on the back of a strappy little top?

i ;-) (That's the emoticon for irony.) Danny

"I think," Monkey said, "that I am going to leave the Fiendish Thing alone. I'm going to call Keno, then I am going to walk home so as to feel the ground under my feet. I am going to take a long shower, put on clean clothes, and lie on the futon in the sunroom under the swamp cooler. I will be using my superb Vulcan mind control to only think about you every twenty seconds instead of every five."

"And I," Nell said, "will walk home for the same reason, buy groceries, offer to cook dinner for Shiloh and Diamond, and use my cold-hearted MBA discipline to not send you a thousand emails."

Monkey tried. He really did. He was showered, shaved, and fed. He had on his tie-dyed soft cotton pajama pants. Jackie was snuggled next to him on the futon. She pulled the pin on the marital grenade.

"I like Nell," she said.

"She's cool," he said.

"But you better not like her," Jackie said, "better than I like her."

She looked up at him. His jaw tightened. His voice changed into what she thought of as his EMT-restraining-psycho-crackhead voice.

"I'm curious," he said, "have you upped your booze?"

"Oh shut up."

"I've been thinking," he said, "it might be a good idea for you and me to cut back on the relaxants, maybe start up a health regime—not so much fried stuff, no cookies."

Jackie sighed. "Don't change the subject. What about Nell?"

"Smart computer nerd. Not my type. And, who do I sleep with every night?"

Jackie looked away.

Monkey tried to slip into the Good Husband compartment and raise the watertight seal. There was no compartment, there was no seal.

"You know," he said, "forget this conversation. It's about nothing. I think I'll go catch some tunes."

Jackie rolled away from him. "Your call, babe," she said. "I'm going to check email."

"Yeah," he said, "leave the computer on. I might beam in later."

It wasn't till Monkey had smoked a bowl and worked on a music mix for Nell that he remembered he was supposed to call Keno. He stepped out on the patio and dialed.

"My brother," Keno said cheerfully. "Want to help me with a little project?"

"Fun?"

"*Muy* fun. I'll pick you up at eight a.m. at the Biz."

Nell stayed in the office long enough to call Shiloh and Diamond, get their menu requests, internet search the kappa, and write Monkey.

To: oilinmyvessel47@yahoo.com
Subject: water on the brain

The kappa is the Fourth Stooge. It looks up women's kimonos and loves to fart. Like Larry, it is hair-challenged. There is a water-filled depression in the top of its head. This is surrounded by scraggly hair. The kappa draws its incredible strength from this water. If the water spills, the kappa is doomed.

Hence, since Japan is a country held together by etiquette, the human threatened by a kappa has only to bow. The kappa must respond with a bow. The water spills. The kappa is immobilized.

Imagine an aquatic monkey with a turtle shell. Imagine how it swims the undercurrents of a desert river.

Imagine a sea horse that is silver that is kelp. Imagine how it drifts through the sea grass beds in the ocean off the coast of Southern Australia.

Imagine the faces of the Bosses are infinite.

n

She saved their email exchanges to her flash drive so she could print them later at the computer shop and logged off. She was in the LeSabre when she realized she had left out something essential. She went back in the office, logged on, and copied her first papercut55 emails to herself to the flash drive. It felt as though she had written them a decade ago.

La Paloma was quiet. Nell unpacked her groceries and set to work. Shiloh and Diamond came in from the backyard. "Our own cook," Diamond said. "Maybe we better think about gating this place."

Shiloh sat at the table. "We've been having the increasingly tedious talk about money. Three adult care homes in the Basin have gone down, the other safe house, and the mobile clinic for street kids."

"La Paloma is okay, just okay," Diamond said, "due to the fact that we became superb investors. The market has changed. And too many of the current crop of easy-bucks young retirees doesn't seem to give a shit for its own generation or anybody else. There used to be charity balls and all that jive rich people keep themselves busy with instead of just writing a check, but even those are fading away."

"Now that the legit agencies are reduced to chump change, the new breed of what would have been *our* donors have begun siphoning their surpluses to them," Shiloh said. "That way they can get tax write-offs and their photo in the paper."

"I know," Nell said. "That was part of my job. To make sure the papers were all over our press releases. The press liking us had very little to do with how craftily our self-congratulations were written, and much to do with who dined on what with whom. Or received a superb blowjob, not given by me, but certainly delegated by someone in the chain of command. Sometimes, that was two degrees of separation." She scattered cilantro and red pepper slivers over the greens. "We have," she said, "either salmon or chicken, feta or ash-dusted chevre, almonds or pine nuts."

"I for one," Shiloh said, "shall be glad to be a whom who dines with you. Dish up the greens and we'll customize them."

Nell left Shiloh and Diamond washing dishes and went to her room. It was not yet fully dark. The walls and objects in her room seemed to float in underwater light. She opened the laptop and logged on.

To: papercut55@yahoo.com
Subject: Kappa, re: Terminal Good Manners
Are you saying that good old-fashioned Southern courtesy can be fatal?
m

She left the message open and put the computer to sleep. She wished she could put what she was feeling to sleep. It was not possible. Not by her intent, nor any others'. She might as well try to put the future to sleep. That option was long gone.

The wail of a *mariachi* singer's voice rose from the alley. She thought of Chris Whitley and his cover of "China Gate." The mariachi singer, his lament echoing across the night; Whitley, his voice now only an echo, their music trails of smoke and tears.

She left her chair, crawled into bed, and fell instantly into sleep. There were no dreams, nothing drifting against the dark.

25

Nell woke at first light, brought coffee up from the kitchen, and reopened Monkey's last email. *Are you saying that good old-fashioned Southern courtesy can be fatal?*

She hit Reply.

To: oilinmyvessel47@yahoo.com
Subject: Duane A.
Good manners can eat you alive.
n

The Biz was locked. She let herself in and found a scrawled note from Monkey. *Keno needs me to make a run over to Yucca. I'll call later.*

Nell printed out the work orders and a few backdated bills. Danny's *Science* piece lay in the South Park hat. She opened the article and read every detail. The earth's magnetic core was weakening. Patches of it had already begun to reverse. When they reached critical mass the magnetic core would flip polarity. The electromagnetic shield around the earth would disappear—the shield that filtered out solar radiation. Minus the shield, mutagenic processes would escalate—kittens with three eyes, fish with no gills, cancer. The flip would occur sometime in the next two thousand years. It would not be the first time.

A scientist had studied lava striations exposed in a mountain in Oregon and found the evidence. The authors' credentials were impeccable. Nell imagined pressing her hand against warm black rock and running her fingers over tens of thousands of years.

Mariah called. "You still with us?"

"I am."

"I'll see you tonight."

"All you have to do," Keno said, "is keep your mouth shut and your eyes open."

He and Monkey walked into the gloomy interior of the Mexican suck-in-the-tourist store. The white fellow behind the counter was in his late fifties. His belly preceded him by about six inches. He sported a sombrero, a mustache, and a South Jersey accent. "G'ahead. Look around. Get a nice souvenir for the wife. Or your girlfriend."

Keno leaned over the desk and grabbed the guy by the pleats of his sweat-stained *guayabera*. "No wife. No souvenir. What I'm looking for is the prick who sold my cousin a very expensive funeral package for her dead beloved father."

"I got no idea what you're talking about, cabron."

Keno nodded at Monkey. "Associate, would you shut the door?"

Monkey closed the door. The place went subterranean dark. "Lock it," Keno said. "Both deadbolts.

"So," he said. "We've got maybe five minutes before somebody tries that door. I know the backdoor is open. I know these streets like I know the veins on my dick. And I have no hesitation about killing you."

The guy's face went blotchy. He started to reach for Keno's wrists. Keno shook his head.

"What I need to know is the name and address of some guy they call *El Mago*. His license plate number would be a bonus. You give me this information and we leave. And, you are guaranteed that the investigation that is being done specific to your son, the undertaker, and his documented internet pedophilia will remain a secret between you, me, and my friend here.

"Oh, and I know about the button under the desk upon which you have undoubtedly stepped. You have a choice here: the cops can be investigating a murder, or they can find a guy who says, 'Oh shit. I accidentally stepped on the alarm. Let me contribute to the Retired Policeman's Fund.'"

Within an hour, Keno and Monkey were back on the road to Twentynine. They had a bag of taquitos between them and a cooler of beer on the floor. Monkey was counting the wad of hundreds Keno had asked him to check. The horizon on their right was auditioning to be a storm. Blue-black clouds scudded south.

"Seven thousand, seven hundred," Monkey said.

"Good."

"Now what happens?"

"I give the money to my cousin. She can now afford to make a down payment on a little trailer she's had her eye on about a block from where she works. She'll have enough left over to feed her and the kids while she registers at the community college for ESL classes. She will be able to work and go to school and raise the kids without going fucking nuts."

"Anything else?" Monkey asked.

Keno grinned. "El Mago will beat up one of his *putas* and punch out his smallest flunky. He will use up a chunk of the product he was supposed to sell and spend the comedown trying to figure out a lie his *jefe* will believe."

"And what's going to go down for you? That is, us?"

"Nothing's going to go down for us. I have too many relatives in this place." He popped a taquito in his mouth. "These scumbags are fuckin' vampires. When an undocumented guest of your country dies, his friends and family do everything they can to send his body back home. They'll pay anything.

"Bam! Some greedy fuck moves in on 'em, sells them body pickup, embalming, casket, shipping container, and airfare—all for about three times what a *gringo* would pay.

"I didn't tell you the details on the way down because I know how you are. You're a bouncy hand grenade with the pin pulled, *compadre*. I needed you to be cool."

"Let's turn around," Monkey said. "Surely, there is more we can do to encourage a sense of fair play and justice in El Mago's business practices."

"Ah, my point is made. Put your pin back in. We're going home."

The Biz office was an oven. Nell turned on the swamp cooler and leaned back in the chair. The chair's back lurched and righted itself. She remembered a yoga teacher who had taken a group of Corp executives through a weekend. "We are each a gleaming intersection on Indra's web. You and me, the tops of the cypress we see outside the window, the window, the light, the seeing. All gleaming jewels. All linked."

She thought of the layers of time in an Oregon mountain. She sat in a tilting office chair on linoleum over a stone floor on hardpan over rock over liquid iron and nickel. The geomagnetic nature of the liquid core was weakening. She searched liquid rock and planets, and was sent to Josh Simpson, glassblower. He had found old handmade marbles outside his kitchen door, their colors still shining, thought of the longevity of glass, and decided to make tiny glass planets and hide them places, first near his house, then eventually all over the world.

He wrote: *I hope future archaeologists will be confused about the meaning and purpose of the little spheres, wondering what they are and how they got there. When I think of them puzzling over Infinity Project Planets, I remember the story about peculiar little glass goblets found in ancient sites throughout the Mideast. For years, archaeologists were stumped as to their purpose...It turned out that they were meant to hold water and seed for caged birds. The archaeologists had never even been close...I like the idea of reaching a totally new audience for my glass— not just a socially or culturally different audience but potentially people separated by hundreds of years from present time.*

A message from the past to the future, a message the archaeologists had not been able to decode. Who was talking to Monkey? How did they know what was coming? She bet whoever or whatever the Bosses were, it would take more than an archaeologist to figure them out. Nell punched *ozone depletion, 2007* into Google. The news was grim. She clicked on a link to ultraviolet radiation. The news was worse. She opened her Yahoo account.

To: *papercut55@yahoo.com*
Subject: *ameliorating the Future*
The geomagnetic core is weakening. There will be a reversal. We did nothing to cause this. We cannot stop it. When it occurs, solar radiation will blast the planet.

All we can do is ameliorate the future. If we begin sixty years ago to change how we live—we, the metastasis in the earth's body—then we can affect the ozone layer and restore a fraction of what was once robust species diversity.

What Monkey sees is the future without our sacrifices. Terminal mutagenesis. Not an evolutionary leap but a pratfall.

n

To: *oilinmyvessel47@yahoo.com*
Subject: *forestalling*
I left Danny's Science article on the seat of your truck. Don't smoke before you open it. I can't imagine that you will be able to resist the invitation to move through these portals if you are stoned.

You need these coordinates before you launch again:
The earth's geo-magnetic core is weakening. It will reverse. This has happened before. We are overdue for the Big Flip.

When it flips, the earth will lose its protection from solar radiation. Mutagenic processes will escalate.

Imagine how the degradation of the ozone layer and species diversity will add to the attrition.

Imagine how humans might not so much forestall what is coming, but ameliorate it.

n

She put the computer to sleep and opened the first drawer of the file cabinet. It held a frisbee and three improvised soda can bongs. "I definitely have my work cut out for me."

Keno turned off the main highway and headed up Adobe. "I want to stop at my mom's and tell her I'm back. She thinks I was visiting her *abuela*. You want to go back to the Biz?"

Monkey didn't answer.

"Hey, *mono loco*, you on the planet?"

"Sorry. I gotta say I got a bad feeling about what went down back there."

Keno slapped his hands over his ears. "Lalalalalalalalalala, I can't hear you. Don't speak no evil, my friend."

"Jesus, get your hands on the steering wheel. You remember that movie we watched, *The Long Good Friday*, how those guys fucked with the IRA and brought a shitstorm down on their heads?"

"They were Limeys. They love shitstorms. My people love love—speaking of which, did you meet that new Asian dancer over at the Totally Naked Girls joint? The one that told me about the kappa?"

"You're a kappa," Monkey said. "And big as you are, you better hope you're a lucky one. Or that whoever El Mago sends doesn't know you have to bow to him."

"Come on, we'll let my moms feed us. Then we can retire to the soothing dark of the Totally Naked Girls joint."

"Is that the new name of the place?"

"Yeah. I find it refreshingly honest," Keno said.

"Tell you the truth, I got two women on my mind and one is a wild card, so I'm full up for rats."

Keno looked at him. "Two women?"

"Yeah, my computer geek and my lovely wife."

"That's it? That's what you got to tell me?"

"That's it," Monkey said. "But while we're on the subject of intimate relationships, did you ever hear from your true love?"

"Who's that?"

"Amber."

"Who?"

26

"Mariah's here," Shiloh called up the stairs. Nell grabbed her bag and laptop and went down to the kitchen. Mariah was showing Diamond and Shiloh new pictures of Punkin. The baby wore a red bow, tiny red sneakers, and a wicked grin. Nell wondered how it would feel to pass over a photo of a kid as though it were a precious jewel.

"Look at those eyelashes," Diamond said. "When she's fifteen, you're going to have to lock her up."

"More like twelve these days," Mariah said. "These young kids are even crazier than we were in my day. You ready, Nell?"

"I am. Should I follow you in my car so you won't have to drive me back?"

"That car," Mariah said, "will hardly make it out of Twentynine, much less to where we're going. Besides, I want to tell you some things on the way over."

Mariah drove west on the main highway. "Did you know the locals call this Death Highway? Creepy."

"Why?"

"You got drunk Marines racing their asses out for fun on the weekends. You got tweakers wired out of their gourds. You got backdated New Agers thinking the lights from the base are UFOs—you got fatal."

They were just past the motel row when a pale yellow car cut in front of them. Mariah laughed. "Here's your classic Twentynine Palms, this guy driving a '98 Plymouth Fury III with day-glo on the back window: *Real Estate Investor. Will buy your poperty or develop.*

"You've got to love people with big dreams," Mariah said. "They're everywhere out here."

She turned north on an unsigned hardpan road. "Those U2 boys got it right about us: 'where the streets have no names.' My grandma never used street names. She'd say, 'You go out past that old rusty washing machine on the corner where your uncle rolled his motorbike into that big wash, thank goodness he was too dumb to get killed.'

"She was a plant lady. She knew every kind of plant you can use for medicine. And you could drop her just about anywhere around here and she'd know right where to go to find what she was looking for."

"My mom and I moved around so much," Nell said, "that I didn't get to know anywhere till I was in my teens and boarded with a family up in Utah."

"I got boarded out too when I was in my teens, but it wasn't with a family. A lot of us Indian kids did. Still got the scars."

Nell kept her mouth shut. Mariah drove in silence for a few minutes.

"I like these back roads a lot better than Death Highway," Mariah said. "There are lots of good memories here. Me and my baby sister stayed a few months with an old lady while my mom and dad worked up in Riverside. Her trailer's gone now—it was one of those little bitty travel trailers—but you can still see the fence right over there. She made it out of brush and rope she twisted from wild grapevines. Things last out here. Sun doesn't take stuff down like water does."

The road became hardpan, cut right, then left, straight-lined away from Twentynine, turned dirt, then into two tracks in the sand. The light had cooled, the last of the sun throwing long blue-black Joshua shadows across the creosote. "It's so pretty now," Mariah said. "No matter how bad the glare is during the day, when it gets all soft purple like this, I think I could just walk out there and keep going. It used to be pretty safe to wander around out here, even a lady alone, but right now I won't go out by myself. It makes me so mad."

"Were you ever afraid when you were alone?" Nell asked.

"Only of people," Mariah said. "Even the rattlers—you leave them alone, they'll leave you alone. Once you start paying attention, you can read this desert like a map. So, let me tell you a little about this meeting. This guy Leonard is coming over from the rez. He taught a lot of us in Twentynine about the songs and the trail. Just keep your ears open when he talks. You'll learn more than I could tell you in a hundred years." Mariah checked the rearview mirror. "Shit! There's headlights behind us. Nobody hardly drives out here. I hope it's my sister Jenella, but we're taking a little detour just in case. Hang on."

She cut the lights, pulled a hard right, barreled down into a shallow wash and out, drove back the direction they had come, re-crossed the wash, and came up on the two tracks behind the other truck. The brake lights ahead flashed four times. "It's Jenella. We're okay.

"So, all you need to do is listen and watch. I'll introduce you. If you're with me, nobody will wonder why you're there."

Jenella had pulled up in front of a white ranch house. "Hey, baby sister," she called out. "Good to see you."

Mariah leaned out her window. "This is Nell," she said. "She's a computer nerd."

"Lord knows we need one," Jenella said. "Good to meet you, Nell. You can call me Number One. Mariah's Number Two."

"Sure," Mariah said. "Dream on." She took a covered pan from the back of the truck. A broad-shouldered man opened the front door of the house.

"What's the secret code?" he said.

"Fry bread," Jenella said. "Let us in, you idiot."

A woman and four men sat around a dining room table loaded with casseroles, salads, soda bottles, and pitchers of iced tea, none of them younger than forty-five, all Chemehuevi except for a lanky guy with an eagle tattooed up one arm and a full-color sled dog on the other. The broad-shouldered man pulled up extra chairs. "Mariah, Jenella. Good to see you."

"You too," Mariah said. "This is Nell. She's a computer genius and a marketing shark."

"Yes!" the woman said. "We need you. I'm Alice. Give me the fry bread. I'll warm it up. Grab a plate and let's get going."

The broad-shouldered guy said, "Nell, we're all starting at the ground floor on this. Leonard's going to catch us up." He nodded at a sturdy warm-eyed man. "Maybe we could go round and say names and why we're here."

Leonard nodded. "I'm Leonard, I'm Nuwuvi, Chemeheuvi. That's why I'm here."

The broad-shouldered man said, "Eddie. I'm a veteran. Vietnam. I didn't fight for America. I fought for this place right here."

Jenella grinned. "I'm Jenella. My mom taught me right, that's why I'm here."

"This is not the first time our land has been threatened," the thin man next to Jenella said. "Time and again, the white man has taken the best of our places and left us with next to nothing. I'm Jones and that's the reason I'm here."

The white guy said, "I'm Jeff. I'm a wildlife biologist. The tortoises, the migratory birds, and everything that they need to survive are the reason I'm here."

Alice came in from the kitchen. "I'm here because my history teacher at the college has been educating us about how we Indians have got too much white man in our brains. I want my real self back. And I heard my daughter asking one of her aunts what we could do. My sister said, 'We've always known what to do. We just haven't done it enough. It's time.'"

"I'm here," Mariah said, "because I have grandkids. This is for them." She turned to Nell.

"I'm Nell and I'm here because I'm a computer nerd and a marketing shark."

"Thanks everybody," Leonard said. "You all know the other reason each of us is here. Somebody—or some thing—is poking around near Quail Wash. Their survey trucks have already messed with a couple of the gateway rocks to the wash. Cesar down south thinks it's the solar power guys. He and his folks down there got trouble near the old sacred geoglyphs.

"I want to make it clear. The tribe isn't opposed to solar power, not at all. We're at the beginning of figuring out where and how we can build our own solar power arrays. We'd be crazy not to. But there is a right way to set up solar panels and a wrong way. Right way is small. Wrong way out here could spell destruction of the Salt Song Trail. And you know what that means."

"It means genocide," Alice said. "And it means evil spreading out everywhere from the damage. This isn't just about us. It's not just about what we believe about Mother Earth. It's tortoises and creosote and water and birds. It's science."

"I'm going to ask one thing," Leonard said. "For now, let's keep our anger here in this room. There may be time in the future to walk harder, but for now we need to step soft."

Monkey should have kept his mouth shut about having two women on his mind. Keno wouldn't talk. That was part of their deal. But saying it out loud had locked it into his brain and heart. It was seven and he was still sitting in the office working up the enthusiasm to go home. He'd read Nell's messages about the polarity shift, read the article, fired up a bowl or two, slammed down the last of the Biz coffee, and stared at the blue and gold web of energy until his eyes ached. No revelations. No trance. Nothing but slowly realizing he was a man lurching out of control.

Monkey closed Nell's last message and typed a name into Google. Sara Townshend, RN. A few links appeared, one on Facebook, another on something called LinkedIn, a third as part of a newspaper article on honoring Vegas nurses. He clicked the Facebook link. There she was, the same clear eyes, the gentle smile, her auburn hair pulled back into a topknot. There were a few other photos of "friends," but almost no other information.

Monkey logged off and walked to the back of the garage. He'd set out a camp chair where he could sit, put his feet up on a concrete block, and look at the southern mountains. Their tops glowed blood-red. Sara had loved watching the light change on the mountains around Vegas. On autumn dawns when their shift was over, they'd ride the elevator of the old Flamingo Hotel to the top floor and watch silver-gold morning glow on the blue-black rock. "I'm sorry, girl," he whispered.

He wondered if she even remembered—the delicate beginning, a flirtation that was barely more than a few words and smiles; the realization that they really liked each other and the promises that it would go no further than friendship, his insistence stronger than hers; his fear as he sensed that she wanted more, that she had begun to rely on him, need him; and then the three a.m. when she pulled him into an empty examining room and quietly told him that she couldn't continue. "I'm so lonesome," she said, "and being so close and not all the way close is tearing my heart." She had kissed him on the cheek and left the room. She had moved on to another job within weeks.

Nell was a lonely woman, had been for a long time. What if she began to want more? What if he found himself with not one, but two women wanting more than he had to give? The sliver of red above the mountains was gone. The stars seemed ice crystals. He pulled up his collar and went back into the Biz to kill a little more time and brain cells.

It was 11:30 by the time Mariah drove them back to town. Nell's mind was full—of words, of the desert photographs Leonard had spread out on the table, of old stories that were living history, of the taste of chili beans and fry bread, of the way a meeting could be run not by rules of order, but by each person having time to talk, listen, and sit with silence.

"That was pretty good," Mariah said. "Especially the food. Well, mine anyhow. And we've got a plan."

"Thanks for taking me. There's hard work ahead of us."

"And thanks," Mariah said, "for saying 'us.' I know we have other white allies we can count on—the Land Trust, a scientist who moved here recently—but there aren't many. Truth be told, there aren't that many of us Indians on this yet. I figure that's our job. Educating. Getting people riled up. Reminding them of who they are. Reminding the white people that they owe us. And if that doesn't work, teaching them the potential threats to the wildlife. They'll go for the animals over the Indians."

She pulled onto Smoke Tree. The light in the Biz glowed icy blue. "I told you," Mariah said. "Bet he's stoned loopy."

"You better drop me off," Nell said. "He's usually home by now. What if he's in a trance and can't come out of it?"

"He's a big boy," Mariah said.

"You don't like him much, do you?"

"It's more that I like Jackie a whole lot." Mariah pulled over. As Nell opened the door, she put her hand on Nell's arm. "He's messing with dangerous things," she said. "I told you that those old medicine people learned from people who'd learned from all the old ones before. Nobody's taught him respect for the plant."

"I'm going to talk with him about that," Nell said. "And if you think it's right, I'd like to ask him to tell what he's seeing to the group."

"Let's see what happens," Mariah said. "Call me tomorrow."

Nell stood at the door. There was a sudden soft thrum to her right, as though a bird had taken off from the sand and flown up past her. She tapped on the door. There was no response. She went in.

Monkey was slumped in the office chair. His eyes were closed. The computer was open and asleep, the *Science* magazine in his lap. His pipe had fallen to the floor. Nell picked it up. It was cold.

She touched a computer key. The screen glowed. There was an unfinished email to her.

Subject: She calls it "Phenomena"
Go to here: http://www.nytimes.com/2007/06/12/science/12frankel.
html?ex=1184385600&en=87e3c4f49cdec94a&ei=5070
Surf slide show
I'm on the seventh pic. I've be

Nell clicked on the link. There was a photo of a smiling middle-aged researcher who photographed scientific phenomena. The photographer spoke, her voice pleasant, her explanations of the images reasonable, as though she were an NPR reporter narrating a walking tour through Hieronymus Bosch's *Garden of Earthly Delights*.

Nell scrolled through the slides till she found the seventh. She looked into an asymmetrical nexus of glistening black and greens. She willed herself to enter, to be taken, to find Monkey wherever he might be and go with him. Her peripheral vision began to blur. Her heart hammered. Then Monkey shuddered and his icy hand brushed hers.

She pulled herself back from the screen. "Monkey. Can you hear me?" He had gone motionless except for slow, deep breaths. Nell put the computer to sleep, tossed the coveralls on the floor, sat and rested her hand on Monkey's icy wrist. His skin warmed under her fingers.

The street was quiet. She had a moment of wondering what she was doing. She remembered the whisper that might have been a bird's ascent. It had been fifty years since she had spoken a prayer. "Desert," she said, "I ask you to tether me as I tether him." Time shrank in on itself.

Monkey's breathing quickened. He raised his head. "Can you see the last gate?" he said. Nell got to her knees and looked into his half-open eyes.

"No, I can't."

He opened his eyes all the way. "Can I come down next to you?"

Nell offered her arm. He leaned on her and lowered himself to the floor. "It's a good thing you're one of those women warriors."

He stretched out and put his head in her lap. "Sorry I didn't bow. Couldn't risk losing what's left of my vital fluids." He closed his eyes. "This will help. The cold was everywhere this time."

He shook his head. "Nell, it's real, isn't it?"

"It is. It's more real than anything we know."

He pressed her hand to his chest. "Give me a second. My heart's still cold."

He put his hands over the hand she held over his heart. "There was one on-planet moment. I was on the edge of a basalt canyon I've been on before. I was going to step off. I wasn't afraid.

"Then a bird swirled around me and held me fast. It moved me slowly away from the edge and lifted me. I realized that the sound of its wings beating was keeping me alive. It carried me down until I stood in that wash next to Magic Electric.

"There was more," Monkey said. "There were these things, energies, beings who watch us. They are interested, only that. No tests. No mercy. We feed them when we love."

He sat up abruptly, his eyes distant. "Gag me with a crystal. That's enough. I need to go home. I need to sleep in my bed."

"Do you want to see the portal?" Nell said. "It's still on the computer."

"Look," he said. "I told you I've had enough for right now. You trust this gobbledegook more than I do. I smoked a little too much dope. There was a groovy picture on the computer. I passed out." He looked away. "That's all."

Nell's gut tightened. She knew, as she had known with David, as she had known the instant she received the call to check in with HR, that an ending was beginning. Her hands went numb. She said before she could stop herself, "What's wrong? Why'd you go so far away?"

"I'm right here. Don't go chick on me." He grabbed the edge of the desk and pulled himself up.

Nell looked at the face of a man she had thought she knew. She couldn't find Monkey in the sleet-storm eyes. He dropped into the chair. "Fuck sake, Nell, not everything is a big cosmic deal. I feel a little weird is all."

"What's going on? Why are you shutting me out? I came here to see if you were okay and to tell you that there are other people who need to know what's happening. Jackie, for one."

"Nell, my dear employee, I believe I told you that managing my marriage isn't part of your job description."

"That's not what this is about," Nell said.

"Then what?"

"I want you to give her a chance to be part of this. And some others. This is too big for just two people. We're not the only ones who are getting this information."

"At the moment," Monkey said coolly, "I may decide that just one person is going to deal with this—me. And Jackie? Oh please. She thinks the things I'm interested in are crazy. She needs our home and our marriage to be ordinary. She needs to be an ordinary wife and me to be an ordinary husband. This kind of weirdness would terrify her."

"I saw her paintings," Nell said. "She talked with me about them. We have to open this out to other people. Mariah…" She stopped herself.

Monkey slammed his fist on the desk. "These trances are mine. That's it. I can decide if they're something that needs to be told to other people or something that's the product of cannabis and a screwed-up brain. They are mine. If I decide that Monkey and Nell and who the fuck else can save the world through messages from the future, you'll be the first to know.

"You're an ally, a witness. That's all. I'm the radio. I'm the fucking antenna. I'm the one who gets my wires stripped. I'm the one with a hole in the top of my head. I'm the fuckin' *kappa*.

"You haven't gone into the trances. You're not leaking energy or whatever—I don't even know what it is—that freezes you to the bone. You're an observer. That's all. You're good at that, aren't you? Watching. I should have paid attention when you told me that."

Nell backed away from him. "I need to go." She turned and opened the front door.

"That's right," Monkey shouted. "Bail. Watchers always get to bail. Listen to me. Jackie could not handle the trances. She's fragile. She's a little girl. I am right. About this, I am fucking right.

"And listen up. If anything gets between her and me, I guarantee you I will pour Everclear on it and light the match."

Nell walked back to La Paloma through the dark quiet streets. She stopped to press her fingertips to something real—an adobe wall, a cool window, the brittle leaves of a half-dead creosote growing in a vacant lot. She stood in the middle of the lot and looked up at the sky. There was no moon. Wisps of cloud drifted above the ambient glow. She pressed her palms to her face. Her skin was hot.

It's true, she thought. *I do watch. I don't get my hands dirty. But the man who just said that to me was not the man to whom I once told that information, the man who said a month ago, "And I watch. I am always a millimeter removed from the mess. You and I are made from the same DNA."*

La Paloma was dark. Nell let herself in, poured a glass of milk, made toast, and sat at the kitchen table. The sink was full of dirty dishes. She finished the milk and toast and ran hot water in the sink. She slipped the plates into the soapy water and remembered the first time she had washed dishes here. She had believed she'd never again feel the clarity she'd felt in those moments. She'd been wrong. The warmth on her fingers, the plates shining in the rack, the scent of desert drifting in the open window—all of it slowly restored her to herself.

Nell finished the dishes and went up to her room. She drew back the curtains and sat in the soft air. She wasn't sure what time it was. There were no tears, nothing but knowledge. She let her breathing slow. It was simple. If Monkey told Jackie about the trances, the entire truth about the trances, he would be telling her the entire truth. A lie could be an enchantment. A way to ensorcell, to protect what would be impossible to sustain with truth.

And the other? The ice voice, the eyes colder still. Monkey was one of two scarred people who'd been granted respite. The memory of a young Stevie Winwood came to her, his passionate voice crying out, "You are the reason I've been waiting all these years..."

Monkey was not David. And she was no longer the Nell that could have been enthralled by David. This was going to be much harder.

She opened her laptop. It was 1:20 a.m. She logged onto her email. Two messages:

Subject:
I can't calm down. I've tried everything that usually works. We've

got to do something about this. You've got to trust me.
I can't worry about how you're going to feel every time I open my
mouth. You've got to ease up. I love your intensity but not non-stop.
What's more: I repeat. If anything or anyone starts to come between
me and Jackie, I will burn it, him, or her down.
m

Nell hit reply:

Subject: bridge arson
It is not in my job description to consider what might come between
you and Jackie. I must consider the bridge between partners. It takes two
to set that fire. One will pour the Everclear. One will strike the match. It
will be an action the partners have discussed and agreed upon.
n

The second message was from Mariah.

Subject: ?
So? A stoned monkey?
Mariah

Subject: It was
and mean, had its fangs out. I'm paying attention. Thanks.
Nell

Subject: Sit tight.
Might be time to think about making that map.
Mariah

Nell lay down on the bed. She took the lightning glass from her
pocket, held it in her palm, and began to drift toward sleep. She was in
the wash with Monkey. He'd just handed her the glass. The last thing
she heard before sleep was the whirr of bird wings rising up and the
Leafy's voice.
The time of ordinary seeing is over. Your eyes have become
lightning glass. You walk into a room you thought you knew to find it

is changed beyond human description. You look at a man you thought you knew and he is gone.

You humans think you know what the next second will bring. You imagine coordinates. Then you are lost. Breathing as though you have at last been found.

Nell came awake. She knew what she could do. She'd make the map. Words to begin with, then colors.

27

The backup bell on the ambulance was stuck. Monkey crouched over the kid. A kid's face was not supposed to be blue. A kid was not supposed to have deep cuts around the rectum. A kid was not supposed to sit up when he was dead and whisper, "*Tengo mucho miedo. Tengo mucho miedo.* I am afraid. I am afraid."

The dead boy twitched with the terrible clangor of the bell.

Jackie snored. Loud enough to bring Monkey up out of the dream. The phone kept ringing. He reached over her and grabbed it.

"Monkey. This is Rella. Keno's sister. You gotta get over here…" the voice trailed off.

He heard a woman's sobs.

"Yeah," he said. "Can you talk?"

"Yes. The cops found Keno's Bronco in a wash up near Landers. It was burned down to the frame. He wasn't in it."

"I'm on my way."

He pulled on his pants, grabbed a mug of leftover coffee from the pot, and stopped. "Everything okay?" Jackie called from the bedroom.

"No problem," he said. "Just heading out to walk off a bad dream. No big deal."

"Old stuff?" she said.

"The usual."

He slipped into the sunroom and logged onto the computer. *Bridge Arson.* He read the message. He logged off and stared out the east window. The sky was pale pink. Monsoon clouds had already begun to drift over the mountains. He remembered a summer when he and Keno had been loco kids. They'd gone out into a wash during a thunderstorm.

The rain had suddenly ripped in. The filthy water flashed. They somehow hauled themselves out, just before a dead dog and a motorcycle tumbled by. Keno had shivered next to him. "It's too freaky," he had said, "how fast shit comes down."

Rella greeted Monkey at the door. Her real name was *Estrella*. She'd made it into a *chola* gang for a while and had *Rella* tattooed on her upper thigh. She'd left the gang, but she figured she didn't deserve her given name till she'd undone the damage she'd caused. It looked like that day had come. She sat on the couch with her arms around her mother. "Thank you, Monkey," she said. "Thank you for coming."

Mrs. Martinez looked up. "My boy," she said. "My boy. I named him *Refugio* because the night before he was born I dreamed he was going to be like a Pancho Villa, like a Robin Hood. How could anyone want to hurt him? He went just yesterday to help his abuela. He told me she hadn't been home, but he had left some money for her daughter."

Monkey pulled a chair up near the two women.

"Rella," Mrs. Martinez said, "bring some coffee for Mr. Barnett. There are *empanadas* and *cuernos* in the kitchen. Warm them and make a nice plate for him."

Rella left. Mrs. Martinez leaned forward. "So. What do you know? You are his best friend. What do you know about that *gusano*, El Mago? What really happened yesterday?"

"Keno straightened some unfair things out," Monkey said, "with the *pendejo* that ripped off his cousin for her father's transportation to Mexico."

"*Refugio*," Mrs. Martinez said. "He is named well."

Nell made herself eat breakfast and headed for the Biz. The door was locked. Nell let herself in. No sign of Monkey. She wondered if he was deliberately staying away. She wondered if he had written. Something had begun to move very fast. The only new message in her email was from Mariah.

Subject: Meeting at 8
We're going out to explore a little. I'll pick you up.
Mariah

Nell wrote back.

Subject: *Moonlight hike*
I'll be at La Paloma. Time to get boots, right?
n

Mariah fired back her response.

Subject: *Goody. More shoes*
You'll want to go to Big Lots in Yucca—if that car can get out of
Twentynine. LMAO. See you later.
Mariah

Nell searched "bees leaving." The news hadn't changed. Bloggers and commentators had dozens of suggestions about what was happening. Scientists guessed everything from global warming to moving bees a thousand miles away from their native habitat. She checked out Leafy Seadragon and found a new report: their numbers were decreasing. Scientists guessed everything from global warming to poachers working to fill the demand for rare aquarium species. She searched for more: *Chemehuevi. Salt Song Trail. Mojave Desert tribal politics. Mojave solar power installations. Mojave wind farms. Marijuana psychosis. Predictive Trance. Apocalyptic Visions.* When the tough felt hopeless, the hopeless googled.

Four hours later, she copied the most recent of Monkey's and her emails into one document, transferred it to her flash drive, and erased the emails from her account. She put a note on the door and drove to the art supply shop. She bought a roll of butcher paper, a box of watercolors, scissors, and glue and drove back to the Biz. If he came in, she would show him what she was doing. She would explain the nature of a map that was made of words, colors, and time. If he was the man who had sat with her under the Joshua tree, he would crouch on the floor and run his fingers over the words. He would find what was hidden, what was missing. If he wasn't that man, she would know.

Nell spread the butcher paper out on the floor of the office. She printed out the emails and the information she'd culled from dozens of articles. She began to draw an arc and realized she couldn't. The trail was going to have to shape itself. She brought a mug of water from the bathroom and opened the watercolors. The pinks and greens and silvers would flow onto the paper. She would not have to decide anything.

She began by pasting scraps of emails on the map, then brushed a wash of clear water over the first few pages and let it soak in. The first colors would be cloudy. They would be currents and eddies. They would twist like lightning glass. She filled a brush with red and trailed it over the wet paper. The color diffused and concentrated, shell pink and rose, the radiance of the heart of dawn. Green came next. Then, silver.

Later, when the paper was dry, she'd paste in more scraps from the emails and the blue and gold polarity grid. She could use Photoshop to transmute the bees, the Leafy, and the nexus into phantoms and mirages.

She understood that the map was only about the recent past. Someday she would make another map, a trail that led to Twentynine. The phone rang. Nell closed the paintbox and answered.

It was Jackie. "Is Monkey there? He went out early this morning and he hasn't come back."

"I haven't seen him," Nell said. "I came in about eight. I ran an errand but I left a note on the door. It was still here when I got back."

Jackie was quiet for a minute.

"Nell," she said, "would you come over? I called in to work and told them I needed the day. I need to talk to somebody besides Monkey and his family. Jerilynne's at her mom's in Palm Desert and I don't think I can wait till she gets back."

I want you to give her a chance to be part of this.

"I'll lock up and be over in five minutes," Nell said. "Should I bring anything?"

"I've got leftovers for lunch. Just bring yourself."

Nell packed the map, printouts, paint, and brushes in the back of the car. She'd work on it in her room, live with it a few days and nights, and bring it back to the Biz.

The cops knocked on the Martinez door. Rella answered. Mrs. Martinez drew herself up straight, pushing a gray curl away from her face.

The first cop took off his hat. Mrs. Martinez froze. He stepped back and jammed the hat on his head. "Oh. No. Sorry. Nobody's dead. That didn't mean anything but respect for an older woman."

Mrs. Martinez smiled tightly.

"Person," he said. "Woman. Oh jeez. I'm Officer Gearheart."

A big Chicano in a SWAT team shirt pulled him back. "Cabron," he said. "Excuse my language, *senora y senorita. Yo son oficial Valdez.*" His voice was calm. He gestured toward Monkey. "*Este hombre es un amigo, si?*"

Mrs. Martinez nodded.

Valdez continued to speak in Spanish. Mrs. Martinez listened intently. Monkey heard *director de funeraria* and *problemas* and *Es ciertamente razonable.*

Mrs. Martinez answered in English. "Thank you for what you are doing. I know of no dealings with an undertaker except for a man in Yucca who my niece paid to transport my husband's brother's ashes to Chiapas."

"Perhaps," the younger cop said, "you might know his name?"

Mrs. Martinez hesitated. The big cop cleared his throat. "It could be arranged for your niece to be brought discretely to a place where she might feel safe to offer that information."

"Yes." Mrs. Martinez folded her arms. "And it could be that those *pendejos* who know the whereabouts of my beloved son Refugio are watching my home and saw you arrive."

"It could be," Officer Valdez said, "that I would write the name of a store in Yucca Valley on a piece of paper which might fall from my hand and you would be there in an hour and a woman would strike up a conversation with you. She might be carrying a Vons bag. She'll ask you a question. You will tell her the name of a man. She will request the phone number and address. It could be that your friend will wait here for you. And I will give each of you an untraceable cell phone in case you need to speak."

"I'll call my niece. She'll drive me," Mrs. Martinez said. "Our friend and my daughter will wait here. They can keep an eye on my home."

28

Jackie sat on the front stoop of the house with a frosted pitcher and two glasses of ice next to her. Hulk was curled up under a low bush. A longhaired ginger kitten played with the tip of Hulk's tail.

"He's new," Jackie said. "I named him Robert."

"Plant," Nell said.

"Yep. I would leave my husband for that guy—wrinkles and all."

She poured them iced herb tea. An astringent scent drifted from the bushes. "That's creosote," Jackie said. "You just missed the flowers. They're gorgeous. Lemon yellow." She set down her glass. "Okay, call me a possessive bitch, but I need to ask you a question."

Nell looked down. "Go ahead."

"Is Monkey sleeping with somebody?" She touched Nell's shoulder. "Please look at me. I'm strong. I need to know what's going on. He's always been weird, but this last year has been the worst year of my life. He watches me like a hawk. He's got a million ideas for how I could improve. There's more—or maybe less. Especially in the last few months. You're a woman. You know."

Her eyes filled.

"No," Nell said. "He is absolutely not sleeping with somebody else. I guarantee you that."

"He doesn't talk to me anymore," Jackie said. "Shit, I bet he talks to Keno more than he talks to me."

Nell was quiet. She could see the soft rose spreading across the black and white words on the time map. She could see Monkey's hands on the steering wheel of the truck.

"It's not a woman," Nell said.

Jackie buried her face in her hands. When she looked up she was grinning. "Knowing Monkey, it's not a guy."

"No," Nell said. "It's a swarm of bees and an Australian seahorse and a chemical nexus and an old Traffic poster. That's the finest of it. The worst of it is that he's smoking pot every night. And I think he's walking through doorways he isn't trained to even so much as unlock."

"I know about the pot and the trances," Jackie said. "He doesn't think I do, but one night I heard this weird laugh from the living room. I went in and found him paralyzed on the couch. He had his hand over his heart. When I touched his chest, it was icy.

"I almost called 911, but he moaned and opened his eyes. He asked me to sit next to him. I held his hand. 'Weird trip,' he said. 'Free ride on the cannabis express.'

"We held each other for a while. He never said another word about it. He's got this idea I get scared when he tells me stuff he thinks is weird. I don't. Sometimes I think he doesn't know me at all. It's as though he's talking to a mirage woman who's standing between him and me."

Jackie picked up the pitcher and her glass. "Come on in. I've got salad from last night and a disgustingly wonderful dessert."

They finished their salads. "Let's take dessert to the patio," Jackie said. She dished up homemade custard and caramel sauce. "Despite what you're about to eat, I want you to know I hate to cook."

"Me too," Nell said. "I used to live on yogurt, jazzed-up smoothies, and takeout. Those are the L.A. Wonder Woman Basic Food Groups."

They settled into the shade at the edge of the patio.

"So," Jackie said, "are you just a little bit in love with my husband? You wouldn't be the first. He doesn't think I know about the adoring nurse."

Nell kept her face neutral. Her staff at the Corp had called her—among everything else—Nefertiti, the Unreadable. "Before I tell you that I am a little bit in love with your husband, I want to show you something. Can we use the computer?"

They looked at the bees, the Leafy, the Salt Song Trail video, and the geoglyphs. "This breaks my heart," Jackie said. "The songs, the children, the bees disappearing. It makes me want to make art again. I can use the bees—or the not-bees—for my new work, put tiny mirrors where the bees once were. I wonder if Mariah would talk with me about those petroglyphs."

Nell opened the nexus. "Oh my god," Jackie said. "Don't you just want to dive into that?"

"Monkey did."

Jackie sat in silence for a long time. Nell petted Hulk. She took the lightning glass from her pocket. "Monkey took me out to a wash with a lightning-struck Joshua. He found this."

"Lightning glass," Jackie said. "Mariah says it's dangerous. It can bring down lightning on a person."

"Maybe Monkey and I were struck," Nell said. "Maybe it had

to be like that so I'd believe him about the trances. Mariah…" Nell remembered her promise not to tell anyone about the meeting. "Is Mariah working today?"

"I don't think so. I've got her cell number. Want me to call?"

"That'd be good. I'd like her to be here for the rest of this conversation."

Jackie picked up her cell. "I'm on it."

Mariah was in Yucca running errands. She'd be in Twentynine as fast as she could. Jackie pressed the icy glass to her forehead. "Do you mind if I smoke? I'm supposed to have quit. Monkey hates it that I smoke." She took a pack of cigarettes out of a sack of fresh kitty litter. "It's guaranteed Monkey would never find them here. I don't think he's changed the cats' litter the whole time we've had them." She lit up and inhaled. "Better than yoga. Breathe into your center, blah blah. You ever smoke?"

"I quit twenty years ago because I had to and I miss them every day. There is nothing—absolutely nothing—like that first drag."

"Tell me more about the lightning strike."

"I think the normal walls people have around them had to be vaporized so we would know deep parts of each other quickly, maybe so we could trust each other in the presence of a mystery. Neither of us are New Age types. Maybe that's part of why I trust what he's learning.

"He's told me what he's being told in the trances. It isn't random. It fits with predictions scientists are making now about the weakening of the earth's geomagnetic core. It fits with an ancient Mayan prophecy about some kind of global transition in 2012. The messages fit with the bees leaving, yuccas growing further and further north, and with the climate of Kansas heating up to the point that sunflowers won't grow there."

"It's not just bees," Jackie said. "It's frogs and birds blipping out everywhere. I'm an animal nut. I pay attention to this stuff. But who's talking to Monkey? *What* is talking to Monkey?"

"I don't know," Nell said. "We call them the Bosses. There was a time I would have believed it was something like repressed guilt or brain chemistry and a new industrial-strength strain of pot. Now, I find myself wondering if the messages are coming from the future—

generations to come, broadcasting back to us. They tell him they've seen the cataclysm. They're looking back at us, seeing us headed for annihilation. They're warning us. He's not the only receiver."

Jackie leaned back in her chair and closed her eyes. "He's not crazy, is he?"

"Not yet."

"What do you mean?"

"I'm not a drug counselor," Nell said, "but I think using pot every day isn't good for him."

"Shit," Jackie said. "When we started arguing so much, I just wanted peace so I didn't say anything. When he's high he's so easy to be around."

"Disagreement Lite," Nell said.

"He told you?"

"He showed me."

Jackie shook her head. "When he gets like that, nobody can reach him."

"I saw Keno talk him down from it one time."

"I think he really gets like that with women—he's railed at his mom the same way. But he went after his brother Deacon more than once. They'd been best friends. After the last blow-up, things changed between them." She sighed. "I don't know what to do."

"Me either."

Jackie touched Nell's hand. "Thanks for the truth. I thought I was going crazy."

"No," Nell said. "Not crazy. Not you."

"Why didn't you sleep with him?" Jackie said. "I know how charming he can be when he wants something. That's part of why his rage hasn't driven me away."

"I don't really know," Nell said. "He wasn't direct. Maybe if he had been, it would have been different. But maybe not. I ran away from a life of absolute logic and calculation to come here, not even knowing I was headed here. My life had no magic, no surprises. Till there was a married guy, a few months of surprises and magic—then nothing."

Jackie nodded. "Once bitten..."

"...twice lonely," Nell said. "I met Monkey and was enchanted. I've never met a man as smart as he is, not just book smart, but music smart, street smart, soul smart."

"Not emotion smart," Jackie said. "Not negotiation smart."

"No. That wasn't apparent at first. That was part of what hooked me. It was so easy."

"It's always easy at first," Jackie said. "Always."

"So," Nell said. "Lightning struck. It melted our cells and burned out cynicism. It gave us the trances."

"I wish he'd told me about the trances," Jackie said. "I would have understood. I'm in a trance when I make art. I've never told Monkey that. I wish I had. It might have made it easier for him to talk to me. I was afraid he'd think I was crazy."

A truck roared into the driveway. "I'd recognize that bad girl engine anywhere," Jackie said. Mariah walked through the house to the patio.

"You two are up to something, right?"

"Could be," Jackie said. "There's pudding and caramel sauce in the fridge. Help yourself and bring a glass. I've got iced tea out here."

Mariah dumped her purse on the chair next to Jackie, kicked off her shoes, and went into the house.

"I need to talk to her for a second," Nell said and followed.

Mariah turned from the cupboard and put her hands on her hips. "You tell her?"

"No. But I hope you will. She knows about Monkey's trances. And she knows there's really bad stuff brewing. I showed her the Salt Song video."

"I trust her," Mariah said. "You clean bedpans together, you have to have trust. You think she'd join us? She's a killer artist. I'd love for her to help us with a website."

She spooned custard and sauce into a bowl.

"Yeah, and she'll be a great addition to the potlucks." They went back out to the patio.

"How's Hanoi Eddie?" Jackie asked Mariah. "Hanoi's an old Nam vet biker, Nell. His brain probably looks like somebody took a welder's torch to it."

"Mellowed out," Mariah said. "I persuaded his doc to take him off all but one of the drugs they had him on, brought him an iPod with a bunch of oldies on it, and he's a new man. That much for dementia. I figure it was rock and roll withdrawal."

The phone rang. Jackie checked the i.d. and answered. "Oh no," she said. Her face went pale. "Do what you got to do. We'll eat when we eat."

She hung up. "Monkey. Keno's Bronco was found burned out in a wash northeast of town. There's been no sign of Keno. Monkey's staying with Keno's mom and sister. He didn't sound good."

"They can't find Keno?" Nell said. She saw the wicked grin, the soft eyes, the huge body she once would not have wanted to see coming toward her down a dark alley.

"No sign of him," Jackie said. "Goddamn it. He lives in about five worlds. Four of them can go deadly in a heartbeat."

"Oh shit," Mariah said. "He was helping us. That probably added to the deadly worlds. This is getting bigger."

"What can we do?" Nell asked.

"We're probably doing it," Mariah said.

Jackie refilled their glasses. "The only good thing about that call is it gives us time to talk."

Mariah told Jackie about the Salt Song Trail, the double threats of solar and wind farms, the certainty that if the sacred places were destroyed, the consequences would ripple in a toxic tide through humans, animals, and the entire web of earthly life. "And Monkey needs to talk with us," she said, "as much as we need to hear what he's learning."

"Why?" Jackie said.

"He may be in danger. The cold he feels in his heart could be a sign. I haven't been formally taught, but I've listened to my aunts and grandma talking. They knew the old people, the ones who remembered."

"What danger?"

"Not from the ones who are talking to him—at least right now— but from how he's using the dope. If—what did you call them, Nell?"

"The Bosses."

"If the Bosses are watching, they can see that he's not fully formed. Nobody's taught him the right way. They'll stop teaching him—or if he keeps doing what he's doing, they'll send him terrible visions. They won't harm him, though the visions will seem real enough to scare him so that he'll think he's going crazy."

"That may already be happening," Nell said. "I found him in a trance last night. He wouldn't talk about it. I asked him to tell Jackie about the trances. He was furious. He talked about the trances being only his, that the suffering they bring is only his, so why should the rest of us get to know what he's being told."

"I'm not surprised," Mariah said. "The old medicine people served long apprenticeships before they were even allowed to approach a plant. There were ceremonies they had to perform, ways to talk respectfully with a plant. They were taught that the messages were for the people, not just for them. Monkey has no teachers. He's a child."

"We need to know what he's seeing and hearing," Mariah said. "It could be really important. It could help us build our case."

"Do you think the feds will listen more seriously to Monkey because he's a white guy?" Jackie asked.

Mariah laughed. "Spare me, Jackie. If the feds don't listen to people who have been here a hundred times longer than they have, do you really think they're going to listen to a whacked-out white man, much less a stoner whacked-out white man? No, I want Monkey to talk with the group because a few of the folks have been taught a lot of the old knowledge. They'll listen for clues in what Monkey says, guideposts we can use."

"If he won't talk," Nell said, "I will. I've written down everything he's said."

Rella paced back and forth from the kitchen to the living room. "I can't keep doing nothing," she said. "I'm going over to one of my girlfriends. Help yourself to more food if you want. There's beer in the fridge."

"No problem," Monkey said. His palms went sweaty. He'd have to be alone in the house and his dope was back at the Biz. You couldn't fool the body.

Rella looked at him. "You sure? You look funny."

"Hey, my best friend's ride is a torched skeleton. He's who the fuck knows where. You think that's enough cause for me to look 'funny'?"

"Whoa, sorry. I just wondered if you'd be okay alone."

"Sorry, Rella," Monkey said. "My butt is full up for rats."

"*Pobre niño*," Rella snapped. "I'm out of here." She slammed out the back door.

The house was instantly creepy. Monkey knew that morph—even his own home went alien when he was alone in it. He flicked on the TV, flicked it off. He thought about calling Jackie. There wasn't any point. She wasn't next to him. Her voice wouldn't be enough. He needed to be in her arms, to lose himself in her soft shelter.

There was Nell, but he couldn't need her, not if there was the possibility she would need him back. And Keno—there was no Keno. Ever again. He knew it. Monkey sat tight. Maybe he could do this. The silence closed round and locked him in with his memories—not blood or shattered bone, not the stink of rotting flesh, not the question in a dying woman's eyes, none of that. Monkey sat with all he could have done and hadn't.

"Jackie," Mariah said. "We're going exploring tonight. Will you come? I can pick you up."

"Sure," Jackie said. "Though maybe I better drive my own car. I've got a hunch Monkey's going to need me at some point."

"We'll see you at eight," Mariah said. "I need to go. I promised Hanoi Eddie I'd teach him how to download iTunes." She carried her glass and bowl into the kitchen and left. The bad girl truck roared. Jackie lit a cigarette and leaned back in her chair.

"So, why didn't you fall all the way in love with him?"

"I started to," Nell said. "Then I saw your *only connect* patchwork. You showed me the paintings. Mariah told me you'd walked him through a bad time when he was an EMT. She said you're a strong lady."

"I must be," Jackie said. "If I lived through that time. Do you know what happened?"

"He told me."

"Did he tell you all of it?"

"The young woman and Custer?" Nell said. "I'm afraid he did. He said you didn't know."

"I thought," Jackie said, "that was just between him and me. I guess I was wrong. It's funny. I'd feel better if he'd slept with you."

Jackie looked away. "He lies. You might not know it, but he lies. It wasn't just me that got him through that time. His mom, dad, and

Deacon got both of us through." She sighed. "Girl, I sure could use a Tanq and tonic. How about you?"

"Oh yeah," Nell said. "But listen, Jackie. My decision to not go further with Monkey had almost nothing to do with me being Saint Nell, the Feminist True to a Sister. He'd go cold now and then—like a cop. I grew up being terrified of the police. I saw him flash into Disagreement Nuclear—with you, Keno, with me. Then when he flipped out last night, I knew if I let things go further, I'd destroy what little of myself I'm finding here. I wanted to lie to myself almost more than I wanted this new life. I couldn't."

"What next?"

"I don't know. I need to keep working for him until I can find something else. I don't think it'll be a problem. He'll just tuck whatever connection we had in one of his lockboxes."

"What about Mariah, what about the group?"

"I'm in. I can stay at La Paloma as long as I want. I'm in this for the long haul. What about you?"

"First, those Tanqs and tonics."

Jackie brought out their drinks. "I'm going to work with you guys. I know exactly what I can offer."

"Your art."

"Designs, posters, a logo—and I'm learning how to make websites." They were quiet a while. Nell felt the icy gin warm her throat, ease the knot that was always in her chest. She found herself telling Jackie the secret: a mother triply lost, once over and over again to pot, once to dementia, once to a daughter who couldn't bear to sit with the shell of the woman who'd been the only parent she'd ever had.

"But it's strange," Nell said. "Ever since I came out here, I keep almost remembering something—one of these crazy sunsets, the way light hits the corner of a building, scents—especially how it smells down in a wash, as though sand and sun create something new. There's an echo of my mother in all of it. It's as though I've been here before. But I'm pretty sure I haven't."

"Your mom didn't bring you out this way?"

"I don't think so. Or maybe I don't remember. There's a lot missing. Maybe that's good."

"Yeah," Jackie said. "I know I've buried a lot from when I was a girl."

"It's no wonder neither of us wanted to have kids," Nell said.

Jackie raised her glass. "I'll drink to that."

They drank to more, to the way there were no highway signs on any true path, no topo map, most certainly no GPS or 911. And they drank to two women in their bare feet, sitting under a patio umbrella, watching a crazy orange sun drop behind thunder clouds; both women loving and loved by the same man; one woman saying out loud the shape of her next piece of art—"I'm going to silkscreen the spaces for the bees, put this sunset behind them, pomegranate on plain cotton. I've got some cobalt satin scraps for the clouds."

"And the bees made from mirrors?"

"Yes," Jackie said. "The creatures need all the mirrors we humans can look into." She walked Nell out to the LeSabre. "Should I tell Monkey I know about the trances?"

"That's not my call," Nell said. "As Monkey pointed out to me when I urged him to tell you, managing your marriage is not in my job description."

Nell drove home. As she turned onto Two Mile Line, something white flickered in a side yard. A white horse had been tethered next to a storage shed. Nell pulled over, wet the tip of a forefinger, touched it to the palm of her hand, and tapped the wet spot with her fist. "I wish to know more," she whispered. "You win again, Mom." Her mother had taught her dozens of magic spells and charms. You always wish on a white horse. If two people say the same word at the same time, you link little fingers and one of you says, "What goes up the chimney? Smoke. We hope our wish never is broke." You never ever told what your wish had been.

She thought about going to the Biz and playing with the pictures of the bees and the Leafy for the time map. She headed home. She didn't want to find Monkey in the office. And she was tired.

Nell parked at La Paloma, sat on the stoop, and unfurled the time map. The street lamp's thin green light fell on the paper. The shell pink and rose went gray. They swirled like a desert river, words rising out of the current:

I seem to believe that I can disappear.

Marginal Irony

You'd look good.
silver wings portals
we would both know we weren't crazy.
from trans- 'across' + portare 'carry.'
The pink bled out just after *carry.*
Mariah pulled up and waved. "Be there in a second," Nell called.
She rolled up the map and took everything to her room.

29

Monkey drove back to the Biz. The cousin had brought Keno's mom home and sat with her while Mrs. Martinez called two of her brothers and Rella. Ten minutes later the cops showed up. The young cop had suggested that Monkey might want to keep everything he'd seen and heard to himself. Monkey had agreed. "Keep your nose clean," the big cop had said and given Monkey his card. "Call us if you think of anything."

Monkey let himself into the Biz office, grabbed the tampon box out of the drawer, packed his pipe, and fired up. "Keno," he said. "The last thing I'm going to do is keep my nose out of this. The cops don't know shit."

The dope kicked into his bloodstream. He laughed. "Git the funk outta my face." He dialed home. Jackie didn't pick up. He left a message: "Running a few errands. Back around ten. Be good."

He pulled his old trail bike out of the shed, checked the Sig Sauer he'd brought south from his Vegas days, dropped the gun and his ancient Walkman into the pack, and grinned. "Lock and load." He closed up the Biz, put the earbuds in, and climbed on the bike. It was a hump up to Landers, but there was a full moon and he, Monkey, was bulletproof for the first time in too fuckin' long.

Eddie hauled himself down out of the truck bed. "Feels like I'm a kid again," he said. "All of us jammed into the back of my pop's truck—except back then I would have jumped out instead of being all creaky like this."

Jones laughed. "Remember when the hippies said not to trust anybody over thirty?"

Leonard crouched on the tailgate. "It's the ladies I don't trust. They sit in the front and make us ride in the back."

Mariah climbed out of the truck. "Suffer," she said. "And we need to keep it down a little. Who knows who's out there."

"Yeah," Eddie said and set the dinosaur down on the sand, "but we've got us a T-rex. Nobody messes with a T-rex."

Jenella pulled up. "Missed a turn," she said. "This one was telling stories and I got laughing so hard I wasn't paying attention." She and Alice stepped out next to Mariah and the men. "Where's Nell?"

"In the truck on her cell," Mariah said. "She's talking Jackie through getting here. She lost us at the second fork."

"So what's the plan?" Jenella asked.

"Wait till Jackie's here," Mariah said, "ask for guidance, and do what we're told."

Nell joined them. "Jackie's almost here. She said to get started without her. She'll catch up."

They sat in a circle on the sand.

"It's better if we start together," Mariah said. "We can check in while we wait. I've got news that isn't good. Jackie already knows. Keno's disappeared. His family found his truck burnt out up near Landers."

Eddie shook his head. "It's like the old folks told us: this is war."

Nell had walked away from the others. She sat on the edge of the wash. The full moon cast long black shadows on the gleaming sand. A dark shape crept along the wash and turned its head. Eyes shone silver-yellow. She was surprised she wasn't afraid. The silence was flawless, the air sweet, the only human light the phosphorescent glow hovering over the Base.

She looked behind her. Her tracks were as clear as they'd have been in daylight. The scent of burning pine drifted around her. Leonard had lit resin in a little clay bowl. The others had washed the smoke over each other and Nell. She remembered her mother lighting a cone of piñon incense. "Someday," she had said, "you'll smell pine smoke and you'll remember the night we slept near the Chama River." She'd set the incense on the sand in front of them, wrapped Nell and herself in the old threadbare sleeping bag, and held her till a crescent moon had risen from the black mountains.

Piñon, sandalwood, Tibetan incense; the Chama, the Missouri River, the time they'd found a ramshackle picnic ground near the Gila in Arizona—maybe there were trails everywhere, of scent, of water, intersections of light and weather, trails of touch: the way warm sandstone felt against a girl's palm—or the satin of desert chert held to a woman's lips.

Nell heard footsteps. Mariah sat down next to her. "In the old days, my people lived outdoors most of the time," she said. "They knew how to make a temporary hut if they needed it from branches and brush. Too many of us have lost that knowledge, not so much in our minds, as in our hands—where we need it."

"My mother taught me how to always find a place to sleep," Nell said. "We had a couple of old sleeping bags and pillows. She said that was like having our own bedroom in our own house."

"Wasn't it dangerous?"

"It was easier back then," Nell said. "We were never hassled, even though we were on the road most of the time." She was grateful Mariah wasn't asking about her dad.

"Is your mother still with us?" Mariah said.

"Yes."

"Is she here in Twentynine?"

"No," Nell said.

"Do you wish she were?"

"I'm not sure. I keep having this feeling that she and I might have been here before. I told Jackie that something—a Joshua tree shadow, hearing doves, the way light ribbons across the tops of the mountains—moves in my cells. At first it was weird. Now it's happening so often that I'm just curious."

"Can't you ask your mom if you and she traveled through here?"

"She wouldn't be able to tell me. She's in a memory unit in a nursing home in Long Beach," Nell said. "I haven't seen her in nearly ten years."

Mariah shook her head. "I'm so sad for you."

"I wouldn't let myself feel sad about her—till now. I didn't let myself feel anything about anything for a long time, then all I could feel was shame—and embarrassing amounts of self-pity. So I stayed away. I haven't told anyone but you and Jackie about this."

"Do you miss her?"

"Not really. There were good times when I was little, more than a few, but most of the time she was so stoned I felt like her mom."

"One of my sisters," Mariah said, "is an alcoholic. Jenella and I took turns raising her kids. We did the best we could, but those kids are hurt. It doesn't always show, but I can tell."

"I'm not a kid anymore," Nell said.

Mariah nodded. They were quiet for a while.

"I need to tell you something," Mariah said, "that no one else knows. I can tell you because you're not one of us. And maybe because you told me about your mother. About feeling ashamed.

"I don't want this secret anymore. It's too heavy for one person to carry. The men who hit me weren't white. They were Indians. They were my own people. They used the Chemehuevi word for granddaughter. I should tell the others, but I'm afraid to. I'm afraid of what it could set off between my people. Like Eddie said, 'This is war.' And some of my people have joined the enemy." She shook her head.

A shadow slipped past them. "Get down in the wash," Leonard whispered. "You know where. Fast."

Mariah grabbed Nell's hand. "Just follow me, quiet as you can."

Leonard, Jenella, and the others had tucked themselves into a cluster of boulders. Mariah and Nell slipped in next to them.

"Listen," Leonard whispered.

Men's voices ratcheted in the night air. "What the fuck? I could have sworn I saw somebody here."

Somebody laughed. "You're paranoid, Buckley. You gotta lay off the wacky weed. It's just kids. Check this out. Somebody's out there somewhere having himself a piece of ass."

"Somebodys. There's two trucks over here."

Eddie winked at Jones. Jones raised his right fist in the old power sign.

"Fuck sake, Buckley," the guy said. "We ought to call you Fuckley. Next time you call us with a terrorist sighting, make sure you haven't smoked a bowl before you decide to play ranger. I'm not going to tell the boss this time, but do not screw up again. This isn't a game."

Two truck engines roared, then faded into a whine and disappeared.

Eddie and Jones stood up. "It's now official. We are the brains of this organization."

"What?" Mariah said. "No way."

They made their way up the side of the wash and gathered at the back of Eddie's truck.

"What happened?" Mariah said.

Leonard laughed. "You know how Jones has that super-vision?"

"Yeah," Jenella said. "Especially for the women."

"No," Eddie said, "seriously. He spotted a light way off up the road. I couldn't see a damn thing, but he told me to do something."

"So," Jenella said, "Eddie rolled the window down in your truck, Mariah, and tossed something in on the seat and we took off down into the wash."

"I don't get it," Mariah said. "What'd he toss into the truck?"

"Two empty packs of Trojans," Jones said. "And it's a good thing his moms wasn't here."

Monkey peddled up Avalon Road to Winters, made the quick turn onto Landers, and headed north. His chest ached, his breath was fire in his lungs. "Leave me alone, Bosses," he muttered. "No fuckin' cold heart. No space launch. I'm fuckin' here—on a road I know like my wife's body." He cranked the volume on the Walkman. "You can't get to me, you can't get past James Brown screaming in my ears. This is mine."

Orange flares burst in the eastern sky. Explosions echoed off the mountains. "You can't scare me, you boy soldiers," Monkey said. "I know what you are. You're not from outer space. You're nothing but humans practicing how to kill each other."

Then there was James screaming about a man having to go back to the crossroads, Monkey's leg muscles howling. Nothing but music and pain and a loss bigger than the huge black sky. The tape in the Walkman jammed. "Fuck you," Monkey said. He pulled the plugs out of his ears. "Fuck everything." Nuclear glare blasted him. He swerved off the road into the sand. The bike toppled. He slammed onto the ground. "Keno," he whispered. "Keno. Where the fuck are you? I can't do this alone."

The stars raced toward each other, coalesced, burned down into his eyes. There were voices from far away.

"Did I hit him?"

"No, he veered off. He's over there."

"He's screaming. I must have hit him."

"No, he's okay. He's either drunk, tripping, or crazy. Call 911."

The light swallowed the voices and Monkey was gone, out toward the spinning rods.

Mariah had dropped Nell off at home. Nell unrolled the time map and went to work. The stream of color had shifted from rose to green to tourmaline to a smear of faintest gray over the words: *if anything or anyone starts to come between me and Jackie, I will burn it, her, or him down.* The map was finished. She left it on the floor to dry, undressed, and lay down on the bed.

She closed her eyes. A soft drift of air from the window cooled her naked body. The withered orange and the lightning glass lay next to her laptop. In the blurred light of the full moon, it could have been an altar. When the Leafy began to speak, she was prepared.

There was no solace revealed, no coded message of a sweet future. There was only beauty and astonishment, humor and tenderness, and the immutable: a rock, a whirlpool, and no way in between. Instead, a desert wash curved forward, gleaming silver.

Nell got out of bed, turned on the light, sat in front of the time map, and painted a silver moon melting into the gray, its radiance washing forward into what couldn't be known.

The emergency doc ran Monkey through enough tests to know there was no serious damage and sent him home a little after ten. The EMT had stashed his bike next to him in the ambulance and left it at the ER desk along with his gun. "Hey Monkey," the triage nurse said, "you're lucky you got a permit. You tell Jackie I said she needs to put that piece in the freezer…maybe you, too."

Monkey saluted. "Yes, ma'am."

Monkey wheeled the bike out past the cold green light of the parking lot security lamps into the sweet wash of moonlight. He rode down the side road to Death Highway. He couldn't remember ever feeling so tired. The thirteen miles to Twentynine felt like thirty. All he wanted was to crawl into his bed between Jackie and Hulk and sleep for a year. He had one thing to do before he got home.

Later, he turned up his street. Jackie sat on the front stoop. She held up a cup. "Want me to nuke you some coffee, babe?"

Monkey dropped the bike to the driveway and sat next to her. "No coffee. I don't know if I'll sleep as it is."

"Leeann called from Emergency," Jackie said and held out her hand. "I'll take the gun."

"No gun. I tossed it away out by the hospital."

They sat in silence. By the full moon's light, Monkey could see every shining creosote, yucca, and boulder in the yard. Hulk pushed the screen door open and crouched next to them. Jackie petted his big head. "We're okay, buddy," she said. "At least for now." Monkey watched the subtle shifts in the moonlight, the creosote's lacy shadows on the sand.

"I went to a meeting tonight," Jackie said. "Nell, a wildlife guy, Mariah, and a few other Chemehuevis. We're going to stop the solar plants. They want my art, Monkey. I can already see the website for the group. There is a Joshua growing out of a spiral. There are ugly ripples moving toward them. We don't even have a name yet, but I can already see the colors of the sky behind the Joshua."

"About time," Monkey said.

"Excuse me?" Jackie said. "We've got a few things to straighten out. The first one is that my art is my business."

For the second time that night, Monkey saluted. Jackie laughed. "Come on, Monkeyboy, let's get some sleep."

Jackie woke later to Monkey's face burrowed into her neck. "Please hold me," he said. "Just hold me."

She slid her arm under his trembling shoulders. "I had a nightmare," he said. "I went into the sunroom to try to sleep. I knew I probably couldn't."

Jackie smoothed back his hair and kissed the top of his head. "I fired up a bowl so I could sleep," he said. "It didn't work. I lay there drifting in and out of time. It wasn't a trance." He fell silent. "I mean a dope blackout."

"I know about the trances," Jackie said. "We'll talk about it later."

"Do you think I'm crazy? Do you think I'm a guy in some mid-life crisis psycho episode?"

"No," Jackie said. "I know you aren't. But this last year, I haven't known who you are." She expected him to pull away from her body. She waited for the finger jabbed in her face and accusations rattling like machine gun fire. There were none.

"I don't know who I am," Monkey said. "Do you know about Nell, too?"

"Yes. She was here. We talked woman talk."

"We didn't fuck. I swear we didn't fuck."

Jackie laughed. "Guys. They're hopeless."

"Ah shit," he said. "What in sweet Jesus' name is happening to me? To us? To everything?"

"I don't know," Jackie said. "What was the nightmare?"

"I was sitting on the floor in the gibbon lair. I was filthy. I stunk. My hair was tangled worse than a street bum's. My fingernails were long and broken. I looked like fuckin' Howard Hughes. All the pictures in the family collage were torn to shreds. All my mix CDs had been shattered. Hulk was chopped into pieces. You were gone.

"Somebody knocked on the front door and opened it. It was Deacon. He didn't seem shocked. He walked in and started to talk to me. I could not understand a word he said. He spoke English, but it might as well have been Chinese. I knew I had gone completely insane."

He pulled back and looked at her. "I am so scared I'm going in that direction. Disagreement Nuclear happened with Nell night before last. I got lost. Rage. I heard things and saw things, terrible things. It wasn't a trance." He flinched. "God, I am so tired."

Jackie pulled herself up on the pillows. "I don't know what's happened between you and me and I sure as shit don't know what the trances are about, but I'm not leaving. You're not going to wake up crazy and find me gone."

"And Nell," he said. "What about Nell and me?"

"That," Jackie said, "will be up to her."

30

The Biz was locked. Nell let herself in and sat in the quiet office. A pipe and the tampon box lay in front of the computer. The box was empty. There were three invoices in the South Park hat. She logged on and entered them into the spreadsheet.

She checked her email. Two messages sent early in the morning.

Subject: late meeting
Leonard has to drive over, so we're at my house at 9. Diamond and
Shiloh know the address. CU.
Mariah

Nell wrote back that she'd be there. The second message was from
an unknown address.

OKeefecat52@msn.com
Subject: What women know
He knows.
What comes next nobody knows.
Jackie

Nell hit Reply:

Subject: Sol y Sombre
These aren't my words. They're from a poem by Juan Ramon
Jimenez:
"What an immense rip
in my life and in all things,
in order to be with my entire self,
in everything:
in order to never cease being,
with my entire self, in everything."
Nell

She had believed that she and Monkey were in everything, that
they were being given information from a vast network that held
the simple rules to bring the bees home. She clicked on the Mayan
Prophecies and considered the nature of wishful mysticism—this
world is fucked, an instant transformation will fix it; no sacrifice
or effort on anyone's part required; you can keep on living just as
you have, grasping and glutted. She re-read the *Science* article. As
she studied the radiant blue and orange geomagnetic tangle, she

understood without question that there are phenomena over which humans have no control. The rules *weren't* simple. And to live by them would undermine the world that most Americans believed was theirs.

She sent the articles to Jackie and opened the Blythe Intaglio images. A stone giant lay across the desert, his body drawn with lines of rocks, his arm cross-hatched with ORV tracks. She remembered the delicate tracery around the desert lily, how wind and leaf had made a perfect circle. She touched the outlines of the giant. "I'll come see you some day," she said, "and feel the sun hammering me to my knees. For now, the battle is here."

The office door opened. "It's me." Monkey walked past Nell into the garage. "I'll be back in. I've got to check the weld job on the VW."

"Do you want coffee?" Nell asked.

"Sure."

She put the computer to sleep, made a fresh pot of coffee, and sat down. Her hands felt heavy. There was nothing for them to do. She wanted to run, but her running days were over. Monkey came in and sat on the tires. "Hey," he said.

"Hey."

"You talk to Jackie this morning?"

"She emailed me," Nell said.

Monkey pulled off the head rag and wiped his eyes.

"Full up?" Nell said.

"Close to exploding."

They fell silent. The coffee maker hissed. "You want a cup?" Monkey asked.

"I'm okay. So, Keno?"

"No sign of him."

"Oh, Monkey," Nell said. She wanted to wrap her arms around him. He hunched his shoulders. "Yeah, but if he was here, he'd congratulate me on being the Guinness Book World Record fuck-up with women."

"Takes more than one to fuck up," Nell said. "But it didn't feel like fucking up. What we had felt like the most sane thing I've ever done."

"Didn't? Had? Past tense?"

"I'm afraid so."

"We didn't really do anything," Monkey said.

"I clearly deluded myself," Nell said. "I thought you were smart, not just intellect smart, but soul smart. 'We didn't do anything.' Are you serious? You sound like a teenage boy."

He poured himself a cup of coffee. "I feel more like an eight-year-old. Or maybe eighty. Nell, it was real. It was."

"Was? Past tense?" She smiled.

"Dragon Lady smile," Monkey said. "I forgot how businesslike you can be."

"I'm not businesslike. I'm in shock."

"Look, we can just go back to being who we were—funny, fascinated, brain melds, almost all of it," he said. "Jackie won't really mind."

"I can't."

"Is it Jackie?"

"She's part of it," Nell said. "But more of it is what I felt two nights ago when you told me the trances were all yours. 'You're an observer,' you said. 'You're good at that, aren't you? Nell watches.'"

"I didn't say that."

"Monkey, I'm a woman. We remember everything. You're a stoner. They forget what they want to forget."

"I know what I said and didn't say." His eyes had gone cold. "So tell me, how did you feel when I apparently innocently said something that you freaked out over?"

"I felt that you were gone. What we had been was gone. Whatever had been carrying us had pulled the plug," Nell said. "We were a team. You were the antenna. I was whatever amps the signals down. You were like that fetus floating in space in *2001*—until you opened up to me. Then you and who knows what else made me part of it."

"You're still part of it," Monkey said. "Jesus, Nell, cut the drama. You're making too big a deal out of this. I was stoned. I needed space. You were acting like an insecure girlfriend. I was being honest. You're the one who told me I could be honest with you, right?" His voice was a razor.

Nell suddenly remembered an Elysian communications trainer telling the managers that some people use the excuse of "honest communication" to be cruel. David. Monkey. Herself. She felt as though she was on the edge of an abyss. She remembered the year after David went cold. The death-in-life. Never again.

"Why do women always have to jack up the intensity?" Monkey said. "Are you doing this to—I don't know—maybe stake some kind of claim on me? I told you. Anything that gets between me and Jackie is fucking doomed."

"No," Nell said. "I'm not. It's just over. I learned something last year when I was fired. When something's over, it's over." She realized that she had stepped off the edge of the cliff. There wasn't going to be any pretty saying on a sappy inspirational poster to buoy her up. And she could only hope that what lay below wouldn't kill her.

"One last chance, Nell," Monkey said. "I've got the Everclear right here. What we have is damn weird and wonderful. Part of it is your independence. That's what I like about it. I've never felt this close to anybody. But I've got one little girl needing me. I don't need another one. *No mas.*"

Nell stood up. "I have to go. You can put down the Everclear. It's nothing but a metaphor."

He shook his head. "You ever see a dog do this? Shake off pain? You ever see that?"

Nell was quiet.

"Now what do I do?" Monkey asked. "Am I supposed to fire you?"

"It's not necessary. I quit. And what you can do? You could stop smoking pot whenever you can't handle something. It's going to turn on you. The trances are going to go bad. You've never been trained to explore what and where you've been traveling."

"What? Who gave you a crystal ball?"

"Mariah told Jackie and me about the danger you're in."

Monkey stood up and walked to the door. "Mariah? I ought to just get the fuck out of this hallucinogenic town. It's like something in a bad trip. Twentynine is so full of senile old desert rats, burnt tweakers, woo woo Indians, and freaked out yuppies running away from reality that nobody can string two logical sentences together, much less thoughts.

"This is some wannabe Injun woo woo, Nell! I'm a redneck in case you haven't noticed, a former Holy Roller boy. But I'll bite. What did Mariah say and how come she's an expert on my brain and smoking habits?"

"Ask Jackie. I need to get out of here."

"Now?"

"Now."

"Nell," Monkey said.

"What?"

"Are you staying in Twentynine? Am I going to have to deal with seeing you every fucking where?"

"I don't know yet. I've got some business to attend to."

"Nell."

"Oh for chrissake, what?"

"I'm sorry."

Nell opened the door. "I am too, Monkey. I really am."

She stepped out into a razor-edge glare that cut into what was left of her composure. She didn't want to go back to her room at La Paloma. She didn't want to talk with Shiloh or Diamond or anybody else. All she wanted was to go back out to the wash where Mariah had told her about the Song Trail. It was more than wanting. She had to go. One hundred and eight degrees or not.

She looked at the LeSabre. "You and me, pal," she said. "I don't know if we can do this, but we're going to try." She drove to Stater's, bought three gallons of water, an orange, and a cheese sandwich. She'd find a hat at Noo to Yoo.

Danny was crouched on the floor of the display window. "Look," he said. "What do you think?"

"I think a recreation of the front of the MGM Grand in miniature in costume jewelry is a work of true vision," Nell said.

"It's an offering for Luisa's sad little spirit, so now she can have all the fun she didn't have in this world. I have no idea how a person can miss such an irritating human being."

"I may be in the same position," Nell said.

"Ooooooh, gossip. Dish it, girl."

"You first. Did the suit sell?"

Danny stepped out of the window display. "I told you it would— to an earnest professor of Gender Studies at UCLA. She thought it might help her get tenure. Poor deluded creature."

"I need a sunhat," Nell said.

"We just traded for this snappy number," Danny said. He handed

Nell a tan broad-brimmed floppy hat. "Now the gossip. Right now."

"I lost my job."

"I know that. Jackie was in earlier."

"Did she tell you details?"

"No. She is always the soul of discretion. But I can guess. Did you disagree with Monkey?"

"I did."

"And it wasn't lite?"

"Jesus, Danny," Nell said. "Does everybody know everything in this town?"

"Welcome to the Morongo Hotline, sweetheart. My business is your business is everybody's business—five minutes after you tell a secret."

"That means there are no secrets in Twentynine."

"Absolutely. I have a fabulous idea. Let's eat lunch at Sally's—my treat—and you can unburden your heart."

"Actually," Nell said, "disagreeing with Monkey unburdened my heart—I lie. I'd say that I'm too heartbroken to talk about it, but I can't turn down free food. It's a childhood habit."

"Even more to talk about. Wait till you hear about my fun with mom and dad. I have a feeling that a woman of mystery is about to tell me who did it, where, and with what. Let me lock up and let's go."

"I'll drive. It's too hot to walk."

"In the LeSabre? Should I put on my Hazmat suit?"

They settled in at a back table and ordered. "You're right. Monkey fired me because we disagreed about something," Nell said. "Though it's more like we both got fired."

"'Something?'" Danny said. "That's riveting. Come on, girl, the details."

"Remember the article on the Mayan prophecies?"

"I do. I've learned lots more. The exact date the glorious cosmic butterfly is going to emerge from this current human mess is December 21, 2012. I personally cannot wait."

"They might be right," Nell said. "Monkey's been going into trances. He's getting messages from some big Whatevers about a cataclysm on its way. And the Whatevers are telling him that only humans can forestall the disaster."

"Monkey? That boy smokes too much dope."

"There seems to be a consensus on that," Nell said.

"So tell me about Monkey's adventures."

Nell told him everything.

"I tripped so much a few years back that nothing surprises me," Danny said. "But here's more. One of the guys I go out dancing with is Chemeheuvi. Rick's the nephew of a woman who's started meeting with some other people. They're worried about all the solar power plans for here. They think the solar development can hurt some ancient pathway that they have. And if that pathway is damaged, we're all wiped out. Not just humans—everything."

"I was told about that," Nell said. "But I wasn't supposed to say anything."

Danny laughed. "Remember, the Morongo Hotline rules."

"Do you know about the attacks?" Nell said.

"Rick told me," Danny said. "But you still haven't told me what the disagreement with Monkey was about?"

"I wanted him to tell the Chemehuevi people about the messages. Rick's aunt thinks they might be able to find some information in them—maybe some ideas to help fight the solar power companies. Monkey doesn't want to tell anyone."

"That's it? That's why you broke up. I mean, got fired."

"And the usual."

"The usual," Danny said. "Oh, as in *the usual*. Don't I know!"

He tapped her hand. "Nell, what's with you? No tears. Nothing in your face but the usual."

"Danny, I was cried out long before I moved here. Cried out and raged out. All that's left is being scared."

"About?"

"Being alone the rest of my life, about wondering if I'm crazy." She laughed. "And whether or not the LeSabre will start when we're done eating."

"Plus what are you going to do for work?" Danny asked. "You can't live on selling your clothes to secondhand stores."

"Pound the pavement," Nell said. "LeSabre probably has a few trips back and forth to J-Tree and Yucca left in it so I can job hunt."

"I can't promise anything," Danny said, "but our files are a mess.

And I could use some backup when people bring in clothes to sell—we've already established that you had fashion sense."

Nell pointed at the beige hat. "Had?"

"Really. And I'd love to have a website for Noo. I'll love to ask the Head Wizard."

"I'm in if the Wiz is."

"That's settled then," Danny said. "By the time I'm done telling him about you, you'll be that Apple guy and Diana Vreeland rolled into one. Now—what about the end of the world?"

"I'm working with Rick's aunt and the others to stop the solar corporations," Nell said. "Between Monkey's trances and the stories Mariah has told me about the trail, I have to."

"I already told Rick that I can help raise money," Danny said. "No way I want to see those Manolo Blahniks wiped out in some hideous apocalypse. I told him that I and some of the other queer souls here can put on a benefit. I'm thinking a series of cabarets at the arts center in J-Tree. I know the owners. They'll go for it. Plus, I do a great Cher. I'm absolutely terrific."

"And you've got just the shoes for your act," Nell said. "You can call it *Save the Manolo Blahniks*. They can star in the show—and maybe on December 21 in 2012 for the big day."

"You and I can beam up together," Danny said. "The energy of our soles will unite us."

It was late afternoon by the time they left Sally's. Nell dropped Danny off at the store and gassed up at the Circle K. She stopped at La Paloma, unhooked the pearl from the doorknob, and dropped it in her bag.

She drove west on Death Highway, pulled off into the web of dirt roads, patted the LeSabre on its dashboard, and murmured, "You can do it, sister." Light flashed ahead of her to the northeast. She remembered the shattered windows in an old Airstream. Four crossroads up, she'd need to turn west, then north at a cluster of five Joshua trees, then go another crossroad till she could see the Magic Electric pole.

She drove slowly, partly out of respect for the LeSabre, but more because she was feeling something she'd never felt before. "I know where I am," Nell said. "Even if I don't dare rest my arms on the windowsill because I'll get a third-degree burn, even if my brain has boiled dry so that I'm talking to a babyshit-green LeSabre. I'm home."

31

Nell parked next to the Magic Electric sign and sat for a few minutes. She wondered if she should be afraid. Why worry about it—she was always afraid. She climbed out of the LeSabre and walked north on the dirt road. The sky over the western mountains was liquid fire, the last ferocious stand the desert sun takes before it sets. *I know that now,* she thought. *And I know that the moon rises at a different time each night, that these tracks in the sand are a lizard's, and that Joshua tree flowers smell pale green. And I know that if I know all of that, then I know where I am. If I know where I am, I have no reason to be afraid.* She patted the cell in her pocket. *Plus, there's signal.*

A pale yellow shack with no windows lay ahead. She walked toward it. The heat sucked away her breath. She slowed down. I have time. Time to cast my bones into the future. They brought me here, to a place that is merciless and molten. To these empty houses.

She walked up a path of gray paving stones. One big nail held the cabin's door shut. There were words painted in flamingo pink:

PEOPLE! If you are the ones that stole the chair,
go ahead and break in again. There is nothing left to
steal.
Hey, Dougie, here's the phone number...
...628-7543
...call...
...if you want...a shower.
EVERYBODY!!! BEWARE OF SNAKES!!!

Nell began to try the door and stopped. It was not the possibility of snakes that stayed her hand. It was the abrupt certainty that the lives of the people who had written on the door were none of her business. It was the dozens of abandoned shacks, houses, and trailers, the currents of lost hope and despair that wound through those phantom neighborhoods, and the secrets she knew needed to belong to people who might have lost everything.

She walked back to the wash. She'd gone no more than fifty yards when she saw a coil of jade-gray gleaming in the sand. The snake lifted its head. It flicked its tongue and tasted what might be coming toward it. Nell stepped back. The snake uncoiled and rippled away. "Sorry," Nell said. "This is your neighborhood."

The western light had begun to cool. She switchbacked down into the wash's shadow. She came to the boulder Mariah had spoken to and kept walking. The rock was Mariah's place, not hers. She walked past the dry stalks of desert lilies, patches of datura, a busted-up baby stroller, and pebbles stuck into the side of the wash that spelled out *QForce Was Here*. The glow above the western edge of the wash went pale yellow, then sea-glass blue. She had forty-five minutes till the moon rose. She followed the delicate light shimmering along the western edge of the wash, came around a curve, and found a low stone ledge.

Nell sat, peeled the orange, unwrapped the cheese sandwich, and checked her cell. No signal. She'd come this far. She wasn't going back. The first star flickered in the sky. A pack of coyotes yipped somewhere to the north. She remembered the bones of a story Leonard had told at the first meeting, how Coyote had set the patterns for human work and living. "I'm glad you're out there, desert dog," she said, "to help us remember."

She ate, and drank water. There were long moments of perfect silence. The evening breeze drifted down into the wash, the scent of creosote and earth surrounding her. She could hear bushes rattling in the wind. She dug her fingers into the still-warm sand and trickled it over her bare legs. The sense of familiarity returned. Her mother. Her mother walking her down a long desert road at twilight and sitting them both down on a boulder, her mother laughing and trickling sand over Nell's bare legs. The scent of creosote. Silence. Then coyotes yipping in the distance.

"They're partying, Nell," her mother had said. "Because they're so happy the long hot day is over. It's evening and all the scrumptious little creatures come out of their burrows." She had laughed and opened the bag of cookies she had shoplifted from the supermarket. "We've got Oreos and milk and coyotes singing. What more do we need."

Nell had snuggled into her mom's warm side. "We're travellers, you know," her mom had said. "It's a true thing. My grandpa came over from Ireland. He and his people called themselves Pavees. They lived in trailers like we do sometimes. They never stayed anywhere long, like we do most of the time.

"See, Nell, the road is our friend. As long as we have it and each other, we don't need much else—except cookies, of course. The road loves us and the earth that the roads tangle over loves us."

"And we love us," Nell had said.

"That most of all," her mom had said. Later, they had walked in the moonlight till they found an old Joshua tree. Her mother had spread their blanket out on the sand and laid Nell down.

"What about snakes?" Nell had said. Her mother scattered Joshua pods around their blanket.

"We'll hear a snake if it bumps into those. Then we just lie still and it won't hurt us. We'll watch the moon till our eyes close and our dreams come."

Silver glowed just above the eastern edge of the wash, just as it had over the mountain range that night. Nell stood. The waxing moon was a sliver of cool light just above the low mountains. She understood now a little about the workings of the Salt Song Trail, how an intersection of moon, tree, and the scent of sand in late summer evening air could transport a woman in time, could anchor her and bring her home. "Mom, I know now. And I know what comes next."

She took the black pearl from her bag and dropped it in the sand. Maybe someone else would walk here. Maybe they would find the pearl. Maybe they would wonder who had dropped it. And if no one came here, the pearl would lie under the sun and moon until the desert winds covered it with sand.

The moon lit her way back to the trailer. She climbed up out of the wash. An old Joshua had fallen to the ground just beyond the Magic Electric sign, its seedpods scattered on the sand. She picked up two of them and climbed into the car.

La Paloma was quiet. Nell wrote the letter to Monkey by hand.

Dear Kappa,

As you know, I came to understand that "forestall" was not the operative instruction. I think the Bosses' message itself is the text. As I re-read the geomagnetic article this morning, I saw again that the reversal will strip the earth of a layer of solar radiation protection. There will be more cancer. There will be more mutations. There will be no forestalling. And our species seems incapable of stopping itself.

Consider the workday traffic on I-10. Consider the human infestation at the park. Consider how much a Hummer seems an Android. Consider all the lists of how to save the earth that have been published since Earth Day.

For a few months, I believed we could help our species find our way home. I believed we might be the ones who held the key. You would be the antenna and receiver; I would broadcast what you were given. I once had access to a huge, complex, and easily manipulated public relations complex. I believed I could create another.

Now I know it is not that simple. The core will shift no matter what we do. An insecure rich guy will pay cash for a Hummer and an eight thousand square-foot house. I will drive seven hundred miles to sleep on slick rock, bathe in an August thunderstorm, and thank a wild place— my car will have sucked gas and spit poison. You will buy dope from a guy who knows a guy who knows a guy who owns a bundle of shares in Walmart.

We are all culpable.

"Rave on, John Donne."

Much was given to us. For that, I'm grateful.

n

p.s. Mariah was attacked in the desert a few months ago. The attack was a warning. She was told that if she returned to the place or told the cops, her granddaughter would be taken. We believe it was connected to the solar development plan. Keno stepped in to protect her and her granddaughter after the attack. Jackie has Mariah's cell number.

p.p.s. You'll find a map in the garage. It is our trail.

She unrolled the time map on the floor and took out her watercolors. She dipped the brush in water and blurred the edges of where the silver washed out from the moon, then trailed them forward. Where the silver faded out she wrote *gate gate paragate parasamgate.* A thread trailed forward from the last curve of the *e*.

She sat at the window while the paint dried. Smoke from the man's cigarette spiraled across the yard. The goat lay curled asleep. The man looked up. "Hey, neighbor," he said. "I see you every night. Good evening."

"I see you too," Nell said. "Good evening to you and your goat. Does it have a name?"

"She is Goat. She is old. As am I."

"As am I," Nell said. "Who would want the alternative?"

The man laughed. "Not Goat, that's for certain. Goodnight."

"Goodnight," Nell said.

She put the letter in her bag and rolled up the time map. If Monkey was in the office, she'd hand them to him. If he wasn't, it would be easy. She had forty-five minutes till the meeting, enough time to do what was necessary.

The Biz was locked. Nell let herself in. She taped the letter to the computer and looked around the office. The coffee maker was clean, the South Park hat empty.

She unfurled the time map across the windshield of the Firebird '83 and held it down with a spanner and the South Park hat. She breathed in the honest stink of the garage. Her mother's voice drifted in her mind: "Always fall in love with a good mechanic. At least that way, you'll get your car fixed for free. And, sweetie, if you end up being your mother's girl, you'll always drive a car that needs fixing."

Nell straightened the edge of the time map. "Thanks Mom, I owe you." Her heart felt swollen and hot. "I hope he shows. I hope he doesn't. I wish there were a passage between the rock and the whirlpool. I would dive in. So deep."

The Biz was quiet. She waited a few lifetimes, then checked her watch. 8:30. The meeting was at 9:00. There was nothing left to do but go.

Monkey pulled up to the Biz. The office light was on. He unlocked the door and stepped in. She had, of course, left him a letter. He sat and read. "Why," he whispered, "did it have to be an amputation?" He sent her a message and wandered out into the garage. A drawing lay across the hood of the Firebird. He carried it into the office and spread it out on the floor. It was all there. All of it.

He set his pen on the thread trailing out from *parasamgate*. *Much*, he wrote. *So much has gone to the other side, never having left*. Some day he would leave the scroll at La Paloma. Some day in a future he couldn't envision.

Monkey waited. Nell didn't come back. It was quiet in the Biz, too quiet. There was no dope, none left in any of his secret stashes. He tried to work on the VW and couldn't figure out what the fuck was wrong with it.

He told himself he could go home. He could load a bunch of CDs in the system, grab Hulk, and hang out with him on the couch. He could lie there with a twenty-pound cat purring on his chest until Jackie came home. He could run over his head with his truck. The walls on the waterproof compartment labeled *Nell* had crumbled. The walls in his waterproof life were down.

The phone rang. "It's Rella. They found him. I'm at my mom's. Please come quick. It's very bad."

"I'm there."

Rella opened the door. "Thank you," she said. "My mother keeps asking for you." Candles burned on every table and shelf. Mrs. Martinez sat on the couch, her back straight, her hands folded in her lap. "Monkey," she said. "*Mi hijo fue destruido*. They broke him everywhere. All his bones. His beautiful face."

She patted the couch. "Sit here. Rella, please bring Monkey some coffee. And some whiskey."

Monkey sat. "We are the only ones here," Mrs. Martinez said. "Later, my house will be full of family. But, for now, only you."

"I have no words," Monkey said, "for the sorrow I feel."

"How could you have any words?" she said. "He was your brother."

Rella handed Monkey his coffee and a shot glass filled with whiskey and set a plate of *biscochitos* on the cocktail table.

"Thank you," Monkey said. He threw back the shot.

Rella sat on the other side of her mother and took her hand. "We hope you might know something that will help us find whoever did this. The police say they are trying, but this is a family matter. My other brothers and my cousins are coming over from Riverside. We don't care about revenge, we care about justice."

"What about El Mago?"

"No," Mrs. Martinez said. "He talks big, but he's a coward."

"We know that Refugio was helping some Indian people," Rella said. "Guarding them—a woman and her granddaughter. He didn't tell us much, but he said that there was an injustice going to happen."

"That's true," Monkey said. "All of it. A Chemehuevi woman and her granddaughter. We think…" He heard himself say we. "We think that big energy corporations want to put solar panels in the desert. That will cause damage to Chemehuevi sacred sites, to the wildlife, to more than can be imagined. This woman Refugio was protecting was attacked in a place that the energy companies might want to develop."

"Is there any proof that's who attacked her?" Rella said.

"No. But there have been other attacks."

Rella picked up her cell.

"No," Monkey said. "Not the police."

"Yes," she said. "Not the police. I'm calling some friends who understand justice. And you, you are not to do anything crazy. Understand?"

"I do," Monkey said. "But there is something I *will* do. For your son. For my brother."

He called Jackie's cell. She didn't pick up. He left his message on her voicemail. "Keno's gone."

Nell drove up to Alice's. A campfire burned in the front yard, dark figures standing around it, their faces fading in and out of the flickering light. She pulled in behind Mariah's truck and stepped next to Jackie. "It feels better to be outside tonight, Nell," Mariah said. "It's easier to pray for our friend, Keno."

"What happened?"

"He was murdered."

Leonard passed gourd rattles around to the Chemehuevi. "We sing for our people to help their souls go forward on the Salt Song Trail," he said. "This isn't one of those songs, but I wrote one especially for Keno. He was a good friend to us and a brave man."

The *hush hush* of the rattles was the sound of dry branches in a gentle desert wind. Leonard's voice rose into the night. The others joined in. Jackie reached for Nell's hand. Later, Nell would remember the scent of mesquite smoke and how the song and smoke spiraled up into the huge sky. She would remember the rattles in the men's hands, the spiral designs, the carved animals on the handles. And she would remember what followed their song: a plan exquisitely sophisticated in its simplicity, a plan that might dump the solar corporation on its ass.

The house was dark. Jackie had left enchiladas in the microwave for Monkey. He nuked them, grabbed a beer, slid CDs in the shuffler, and sat on the couch. Hulk wandered in and jumped up beside him. "Be cool, little brother," Monkey said. "I'm having a wake here."

Hulk insinuated himself between the enchiladas and Monkey's lap. "Ah fuck," Monkey said and fed him a piece of chicken. "I've got to do something I don't even believe in. What do you think of that?"

Hulk nuzzled the plate. "Right," Monkey said. "Business as usual."

The front door opened.

"You there, babe?" Jackie called out.

"Me and Hulk are in here," Monkey said. "Where you been?"

Jackie sat down in the big recliner across from him. "I'm whipped. I worked all day and then we had a meeting about the solar stuff. But you probably don't want to hear about that."

"Not true," Monkey said. "And I need Mariah's number."

32

Nell knocked on Shiloh and Diamond's door. "I'm making breakfast," she said. "The coffee's on."

She went into the kitchen. Aside from dumping salad and fixings in a bowl, she'd done nothing in the way of feeding anyone during her stay except to put takeout in the fridge. Once an L.A. Princess, always an L.A. Princess.

She opened the refrigerator. There were eggs and havarti cheese, andouille and homemade salsa. There were apricot sweet rolls in the breadbox. Not much of a challenge for the cooking-impaired. Nell set coffee brewing and hunted through the cupboards for a cutting board and frying pan. She was breaking eggs into Diamond's favorite red bowl when it occurred to her that she was about to have a life in which there would be more than enough time to cook, more than enough time to eat, more than enough time to feed friends—in fact, to have friends. More than enough time to sit on the front stoop of La Paloma and let the dawn give her invitations she wouldn't refuse.

Diamond walked in and filled their coffee cups. "You want cream?"

"Milk. No sugar, thanks."

Shiloh came in and sat down. "What's the occasion? I was in the shower when you knocked."

"I've got an errand to run in L.A." Nell poured the eggs into an old iron skillet. "I'll be back tonight. I figured it's time for me to start pulling my weight around here."

"Don't worry," Diamond said. "How many dishes you figure you've washed? And you'll be pulling weight you'll wish you hadn't picked up. You haven't heard our plan for you yet. And go easy with that skillet. That was my nanny's. I hauled that thing everywhere, even when I didn't have a place to use it."

Nell laid andouille, green chilis, and cheese across the omelet and folded it. "Where'd you get andouille in Twentynine?"

"Palm Springs," Diamond said. "You can get anything you want in the Springs—mojo bags, couscous, Filipino psychic surgeons, rhinestone-encrusted cowboy hats, your wish is Palm Springs' command. All you have to do is give the genie your money."

Nell dished up the eggs and sat.

"Here's the deal," Diamond said. "We could use a business manager."

"And bookkeeper!" Shiloh said. "You found us during a lull, but when the effects hit of those two other safe houses closing down and the long winter nights driving everybody crazy, it'll go berserk here. And our funding is shakier than it's ever been. Could you handle a second job?"

"Nice timing," Nell said. "I can. I'm no longer employed at the Biz."

"Oh?" Shiloh said.

"Leave her alone," Diamond said. "Maybe she needs a new challenge."

Nell laughed. "You can only type in work orders and bills for so long. I need to do what I'm good at. Raising money. Guarding money. Keeping track of money. Making connections while I pretend I'm not making connections. I'd love working here. That way I wouldn't feel so guilty about taking up a room until I can find my own place."

"You're hired," Shiloh said. "Part-time. Minimum wage under the table, room with a view, and all Diamond's cooking you can eat. And don't be in a big hurry to leave us."

"I won't. This is perfect. Danny asked me to do some part-time work for him. Shelter, food, and all the t-shirts a girl could possibly want. I'm set. Except for one thing."

"Which is?"

"Are any of the old peoples' homes set up for dementia patients?"

"The two that are left are. And the care and security are ten times what you'd find in a commercial home. Why?"

"My mother is in a good home in Long Beach, but I need to bring her here."

"Your mother?"

"My mother. I think she'd be happier here."

"And you?" Diamond said.

"I hope so."

"Nell?" Shiloh said.

"What?"

"You could have told us. We could have done something sooner."

"I wasn't ready. I am now."

Nell tucked the San Berdoo orange in her bag and put the lightning glass and one of the seedpods in her pocket. She read through the little budget book and smiled.

When she logged on to her email, there were messages:

Subject: Stop.
You can't do this. It's an amputation. We can figure something out.
Monkey

She considered how it would be to stop at the Biz before she headed to L.A., how it would be to re-enter something that would, at best, wear her away as steadily and cruelly as being shoved through a basalt tube—and at worst would bring a cataclysm roaring toward three people.

She hit Reply.

Subject: No
Not an amputation. It is the work of the bees.
And far more prosaically, I am a woman. I imagine you will occasionally receive wistful emails from me, in which there are references to nexi and Chris Whitley and the end of the world as we know it (hint: on the Greenpeace album).
See how I am?
Nell

She checked her watch. If she wanted to get to the lawyer's before five, she needed to leave soon.

Subject: very pretty bullshit
You said one of us would pour the Everclear; the other would strike the match.
You were wrong. I poured the Everclear. I strike the match.
Monkey

Nell sat by the window. The goat had curled up in the shade under the man's chair. Birds pecked at its feed. She knew she was looking for a sign, a divine intervention from a hypothetical Divine distinctly incapable of intervening. She hit Reply.

Subject: What is
I told you. Everclear is only a metaphor, as is the match. These are the realities.
1. You are married.
2. I nearly destroyed myself with a married man, unlike you in many ways; like you in ways I mustn't ignore.
3. You can't be alone.
4. You're mean.
5. I won't respond to anything you send me while you play with a sacred and for you, dangerous plant.
6. There was Much.
7. My real name is

Nell Walker

Five minutes passed. A new message appeared:

OKeefecat52@msn.com
Subject: Testifying
The good Baptist boy is going to tell the group what he's learned in the trances. We're meeting tonight at 9:00. Mariah asked me to tell you. See you there.
Jackie

So much for dramatic farewells. She'd see Monkey again. And again. And again. She wasn't leaving Twentynine. And maybe over time, when she saw him, he'd be just another guy. Not the one who held the key.

There was a new message:

oilinmyvessel47@yahoo.com
Subject: Reality 8.
Quid pro quo.
Gate gate paragate parasamgate. It is Sanskrit. You know what it means. It is called the Heart Sutra. I still can't remember where I learned it. Probably from my wise brother, Deacon.
Much, Carl Luther Barnett

She logged off and closed the laptop. How strange that fragments of her lived in computer circuitry, past and present, heartbeats and tears flashing on and off in an etheric grid. She remembered Indra's web, a vast cosmic network in whose intersections tiny jewels glowed. Everything that was—every petal unfolding and carrion beetle feasting, every caress and punch, every molten sunset and cloud-drifted moonrise, every loving thought and cruel impulse—was the flash of a turquoise, a garnet, an opal.

Her phone rang. "Hey, it's Mariah. I hear you're going over to L.A."

"What? I just told Diamond and Shiloh five minutes ago."

Mariah laughed. "Girl, you know you're on the Morongo Hotline now. Your business is our business. Ours is yours."

"Why doesn't that reassure me?"

"It shouldn't. Have you got time to stop by my place before you leave?"

"I can do that. I just have to get to L.A. by 1:00."

"You've got plenty of time. See you in a few minutes."

Nell hung up and went down into the kitchen. Shiloh and Diamond looked up at her. "That was Mariah," Nell said. "Is there no privacy in this town?"

"I like to think of it as community," Diamond said. "You know, folks watching out for each other."

"Oh that," Nell said. "I kind of forgot about that for a few lifetimes."

"Huh!" Shiloh said. "Good thing you fucked up in L.A."

"Easy for you to say."

"Monty Python, right? Where are they when we so desperately need them?"

Diamond handed Nell a paper bag.

"What's this?"

"Fried chicken, corn bread, and a hunk of sweet potato pie. No friend of mine would travel without them."

Nell sat down. "I don't know how to thank you guys."

"First off," Shiloh said, "we're not guys. Second off, when you start to dig into the mess that we call our bookkeeping, you'll understand."

"I feel less guilty now."

"Call us when you get to L.A.," Shiloh said.

"*Si, mi gallincita*, I promise."

Mariah's house was an old tile-roofed adobe at the base of Copper Mountain, the front yard filled with ocatillo, yucca, and wind chimes. She opened her door. "You got time for coffee?"

"Always."

They took their cups to the shaded backyard.

"I've got a lot to learn," Nell said. "I can spot a Joshua, quail, creosote, and desert lily. I know you shouldn't walk the streets at night. But I've never seen a desert tortoise and I still don't know what makes up that pink vapor that floats over us at night sometimes."

"I try not to think about it," Mariah said. "It's most likely tweak fumes."

"I'll be back tonight for the meeting," Nell said. "I suspect you know everything else."

"You're catching on. So you quit the Biz?"

"We came to a mutually agreed-upon parting of the ways, as they used to say in my old life."

"You're going to need work, right?"

"I'm okay. Danny's hiring me part-time and Shiloh and Paloma made me an offer I couldn't refuse."

"I hope you'll have enough time for a third job," Mariah said. "Leonard and I talked. There's a little money, not much, that came in from an anonymous donor. What if you put in a few hours a week helping us with the computer stuff? I've got all the paper files in my house. Be good if you worked over here. I know the corporations are going to start monitoring everything we do—if they haven't already. This way you and me and the other Sacred Sites folks have a way to communicate immediately—under the radar."

"Twist my arm," Nell said.

"There are even benefits," Mariah said. "There are so many beautiful places we can walk to from here. I think we'll be safe now. The two Chemehuevi men who grabbed me came to talk with Daryl and me right after Keno was found. They were scared it'd get pinned on them. And they told us they'd each had a run of really bad luck since they threatened me. They figured it was tied in with what they'd done."

"Bad luck?" Nell said.

"Sometimes those old ones remember useful things," Mariah said. "My mom and my aunts do.

"The guys said that FreegreenGlobal had paid them each a few hundred bucks. They asked if they could make up for what they'd done by helping us out. Leonard told them that there would be work for them to do in the future, but for now they would have to prove themselves and give the Judas money to our group. They'd spent most of it, but they started paying us back right away."

"What about the other attacks?" Nell said.

"We don't know. It wasn't these fellows. I'm thinking maybe brain-dead tweakers. Maybe desperate guys without jobs. Maybe just racist shitheads."

"And Keno," Nell said. "What about Keno?"

"Nothing so far. I don't think it was local. Maybe company goons. Maybe El Mago got some balls on him. We may never find out. One of my nephews is a cop up in Vegas. He says that mostly if they don't solve a case within thirty days, they don't solve the case. What a loss for all of us, but mostly for Monkey."

"I hear he's agreed to tell us about the trances," Nell said.

"Congratulations," Mariah said. "Now you're in the Hotline."

"Jackie emailed me."

"We'll get a few of the older folks—what's left of them—to the meeting and see what they think," Mariah said. "There could be signs in what he saw and heard; there could be nothing but stoner gobbledegook."

"It all made sense to me," Nell said. "Which really didn't make sense to me."

"One thing the old people teach us," Mariah said, "is that we don't know much. Or maybe more like we used to know things that mattered and now...damn it, I'll just piss myself off if I keep talking about this."

"This'll cheer you up," Nell said. "When I left my job, I liberated an illegal program that takes you into all the connections between the boards and major investors in the big corporations. We've got a network of names that we can use."

"If we can get to the investors," Mariah said, "maybe we can influence them. Changing government rules these days is an illusion. By the time we have an effect—if any—the trail will be paved over. Still, we've got a mole over at the BLM. It's time for us to lean on them— for what it might be worth. But people, even rich people, maybe we can get to their hearts. Remember, that's what Mr. Eddy says when he teaches Salt Trail songs: 'But before I teach you this song, I need to break your heart.'"

"If they have any hearts," Nell said.

"You were one of them, right?"

"I was. I had a heart, but it was buried deep, so nobody could find it."

"It got found," Mariah said. "That's the point."

"Heart, no heart," Nell said. "I'm in on anything to save this desert. I owe it." She stood. "Thanks for the coffee and catch up. I need to get moving. Did the hotline tell you that I'm going to see my mother in L.A.?"

"It missed that detail," Mariah said. "I'm so glad. It's not good for the old ones to be so far from their children." She grinned. "Even if the old ones can sometimes drive their children nuts. Believe me, I know."

"You're part of my wanting to do this. Thank you for talking with me the night we found the FreegreenGlobal markers," Nell said. "I went back to the wash next to Magic Electric. I walked up past where you and I talked and found a place to sit and watch the moon rise. I remembered that my mom and I were out here when I was a kid. Our time here was one of the sweet times. I'm going to bring her here."

"To live with you?"

"No, she loves to wander too much. Shiloh and Diamond told me about a memory home. There's room for my mom."

"I hope to meet her," Mariah said. "You know those old ones who seem to be so far away in their minds, sometimes I wonder if they aren't just remembering things we've forgotten. They sure do seem to be able to travel back in time."

"I haven't seen my mom in so long, I don't really know how she is. I'm a little scared."

"You'll be okay," Mariah said. "She's just your mom. Always was, always will be."

Nell looked out the west window. Hummingbirds played badass around a feeder, ruby pilots flashing in the sun. "I had a hunch you'd want to be our paid computer geek," Mariah said. "So I put up the feeder. Those guys are good luck."

"You've made what could have been so hard, so easy," Nell said. "I had no idea my life could be this easy. Thank you again."

"But you had all that money?"

"Money makes some things easy, but in the long run…"

Mariah laughed. "Only rich people say stuff like that. Good thing you're not rich anymore."

"I better get on the road. Pray for the LeSabre. If I break down on the Ten, I'll wish I were still rich."

"You'll be back in time for the meeting?"

"Ask the LeSabre. It rules."

"Travel safe, Nell. Do you need food for the road?"

"Thanks, I've got enough food for a week. Diamond is my foster mom. See you soon."

33

Jensen's office was quiet, the receptionist, Mackenzie, on her cell, the lawyer's door closed. Mackenzie waved Nell to the waiting area. The pale jade curtains over the huge eastern windows had been pulled back and tied with swatches of darker jade linen. The black leather couch was strewn with jade and wine-red pillows. Mackenzie's desk was a slab of polished rosewood, illuminated by a bronze and jade lamp. There was no dust, no clutter, nothing but shining surfaces and the faint scent of cedar from a fat candle burning next to the espresso machine.

Nell sat on the couch and ran her fingertips over the brushed metal coffee table. Nothing had changed since her last visit. She hadn't been in a room like this for six months, a room crafted to lead one to believe that everything was under control.

Jensen stepped out of his office and walked toward her. He wore a black Harley logo t-shirt, carefully faded jeans, and a black leather sport coat. "Nell Walker, I was beginning to think you'd disappeared. How are you?"

Nell stood and took his hand. "I'm very well," she said. "Very well and working." He'd been something of an ally as her former world had imploded.

"Of course you are," Jensen said. "You're too valuable a player for someone not to have snatched you up. Come in and tell me what I can do for you."

It was 3:30 by the time Nell pulled onto the freeway. Forty-five minutes to Long Beach and who knew how long with her mom. Jensen had been startled that she wanted to move her mother from Ocean Palms, baffled that the foster home was in Twentynine Palms. "But it's your call. It'll take about a month or so to put the paperwork in order. I can't imagine there'll be any problems."

Nell's mouth was dry, her thoughts hurtling ahead of the LeSabre. *My mother will drool. She'll smell. She'll look at me with a crazy grin.* It was good that she had to be back in Twentynine at 9:00. If it were a nightmare, she wouldn't have to stay long. She set the Joshua seedpod and the lightning glass on the dash. A lightning strike would have been welcome.

She couldn't remember being so frightened. What if her mother looked into her eyes and, suddenly lucid, said, "Where have you been all these years?" Traffic slowed ahead of her. What once would have driven her frantic—rush-hour freeway gridlock—seemed like a blessing. There was nothing to do but pull up behind the stopped car ahead of her and wait.

Nell parked in the shade of the old eucalyptus grove at the far end of the Ocean Palms parking lot and put the Joshua seed in her pocket. There was an herb garden in the middle of the grove. She walked to the bench in the center of a mandala of cilantro, mint, and rosemary. A carved stone at her feet reminded her to *Love Life*. "Shut up," she said. "I can do this without your advice." She took the Joshua seedpod from her pocket and walked toward the entrance to the Memory Unit.

Her mother sat in a chair on the patio outside her room. Her old patchwork quilt was spread over her legs, her long white curls gleaming. Nell stopped. It would have been easier to believe she saw a ghost. Her mother's cheeks were pink and she was smiling at something. A nurse walked out of the building and waved.

"Can I help you?"

"I'm Nell Walker. I've come to see my mother…my mother…she's right here."

The nurse reached out her hand. "I'm glad to meet you. Mr. Jensen said to expect you." She set a chair next to Nell's mother. "Tara, you have a special visitor."

Her mother didn't move. Nell touched her shoulder and sat down. The nurse wrote something on a scrap of paper and handed it to Nell. *They become more confused later in the day. She may not respond.*

"Thank you," Nell said. "I'm fine if we just sit here."

The sun dropped behind the eucalyptus, went copper, then fire. Thin cobalt shadows stretched across the lawn. Silence, her mother motionless beside her. Nell couldn't think of anything to say. It was easier to watch the sunset, the shadows, to feel the cool air on her skin. There was nothing to say. Nell took her mother's hand and placed the Joshua seedpod in her palm.

Her mother was still. Nell reminded herself to breathe. The sun went pale salmon above the eucalyptus. Time moved as slowly as the fading light. Nell put her hand over her mother's. A small breeze drifted over them, carrying the scent of salt and twilight.

Nell's mother looked down at the seedpod. She raised it to her nostrils, breathed in, and smiled. She lowered her hand to her lap and set her other hand gently over the pod.

"I'm glad you like it," Nell said. "I think you know what it is. You'll be living where you can see the Joshuas and hear the coyotes. You'll get to watch the moon rise. I'm taking you there soon. Our lawyer said it will take a few weeks."

Her mother was silent. Nell kissed the back of her mother's hand. "Thank you," she said. "Thank you for being my mother."

2. The Long Run

John Maynard Keynes said, "It's a struggle to survive..."
—Walt Richardson, "Always Was and Always Will Be Love"

1

The usual group sat around the dining room table, the usual artery-annihilating feast spread out before them. There were a few new people: an old woman in a dark red pantsuit next to Eddie, an old man next to Leonard, his dark face laced with wrinkles, his black eyes cloudy. He was the man from the desert intaglio resistance video.

"We're waiting on Jackie and Monkey," Mariah said. "Take some food. We already started."

Nell sat next to Jenella and filled a plate with stew, frybread, and beans. "I'm sorry I'm late. That Ten is insane. Bumper to bumper for twenty miles out of L.A."

"People got to be crazy to live over there," Eddie said. "I been in L.A. once, after I got out of Iraq. It made me damn near puke."

The old woman glared at him.

"I'm sorry, Mom," he said. "I'll watch my mouth."

"You will," she said.

Jackie and Monkey came in through the front door, Jackie smiling, Monkey locked up tight. Nell was grateful she was exhausted from the drive. She didn't have the energy to feel as bad as she suspected she felt seeing him and his damn shoulders, his damn glacier eyes.

"Alright," Leonard said. "We can get started. Since we've got some new folks, let's go around and say who we are."

The old woman nodded. "I'll start. I'm Della. This is my son here." She patted Eddie's arm. "And I'm Punkin's godmother. I want her to have a way to follow."

The old man smiled. "I'm Cesar, Leonard's uncle. I love to hear stories."

The regulars checked in, then Jackie said, "I'm here because of the animals."

Monkey glanced at Nell. "I'm Monkey and I'm here because my friend Keno was killed."

"I'm sorry your friend died," Leonard said. "That was a serious loss to our community, not just because he protected us, but because he was a man filled with joy."

Monkey nodded. "If it's alright with you all," he said, "I'd like to just say my piece and get out of here. I'm not much for politics—or crowds."

"Me either," Leonard said. "If I had my way, I'd be home hanging out with my grandkids and working in the garden. Go ahead and tell us your story. Could you speak a little louder though? The older folks' hearing aids aren't that good."

"I'll do my best," Monkey said. "But first I want to say that most of the time I don't believe in this woo woo stuff. I think our minds can play all kinds of tricks on us."

Leonard grinned. "So, now that you've straightened us out, maybe you can tell us about a few of the tricks your mind is playing."

Monkey talked about the spinning rods, the disembodied voices, the animal/human mutations, the huge lonely space beings, the warning that a cataclysm was coming and that humans were the only creatures who could stop it. When he'd finished, he looked at Nell. "Did I leave anything out?"

"There was something about a last gate," she said. "You asked me if I saw it and you asked me if I could I see through you? And you heard music and your grandpa's voice."

"I don't remember the gate. I do remember the music. It was seventies rock and roll."

"Well, it would be," Eddie said. "What else are you going to find in heaven?"

"Would you please repeat the part about the animals?" Della asked. Monkey told them again about the javelina-person, the coyote, the lizard, the crow, and the rabbit. "We believe," Della said, "that the animals were here before humans. They are the oldest ones. They, especially Coyote, taught us how to be."

Cesar nodded. "That was a pretty good story." He looked at Della. "I think we will be sitting with it for a while, talking about it, maybe praying. Can we ask you questions if we think of any?"

"Sure," Monkey said. "And I'll stick around if I can have some of that fry bread."

"Thanks," Leonard said. "You know it can be really hard to be the person who gets talked to. I hope you have a good teacher."

Monkey glanced at Nell. She looked down at her plate. "No," Monkey said, "but I've had a friend to talk to. It helped."

Nell wanted to reach across the table and smack him. She should have remembered that laying guilt trips was the bedrock of Baptist-think. Jackie nudged her. Nell took another piece of fry bread and drenched it in honey.

"When in doubt, go carbohydrates," Jackie whispered.

"Reports," Leonard said, "then money. Anybody want to catch us up?"

"Just one thing first," Mariah said. "We need to get moving on finding out what the BLM is up to. I want to be sure that's on our agenda."

Alice made a note. "We'll get to that a little later. Meanwhile, here's what I've found." She handed out a list of FreegreenGlobal investors who lived in L.A. and Palm Springs. She tapped the third name on the list. "What if we target this guy in Palm Springs and hold a gathering in front of his house? We can put in a couple hours there and head over to the BLM office later."

"I like it," Jones said. "I can get a few of my grandsons' friends. They're good singers." He laughed. "And they look pretty scary, got those baggy pants, head rags, and tribal tattoos everywhere."

"Somebody needs to check into the laws about protests," Leonard said. "This is about getting attention. It is not about getting busted."

"I already did it," Alice said. "We're okay on the grass between the street and the sidewalk. Same thing with the BLM. I'll keep checking out the BLM and Fed permitting laws. We'll have to go legal pretty soon and we need the information to do that."

"We got a lawyer?" Jones asked.

"Not yet," Mariah said, "but my Havasupai friend who's working on stopping that uranium mine up by the Grand Canyon said she's going to ask around."

"Next," Leonard said.

Jackie glanced at Alice. "Are we all set up?"

Alice grinned. "We are good to go." She brought a laptop from the back of the house, set it in the center of the table, and turned it on.

"Do you want to run it, Jackie?"

"I do. Close your eyes, it's going to take me a few seconds." Alice turned off the lights. "Okay," Jackie said. "You can look now."

The desert glowed in front of them, a cluster of datura pale against dark sand, a Joshua tree throwing shadows at the edge of a wash. The soft gold and green melted into the figure of a man written in desert varnish, who shifted into a line of crushed mica leading up a narrow trail, the trail twisting into letters: *Salt Song Warriors*.

"This could be our website," Jackie said. "I took the idea from your video, Leonard. It doesn't have to be Salt Song Warriors, but this is a beginning. I'll put in our story, how to reach us, how to donate. I'm thinking some of you can work on the writing. I'm your tech."

"This is beautiful," Leonard said quietly. "I have photographs we might use. I usually just get pissed off at having to use the computer, but you've showed me it can become part of a song. Thank you."

Jackie looked down at her hands. "It feels good to do this." She closed the laptop. "There's a little more. I've started talking with other artists around here. We think we can pull together an art festival for late October. That's when the tourist and climbing season picks up, and it gives us two months to find a venue, collect art, and set up the music."

Jones laughed. "We sound like the old ladies in my grandma's church. They were always putting on fry bread sales and potluck suppers. Back in the day, we called them AIM ladies. American Indian Moms."

Eddie shook his head. "That's the reality. Did you ever see that dumb-ass movie, *Thunderheart*? First off, they got a white guy playing the hero. Second off, at the end the good Injuns are boxed in with the FBI about to off all of them. All of a sudden a whole bunch of bloods show up and save the day. Pure white boy fantasy. Real reality? Us."

"Yeah," Della said, "but how about when that badger rips the shit—sorry, son—out of the cop's hand?"

Eddie pounded the table. "That's my mom."

"I hate to ruin the fun," Jones said, "but there's one more thing. Somebody busted out my truck's rearview mirrors and brake lights last night. And took a shit in the truck bed. I wasn't going to say anything, but now that you mention it, we need a badger."

Monkey's jaw tightened.

Jackie poked Nell and whispered, "Monkey inferno alert."

Nell looked up. Monkey's shoulders were rigid. He stared out the window. Leonard followed Nell's gaze and nodded. "Jones, maybe you and me can have a cup of coffee tomorrow and figure a few things out."

"Works for me," Jones said.

Monkey had made himself sit quiet. His head pounded, his fists were clenched so tight they ached. What the fuck was going on? He didn't know Jones from Adam and all he wanted to do was wreak some serious Samuel Jackson Kahuna Burger wrath on somebody. He excused himself to go to the john and walked outside. A few minutes later, the meeting broke up. He headed for the truck. Leonard fell in beside him.

"Let's take a minute," Leonard said. "Come on around the back."

Monkey followed him to a couple lawn chairs near the garage. "Let's sit for a minute," Leonard said. "I hope you don't take offense, but I need to explain a couple things. You okay with that?"

Monkey nodded.

"Here's how it is," Leonard said. "I saw your eyes when Jones spoke. I feel the same way. But this slow way is how we do things. First, we recognize that there's a problem. Then we talk with the old folks. Then we do what we can to educate ourselves and other people. This is *our* battle. Those AIM days are long ago. Those AIM ways won't work for us with this mess." He grinned. "For now."

La Paloma was quiet. Nell sat on the stoop for a while. She was too wired from the L.A. drive and seeing Monkey to sleep. She took her bag to her room, put her cell in her pocket, and walked toward downtown.

Sally's was still open, the big front windows glowing pink-gold, the candles burning in front of the altar. A woman sat alone, looking into the mirror behind the little bar. Two men talked at the kitchen door, one of them taking off his waiter apron. Sally looked up from the register and waved. Nell leaned in the door.

"See you soon."

"You better," Sally said.

Nell walked across the parking lot to a quiet side street. Headlights floated ghostly amber in the smoky air. She walked next to the chainlink fence of an autoyard, stepped away from its security light, then back along the fence. The headlights brightened and moved past.

Heavy metal music shook the air. A doorway glowed orange ahead, the music pounding out of the light. A tall skinny man, veiled in smoke, crouched, straightened, reached up, and crouched again. Dancing. Playing air guitar. Being anything but a lonesome guy in a warehouse in a hard little desert town. She had once looked through the garage door and seen Monkey, eyes closed, head thrown back, playing the living shit out of an invisible guitar. The man bent again and she saw that he held a paintbrush. He straightened, swiped once across the top of the doorframe in rhythm to the music, and moved out of sight.

Nell waited. The man didn't reappear. There was only the dark building, the empty asphalt parking lot, a sign that made it clear that no alcohol, drugs, guns, or troubling behavior were welcome beyond the locked gate, and a refrigerator on which a black peace sign had been painted and the words: *If you enter, you will be subject to search.*

The music stopped, then the intro to "Mr. Brownstone" ratcheted in. Nell leaned against the fence. That's how it was. Money, dope, power, romance, control, the illusion of control—you try for forever, you end up with nothing but the dead past. She remembered a little club in a Southwestern city, a reggae band, Morningstar, the lanky dreadlocked singer leaning into the microphone. *And in the long run, we are all dead.*

In the long run, Nell thought, *I was given a second chance.* She turned on Smoke Tree. A gray shadow crossed in front of her, stopped, and looked back over its shoulder. It was a coyote, chunky, its coat shining in the Biz security light. Nell slid her key under the door. The coyote watched her. "We're crazy, you know," Nell said. "We humans. It's because nobody taught us how to be shadows."

The coyote loped down Smoke Tree. Nell pressed her fingertips against the Biz window. There was a faint print on the dusty glass. "You won't know I'm here," she said, "but I will be, at least till you clean the windows. That could be a long, long time."

Shiloh and Diamond were in the kitchen, stacks of paper and files covering the table. Shiloh had her head in her hands. Diamond was eating peanut butter cups as fast as she could unwrap them.

"See what I meant, Nell," Shiloh said, "about you earning your keep?"

"Eight years of records," Diamond said. "None of it in the computer, which died yesterday." She tossed Nell a peanut butter cup.

Nell sat across from them. "I'm on the clock," she said. "And I'm in charge."

"Thank you," Diamond said. "Oh dear Jesus, thank you."

"Jesus has nothing to do with this," Nell said.

"What'll you need?" Diamond asked.

"We need a good computer. I like Macs. How about if I go out tomorrow and price them?"

"Go local," Diamond said. "That includes Yucca Valley."

"Local for sure, and one more question. Did you get any info on a memory unit?"

"I told Barbara over at the old folks' place on Indian Cove to keep a spot for your mom," Diamond said. "It's not too far from here and the view is great."

"Perfect. Now here's what you need to do. Get up from the table, go upstairs, get into bed, go to sleep, and forget about all of this."

"Thank you," Shiloh said, "she who must be obeyed."

Monkey sat on the patio, no shirt, no shoes, just his pajama pants and head rag, Hulk coiled around his feet.

"What I need to know," Monkey said, "is how I'm going to want to stay alive without the killer weed? Without Keno. And how I can so badly miss someone I barely touched?"

"As you so often point out to me," Jackie said from behind him, "cats can't understand human."

Monkey jolted. "Shit, I don't understand human."

"You could try being human," Jackie said. "You could let me be human."

"What?"

"You think I'm some My Little Princess doll."

"I'm an Okie gentleman," Monkey said. "We take care of our women. Besides, you know you've got a few problems."

"Such as?"

"Well, whatever you've got in that pop can besides pop. And

whatever you take in order to sleep. Right? Am I right?"

"Wrong. You are wrong," Jackie said.

"Prove it. Give me the can."

Jackie put the can down and reached for Monkey's hand. "No. If you don't trust me after twenty-five years, you'll never trust me. I'm not going to defend myself. Not now. Not ever again. If we're going to make it much beyond twenty-four years and eleven months, we've got to tear down most of the last five years and see what's left."

"What are you talking about?"

"I'm talking about a dead marriage that we both helped kill. I'm talking about the fact that I love you, but I don't like you. I'm talking about the possibility that the love may get us past the don't like."

"I didn't do anything with Nell," Monkey said. "That's what this is all about, right?"

Jackie let go of his hand. "No. When's the last time you smoked?"

"What's that got to do with it? My wife threatens me with divorce and all of a sudden I'm the one that has to answer questions."

Jackie was silent.

"Am I going crazy?" Monkey said. "I fucking did what you wanted me to do. I talked to your friends. I risked everything. I sat in that room with you and Nell which was weirder than shit. What more do you want?"

"I want the man I liked back," Jackie said.

Monkey shook his head.

"I want the next twenty-five years," Jackie said, "with that man."

"I want a cigarette," Monkey said. "Even if this isn't exactly post-coital. Jackie, I don't know where that man is."

Jackie shrugged. "What's more…"

"Don't say it. Do not say it. 'Sex won't fix it,' right?"

She grinned. "No, but you could reach over here and take my hand."

She watched Monkey hunch down into himself. She knew him. She could wait him out. He reached down, scratched Hulk behind the ears, straightened up, and looked out over the fence to the silhouette of the mountains.

"It was up near where they found Keno," he said. "That was the last time I smoked." He moved his chair next to hers and took her hand. "I don't know anything more than that, Jackie. I don't fucking know much of anything right now. Except that I don't like me either. That's for sure."

"I know something," Jackie said and ran her bare toes over his foot. "You could start changing the kitty litter every other time. That's a great beginning to the next twenty-five years."

2

A month passed. It was a joy for Nell to work with Shiloh, Diamond, and Danny, far from a joy to dig into research on the corporate sustainable energy cabal. Nell should have known. She had spearheaded campaigns to co-opt peoples' best impulses. Nothing had changed. Go green! Renewable solar power! You can consume till you explode and give up nothing! The energy corporations were wrapping themselves in Sierra Club t-shirts and storming into the desert—where, as far as they were concerned, there was nothing.

Nell checked out the memory home and care center off Indian Cove. Barbara, the director, was a petite woman in her mid-sixties. She took Nell on a tour of the bright and immaculate ranch house.

"Your mom's room can be back here, no stairs to deal with, and she'll have this window looking out at our granddaddy Joshua and the mountains." She'd shown Nell her art—framed cross-stitched desert flowers, pillows stitched with mandalas and eyes, a crazy quilt on the bed. "I embroider with a vengeance," she had said. "People don't realize that Eastern European women snuck goddess figures into their embroidery back during the Inquisition. Some days, it seems to me that we never left those times, so I'm a secret agent in my art. I love it when somebody sees a cross in one of my pieces and I get to tell them she's a goddess with her arms raised in blessing."

"You've sold me," Nell said. "My mom was one of our first secret agents."

The group decided at their next meeting to call themselves Twentynine for the Mojave.

"I don't know," Eddie said. "There's really only eleven of us. The enemy is going to pick up on that."

"We only need eighteen more, Eddie," his mom said. "They must have taught you that in school."

"I'm just sayin'."

"Just say something useful. You know better."

"We're enough for now," Jenella said. "But I've got an idea to bring in more people. What if we postpone the Palm Springs events till we've established a name for ourselves. Let's hold our first gathering outside the Twentynine City Hall. We could start there next week, see how it goes, and use local media coverage and the website to spread the word about us. The *Hi-Desert Star* and KCDZ are always looking for real news."

"I like it," Alice said. "We've already got contacts up here, and I was going to tell you guys that it'll take a few months to pull something together for Palm Springs. I'll look into permits. They've got that big lawn out front. We can park and set up in the back lot next to the library."

"We've still only got eleven of us to show up for this demo," Eddie said. "How about if Jones and me see who we can scare up?"

Jones grinned. "Scare up is right. I told you guys I know that some of my grandsons' friends would love this. They got those tribal tattoos and baggy pants, look great next to us sweet little old elders. Solidarity and all." He winked at Monkey. "They got those head rags, too. You'll fit right in." Monkey almost smiled.

"I can get some of the ladies from my beading group," Della said and nodded to Alice. "You know how Charletta's always shooting her mouth off about how we women need to get more mouthy?"

"She should know," Alice said. "I'm thinking maybe some of the Indian kids over at the college would be interested. Jenella, can you talk it up a little?"

"I already have. And some of the white kids are climbers—they don't want their playground messed up. There's an older guy climber, Brock somebody, who said he'd round up his friends."

"Me and Leonard can round up some singers from the river Rez, maybe up from Coachella," Cesar said. "I'm feeling good. Seems like we know what we're doing."

Mariah looked at Jackie, Nell, and Jeff. "Can we find a few more white folks to stand with us?"

"My artist friends and I will make signs," Jackie said. "Just tell us what you want. This will give us advance publicity for the Art for Our Home festival."

"Danny at Noo to Yoo is already on board," Nell said. "I'm sure Shiloh and Diamond are too."

"We may have some new allies," Jeff said. "It's turning out that the wind turbines aren't the big green blessing people hoped they would be. They're chopping birds to birdburger. Some folks called me from over near Tehatchapi. I'll let them know."

"I'm guessing that this thing's going to drag on and on," Monkey said. "You all know that. We're going to need money. I'd like to give free tune-ups to anybody who donates a hundred bucks or over. Might be good to see if some other local businesses would do something like that. I can ask around." He glanced at Nell. "I'm in for the demo." She figured he was choking on the words.

Nell looked at him. He had his cop gaze on. She saw how he was not handsome and she couldn't not want to look at him. She hoped her face was as unreadable as his.

"We need to get started right away amping up our online presence," she said. "Facebook, Twitter, post some comments on some of the enviro and Native American blogs. Maybe Jackie, Mariah, and I can start working on that."

"Looks like it's time to join the Evil Empire," Jones said. "As long as I get my handsome picture on Facebook and it says I'm single."

Della groaned.

"So," Mariah said, "we start getting the word out for the gathering. Saturday, October eighteenth. I'm thinking noon. That's when more tourists are in town. And Jones, I don't want to hear one word about those cute climber girls."

They finished up at eleven. Monkey left first. Nell found him leaning against the LeSabre.

"I know the rules," he said. "Will you break them long enough to let me give you this?" He held out a CD. There was a watercolor of a kappa on the label and the words *Bowing to the Future.*

Nell took the CD. "Thank you. But please, no more."

"I know. I told Jackie I was making it for you. She said it wasn't any of her business and that it was up to you. She knows I'm done with lies."

"Me too."

"One last thing, okay?"

"I'll listen."

"Mariah was right. Dope turned on me."

"She's coming out the door," Nell said. "You could tell her."

He shook his head. "No can do, dear Nell. I am fuckin' full up." He walked past her toward his truck.

"Hey, Monkey," Mariah yelled. "I love the idea of the tune-ups. Daryl already told me he'll kick in a hundred bucks of plumbing work for our high rollers." She caught up to Monkey and Nell.

"It's for Keno," Monkey said. "But thanks. See you later."

Nell drove out to Magic Electric. The roads cut dark across the platinum desert, near full moon washing over the old shacks and creosote. She parked next to the trailer, opened the windows, slid the CD into the player, and hit Pause.

"You know, Monkey, you know what this'll cost me. Listening to this is my match to the Everclear. I don't want to do this. I don't want to hear what comes next."

She turned the CD to the songlist and hit Play. Monkey had written at the top of the list: *Needs no translation*. The first song kicked in, a hard rockabilly beat and the singer's nasal whine: *Strap them kids in, give them a little bit of vodka and a cherry coke.*

"Okay, pal," Nell said. "I'm in this soundtrack. I'm in your movie for now."

She read down the songlist: "James McMurtry's 'Choctaw Bingo'; Little Feat, 'Rock and Roll Doctor'; Eel's 'Woman Driving, Man Sleeping'; Chris Whitley, 'Perfect Day'; Roy Orbison, 'In Dreams'; Bonnie Raitt, 'Tangled and Dark'; Van Morrison, 'Into the Mystic'; Ray Stevens, 'Purple People Eater'; Jackie Wilson, 'Lonely Teardrops'; Robin Trower, (You name the tune); Van Morrison, 'Western Plain'; a surprise."

The music filled the car. She stepped outside and sat on the back fender. A Joshua rose up on the western bank of the wash, star dazzle caught in its branches. "Perfect Day" could have been a cool breeze in the midnight air. Nell went to the edge of the wash and sat. Roy Orbison's satin rasp held her.

"I always wondered what the candy-colored man looked like, Monkey. Now I know. He's getting bald and his eyes can turn to sleet."

She didn't begin to cry until "Lonely Teardrops." "Leaving Las

Vegas, my friend," she said. "As if you could." The first notes of Robin Trower echoed in. "'Daydream,' Monkey," she said. "Not a subtle message, but a true dart to the heart." By the time Van Morrison sang about the shack burning down with no water around, she was pissed off. "Too little, too late, damn it. And please don't let the surprise be 'The End,'" Nell said. "Don't be that obvious."

The last song began, *I'm warped by the rain...*

"Well, fuck you, Monkey," Nell said. "I should have tried to find Tanapall."

She turned off the music, locked the car, and went down into the wash. She walked south, away from Mariah's boulder, away from where she had left the pearl, away from the sweet ghosts of a mother and little girl. The sand was pale satin, threaded with snake and lizard tracks. She walked slowly, studying the ground, stopping to look up at the moon. "I wish it wasn't like this, Monkey," she said. "I wish I were talking to you, not to myself."

Beer cans glittered ahead, scattered around the skeleton of a convertible stripped of everything but its chassis, driver's wheel, and seats. Nell thumped the driver's seat. "Whatever's in there that stings, get out." She sat and took hold of the steering wheel. *Woman driving...*

"If you were asleep beside me," she said, "I'd talk to you. I'd tell you that someday much too soon, I'll miss you. I'll miss what we made, or maybe how we were being made. I don't know what that means because I don't believe in anything that could bring two people together to be more than friends, more than lovers beyond sex, more than partners beyond promises; some huge unknown that could alchemize a man and woman into a flesh radio.

"I'm sorry I knew more than you about what was happening and didn't tell you that I knew. Not about the Bosses, but the ordinary human fumbling. I'm sorry I pretended I knew less. I'm sorry I wanted flesh radio to go on receiving forever. I'm sorry I became scared when it felt like it was fading. I'm sorry I needed you."

She leaned back and closed her eyes. "I'm sorry we never made love. Now you know everything. Now I've really gone down where it's tangled and dark."

She left the car and walked a long time in the wash. The moon began to arc toward the western mountains. She wrote in the cool packed sand of the side of the wash. Fingernail gouges in car wax, fingertip prints on a dirty window. *I was here. Thank you.* She doubled back. It was nearly dawn by the time she came up out of the wash to the car.

Nell leaned in and ejected the CD. "I have to do this, Monkey," she said. "If I don't, I'll play it again and again, and each time I'll want to be with you. You know what that means." She folded the CD slowly in half. It snapped in pieces, a shard cutting her palm. She gathered up the shards and buried them at the base of the Magic Electric sign.

The cut was shallow, her blood dark against her skin. She pulled her sleeve down over the cut. The moon was gone. Gray-green light shimmered above the eastern mountains. She started to say something to Monkey about the perfect beauty and stopped. After all, how could a woman go home if she couldn't turn her back on a vanishing shoreline?

3

Jackie picked Nell up. The back of her truck was filled with fluttering signs and banners, blazing red words against a basket-weave backdrop: *Twentynine for the Mojave. Honk if you love our desert. Tortoises not solar profits. Birds not corpses. Protect sacred sites. Stop and ask us why we're here.*

"They're beautiful," Nell said. "Even if they're giving me weird flashbacks."

"Mariah's mom showed us her old baskets. I asked her if we could use some of the designs for the posters—the butterfly, the birds, the spirals."

"I haven't done this in years," Nell said. "No, decades. My mom was always hauling me off to peace demos. I hated them. I was so little that all I could ever see most of the time were peoples' butts. By the time I was old enough to have an opinion, I was living with Jack Mormons. The only thing they protested was the Church and they did it by ignoring the bishops."

"I was a wild child," Jackie said. "Especially in my teens. But then my folks said, 'Forget art. Go to business college.' I did, dropped out, got a job at the hospital, met Monkey, and the real Jackie was gone."

She pulled into the library parking lot. Mariah's truck, Eddie's Bronco, and Jenella's pickup were parked in the shade. "Monkey's walking over," Jackie said. "Probably Danny, too."

Mariah, Daryl, Eddie, Della, Jenella, Alice, and Danny stood at the back of the Bronco. Della was passing out water bottles. Danny pulled umbrellas out of his car. Eddie opened a patchwork cloth bag and began taking out rattles.

"We're waiting on the others," Mariah said. "Jeff's on his way from the wildlife center out in Wonder Valley. Jones called and said he's meeting the young guys at Denny's."

"Some of the climber kids will be here later," Alice said.

Monkey walked around the corner of the library, looking like a guy who would much prefer to be undergoing dental surgery. He walked over to them and started unloading the posters.

"I didn't figure he'd actually come," Jackie said.

Nell shrugged. "It's for Keno."

Jones' quarter-ton flatbed wheezed into the parking lot, three boys in hip-hop gear crammed into the front, two girls and two boys clinging to the back.

"Aunt Mariah," a lanky boy yelled and ran toward them. "I finally got my own rattle, check it out."

"Let me see that, Ricky," she said. "Who made it?"

"Jones taught me how." He held the rattle out for everybody to see. "We did it all the right way." He ran his fingers over the roadrunner carved on the handle.

"You guys are going to be famous," Jenella said. "Fox News is coming over from Palm Springs." She smiled sweetly at Mariah.

"When did you learn that?" Mariah said. "Why didn't you tell us at the meeting?"

"They called me a few days ago."

Mariah glanced at Nell and shook her head.

"I'm just teasing," Jenella said. "They called me this morning."

"Fifty years of this," Mariah said. "You ought to know who's first by now."

"Peace, lil sister," Jenella said.

Mariah laughed. "I ought to smack your butt."

"Women," Eddie said. "I was scared for a minute our solidarity was getting shaky."

Leonard pulled in and parked next to Jones. He, Cesar, two couples, and two toddlers climbed out.

"You bring the family?" Alice said.

"Can't start them too young," Leonard said. "I think we're all here. Let's take a minute to circle up and introduce ourselves."

They made a ragged circle, the hip-hop kids hanging back a little.

"Ricky," Leonard said, "you guys want to start us off with a song?" Ricky nodded and stepped forward. The other hip-hop kids moved next to him, the toddlers pushing through them into the center of the circle. Ricky looked down at the ground. The young men waited. The first *hush hush* of the rattle was barely audible. He shook it again. The others joined in, the sound weaving through the hum of traffic on Adobe, a cowbird's squawk from the top of a palm.

Ricky's voice was quiet at first. One by one, the other young men began to sing, then Leonard and Cesar, then Daryl, then the other men. The Chemehuevi women danced in place, a slow side step right, then left. Tears streamed down Della's face. The toddlers spun in the center of the circle.

Jeff pulled into the parking lot. He went to the back of his camper, opened the door, and leaned in. When he emerged, he had an eagle on his wrist. He clipped its lead and walked toward the circle. The eagle sat calmly. Jeff waited at the edge of the circle. When the song finished, he stepped in next to Eddie.

"You brought that old dream flyer," Eddie said. "Good to see her again."

"She's been needing a chance to play diva," Jeff said. The eagle stretched out her wings.

"Thank you for the song, everyone," Leonard said. "Let's check in and get ourselves out front on the lawn."

"Wait," one of the hip-hop girls said. "You left the dinosaur in the back of the truck."

They stood in a quiet line for three hours, Cesar, Della and Jenella holding the *Sacred Sites* banner, the hip-hop kids next to them with the *Honk if you love our desert* sign. The toddlers fell asleep curled around the T-rex. Ricky handed one edge of the *Honk* sign to Nell, the other end to Danny. He nodded to his friends. They stepped in front of the banner and began to sing. There were no cops. There was no teargas. Nobody flipped them off. Only one guy leaned out of his truck and yelled, "Get a job."

A car full of Marines pulled into the parking lot and listened. One of them walked over to the singers. He waited a few beats, then joined in the song. When they were finished, he punched Ricky lightly in the arm. "Hey, brah," he said. "Remember me?"

"KSeven? Juvie in San Berdoo, right?"

"That's me. Good to see you here, man, putting yourself on the line."

"Thanks for joining in. We got some flyers on that table over there. Could you grab a few for the Base? My cousin, Jeanie, is in Communications."

"Done. You got a way I can reach you?"

Ricky pulled out his cell. "Number?"

KSeven punched it in. "Be in touch," he said and headed back to his pals.

A big satellite truck pulled in.

"Look sharp," Jenella said. "Fox is here."

A perky young blonde woman walked toward them. "Hey," she said. "You guys look great." She smiled up at Jeff. "Are you the organizer?"

"Nope," he said.

"Is he?" she pointed to Monkey.

"Nope," he said. "I suspect you want to talk to the lady in the ribbon dress, the one who's glaring at you."

Jenella waved. "I'm Jenella Edwards. I called and talked to somebody in the newsroom a couple days ago. But we're all the organizers."

"Oh my god, I am so sorry," the woman said. "I'm Stacy Marsh. I'm the one you talked to. This is my camera gal, Shawn. How about we start with you, Jenella? Can you tell me what this is all about?"

Stacy Marsh shook Cesar's hand. "It's a wrap," she said. "Thank you so much. We're going to zap this footage right back to the station. That way, it'll be on the 6:00 news. You guys have been awesome."

The camerawoman gave Stacy a thumbs up. Stacy's cell rang. She answered and listened. Her face went gray. "Okay," she said. "Sure, I'll put her on." She handed the phone to Jenella.

"Yes. This is Jenella Edwards. What can I do for you?" She covered the phone with her hand. "What is this shit?" she said to Stacy.

"I am so sorry," Stacy said. "He's an asshole."

Jenella nodded and uncovered the phone. "Okay," she said. "You've made yourself perfectly clear, Mr. Burke. Yep, I've got it. Thanks so much for clarifying—and for your cultural sensitivity." She hung up.

"What?" Leonard said. "What did he say?"

"He told me," Jenella said, "that they'll run the story tonight, but if we ever expect them to come all the hell way out here in the future, we better break a law—or bust up some property—or dress up like real Indians, maybe some of those Aztec headdresses, whatever it is we wear."

She looked down at her ribbon dress. "And I got all gorgeous and ethnic for this demo."

"Well," Danny said, "excuse me for stereotyping myself, but I do like the idea of the fancy outfits."

"What," Ricky said. "You don't think me and my brahs look good?"

"Maybe," Stacy said, "I'm going to get lucky and a six-point earthquake will open up this lawn right where I'm standing."

Jenella laughed. "You were just the messenger," she said. "You aren't the asshole. Even your boss isn't the asshole. It's like there's this big anonymous asshole farting all over the rest of us. Coyote was right."

"Where is Coyote," Ricky said, "when we need Him?"

"He's right here," Cesar said. "Right here with us."

Stacy looked at Shawn. "Let's put our gear in the truck. I'm going to stand with these guys for a while."

A spotlessly shiny white King Cab pulled into the parking lot. A second identical truck followed. They parked so they had full view of the demo. A man leaned out of the first truck with a camera. Monkey walked toward them. The driver of the second truck picked up a cell phone. Monkey slowed, stopped, and watched them.

"Oh shit," Jackie said.

Leonard handed his corner of the banner to one of the kids. He walked up next to Monkey and put his arm over his shoulders.

Monkey bowed his head as Leonard said something. Monkey nodded and they walked back into the circle.

"Good thing you're here, Uncle Leonard," one of the hip-hop kids said. "I was going to stand right out there with the pissed-off white guy."

An old black Mazda truck with a skeleton painted on the side pulled into the parking lot behind the surveillance team. A dark-haired man in his early forties and two little girls who'd clearly dressed themselves that morning—one in a tutu and pirate hat, the other in rainbow overalls and sparkly sneakers—climbed out and walked toward the demo. The man waved to Nell.

"I'm Brock. These are my daughters, Aine and Maive. I know you. You've got that manky LeSabre, right? And you walk around at night by yourself?"

"That's me. I'm Nell."

The man was built like a badger, all shoulders and beat-up muscled hands. He took off his shades. He had one green eye and one brown. "So," he said, "do you guys believe in magic?"

Nell took off her shades and grinned. "Would we be out here doing this if we didn't?"

"Good enough," Brock said. "I climb. I write. I'm a dad. If I didn't believe in magic, I'd be lost."

"Maybe what really matters," Nell said, "is whether or not magic believes in us."

Brock studied her face for a second. "Intense." He reached into his pack, pulled out a faded Tarot card, and handed it to Nell.

"The Fool," Nell said, "bouncing down the mountain."

"My cell number's on the back. If you want to play on some rock, give me a call."

Jones handed over his corner of the banner to Brock. He grabbed it and nodded to the little girls. "Let's do it."

"How about if we put in another half hour," Leonard said. "The sun'll be going down soon."

"I've got to bail," Jeff said. "I need to get Dream back to the center before we close. I'll see you at the next meeting."

Everyone else stayed, Stacy and Shawn holding the Tortoise banner, Jackie in between Mariah and Della, Monkey standing back a little, his arms folded over his chest. Danny moved next to Nell.

"I keep thinking about Luisa," he said. "How the only people at her funeral were me and her folks. How nobody sang for her poor little soul."

Nell knew better than to say something blah blah about God's love or Luisa being in a better place. She put her hand on Danny's arm.

"I wish I believed in something like these folks do," she said. "But, maybe like Cesar said, her song is here, here with us."

Ribbons of pink and orange laced the western sky. Traffic had slowed on Adobe. Leonard held up his hand and said, "We've done a good job. Let's have a last song. Cesar, can you start us off?"

Cesar took off his hat. "I want to say something first. This here—what we've done—it's not the finish of this. It's the beginning. This thing is a war. It's gone on forever. I'll fight till my last breath."

He shook his rattle once, waited and shook it again, waited and shook it again. Nell wondered if the silence between the sounds was also the song.

4

Nell picked up a few trip essentials at Stater's. The checkout line was long, the line at the Coinstar machine even longer. An emaciated couple pushed a shopping cart with a little boy in the toddler seat. The sides of his head were shaved. His mohawk had been dyed orange-red. A four-hundred-pound woman in a tropical print muu-muu rolled her motorized cart up to the kid. She ran her hand over the top of his hair. The kid giggled. The weariness in his parents' faces did not lift. She pulled in line behind them.

People dumped coins into the machine—out of a knit cap, an old nickle slot bucket, a backpack with a faded Dodgers logo. Nell knew the story. The weekend was almost here. The money was all the way over. The kids were hungry. You were thirsty. The jacket-pocket safari yielded enough loose change to make the last trip to the Coinstar worth it. But it would only be enough for a mac 'n' cheese for the kids and a quart of Old Mil for you. Maybe. So you strolled over to the lottery machine, shoved in two bucks, and took a shot on a bigger maybe. *Everybody's a gambler*, Nell thought. *Me, I don't even know what I'm betting on.*

The slow gentle checkout guy carefully packed her cheese sticks and fruit and smiled just as carefully.

"Popeye," he said. "Remember Popeye?" Nell grinned at him. The last time she'd shopped, he'd insisted on helping her put her groceries in the car. As they had walked up to the LeSabre, he'd watched her until she took out her keys to open the trunk. Then he'd raised his arm imperiously, pointed at the trunk and said, "Open, Sesame." Nell had keyed the trunk open with a flourish. "Popeye and Bluto," he'd said. "They're at the treasure cave. Bluto looks puzzled. Popeye says, 'Open, sez me.'"

"Open, sez me," Nell had said and put a bag in the trunk.

The man had laughed. "Sez you."

She drove west through a town no longer unknown, down the long slope toward I-10, through a desert alchemized by October into soft sage and gold. She passed the road into Palm Springs and waved.

"Hey, Harrison," she yelled. "I hope Lady Luck has her head in your lap."

Nell got lucky in West Hollywood. She found a parking spot only four blocks from the house on Kings Road. She locked the car and walked toward what had been home. She'd barely seen the neighborhood in the fifteen years she'd lived there, though two or three evenings a week after work she'd jogged five miles, earbuds plugged in, her gaze focused only on the street under her feet.

Then after the months of futile job hunt morphed into desperation, she'd left her iPod at home, driven to Santa Monica, and run on the packed sand at the ocean's edge. She'd run till dusk, till the fairy lights of the pier began to shine like a little galaxy.

She walked down Orlando to Rosewood and turned onto Kings Road. There were For Sale signs everywhere. The air was soft and damp, traffic noise muted. She was the only person on the street, the only person who watched a sleek tabby cat amble across the road and tuck itself under a hedge to watch her.

A foreclosure sale sign was in front of the little white house. She climbed the three steps to the porch and looked in the living room window. The curtains had been pulled back. The realtor had clearly decided that the place needed the "moving up in the industry" look. There was a new black leather couch with copper and gold throw pillows, a slab of glass on four chunks of sandstone, huge black and white photographs on three of the walls. The picture over the mantelpiece was in color, a copy of Man Ray's *The Rope Dancer Accompanies Herself with Her Shadows*.

Nell sat on the top step. She took the tangerines Popeye had packed for her out of the bag and began to peel them. She waited to feel a sense of homecoming, of belonging, of even a glimmer of longing for this front step, these tangerines, this hope that the parrots would arrive. There was nothing.

She scattered the tangerine segments on the broad porch railing. The parrots would come—if they were still in the palms across the street. She would be long gone.

A frighteningly thin woman in workout gear peeked out the front door of the house to Nell's left.

"Excuse me," she said. "I'm sorry, but do you need anything?"

Nell stood and put the tangerine peels in her bag.

"No," she said. "I'm fine. I used to live here. I just came back to feed the parrots."

"The parrots?" the woman said. "What parrots?"

"They used to live in the palms across the street. I fed them every morning."

The woman stepped onto her porch and studied Nell carefully.

"I don't think there are any parrots over there. I've lived here ten years and I've never seen any. And I don't remember ever seeing you. Maybe you should leave. That house is private property."

I didn't exist here, Nell thought. *And I don't now*. She nodded.

"I'm leaving," she said and went out toward the street. When she was a block away, she looked back. The woman still watched her.

Nell walked slowly down the long sloping ramp to the beach at Santa Monica. The first time she'd seen the fiercely intent young boy with an angel's face skateboard the ramp, she'd been a part-time file clerk at the pharmaceutical company that had metastasized into Elysian. She'd worked twenty hours a week and spent the rest of the time in classes and the lab. Almost every hour, every minute had been accounted for. One afternoon, she bolted and found herself walking down to the beach. The boy flew past her on a homemade skateboard, his ice-blond hair streaming in the ocean wind. He was gone before she fully understood what she'd seen and she'd wondered how it felt to throw yourself forward into nothing known.

Twenty years later, David had taken her to see *Dogtown and Z-Boys*. A bright-eyed boy with a mane of blond hair flashed across the screen. His name was Jay Adams. She searched for him on the internet and found a *New York Times* article. A month before Elysian threw her into the unknown, Jay Adams had been released from a four-year prison stretch. He had headed straight back into skating, his blue-inked face no longer an angel's, his intentions still fierce. "I can't make those mistakes anymore," he said.

You saw what I'm seeing, Nell thought. *The ocean, the web of the ferris wheel against a silver-gray sky. You believed you had forever. Then you caught on.*

She walked forward. She needed to pick her mom up at three, and had one more visit to make once she'd touched the ocean. There were only a few people on the beach. Gulls screamed into the cold sky. She sat at the edge of the packed sand just beyond the waves and took off her shoes.

A wave rippled up within inches of her bare feet. She walked out into the water, scooped some into her hands, and splashed the top of her head, her throat, and her heart. She licked the salt from her lips.

A jogger ran toward her, his hair a mane of dreadlocks, his dark eyes reflecting silver.

"Here," he said. "Put out your hand."

She held out her hand. "You can use these," the man said, "when you're not here in this blessed place and you need to remember who you are." He dropped a bracelet of tiny skull beads onto her palm. "You are a ghost becoming a ghost. Whenever you touch these beads, you will find yourself saying the only prayer that counts: *Thank you.*"

Nell slipped the beads onto her left wrist.

"Thank you," she said. "Looks like they're already working."

He laughed. "You're welcome. Peace and love, sister."

She had almost forgotten how it felt to be boxed in front and back, left and right, by cars driven by people whose jaws were set, whose gazes were straight ahead, people she had been one of for at least twenty years, and apparently, from the ache in her jaw, still was. She slowed, dropped into the far right lane, and stretched out her shoulders.

The 2008 pretending-to-be-a-Mustang ahead of her slowed to a crawl and stopped. A guy in an El Dorado tried to slide out of her lane into the one on her left and was blocked. No cars moved in any of the five lanes. The dread 405 was letting the humans know the meaning of chaos theory.

Nell turned off the engine. There was no point in opening the windows for fresh air. Most of the drivers had left their engines running, the better to get the jump on each other once the grid unlocked. She started to slide Johnny Duhan's *Just Another Town* into the player and stopped. That would be for later, for when she and her mother drove up the long slope into the Morongo Basin. She closed her eyes and turned the skull bracelet on her wrist.

It was close to 1:30 when she took the Aquarium exit and drove to the bus station. She parked in the lot, went in, and bought a bag of peanuts and a lemonade from the vending machines. The same sweet-faced young woman was studying behind the ticket counter.

"I'm Nell," Nell said. "I came to thank you."

The woman looked up from her book.

"Hi Nell, I'm Luz. What are you thanking me for?"

"Last April, I didn't know where to go and you told me to visit the aquarium, then take the bus to Palm Springs. You said I might get lucky."

"OMG," Luz said. "My mom always tells me I've got such a big mouth. I'm scared to ask how it worked out?"

"I got lucky," Nell said. "I'm living in Twentynine Palms. I've got three part-time jobs and all the soul food I can eat. I didn't fool around with a married guy. And I'm picking up my long lost mom and taking her back to Twentynine."

"It all sounds great except for the part about living in Twentynine," Luz said. "One of my cousins landed there after he screwed up here. He got so bored he went back to school."

"You know that song?"

"By Robert Plant?" the woman asked.

"He got it right," Nell said.

Nell took the light rail to the aquarium and sat on the bench to eat Diamond's picnic. She finished, ordered a half coffee and half mango ice and sat looking out at the harbor. The air was the same salt cool it had been in April, the bittersweet ice as delicious. She touched the bracelet again. *If I hadn't learned myself so well*, she thought, *I might imagine I didn't need the bracelet, but I'm in the middle part now. I always hated it when my mom and I said goodbye to a place, and loved it when we first arrived in some possible new home. The middle parts were boring.*

In the last seven months, I left everything—wrong, everything left me—and some days, it seems like I've come home to everything. But I'm no good at the middle parts. I never have been. Even goodbyes are better than the times in between. I can't imagine how I stayed at Elysian all those years—I must have been haunted by all those goodbyes. I must have imagined I would find some permanent arrival. And in the long run, I sure as shit am going to need this bracelet.

She swallowed the last of the ice and stood. She had a half hour to spend with the Leafy. She knew that the delicate blue luminescence at the end of the dark hallway would not surprise her. It would appear more like a doorway—or an opening into a desert twilight.

There was no one at the Leafy tank.

"I'm here," Nell said. The Leafies drifted up and down, forward and back, their crystalline fins shimmering against the jade kelp. "Sue me for anthropomorphizing," she said, "but I believe you hear me. I believe you heard me seven months ago. I believe you are beyond human imagining and came to me to keep me alive—so that I could remember how to imagine."

She sat on the floor and rested her forehead against the cool glass of the tank. "I used to be afraid of going crazy. Now I talk to everything. I even talk to the living ghost of a man I love. For thirty years, I never once said the word *love*. I'd listen to the people—yes, mostly women—in my office use that word about chocolate and shoes and haircuts and Facebook, and I knew none of us had any idea what the word meant.

"Now I know. Here is the strangest part of all of this: I seem to be feeling love without anyone giving me instructions. Nobody in Twentynine lectures me or tells me the rules for coming home to yourself. Nobody quotes prophets or shamans or some slick New Age hustler. Nobody suggests I read Deepak Chopra or sends me links to TED talks.

"Sometimes it seems that most of the people I've met have tiny invisible fins that had moved them through their lives toward me. This is not about G-O-D, my shining friends. This is not about the Big Puppeteer in the Sky. This, and this is the best part, is about something I can't and will never be able to figure out, a big nothing as vast, hard, and generous as the Mojave desert, as mysterious as the return to home.

"And you, do you miss your relatives, all those shining aunts and uncles and cousins back in Australia? Do you remember how it is to travel through waving kelp fronds, through a place that is green and gold all at the same time? Do you remember what it is to be free to be moved wherever you want to go?

"Imagine this. There is a woman who learned how to walk in a place she'd believed she'd never been, under a moon she had rarely known, over tracks of creatures she couldn't name. This woman learned that there is a trail made of rock and water and song, and that women and men of her own species have carried that trail in their hearts for time beyond time. And now there are other women and men of her own species who would destroy that trail, that way of being moved wherever a human needs to go."

There were voices in the hall coming closer. Nell stood. A couple stopped next to her.

"Where are Scylla and Charybdis?" the woman asked. "I can't see them."

The man laughed softly. "We have to be patient. It's not as though they can see us and swim up to study our faces."

"I imagine they do," Nell said. "Study us."

The woman touched the tank. "After all," she said, "we only pretend we're at the top of the food chain."

The receptionist called a nurse. "Your mom's ready to go," he said.

"Ms. Norlin will bring her right out in a few minutes."

"Thanks," Nell said.

"While you're waiting," the receptionist said, "check out the new stained glass piece in the west window. Ms. Norlin did it. She's amazing."

Nell turned. An oval of radiance hung in the window, tourmaline and aqua, garnet and opal; a Costa's Hummingbird sipping out of a moon-white datura blossom. A tiny label at the bottom read *Ravenseyestudio.*

"She's a genius," Nell said. "Thank you."

She sat on the Laura Ashley knock-off couch. Everything—the floor, the cocktail table, the windows—was spotless. The carpet was soft rose, just thick enough for comfort, not thick enough to catch a toe or walker. There were fresh flowers on the receptionist's desk. The faintest scent of urine and the morning's breakfast hung under the lemon verbena air freshener.

Her mother and Ms. Norlin emerged from the elevator, her mother smiling pleasantly, the nurse carrying one suitcase and a cardboard box.

"Mom," Nell said. "It's me. Nell." Her mother's expression didn't change. She wore a denim shirtwaist and dark blue walking shoes. Her hair had been freshly cut and permed. In the instant that she touched her mother's hands, a memory leaped up: her mother looking in a motel mirror, taking off one of the eight strands of beads she had around her neck.

"You know, Nell," she had said, "your grandpa told me the last time we visited him that in Paris, women take off one piece of jewelry to get that understated fashionable look." She had laughed and looked down at herself, dark purple velvet vest over a pale green embroidered Indian shirt, a flowing gauze skirt over a pair of velvet pants, three ankle bracelets on her right ankle, a line of bangles up her wrist near to her elbow. She flicked the three earrings in her left ear and shook her head. The bells woven into her long hair had chimed silvery. "You might say I'm a little overstated," she said. She draped the necklace around Nell and slid five of the bangles on her little wrist. "There. We might not make it in Paris, but we're all set for downtown Willetts."

Ms. Norlin handed Nell the box. "We put all Tara's pictures and personal items in here. We found an old seedpod in a skirt pocket. I was going to throw it out, but she stopped me. It's in the box."

Mrs. Norlin handed the suitcase to Nell. "She was such a dear," she said. "So easy. Not all our residents are like that."

Nell laughed. "It was one of her favorite songs."

"Songs?"

"The Eagles. And her favorite line was the one about how the sound of your own wheels can drive you nuts."

"Of course," Ms. Norlin said. "My dad loved that song. We want you to know that Tara is in great physical shape. Her heart is strong. She's a little wobbly—many older folks have balance problems—but walks every day around and around the garden."

"Thank you," Nell said. "We'll be walking every day when I get her home. She taught me that walking was one of the simple gifts."

Mrs. Norlin embraced Nell's mom. "Goodbye, dear Tara," she said. "You're in good hands."

"I hope so," Nell said. "I'm new at this, but I'll have help."

"Please email me now and then and let me know how your mom is doing."

"I will. Do you have a card? I may be in a position in a few months to buy my mom a piece of your stained glass."

Ms. Norlin took a card from the reception desk. "I'd love to do that. Get in touch once things have settled down. Let me know what image you'd like in the glass."

"I already know," Nell said. "A Joshua tree with a moon caught in its upper branches."

"Oh yes," the nurse said. "I lived in that desert a long long time ago. I've never forgotten the nights. The days were something else altogether. That's why I left."

5

Nell settled her mother into the passenger seat and opened the box of pictures. "We'll look at these later," she said. Her mother folded her hands in her lap. "Here," Nell said, took the Joshua bud out of the box, and tucked it between her mother's hands. "You hang onto this for us," she said. "There's a window sill facing east in your new room. You can put it there and watch the moon rise."

She didn't expect her mother to talk. It didn't matter. She was the one who needed to tell stories, to give back memories and—she touched the skull beads—to say thank you.

"We're going on the road," she said. "We have all the time we need."

Nell's mother sat quietly as they drove up through the pass into Morongo Valley. "I think we were here," Nell said. "Maybe we were on a bus, maybe we had hitchhiked, I can't remember. I bet you know. I hope you look at the creosote bushes and the red and gray rock and remember that soon we'll come to a little town, then another with beat-up old motels that don't look much different from when we might have stayed at one of them. More than anything, I hope we were happy here."

She slid the Johnny Duhan CD into the player.

It was twilight when they pulled into the driveway of the care center. Barbara waved to them from the front stoop.

"I've just finished making dinner. You can eat with us, Nell. There's plenty. The other new guest won't come in till tomorrow."

Nell helped her mom out of the car, grabbed the suitcase and box, and guided her mother up the walk. "Hello, Tara," Barbara said. "You don't know me and I don't know you, but I hope you'll like living here."

Tara reached out her hand. Barbara took it in hers.

"Take your mom to her room," Barbara said. "I'll put dinner on the table."

Nell stepped into the room before her mom. She would greet her. She wasn't sure that anything she did made a difference, but she remembered Diamond taking her to her room at La Paloma and how Diamond's welcoming presence had made the room almost familiar.

"Welcome home, Mom," she said. Her mother stepped in and ran her hand over the crazy quilt. Nell pulled the bright red armchair to the window. "Sit here for a minute," she said. "There's an old friend out there." She touched her mother's elbow. "Come on."

Tara sat in the chair, the seedpod in her right hand. She looked down into the yard. Nell watched for a smile. Her mother's face remained serene. "Do you want to put your seedpod on the windowsill?" Nell said.

She saw her mother's fingers tighten around the seedpod. Barbara called from the dining room. "You can take it with you," Nell said. "You can keep it with you always."

Monkey ignored the computer. Maybe it was like a woman. Maybe if you didn't write, didn't call, it would come around. The computer had frozen up when he'd been trying to enter invoices. He'd restarted it three times. No luck. Maybe the computer was exactly like a woman—specifically his former computer nerd.

There was a knock on the office door.

"I'm here," Monkey yelled. He spun around in his chair. Leonard came in and sat on the stack of tires.

"How's it going?" he said. "Me and Cesar been wondering about you."

"I'm going," Monkey said, "but the Fiendish Thing here isn't."

"Want me to help?" Leonard said. "I love those damn things. I've got four million photographs on mine."

Monkey stood and leaned against the door to the garage. "Have at it."

Leonard's fingers flew over the keys. He leaned back and watched. Monkey's spreadsheet came up. "There you go," Leonard said. "You need to get a computer nerd."

Monkey sat on the tires. "I had one," he said. "Didn't work out."

Leonard nodded. "Shit happens. You got a soda by any chance? I'm dry."

Monkey pulled a couple cans out of the office mini-fridge. "Here you go."

"Mmmmm," Leonard said. "Dr Pepper. I love this stuff."

They drank in silence for a few minutes. Finally, Monkey said, "If you want to know more, I told you pretty much everything I know. I haven't smoked in a month. There are no trances. Absolutely nothing."

Leonard nodded and took a long pull on the soda. "I didn't come to ask you anything. Our old folks are still working with what you told us. You never know how long it'll take them."

"This is a social call?"

"More or less. How about we go over to the Greek's and get us a cholesterol breakfast bomb? We can talk a few things over."

"Yeah. How do I get out of this spreadsheet without killing everything?"

Leonard showed him how to save, and put the computer to sleep.

The Greek's was nearly empty, a hung-over Marine staring into his feta omelet, a couple gang-bangers playing hooky from school, hefting their cans of soda like they were beers. Monkey and Leonard ordered. The waitress brought two cups of high octane.

Leonard creamed and sugared his coffee to candy and leaned back. "Me and Cesar been talking about you."

Monkey shrugged. "Must have been a short conversation."

"It was long enough."

"I sure hope Rafael's in the kitchen," Monkey said. "He's the only one gets my hashbrowns right."

"You like 'em crispy?"

"Damn near burnt."

Leonard threw back his head and laughed. "Kinda like you, right?"

Monkey grinned. "Shit, Leonard, that's the first time I've smiled since Keno died. No dope. No happy Monkey."

"Yeah, I know how that is. I sure do miss my beer. Me and Daryl talk about the bad old days all the time. I never would've quit until that shit quit me."

The waitress brought their food. Monkey's hashbrowns were a shade below black.

"Perfect," he said. "And we'll take some hot sauce, please."

Leonard cut up his sausage and dipped into his eggs. "Don't tell my wife," he said. "She's got me on some damn cottage cheese and ferns diet."

"Leonard," Monkey said, "did you come all the fuck over here just to clog your arteries and bitch about your old lady?"

"Nope."

"Okay, I'll ask. Why *did* you come all the fuck over here?"

"Cesar thinks that him and me could maybe take you fishing or something."

"On the river?"

"Where else?"

The waitress set the hot sauce bottle in front of Monkey.

"Knock yourself out," she said. Monkey splashed hot sauce on his omelet.

"Leonard," Monkey said. "I hate fishing."

"Well, maybe then, we could just sit around in the shade in my backyard and shoot the shit."

"When?"

"How about this weekend? Sunday, maybe. I'm thinking about barbecuing up some ribs. The wife makes the best fry bread you ever ate. You and Jackie could come over and take a break."

"We could," Monkey said.

"How's noon?"

"Works good."

"I'll tell Cesar. Now, pass the damn hot sauce. And whatever you do, don't ever tell Mariah what I said about my wife's fry bread."

Nell left her mom with Barbara and drove back to La Paloma. Shiloh, Diamond, and four women sat on the porch.

"Hey, Nell," Shiloh called. "Come and meet the new kids."

"And an old kid," Chelsea said. "I'm baaaaaaaaaack. My old man's middle name is recidivism."

The other women introduced themselves. Nicky. Lola. ChiChi.

"Actually that's a joke," the woman said. "I'm Rachel—ChiChi means titties in Spanish."

"I'm Nell. I'm your housemate."

"There's rhubarb pie in the kitchen," Diamond said. "Grab some and come back out. Chelsea's catching us up on all the Twentynine dirt there is to spread."

"And," Shiloh said, "if you could check out what me and Diamond have done with the website? I have a blog."

"So do I," Chelsea said.

"And me," each of the other women said.

"We made up these totally cool names," Rachel said. "I'm ChiChi, of course."

Nell thought about the hundred million blog voices nattering in cyberspace and said, "That's awesome. I can't wait to read them."

Next morning, there was an email from Mariah. *How about eating with us tonight? You can bring your mom and we can fill you in on the new happenings.*

There was one other message:

OKeefecat52@msn.com

If I thought it was a drag living with Monkey Mota, Monkey clean 'n' sober is soooooo much fun. Monosyllables. Staring off into space. Hugging me as though some therapist told him to.
I need my girl buddy. Let's go get coffee at Crossroads. SOOOOOON!

Nell hit Reply:

You got it. But how about lunch tomorrow? I'm working at Mariah's. We can go over to Thai Joy. 11:30? Before it's crowded.

She logged off. She'd go out to Magic Electric to make sure her mom could make it down the switchbacks. The moon was two days from full. That meant they could be in the wash looking up at the Joshua before it got too late for her mom. And she'd make it back for the meeting. She filled her bottle with water and climbed into the LeSabre.

Nell parked at the Magic Electric sign, pulled on a jacket, and slip-slid down the switchbacks. She imagined how it would be to follow a familiar stranger and not know where you were, to live in a shattered mirror of time and walk on earth that shifted beneath your feet. The air in the wash smelled damp, as though she breathed in cloud. She walked past Mariah's boulder, around the curve, and sat on the low ledge.

She looked up at the Joshua tree. There was something coiled round the trunk. It had been too dark to see it before. She climbed up the side of the wash. Three strands of rusted barbed wire had been wrapped around the Joshua and secured with rusted brads. Bark had grown around the wire in a couple places, but if she worked carefully, she could pull it free.

She used her nail clippers to pry out the brads, dropped them into her jacket pocket, and carefully uncoiled the wire.

"There," she said. "You're free." She laughed. "And none of this is a metaphor." She walked the dirt road back to Magic Electric. The descent into the wash had seemed a little too tricky to take her mom down. She needed to scout out a place she could get her mom to safely. Mariah had told her that there was a near-forest of Joshua trees up by the county dump.

"Head up Avalon to Winters. You'll see."

Nell drove up past Security and Memory, turned west on Aberdeen, then north on Avalon. Winters ran east to the landfill and west to Landers. Nell parked on Winters. She saw a ripple of pebbles in the sand and remembered. Seven months ago, Shiloh and Diamond had brought her here to get desert eyes. A dirt road took off north. She climbed out of the car and started to walk across Winters.

A dead bird lay at the edge of the asphalt, no mark on it, no blood or broken bone. She picked it up. The gray, black, and white feathers were exquisitely soft against the palm of her hand.

"I'll take you where you can go back into the ground," she said, and crossed the road to the dirt road. She found a cluster of ruined rock walls, then an intersection where a hawk nest sat in a telephone pole. She turned east, came round a curve, and stopped. Someone was seated on a fallen Joshua just ahead.

She waited till her heart had slowed. The figure didn't move. She waited. The bird was still warm in her palm. She moved a few steps closer to the figure. It was still. It could have been a gray Buddha. She remembered learning about the natural deities in Tibet, the rocks and trees and river eddies that looked like ogre gods and goddesses. She took a deep breath and walked toward the figure.

The Buddha remained still. She was about ten feet away when Buddha became a stump jutting up from the fallen Joshua. She let out the breath she hadn't realized she was holding and went to the old Joshua.

Nell tucked the bird in a space between the stump and a dead branch. He, for she somehow knew it was a he, lay just below what would be the head of the Buddha, facing east. She remembered one of the old medicine healers telling the Elysian crew that the direction of the afterworld was east. "*Gate gate paragate*," she whispered. "Gone, gone, gone to the other shore, never having left."

She sat on the fallen Joshua. Something white flickered near her left hand. A tiny white spine lay in a crack in the bark. She pulled off her boots and dug her toes into the cool sand. She closed her eyes. The sun was a soft rose blossoming behind her eyelids. Nell touched the skull bracelet and began to wonder. What was the name for the gray, black, and white bird? She had always been a girl who loved names.

Back in her room, she searched the internet for gray, black, and white birds, hooked beak, Mojave Desert. A Loggerhead Shrike appeared. *(Shrikes): Songbirds with hook-tipped bills, hawk-like behavior. Shrikes perch watchfully on treetops, wires, often impale prey on thorns, barbed wire.* Nell was, for an instant, in love with the workings of the human mind. No matter what lay ahead, she knew that she was in love with her mind, with knowledge—and with the pale gold light, the low indigo mountains, the certainty of the moon rising.

"We're going for it, Mom," Nell said. They had stopped at Magic Electric. "Wait here," Nell said. "I'll be right back." She walked to the Joshua tree at the edge of the wash and wrapped her arms around it. She remembered the rasp of the rusty wire in her fingers, the softness of the shrike in her palm. Rough and soft had no meaning. Old and new were the same. Wire and bird were the same. There was only the Great Circling Around.

She walked back to the car. Her mom stood at the base of the Magic Electric sign. "The magic electricity didn't happen, Mom," Nell said. "But the sign's still here. And so are we. Let's head out."

Nell drove off Winters onto the dirt road. "Okay Mom, hang on. All I have to do is stay calm, go just the right speed, which is almost no speed at all, and not panic." Tara held onto the dashboard. "Good call, Mom," Nell said. "You're riding shotgun. Remember you used to say that to me the times we had a car?"

The LeSabre hung up for a second on a sand drift in the road, then eased forward. "Yes!" Nell said. "Noble beast. I have to confess, Mom, I had a fancy car—an Audi—where I lived before. You would have looked at it and me and said, 'Why do you need this?' But by then I never saw you. I hate how people—especially women—say *I'm sorry* all the time. *I'm sorry* are holy words. They should be only said as a sacrament.

"I'm sorry, Mom. About the fancy car, the fancy house, the fancy man, but most of all about not coming to be with you."

She made the turn at the hawk's nest. "But I'm not sorry I got rid of the Audi. The person I was would never have taken it on this beautiful road."

Tara laughed.

They sat on the trunk of the Joshua Buddha, their linked shadows stretching across the pale sand.

"We'll sit here for a while, Mom," Nell said. Mother, daughter, tree, and tiny spine fell away from the last of the day, circling toward the moon.

Tara touched the skull beads. "A man gave me these," Nell said. "He said it would help me remember what's important. Here's what I'm learning, what I have to remember. There are almond groves catching sunset beyond the mountains behind us. The bees have long since left the orchards. No one knows why. Across the ocean, far beyond the almond trees, pink and silver creatures are drifting in salt water and kelp. They're called Leafy Seadragons. Each year, there are fewer and fewer, because the ocean is dying and people kidnap them to sell to collectors. Somewhere near here, maybe even at our feet, there is a trail made of songs. And there are people who want to destroy it, and people who will not let that happen. Meanwhile, deep beneath us, the earth's blood and bones are changing.

"I don't know what you've forgotten and what you remember. I wish I knew. We humans are forgetting and forgetting. I'm beginning to remember. I want to remember as much as I can. Pretty soon the moon will be up, and we'll go into that grove of Joshuas just ahead. I've brought a blanket. We can lie down and look up through the branches at the moon. I hope you remember. I hope you remember how you taught me to save my own life."

Epilogue: In Fact

I owe the idea of this epilogue to John Burdett. He's the author of a series of remarkable crime novels set in Soi Cowboy, the red-light district of Bangkok. In his last two novels, *Bangkok Haunts* and *Vulture Peak*, he included epilogues which detail the facts of the crime industries fictionalized in the books. I came away knowing that none of the meticulously written and horrific details in the novels had, in fact, been fiction. I came away understanding the necrotic conspiracy between big business, little pimps and killers, and the rest of us. And I had learned the ways I could refuse to take part in deadly global business.

Mr. Eddy, a lead Salt Song singer in the Youtube video *The Salt Song Trail*, tells us he will break our hearts before he teaches us the songs. "If your heart is broken," he says, "you can learn the songs." I offer the facts of the potential annihilation of the web of life that is the Mojave Desert and the ancient sacred sites that lie in its playas, canyons, and oases. May they break your heart. Then, you might learn the song.

In fact, in 2010, California native peoples began fighting Solar Millenium's plan to put a huge solar array near their sacred sites by Blythe, California. The project was held off long enough for the company to go bankrupt. There was a brief respite until Next Era bought Millenium's lease and, in 2013, began to acquire the necessary government permits and permissions to go ahead with the development. The danger is everywhere. In 2011, *Mother Jones* reported that the California Energy Commission, which grants permits for large-scale solar plants, found 17,000 cultural sites—not all indigenous—in the southern California desert that "will potentially be destroyed" by past, present, and future construction projects. And the CEC acknowledges that number is probably larger today.

And, in fact, bird deaths are being reported from solar installations—migrating water birds plummeting to their deaths because they've mistaken the gleam of the panels for water, other birds charred to death by the intensity of reflections. Not only solar "factories" are deadly. Eagles, hawks, owls, and other birds are being chopped to pieces by wind turbines; humans living near wind turbines are reporting physical and psychological symptoms; exploratory roads and construction of wind facilities are destroying not only desert habitat, but other places where the wind power industry is establishing its heavy footprint.

In fact, the earth's polarity is shifting. Sometime in the relatively near future, it will flip. A layer of protection from solar radiation will be stripped away—increasing mutagenic processes and global warming. A planet with damaged species diversity will be a dying planet. Humans with damaged immune systems from pollution will be far more susceptible to cancer. In fact, the bees continue to die and the experts continue to conjecture. The *New York Times* 2013 review of the film *More Than Honey* reported that: *In a scene filmed in northern China, where pesticides are heavily used, bees have all but vanished, and peasants are reduced to laboriously importing pollen from the south and daubing it by hand on blossoms.* Global warming, disease epidemics, uprooting bees from their homeground—all of these factors have not gone away; in fact, they have worsened.

As Nell herself writes: *If we begin thirty years ago to change how we live—we, the metastasis on the web—then we can affect the ozone layer and restore a fraction of what was once robust species diversity.*

In fact, December 12, 2012 came and went—with what some people believe is huge and immutable effect, and others believe was nothing.

"*Nothing,*" *as when a person without desert eyes looks at a Mojave playa shining like a dream and says, "There's nothing out there.*"

In fact, Nell and her mother reunited, her mother intact, the reunion given to them by grace and hard inner work.

In fact, Monkey and his trances were once real.

In fact, Nell's heart broke. And she learned the song.

Thank you.

Mary Sojourner
Flagstaff, Arizona, June 17, 2013

You must end where you begin;
and as you begin...you must
go back. What remains?
Detail work. Through eternity
You have to do the detail work.
　　　　　—Swami Vivekananda

ABOUT MARY SOJOURNER

Mary Sojourner is the author of two novels, one short story collection, one essay collection, two memoirs, and dozens of NPR commentaries and magazine and newspaper columns. She teaches writing in private circles, one on-one, at colleges and universities, writing conferences, and book festivals. She lives in Flagstaff, Arizona.

MarySojourner.com

About Torrey House Press

The economy is a wholly owned subsidiary of the environment, not the other way around.
—Senator Gaylord Nelson, founder of Earth Day

Love of the land inspires Torrey House Press and the books we publish. From literature and the environment and Western Lit to topical nonfiction about land related issues and ideas, we strive to increase appreciation for the importance of natural landscape through the power of pen and story. Through our *2% to the West* program, Torrey House Press donates two percent of sales to not-for-profit environmental organizations and funds a scholarship for up-and-coming writers at colleges throughout the West.

Torrey House Press
www.torreyhouse.com
Visit our website for reading group discussion guides, author interviews, and more.